PRAISE FOR THE INV

THE LOST PLOT

"The Invisible Library series never runs short on intrigue."
—RT Book Reviews

"A light and fun series." —*Library Journal*

"Cogman writes with a flair for both the dramatic and the succinct. . . . Cogman combines a beautiful writing style, filled with subtle nuances that the close reader will relish, and a fast-paced thread which drives the story through twists, turns, and pitfalls without ever feeling as if you have stayed in one place too long or longing to remain somewhere else." —Fantasy Book Review

"Irene, as always, remains one of my favorite heroines. . . . Cogman has a way of combining a unique idea with intriguing characters into a story you can't put down." —NovelKnight Book Reviews

"*The Lost Plot* is full of life and wit from the start. . . . A pacy-to-breakneck-speed adventure through prohibition America, *The Lost Plot* is a hi-*gin*-ks read." —SFF World

THE BURNING PAGE

"Funny, exciting, and oh so inspiring, this is the kind of fantasy novel that will have female readers everywhere gearing up for their own adventure[s]."
—Bustle

"*The Burning Page* is action-packed from start to finish and will keep you hooked until the very last page." —Nerd Much?

"Imaginative and suspenseful with a touch of magic and science fiction, the worlds of the Invisible Library are ones I want to visit again and again. . . . What makes this series magical are the incredible scenes and creative imagination of the author. The creatures, portals, attacks, and investigation are all surrounded by a feast for your mind's eye." —Caffeinated Book Reviewer

"Libraries, Librarians, dragons, Fae, chaos, dastardly baddies, and a Sherlock Holmes–style detective all thrown into the mix equal an excellent read. . . . It's packed with chaotic and dramatic adventures and is witty, to boot." —The Speculative Herald

THE MASKED CITY

"This witty fantasy also includes a Holmesian detective, a wondrous magical train, some fascinating Fae politics, frequent funny moments, and a very limited time for Irene to rescue Kai, all making for a thrilling and deliciously atmospheric adventure." —*Locus*

THE INVISIBLE LIBRARY

#2 on the *Independent*'s (UK) Best Fantasy Novels of 2015 List

On *Library Journal*'s Best Science Fiction/ Fantasy Books of 2016 List

"Satisfyingly complex . . . a book in which to wallow."
—*The Guardian* (UK)

"Ms. Cogman has opened a new pathway into our vast heritage of imagined wonderlands. And yet, as her story reminds us, we yearn for still more." —Tom Shippey, *The Wall Street Journal*

"A dazzling bibliophilic debut."

—Charles Stross, Hugo Award–winning author of *The Nightmare Stacks*

"Surrender to the sheer volume of fun that appears on every page . . . thoroughly entertaining."

—*Starburst*

"Fantasy doesn't get much better. . . . If you're looking for a swift, clever, and witty read, look no further."

—Fantasy Faction

"Series fans will be thrilled to learn more about dragon-kind and the capricious Fae, and will be eager for Cogman's third in the series."

—*Booklist*

"Another fantastic adventure . . . fast-paced and entertaining. The books in this series make for light, fun popcorn reads."

—The BiblioSanctum

BY GENEVIEVE COGMAN

The Invisible Library

The Masked City

The Burning Page

The Lost Plot

The Mortal Word

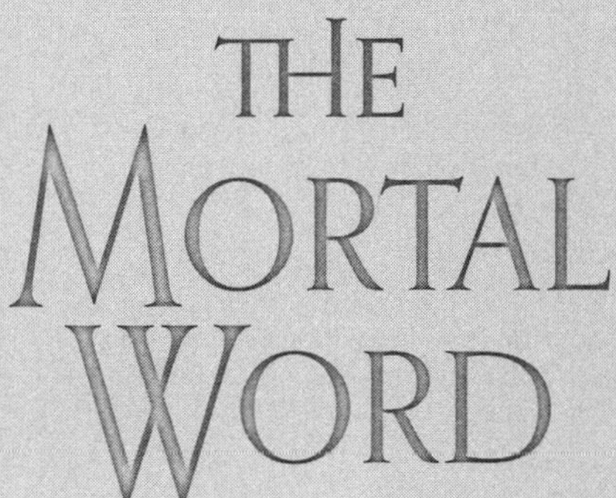

THE MORTAL WORD

AN INVISIBLE LIBRARY NOVEL

GENEVIEVE COGMAN

ACE
NEW YORK

ACE
Published by Berkley
An imprint of Penguin Random House LLC
375 Hudson Street, New York, New York 10014

Library of Congress Cataloging-in-Publication Data

Names: Cogman, Genevieve, author.
Title: The mortal word: an invisible library novel / Genevieve Cogman.
Description: First edition. | New York: BERKLEY, 2018.
Identifiers: LCCN 2018023853 | ISBN 9780399587443 (trade pbk.) | ISBN 9780399587450 (ebook)
Subjects: LCSH: Librarians—Fiction. | GSAFD: Fantasy fiction. | Alternative histories (Fiction)
Classification: LCC PR6103.O39 M67 2018 | DDC 823/.92—dc23
LC record available at https://lccn.loc.gov/2018023853

First Edition: November 2018

Printed in the United States of America
1 3 5 7 9 10 8 6 4 2

Cover images: Eiffel Tower by Titov Nikolai/Shutterstock Images;
daggers by Kuryanovich Tatsiana/Shutterstock Images;
paper texture by Lukasz Szwaj/Shutterstock Images; framework by bomg/Shutterstock Images;
cat by Hein Nouwens/Shutterstock Images;
Colorful Thailand Sky by rattanapatphoto/Shutterstock Images
Cover design by Adam Auerbach
Book design by Laura K. Corless

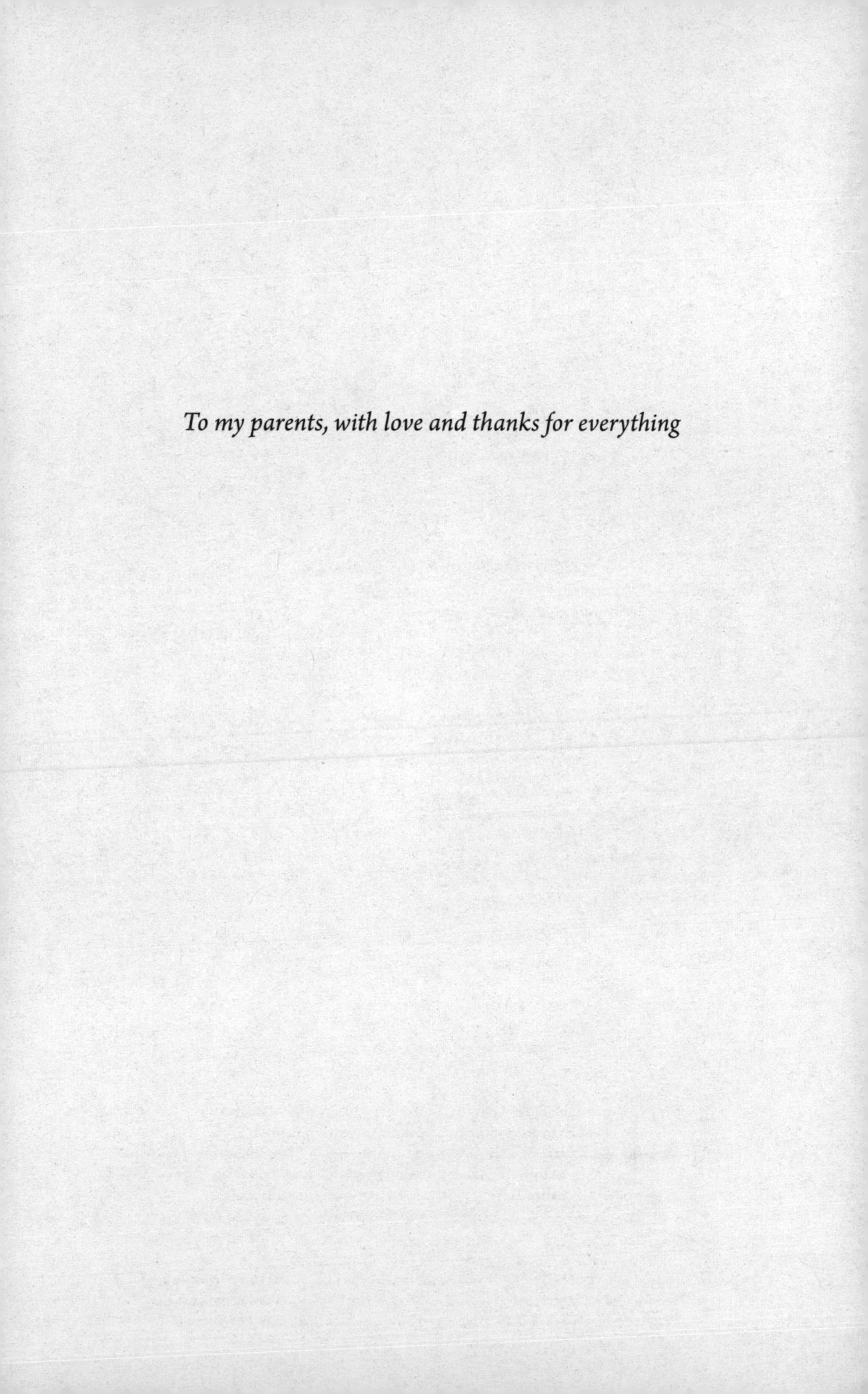

To my parents, with love and thanks for everything

ACKNOWLEDGEMENTS

Many thanks to my agent, Lucienne Diver, and my editors, Bella Pagan and Rebecca Brewer: I greatly appreciate all your help and edits. (And I'll try to cut down on my use of the word *that* . . .)

Thank you to all my beta readers—Jeanne, Beth, Phyllis, Anne, Iolanthe, Phyllis, and everyone else. Thanks to my father for research sources on Belle Epoque Paris, to my sister-in-law Crystal for Mu Dan's name, to Beth and Walter for ways to dispose of chlorine, and to all other contributors of helpful information. Many thanks to my supportive co-workers and colleagues who endure my scribbling notes and muttering at inappropriate moments. Thanks to the authors of the various research volumes which I've read while writing this, whether on Belle Epoque Paris or the Theatre of the Grand Guignol. And thank you to everyone who's read my books and enjoyed them—it does help. It really does.

Thank you to my family for their support and encouragement.

And apologies to the city of Paris and to all its history. Any errors are my fault and mine alone.

THE MORTAL WORD

My lord father,

Please forgive the haste and informality of this letter: you know my respect for you and my obedience to your will. You will have heard that I was expelled from the Library's service under conditions of high scandal and because of personal fondness for one of the Librarians. This is absolutely not true and is a gross misrepresentation of the facts.

Minister Zhao, a high-ranking royal courtier, was assassinated. You will have heard of this, my lord father. The Queen of the Southern Lands then held a competition to fill the minister's position from the dragons who had been in his service. What you may not know is that a junior Librarian was implicated in grave misconduct relating to this competition. And Irene, my current superior at the Library, was tasked to investigate. I accompanied her.

We were eventually forced to give evidence before the queen herself. Irene capably and efficiently identified a member of the queen's court as the guilty party. You would have been impressed by her bearing and her intelligence, Father: though she is only a human, her self-control and courage are truly admirable, and she carries herself with an inner power and strength that reminds me of the best of us.

However, as I am a dragon, and was working for the Library, I was in serious danger of compromising both us and the Library. I was forced to claim I'd joined the Library as a boyish prank, without your knowledge. I told all present that I'd been in human form, so the Librarians were unaware of my true nature. As a result, I had to renounce my position as an apprentice there.

I realize that this is not in accordance with your greater plans, Father. Although my joining the Library was irregular, you had seen advantage in my gaining influence with the Librarians. You have said many times that they are secretive and take full advantage of their ability to hide in their Library between worlds. And while our kindred are not currently hostile to them, more information and access to their secrets can only serve our cause. My lord father, you are the eldest of the dragon kings, and the most respected of all the dragon monarchs. What serves you serves us all. It was my honour to be able to infiltrate their ranks and observe their behaviour.

I do not wish to now disappoint you by failing. I no longer have any formal ties here, but I humbly beg for your permission to remain in my current location, so I can consolidate my contacts. Notably, Vale, a master detective, and Irene, my former mentor.

Naturally I will return at once if you desire my presence, my lord father. Your word is my command. But I would not want to leave my work half-done.

Your obedient son,
Kai

Note at bottom, in different writing—"Tian Shu, the boy's babbling. I haven't heard so many excuses for dubious behaviour since that duel defending his mother's reputation. Find out what's going on, and for the love of gods and men alike, don't let him get anywhere near the peace conference."

CHAPTER 1

The braziers in the torture chamber had burned low while Irene waited for the count to arrive. The stone wall behind her back was cold, even through her layers of clothing—dirndl, blouse, apron, and shawl—and the shackles scraped her wrists. Down the corridor she could hear the sounds of the other prisoners: suppressed tears, prayers, and a mother trying to soothe her baby.

She'd been arrested at about three o'clock. It must be early evening by now: there were no windows in the dungeons, and she couldn't hear the bells in the castle chapel or the village church, but it had been several hours at least. She wished that she'd had a bigger lunch.

The door opened, and one of the guards poked his head in to check that she was still there. It was a pro forma inspection, not serious; after all, she was chained to the wall, in a locked torture chamber, deep under the castle. How could she possibly go anywhere?

His assumptions would have been correct, if she hadn't been a Librarian.

But for the moment, they thought she was a normal human, even if they did believe she was a witch, and she had to play the part.

Irene knew that the people in the small Germanic village next to the castle would be particularly devout in their prayers that night. For another witch—namely, her—had been arrested by the count's guard and hauled off to be put to the question. Otto, the Count of Süllichen—or rather, the Graf von Süllichen—was superstitious, paranoid, and vindictive: he was constantly on the watch for witches and plotters against his rule. The villagers would be afraid that she'd name them in her inevitable confession.

The sound of weeping was hushed as the thump of marching boots echoed down the corridor. Irene swallowed, her throat abruptly dry. This was where she found out whether her plan was quite as clever as it had seemed earlier.

The dungeon door was flung open brutally, crashing into the wall. Haloed in the torch-light beyond, the *Graf* loomed there, his arms folded. His heavy black velvet doublet suggested shoulders wider than was actually the case, but the two soldiers at attention behind him were muscular enough for any manhandling that might be necessary. He considered Irene, stroking his chin thoughtfully.

"So," he finally said, "the newest witch who dares sneak into my domain and plot against me. Have you not learned, wench, that all those who came before you failed?"

"Oh, forgive me, most noble *Graf*!" Irene begged humbly. She knew that her German was too modern for this time and place, but he would probably be only too happy to take it as additional proof of witchcraft. "I was a fool to come here. I cast myself at your feet and beg for mercy!"

The *Graf* looked surprised. "You admit your guilt?"

Irene looked down at the floor, trying to squeeze out a tear or two. "You have chained me in iron, Your Grace, and there is a crucifix on the door. I am bound and my Satanic master will no longer help me."

"Well." The *Graf* paused, then rubbed his hands together. "Well, this makes a pleasant change! Perhaps I will not have to question you as harshly as I did your sisters. Confess all your evil-doings and name your accomplices, and you may yet be spared from damnation."

"But I have done such dreadful things, most noble *Graf* . . ." Irene managed a heartfelt sniffle. "How can I befoul your ears with my confession? You are a nobleman, far above such things."

As she'd hoped, that got his full interest. "Wench, there is nothing you can tell me which I have not already read. You may not know this . . ."

In fact, she did know it—and it was the reason she was there.

". . . but I am the most learned man in all Württemberg. Men come from across Germany to admire my books. Many of the treatises of the great holy men and witch-hunters adorn my library. The *Malleus Maleficarum* of Kramer was my childhood reading. I have studied the confessions of witches from across the world. Yours will be no different."

An idea of how to get rid of at least one guard came to Irene. "Then I beg you to summon a priest, most noble *Graf*. Let me make my final confession to him as well as you, so that I may be saved from the flames of hell."

The *Graf* nodded. "You show wisdom, woman. Stefan. Fetch Father Heinrich here at once."

"But, sire," the guard protested, "he said that he wanted nothing more to do with the questioning of witnesses—"

"Fool." The *Graf* cut him off. "This witch is begging to confess her sins. Hah! This will prove to him that I was right in my suspicions all along. Fetch him and be quick about it . . . I don't care if he's in the middle of mass or the middle of supper, but drag him down here so that this foul wench may cleanse her conscience."

Irene noted that the guard rolled his eyes heavenwards but that he was careful to do it when the *Graf* had his back turned. "Of course, sire," he muttered, and left at a trot, closing the door behind him.

"Now, wench." The *Graf* was practically salivating at the thought of licentious confessions. "Tell me what brought you to my domain and into my hands. And the hands of Mother Church, of course," he added as an afterthought. "Be warned: if you attempt to hold anything back, I will be forced to put you to the question after all. You see those irons heating in the brazier? You see the rack, and the iron maiden in the corner of the room? Many before have tried to keep silent and have failed." He pondered. "Tell me first why your hair is shorn in such an unwomanly way. Did you sacrifice it to your dark master in return for powers of seduction or disease?"

Irene couldn't think of a way to get the second guard out of the room. She'd just have to deal with him before the first one came back. Time to move to stage two of the plan. "He cut it from my head as I knelt before him, most noble *Graf*," she confessed. "He spoke words of power as he did so." Not remotely accurate. Her hair had been cut by her friend and ex-apprentice during a recent excursion to Prohibition America. It was so difficult maintaining a consistent hair-style between alternate worlds. But nobody in this place and time—sixteenth-century Germany—would believe that a woman would *choose* to have her hair cut short.

"Really?" The *Graf* walked over to where a book lay open on a lectern and dipped the quill there in the open inkwell. "Recite his diabolical words for me, so that I can have a record of these spells."

"He said—" And Irene shifted to the Language. The time for pretence was over. **"Ink, fly in the eyes of the men: chains, open and release me."**

One of the many useful things about being a Librarian—as opposed to being a witch—was that Irene could use the Library's Language to change the world around her. Even if she was in manacles and chained to the wall.

Which she wasn't any longer. The heavy iron cuffs fell open, releasing her. She prudently took a few steps to the side before the guard, who was currently rubbing his eyes and howling in rage and fear, could think of attacking where she'd been standing. **"Breeches, bind your legs together and hobble your wearers,"** she ordered. After all, *she* was wearing a dress, not breeches, so the only people it would affect would be the guard and the *Graf*.

"Witch!" the *Graf* screamed, thrashing on the floor with futile kicks.

"I thought you already knew that," Irene pointed out, picking up a twisted piece of ironwork that was probably an instrument of torture. At the moment, the most important thing about it to her was that it was a heavy blunt instrument that could be applied to people's heads.

Two thumps later, and with the room a great deal quieter, she opened the door and stepped into the corridor, fastening her discarded wimple back over her hair. The key—also cold iron—was conveniently hanging on the wall, and she used it to lock the door before going any farther. She had until Stefan got back with the priest. That should be long enough.

Another whimper came from one of the other cells, and Irene found herself torn. Her objective here was to acquire a book from the *Graf*'s private library. It wasn't often that she got to do her job—that is, to steal books in order to maintain the balance of the universe—with such a thoroughly unpleasant and deserving target. She should be focusing on that and not on his lordship's other victims. And if she spent time on them, it might jeopardise her chance of securing that copy of the *Heliand*. Which was much more important than the lives of a few peasants who would never know about the Library or understand its mission . . .

But releasing all the prisoners would be a *big* distraction. It was a convenient counter-argument, which satisfied her conscience and very nearly her sense of duty. Of course, that could just be a specious rationalization. But it meant that she didn't have to abandon the *Graf*'s prisoners, so she could live with it.

Five minutes later, she'd released two prisoners—whom she left in charge of freeing the others as she sneaked up the nearest stairs.

The next obstacle presented itself quickly enough. The guardroom was at the head of the stairwell, and it was occupied. This whole place was like the *Graf* himself—utterly paranoid. There was no cover either: the stairwell was plain rough-hewn stone. And although it was only lit by torches, there were no places where one might hide if the guards ran to investigate the distraction below. But Irene did have one trick up her sleeve.

She marched up to the guard-room door, opened it, and walked in.

The four guards were lounging and sharing an illicit jug of beer, and they stared at her in shock. Fortunately none of them had the wit to immediately shout "Witch!" or launch himself at her, which gave Irene the time to speak.

"You perceive," she said, using the Language again, **"that I am not the witch you're looking for, but just another guard on an errand for the *Graf,* and that it is entirely normal for me to be passing through and not worth your time or interest."**

The headache hit her. Using the Language to confuse people's perceptions was a strain at the best of times, and doing it to four people simultaneously made it worse. But it worked: they gave her no more than casual nods, as their brains reinterpreted her presence as unimportant. Two of them turned back to their argument over dice, while the third returned to polishing his sword.

The fourth kept on staring at her. Irene's throat was dry as she walked across the room, passing between them, concentrating on not doing anything that might shake their delusion. It wouldn't last long in any case. But if that fourth guard had somehow managed to see the truth . . .

"Hey, Johann," he grunted. "Did you have a word with Lise about your sister?"

Irene shrugged and made a noncommittal noise, feeling the flesh crawl down her back. Three more steps to the door at the far side of the room. *Don't notice anything,* she prayed, *don't notice anything . . .*

One of the dice rollers looked up, confused. "Johann?" he said. "That's Bruno."

The original questioner frowned. "No, that's Johann—"

Irene threw herself through the door and slammed it shut behind her. **"Door, lock and jam!"** she gasped. She heard the wards in the lock click into place a moment before someone yanked on the door handle on the other side. The door strained in its frame as more guards added their weight to the handle, shouting in an attempt to raise the alarm.

So much for her margin of safety. Irene ran down the corridor ahead of her. The stonework was smoother here, and the torches better quality. This meant she was getting closer to the *Graf*'s quarters at the top of the castle, but it also meant she was more likely to be noticed. Even if nobody recognized her as the "witch" who'd been brought in earlier today, they would see her peasant clothing and ask awkward questions.

Irene mentally reviewed her experience as a Librarian. From all her years of stealing books, to maintain the balance between order and chaos, what would serve her best? Maxims such as *When in doubt, hide the evidence* or *Deny everything and ask for a lawyer* flickered unhelpfully through her mind.

I want everyone out of my way while I head upwards. So what if they all focus downwards . . .

This part of the castle was for servants. Kitchens, guard-rooms, laundries, bedrooms. The smell of boiling cabbage and turnips coming from ahead of her indicated a kitchen nearby. That would do nicely.

Irene waited for someone to emerge. It was a male servant with a harried look, carrying a stack of folded uniforms. She caught his arm, and before he could react, she told him, **"You perceive I've told you the Devil is loose in the dungeons, and that this is absolutely true. And you must rally the guards to go down there and save the *Graf*."**

Then she let him go and stood well back, taking an alternate route through the servants' passages as the alarm was raised.

Irene repeated the manoeuvre several times as she made her way up through the castle. This place had a superfluity of guards, and they were all converging on the lower parts of the castle. Even if they didn't all believe in the Devil, they did believe in the *Graf*—and in what the *Graf* might do to them if they didn't respond enthusiastically enough. Or perhaps they *did* believe in the Devil. In the febrile atmosphere of panic and suspicion that surrounded this place, it was easy enough to believe in evil.

Finally, with a sigh of relief, she set foot on the stair leading to the *Graf*'s private quarters and library. The plans she'd memorised had proved accurate—so far. There was a great deal of confusion going on below—she had heard screams and crashes, and she thought she could smell smoke—but the focus of interest was still downwards, not upwards. She had a pounding headache, but also some anachronistic aspirin hidden in her bodice, for when this was all over. So far the mission was going according to plan. Well, more or less. Somewhat. She was still alive and nearly at her objective. And if there was a little bit of regime change going on below stairs, well, these things did happen.

She used the Language to open the heavily locked door, closed it behind her to cover her tracks, and wearily plodded up the stairs, admiring the tapestries and embroidered rugs on the landings. Like the rest of the castle, this tower was heavy stone, constructed to last for centuries and keep out both draughts and invaders. It was why she'd devised this whole infiltration. The *Graf* and his guards were too paranoid for her to have entered the place under any normal circumstances. She'd had to lure him into bringing her inside himself.

But getting out was going to be difficult. It all depended on whether the *Graf*'s private "library" was as large as he liked to claim.

The rooms at the top were laid out in a spiral around the ascending stairs, each one heavily locked. As she unlocked and checked each, Irene saw that inside they were scrupulously clean. The shelves were rich with the smell of beeswax, and the heavy covers of the books gleamed with inset jewels or gold lettering. Either the *Graf* did the dusting himself—unlikely, Irene judged—or the maids were escorted up here daily. There was no way any mere servant would have been allowed the keys to the *Graf*'s pride and glory. Oil lamps burned continually in all the rooms, making them much better lit than the rest of the castle below.

Fortunately the *Graf* did have some organisation to his collection. Most of it concerned witchcraft, demonology and diabolism, and horrific crimes (presumably in case any had been committed by witches). But he'd put the few works that were actually connected with theology and hagiology in a small side bookcase in the fifth room. Irene knelt to sort through the books. Since they were all large, heavy volumes, and most had their names on the fronts, not the sides, she had to slide each one out to check it.

The silent footsteps from behind took her by surprise; if it hadn't been for the shadow that fell across her book, she wouldn't have been warned at all. She threw herself to one side, letting the book fall and feeling a pang of guilt as it thudded to the ground, bringing her arm up to shield her face as she rolled. A thin line of pain scored her forearm.

Irene came to her feet, grateful for the loose skirts of her dirndl, and took the other person in. It was a woman: she was in a silk shift, wildly inappropriate for anything except bed, her blonde hair falling loose over her shoulders and down her back. In one hand she clasped a needle-pointed misericord dagger. She was holding it point-up in a knife-fighter's grip, rather than the more amateur point-down position. And, Irene noted with growing dismay, the blade had an unpleasant black stain from hilt to point.

Irene's arm throbbed. Right. Poison. She had to take care of that, but she had to take care of this woman first. She'd heard that the *Graf* had a mistress (it had been the first thing the village gossips mentioned), but she hadn't realized that the *Graf* kept the woman in his private library.

The woman shifted her weight from foot to foot, watching Irene carefully, then slid in for another attack, her blade moving to slice rather than stab. She was keeping a defensive position, going for flesh wounds rather than serious injury.

Irene blocked the woman's thrust with a self-defence move. Something from an unarmed combat class, years ago and in a different world. Irene caught her wrist and twisted hand and wrist round behind the other woman as she kicked the woman's knee out from under her, forcing her to the floor. "Drop it," she ordered.

"Witch!" the woman spat. "Do your worst!"

Irene tried not to consider this a challenge. Instead she simply wound her free hand into the other woman's flowing hair and banged her head against the floorboards a few times, till she stopped moving.

Her arm was really aching now. She needed to get that poison out of her system *fast*.

Prudently she kicked the dagger well out of the other woman's reach, then peeled back her own sleeve. It was a shallow cut, but deep enough for something to get into her bloodstream.

Irene settled back on her knees. **"Poison or any other sub-**

stance on the dagger, leave my body through the route that you entered!" she commanded.

A sudden spurt of blood came from the wound, spattering across her skirts and over the floor. Irene gritted her teeth as she swayed with light-headedness, waiting till the flow had stopped before turning her wimple into a tourniquet and bandage. She couldn't actually *see* any poison in the blood, but then one wouldn't, would one?

The little voice of common sense at the back of her mind pointed out that she was getting distracted. And she needed to tie up the *Graf*'s mistress, find that book, and get out of there.

Irene shook her head and pulled herself together. Priorities. Right.

The book turned out to be on the next shelf down—rather than, as Irene had been starting to fear, the last book on the entire bookcase. (Sometimes the universe had an unpleasant sense of humour.) Her Old Saxon was shaky to non-existent, but the title was clear, and she'd checked beforehand what some key phrases in the text should be. It was the full version of the *Heliand*, rather than the partial ones the Library had already taken from this world—the life of Jesus in verse form, in Old Saxon, composed sometime during the ninth century. And this one, unlike versions of the *Heliand* from other worlds, was supposed to have some interesting divergences from the New Testament that made it unique.

Mission accomplished. Now Irene just had to get out of this castle—and out of this *world*.

The *Graf*'s mistress lay bound and unconscious on the floor. Irene stepped over her and walked to the open door, the book a heavy weight under her arm. She closed it, the iron handle cold against her hand.

Now, would this work or not? Reaching the Library from one of the thousands of alternate worlds required a sufficiently large collection of books. The *Graf*'s library was reasonably large—well, for this time and place—and was certainly dedicated to the function of being a library, rather than simply a showplace or a warehouse. It would make her life a great deal easier if this *did* work . . .

"Open to the Library," Irene ordered in the Language, and pulled the door open.

The room on the other side was as far from the stone tower stairway as possible. A meshwork of metal shelves covered the walls and spun out across the ceiling, firm under the weight of piles of printouts and books bound in gleaming white cardboard and slick plastic. In the centre of the room, a set of computer screens hummed in an electronic Stonehenge of server towers, dark mirrors that reflected the rest of the room.

From the floor, the *Graf*'s mistress gasped in shock.

Irene stepped through the open doorway, but before closing it, she turned to address the other woman. It seemed unfair to leave her with all the blame. "I suggest you tell him that you stabbed me and I vanished with a scream," she offered. "You've got my blood on the floor and on the dagger, after all. And it's a good ending for a story about witches . . ."

And then she shut the door and broke the link to that world.

Several hours later, Irene had deposited the book in the Library's central collections system, where it would be delivered to the proper place for reading and archival. And now that that world had stronger links to the Library, it should be protected against the forces of chaos. She'd treated the cut on her arm with more up-to-date medicine and bandages, taken several aspirin, and changed her clothing. For her next location, her current home, was very different—a vaguely Victorian England with a tendency towards steam power, zeppelins, libertines, and Great Detectives.

And now she was sitting in this Great Detective's lodgings. Peregrine Vale was the nemesis of criminals across Great Britain and—rather to Irene's own surprise—her friend. For whom she was about to do a minor favour.

A society blackmailer had stumbled across a compromising document in Ottoman Turkish, regarding British troop dispositions. And while Vale had been quite capable of getting his hands on said blackmailer's entire stock of private documents, he couldn't read Ottoman Turkish or identify the specific letter. Which was why Irene had dropped by. Well, one of the reasons.

The other reason sat across the table from Vale, sorting through the large pile of documents that had been dumped at the centre of the table, the ether-lights turning him into an illustration by a master ink painter. His dark hair fell carelessly round his face; his skin was as pale as marble, his eyes a blue so dark that it mirrored the lightless depths of the ocean, and his bones could have been the work of a master sculptor.

Kai was Irene's previous apprentice. He was also a dragon prince. He'd had to abandon any career he might have had as a Librarian (though frankly, Irene doubted he'd have made it his final choice) due to political complications, and they had publicly parted ways. But public declarations of *sadly, you are no longer my mentor* didn't cover private meetings in the houses of mutual friends. Irene didn't know how long they could carry on like this. So she was already preparing herself for the moment when the theoretical separation became a reality. But for the moment, she was going to enjoy Kai's company as long as she could.

Except, of course, when the Library sent her on urgent missions. To be honest, she found the timing of the recent *Heliand* recovery a little suspect. Possibly even a subtle hint that she should be spending her time purely on Library business? But the good thing about subtle hints was that one could ignore them as long as the actual work got done. She'd done her work. Now her time was her own.

Irene did technically have a higher purpose. The infinite array of alternate worlds was unstable, veering between chaos on one end and order on the other. Entities from the far ends of this reality—Fae representing chaos and dragons standing for order—threatened to destabilise the worlds for their own purposes. They were capable of dragging them to the brink of war or even destroying them. But the Library maintained the balance between worlds by acquiring and keeping (the keeping bit was very important) unique works of fiction from the different alternate worlds. Usually without asking first. This had a massively stabilizing effect on those worlds. And Irene's duties as a sworn Librarian were far more important than personal indulgences.

On the other hand, there was little she could do in pursuit of said higher purpose at two o'clock in the morning, on a foggy London night in December. So she might as well look over Vale's documents, have a glass of brandy, and spend what was left of the night chatting with friends. And then possibly something else, with Kai.

And when it came to personal indulgences . . . Kai had made it quite clear that he would be pleased to share her bed. But it wouldn't have been appropriate to their mentor-apprentice relationship. Yet now she was no longer responsible for his welfare, well . . .

The ether-lights on the walls had been turned up to full brightness, throwing the black and white of Kai's evening dress into sharp relief and lingering on the battered collar and cuffs of Vale's favourite dressing gown. Kai held up one of the letters to inspect its watermark. He sniffed it, and his nose wrinkled. "This one doesn't give any names at the beginning or end," he reported, "but it's all about romance, the target has scarlet hair, and the writer has an unfortunate taste for sandalwood."

"Probably one of the Chisholm sisters," Vale said, not looking up from the sheaf of invoices he was flicking through. "Put it on the pile to my right. If you've recovered from your journey, Winters, pull up a chair and lend us your assistance. Strongrock and I have made a start, but I would like to get these sorted and cleared before dawn to avoid any possible awkwardness."

"It's always a sensible idea to get things neat and tidy," Irene agreed. And to get rid of any compromising evidence before police can show up and search the place. She pulled the spare armchair up to the table and chose a few papers. "Was it an interesting night?" she asked Kai.

He shrugged. "Sometimes life can be cruel. I had to stand on the roof while other people"—he caught Vale's glance—"ah, acquired papers. If we have to do this again, I'd like to take a more equal share of the job."

"Such an event is highly unlikely," Vale said firmly. "I do not descend to criminal actions—unless the cause is good and the action is absolutely necessary."

Kai and Irene exchanged a sidewards glance but had more sense than to disagree.

Irene found herself relaxing as she looked through the documents. With her own duty put aside for the moment, she was among friends, and that was still a new enough experience that she wasn't completely used to it.

Over the last year or two, she had gradually become accustomed to the feeling that there were people in her life whom she could rely on. Whom she could trust. Even if one of them was the greatest detective in an alternate Victorian London, and the other was a somewhat-out-of-favour dragon prince in human form. Even if she was supposed to have parted ways with the dragon prince, rather than publicly associating with him. But this was her life now, a permanent assignment as Librarian-in-Residence to this world. It wasn't what she'd planned.

But plans rarely worked out.

"Irene?" Kai asked, turning to look more closely at her. "Is something the matter?"

She hesitated, trying to think of what to say. With a mental sigh she dismissed sentiment and got back to practicalities. "Metaphysics," she said with a shrug, "and how we got to where we are now. Nothing important."

Carriage wheels creaked and came to a stop in the street outside, and Vale frowned. He rose and walked across to the first-floor window, drawing the edge of a curtain back to peer out. "A private carriage," he reported. "Not the police, not even Singh. And not Lady Rotherhyde . . ."

He paused, looking genuinely surprised. "Winters, I do believe it is your associate Bradamant. Why would she be looking for you at this hour?"

Downstairs the doorbell rang.

"I don't know," Irene said, jumping up from the table, "but I'd better go and find out. I apologise—"

Vale shook his head. "Not important. But do go and see to her, before she rouses the housekeeper."

Kai half rose from his seat, but Irene gestured for him to stay put. "We're not supposed to be associating, remember?" she reminded him.

Kai snorted. "As if Bradamant's going to believe that." But he sat down again.

Irene reflected on the virtues of plausible deniability as she ran down the stairs. Hopefully Bradamant wasn't here in any sort of official capacity.

The doorbell sounded again as Irene reached the entrance hall at the bottom of the stairs. She hurried to throw back the bolts and open the door.

Bradamant had one hand raised to push the bell again, but she lowered it as she saw Irene. "Thank God you're here," she said. "I tried your lodgings first, but you weren't there and you hadn't left a note."

"I wasn't expecting visitors," Irene said, beckoning Bradamant inside and closing the door behind her. The other woman was muffled in a thick grey velvet mantle trimmed with ermine at the cuffs and collar—slightly out of period for the world and country in which they were both standing, but very warm, and certainly very stylish. Her black hair gleamed with tiny dewdrops from the fog. "Is there an emergency?"

"There is," Bradamant said. "But you're not the only person I'm after."

Irene's mind immediately went to Kai, and her heart sank. Was this some sort of formal separation demand? Had someone in authority decided to enforce a ban between them? "Oh?" she said, trying to control her pulse. "Who else?"

"Vale." Bradamant nodded towards the stairs. "I'm glad to see that he's in. There's been a murder, Irene. We need a detective, and a good one. Or things are going to be even worse than you can possibly imagine."

CHAPTER 2

"Who's dead?" Irene demanded. "Is it someone I know?" She was tempted to add something about how she could in fact imagine pretty bad situations. But then she took another look at Bradamant's face and decided—just this once—not to be sarcastic. Bradamant, normally one of the most cool and controlled Librarians Irene knew, was *worried*. Being witty could wait.

Unless Bradamant gave her a genuine excuse to indulge.

"No, you don't know him," Bradamant said quickly. "At least, I don't think you've ever met him. It's not a Librarian. It's—look, can I just come upstairs and tell you and Vale both at once?"

"Bring your colleague up here, Winters!" Vale called from his room. He'd obviously been listening.

Irene gestured Bradamant towards the stairs. "You know the way, I think." She locked the door, then followed Bradamant up the stairs and arrived in Vale's room in time to see Vale and Kai hastily rearranging the chairs. A spare sheet had been thrown over the table, papers and all, in a vague attempt at plausible deniability.

Bradamant gave Kai a cool glance. "And I suppose you just happened to be in the vicinity," she said.

Kai returned an equally frosty look, and Irene remembered that his protective instincts towards her involved a certain amount of antipathy towards Bradamant—even if she and Irene had technically agreed to be on polite terms now. "I'm visiting my friend Peregrine Vale," he said. "Is there some sort of problem with that?"

Vale regarded the two of them with an expression that was partly a plea for heaven to give him patience, but mostly a weary impatience for them to cut the chit-chat and get on to the gory details. "Madam Bradamant. Kindly take a seat. I perceive that you have recently come from another world where it happens to have been snowing." He flung himself into his favourite armchair. "Strongrock, Winters, sit or not as you wish, but I believe the lady's business is urgent."

"I don't suppose it would do any good to ask to speak to you in private?" Bradamant said. "And how did you know about the snow?"

"Very little good," Vale replied. "And it would make me very curious about why you are trying to keep secrets from my colleagues. As to the snow, while your clothing has had time to dry, the marks on the hem of your dress indicate you have been walking through dirty snow, which left traces on the fabric as it dried."

Irene treasured a little spark of delight at the word *colleagues,* taking a seat in one of the spare armchairs. Kai dropped into another, leaning forward with interest.

Bradamant turned her hands over in her lap. "Before we start," she said, "what I have to tell you mustn't go beyond the walls of this room. And I don't mean the local newspapers. I'm talking about Fae, dragons, or even other Librarians—if they aren't already involved."

"Involved in what?" Irene asked. She'd always tried to stay out of Library politics, but a creeping feeling of doom was suggesting she should have paid more attention. What exactly had she managed to miss?

Bradamant looked at the three of them—Vale, Irene, and Kai—then took a deep breath. "A peace conference has just started," she said, the words spilling out too fast, as if she was trying to complete her statement before someone stopped her. Or as if she was afraid of what she was saying. "Between the dragons and the Fae. The Library's playing mediator. And there might be a genuine chance of it *working*."

"And I suppose," Vale said drily, "I'm to attend as a representative of humanity. Those mere common mortals who people the worlds."

"You must be joking," Bradamant said, dropping all semblance of tact. "They barely listen to *us*. What makes you think they're going to listen to ordinary humans? No, we need you there because the second negotiator on the dragon side has been murdered, and it looks as if the whole thing is going to fall apart. Vale, if you've ever felt you owed anything to the Library, if you have *any* regard for the safety of other worlds besides your own, then I'm begging you to come and help us. The Library can offer you whatever you want. But we need to know who did it, before someone starts a war."

There was dead silence in the room.

Finally Irene said, "When the hell did this happen?" She saw Vale twitch at the vulgarity. "Please excuse my language," she added hastily. "But seriously, *how*? It's only been a few months since the Alberich drama." That was the short way of putting it. It sounded better than *since Alberich tried to destroy the Library, nearly killing all of us. And I can only hope that he's dead and stays that way.* "How on earth is all this supposed to have happened since then too, and how can you keep something like this hushed up?" The dragons and the Fae came from opposite ends of the universe and were creatures of order and chaos, respectively. The dragons embodied pure natural forces, and the Fae represented fictional narrative tropes—so they were polar opposites. And they didn't just dislike each other—they *loathed* each other. Humans were caught in the middle—possessions to be protected, or playing pieces to be used in their games. While individuals from either side might be reasonable and occasionally willing to negotiate, the idea that the two sides might be willing to make peace was something that Irene had never even considered in her most spectacular daydreams.

"What I want to know is how it could have happened *at all*!" Kai was as stiff as a carved statue in his chair. The colour had drained from his skin, leaving him paler than marble, and his fingers dug into the arms of the chair—as though he would break it apart in order to assert reality as he knew it. "And it is *impossible* that any of my kindred would consider peace with such beings as the Fae!"

"These are both valid points," Vale said. He settled back in his chair, calm with the ease of a man who didn't have an immediate personal stake in the matter. Or perhaps he was simply allowing Irene and Kai to act as lightning rods and ask the questions he wouldn't know to ask. While his voice was all smooth reason and logic, his eyes were hard and suspicious. "Maybe you should begin from the beginning. Assuming that we aren't required on the spot immediately?"

"We've got long enough for me to explain this to you," Bradamant said. She folded her hands over each other, stilling their trembling, composing herself. "The scene of the murder's being kept as untouched as possible. It did get disturbed when the victim was found but hasn't been tampered with since then."

Kai swallowed, closing his eyes for a moment as though he didn't want to ask, but it came out unwillingly. "Who is the victim?"

It might be someone he knows, Irene realized. *It might be a friend, or family . . .* She reached across to touch his wrist for a moment, in a vain gesture of reassurance.

"Lord Ren Shun," Bradamant said. "He was a liegeman of—"

Kai's sharp hiss of indrawn breath cut her off. "He's the sworn man of my lord uncle Ao Ji! What was he doing at an event such as *this*?"

"Well, that's part of the problem," Bradamant said. "Your uncle is there too. He's . . ." She looked as if she was remembering something extremely unsettling, and her hands clenched in her lap. "Deeply unhappy."

"My lord uncle has a temper," Kai agreed, his tone as carefully neutral as Bradamant's was carefully controlled. "But how could such an attack have happened?"

"Perhaps if you were to permit Madam Bradamant to tell her story without interrupting, we'd find out," Vale suggested. He was watching Bradamant from under half-closed eyelids, as if he suspected the whole story was an elaborate hoax.

Irene might have agreed with Vale—after all, Bradamant had lied to both of them before—but this time she felt the other Librarian was telling the truth. Those hints of distress were a little too real to be faked. And she could guess why Bradamant was off balance. If she'd been anywhere near a dragon king who had lost his temper . . .

She made her way over to where Vale kept the brandy, splashing some into four glasses, then returned to hand them round. Bradamant took her glass with a nod of thanks, but both Vale and Kai ignored theirs for the moment.

Bradamant sipped the brandy and pulled her usual air of calm composure around her like the mantle she still wore. "From the beginning, then," she said. "It all goes back to when Kai here was kidnapped by the Fae."

"In order to start a war between the dragons and Fae, I thought," Vale said.

"Yes," Bradamant agreed, "but when the abduction went wrong, you could say that it galvanised those on both sides who *hadn't* originally wanted one. A war, that is. When they saw just how close they'd come to being embroiled in a conflict, one that they *really* weren't interested in, just because one dragon princeling had been seized by a pair of manipulators, a number of them reconsidered the status quo. It began to seem like a good idea to get a non-aggression pact up and running. Or so I've been told, you understand. I wasn't actually involved in the early parts of this myself. I only found out about it two days ago."

Kai was still frowning. "And I didn't hear anything about this when I was visiting my family—and that was less than a month ago."

"It must have been kept very secret, even within both sides," Irene said. She considered. "Were the prime movers planning to spring a peace treaty on their allies as a fait accompli once it had been agreed, and hope that they'd go along with it?"

Bradamant nodded. "Or at least the instigators hoped the allies in question wouldn't object too strongly. And once one little peace agreement had been reached, more might have come in time. It was a very tentative bridge. But it *was* a bridge."

Vale nodded. "And when precisely did both sides approach each other? And when—and why—did they approach the Library?"

"I don't know exactly when contact was made," Bradamant said, "but Fae and dragon representatives contacted the Library shortly after Alberich was destroyed—wanting us to act as mediators."

"You mean, once they'd seen that we were safely back on our feet and he wasn't going to wipe us out in a ball of flaming debris?" Irene said wryly.

Bradamant shrugged. "Consider their attitude to be a compliment to us—or rather you—for getting rid of him. Ultimately he was a danger to them as well as to us. Library power in the hands of someone who didn't even pretend to neutrality? Not something that either the Fae or the dragons would sanction." She must have seen the expression on Irene's face. "No, I don't trust either side myself, but what do you actually want us to *do* about it? Stand on our pride? Or accept the realpolitik and do whatever we can, with the goal being to establish a non-aggression pact which both sides would sign up to?"

"You're veering between *peace treaty* and *non-aggression pact*," Vale commented. "Which would you say is more accurate?"

Bradamant paused, then shrugged. "It's still being hammered out. I'd prefer the first one, but I'll take whatever we can get. Lord Ren Shun was doing a lot of the negotiating. To be honest, he and the Fae second in command were getting on a lot better than the two principals."

Vale nodded. "A situation not unknown among human beings. Very well. And your Library was brought in as a neutral party?"

"Exactly." Bradamant sipped her brandy again. "I don't know the full details—I haven't been *told* the full details—but the original idea seems to have been that we organise the location and act as arbitrators. Both sides knew that if we swear to something in the Language, we have to keep our word. That way they could be sure that we'd stay neutral. And I think there are going to be clauses in the final agreement, involving us not 'acquiring' books from treaty signatories . . . which could be inconvenient. Anyhow, we ended up booking hotels in Paris, in a different world to this one."

"Hotels?" Vale queried.

"Three hotels," Bradamant said with a sigh. "One each for the two sides and a third one for negotiations to take place. Both sides refused to share a hotel. And this was as neutral a world as we could find."

"'We' booked hotels . . . ?" Kai said. "I thought you said that you'd only just come in on it."

Bradamant flushed but kept her tone level. "The senior Librarians organised them. I was using the collective 'we.' If I may continue?"

Vale waved a lazy hand for her to go on.

"So skipping over the background, which I can give you on the way there, the crime boils down to this. The second dragon negotiator, Ren Shun, went out yesterday evening—not telling anyone exactly where he was going. He was found the next morning, stabbed in the back in a conference room belonging to the negotiations hotel. The Fae were accused, of course."

There was a shocked—or possibly thoughtful—moment of silence. Kai opened his mouth. Then he shut it again. Finally he said, "While the personal agenda seems obvious, I wouldn't have expected any Fae to be so *stupid*. Unless they actually wanted to cause a breakdown in negotiations."

Irene was conscious of how large a concession that was from Kai, who had absolutely no reason to like the Fae personally, and whose lifelong antipathy towards them gave him every excuse to think the worst. "I'm guessing any Librarians on the spot stressed that point heavily."

Bradamant nodded. "Kostchei—he's one of our lead arbitrators—said that they managed to talk His Majesty out of anything immediate. His Majesty being Ao Ji, head of the dragon contingent. Kostchei promised on behalf of the Library that we'd investigate, as the neutral party, and find the murderer."

"And who put Vale's name forward?" Irene asked. She was torn between pride that they'd come to him and concern for Vale himself. There was no way that this could be described as safe—for Vale, or for his world, if things went wrong . . .

"That I don't know," Bradamant said, so smoothly that Irene was sure she was lying. "But I was told to fetch him as soon as possible."

Vale frowned. "You say the murder was discovered this morning? Or rather, yesterday, since we're past midnight already?"

Irene could see his point. It did seem a curiously long delay.

Bradamant put down her empty glass and spread her hands. "I know we should have reacted faster. But first the senior Librarians present had to decide on a course of action. And then they had to negotiate who'd be doing the investigation—besides Vale—with the parties involved."

Vale's eyebrows rose. *"Besides me . . . ?"* he said flatly.

"It wasn't easy," Bradamant said quickly. "Everyone wanted their own people looking into it. In the end it was thrashed out into a three-person team who'd be assisting you, one person from each group." She sighed. "I know it sounds as if they spent hours talking rather than actually doing anything practical. But it took that long to come to an agreement."

Vale shrugged. "I am not unfamiliar with politically awkward situations. I can work with this, as long as it is understood by all parties that the observers aren't to get in my way."

"Well, at least one of them should suit you." Bradamant nodded towards Irene. "The Librarian member of the team is Irene here."

"Me?" Irene said, then felt foolish. Apparently some responses were hardwired into the human brain, right up there with *this isn't what it looks like* when caught with an open safe and a stolen book. Her second reaction was pure relief that she'd have some influence here—be able to help Vale, to *protect* Vale, and to actually do something to help sort out this disaster. The more cynical third reaction was to wonder why her. "Surely they'd have wanted someone more senior on the job. And I don't just mean the Librarians who've been masterminding this, I mean all factions. I may be competent, but I'm still junior."

"No doubt the Librarians believe you'll be able to sway my judgement, should it prove expedient in some way," Vale remarked, proving that he was just as cynical as Irene. "Or they think having you around will convince me to accept the case."

"But you are accepting it, aren't you?" Bradamant demanded. She clearly didn't like the idea that Vale might even consider saying no.

"I am taking it under consideration." Vale steepled his fingers and regarded his nails thoughtfully. "Were all three factions required to approve all the team members?"

A nasty thought trickled into Irene's mind, spreading like a cloud of ink in water. "Kai isn't the dragon representative, is he?"

Kai straightened in his chair. "But I'm the logical candidate!" he protested.

"How *did* you deduce that?" Bradamant asked Irene wryly.

"You'd have said if he was." Irene put down her still-full glass of brandy. "Besides—forgive me, Kai—the only logical reason for your uncle to choose *you* as dragon representative would be if he thought you could influence Vale." Kai was a very young dragon, after all, and even if he was the son of one of the dragon kings, he was the youngest son, and Irene had heard a number of other dragons describe him as "low-born" on his mother's side. She hadn't asked for an explanation, but it didn't seem a recommendation under the current circumstances.

That didn't mean that she was *happy* to be going into this without Kai. Far from it. But perhaps there were ways around it . . .

Bradamant apparently took Irene's comment as agreement with the situation. "I'm sorry, Kai," she said. "But I hadn't even expected to find you here. According to Irene's report, you'd stopped working with her. I don't even know what you *are* doing here." Her glance towards Irene promised later pointed questions.

"Strongrock is visiting me," Vale put in before Kai could declare his absolute freedom to be anywhere he felt like. "Can you tell me who the dragon or Fae representatives are, Madam Bradamant?"

"No. But they should be meeting us in Paris, at our hotel. I'm assuming they'll be competent."

But competent at what? Irene wondered. *Competent investigators? Or competent politicians who'll just want to cover this up and make sure the treaty gets signed? Unless their goal is for it not to be signed. And if I'm being honest with myself, what's actually more important—the crime or the treaty?*

First things first. Get the facts, then decide what to do next. And hope that there is a next.

"And what are the *other* possible motives for the victim's murder?" Vale asked.

"What do you mean?" Bradamant said.

Vale gestured impatiently. "Do not attempt innocence, madam. It doesn't suit you. We've all agreed it would be extremely stupid for any member of the Fae peace-seeking faction to commit a murder like this. But what about those who don't want peace? And what *has* been suggested as a motive?"

"I didn't want to prejudice you," Bradamant said stubbornly. "And I've probably already said more than I should in front of Kai."

Kai's jaw set in lines very similar to Bradamant's—though neither of them, Irene thought, would have welcomed her pointing it out. "I'm of the opinion you haven't said enough," Kai replied.

Irene rose to her feet. "Kai," she said. "Bradamant has a point. This is Vale's case to investigate. Perhaps we'd both better leave the room for a moment, in case she has something that she wants to tell him. She is his client, after all. And you and I can discuss where you're going after this."

For a long moment Kai stared at Irene. Then he stood. "As you wish," he said. "My coat's downstairs. I'll see you all later. Vale, I hope that you can resolve this situation."

"It has its interesting points," Vale said. His glance to Irene suggested that he knew exactly what she had in mind and that he wasn't going to stop her. Instead he leaned forward towards Bradamant, beckoning her to continue. "Motives—" he began.

Irene led Kai down the stairs to just inside the front door—and safely out of Bradamant's earshot, as long as they kept their voices down—before turning to him. "I want you there," she said softly. "Vale *needs* you there. And I think your uncle could use your help in Paris. But do you think you can actually support a peace treaty like this?"

In the near darkness, Kai's face was troubled. "There was a time when I would have said no," he answered quietly. "The Fae are creatures of chaos, and they aren't healthy for humanity—or anyone else. But I am prepared to consider a non-aggression pact, if *they* are willing to abide by it. And if my lord uncle Ao Ji is in favour of it—he of all people!—then I can follow his lead."

"He isn't usually in favour of such things?" Irene guessed.

"Of all my uncles, he would be the most strongly set against it. He's never made a secret of his opinions. He loathes the Fae. He considers them a pollution that endangers all human beings—and we consider it a duty to protect those humans who dwell in our realms. He would like to see the Fae scoured from the surface of every world they've touched." Kai shrugged. "But perhaps he's decided that confinement is an acceptable strategy. And if he's willing to negotiate it, then I can do no less. So what have you got in mind?"

Irene felt her lips quirking into a smile. He knew her quite well by now. "Since you clearly know him reasonably well, could you realistically feel a sudden need to visit your uncle?"

"Unlikely but not unrealistic," Kai judged. "Of course, the moment I turn up, people are going to suspect collusion."

"Plausible deniability," Irene said firmly. "Try to look innocent. Try really, really hard. Besides, if your uncle thinks that you might be able to exert influence on Vale, he's likely to want you to stay."

"You think that he'll want to affect the outcome of the investigation?"

"Your uncle is a ruling monarch. He isn't going to throw away a possible tool, even if he doesn't end up using it. Wouldn't you agree?"

Kai nodded. "And I can make sure you get reliable information, once I'm there. Or deal with any of my kind who might be trying to sow dissension. That was why you marched me out of there right now, wasn't it? So that I can get there as soon as possible and already be there when you turn up?"

"Pretty much," Irene admitted. "That whole plausible deniability thing. And I suspect Bradamant may not want to admit how much she's already told you. We'll see." She knew that Kai—like all dragons—could travel between worlds to a person he knew well, wherever that person was. He'd probably reach that world long before she and Vale did, since they'd have to travel through the Library to get there. "Play it by ear," she instructed. "And try to keep your options open. Is anyone expecting you to be anywhere else?"

"My father's servant Tian Shu had written to say he'd call on me," Kai admitted. "I think he wants more details about the recent business in America. But I think I can get away with avoiding that for a while . . ."

"If you're sure it won't be an issue," Irene said. "I don't want you getting into trouble."

"It's my decision to make. And I thought the two of us weren't supposed to be teacher and student any more. Or superior and inferior."

Irene flushed. "I'm sorry," she said. "Some habits die hard."

"I'd be a fool not to listen to you." He caught her by the shoulders and pulled her close, brushing a kiss against her forehead. "Be careful, Irene. My lord uncle Ao Ji has little tolerance for impertinence."

For a moment Irene let herself enjoy the feeling of his body against hers, and bitterly regretted abandoning certain plans that she'd had for the rest of the night. But there was, after all, a crisis.

When *wasn't* there a crisis?

"Be careful yourself." She pulled herself away, giving his hands a squeeze. "There's already been one death. I don't want you in danger." She considered exactly what they were all walking into. "Well, not any *more* danger."

"The story of our lives," Kai said with a sigh. He caught up his coat from the rack by the door and strode out into the foggy night.

Irene trotted back up the stairs, hoping that she hadn't missed too much. She knew that Bradamant would realize she'd been talking to Kai. She hoped—for the sake of peace and non-aggression between Librarians for at least the next few hours—that Bradamant wouldn't figure out what she'd been suggesting. She was sure Vale had guessed (that is, *deduced*) what she had in mind, but he'd be glad to have Kai as potential backup.

As she walked back into the room, Bradamant was saying, "And there's the Library's motive."

Irene stopped dead in the doorway. "The Library's motive?" she demanded. "What sort of motive would the *Library* have?"

"I'm no happier about it than you are," Bradamant said bitterly. "But His Majesty Ao Ji says that the night before the murder, Lord Ren Shun said something about a mysterious book. And given that he's now dead . . . Well, who else would kill someone over a book?"

CHAPTER 3

"And you can tell me nothing more of the Fae side except the pseudonyms of their leaders?" Vale queried. "The Princess and the Cardinal?" Instead of spending time scrutinising the Library as they used it to pass between worlds, Vale had been all business. He was rapidly firing questions at Bradamant on the details of the case and growing perceptibly irritated at how little she knew.

Bradamant jerked her shoulders in an angry shrug. "I've told you everything I've been told myself. I'd only just *arrived* there when I was sent away again to fetch you. Kostchei didn't have the chance to give me a full briefing." Her anger, Irene suspected, was more at her own ignorance than at Vale: naturally Bradamant would want to know what was going on. Who wouldn't?

And the biggest question of all, the one that would be troubling Bradamant as much as it was Irene: What was the mysterious book that Ren Shun had mentioned? Was it incidental to his murder, or was it the direct cause?

And what would they do if it *had* been a Librarian who killed him? The Library's reputation would be shattered for good—and its ancient calling would be obstructed at every turn. And without the Library's stabilising influence, warring dragons and Fae could pull apart human worlds with their opposing forces. Irene shuddered.

"It would have been a far more efficient use of time if your superiors had sent someone who'd actually been involved in this conference," Vale finally said. "I mean no criticism to you, Madam Bradamant, but you are sadly underinformed about the pertinent details of this case."

It had been three o'clock in the morning when they had left Vale's London. In order to forge a passage to the Library, they needed a sufficient quantity of books. But all the local libraries had been closed at that hour, naturally. (Well, all the *legal* libraries that Irene knew about. Perhaps London possessed secret societies with highly illegal libraries, which were open and busy at this time of night. But unfortunately Irene didn't know of any.) So instead the three of them had done a bit of quiet breaking and entering, sneaking into the closest public library to Vale's lodgings. Bradamant had opened a door from there into the Library itself. She'd been given a command word that allowed her to access its transfer shift facility, so that the three of them could be moved nearly instantaneously across the Library. It took them from their entry point to a door that would open on the very world where the murder had taken place.

Now they were in an impressive Library room whose ceiling teemed with so much tiled art nouveau decoration that it almost overpowered the shelves of black-bound volumes. The door at the far end, their destination, was sealed and chained shut. They had paused, at Irene's suggestion, to decide where to go first.

"The situation must be quite bad, given what you've said about people's tempers," Irene suggested neutrally. "We're not going to walk out into a war zone, are we?"

"Absolutely not," Bradamant said, possibly a little too quickly. "All parties are trying to keep things locked down, to stop them getting any worse. And let's be reasonable about this: it was easier to send *me* to fetch Vale—and you," she added as an afterthought, "than it would have been to send one of the supervising Librarians here, who didn't actually know Vale or his world."

"And you certainly aren't objecting to being in on things," Irene observed.

"Do I look stupid? Of course I'm not objecting. This is a game-changer. This whole situation might permanently affect how we work." Bradamant gave her a sidelong glance. "You aren't objecting either, I notice."

"I'm not objecting, I'm just *worried*," Irene said. "This would be marvellous if it does work. But there are so many ways that it could fail."

She'd seen what dragons and Fae could do to the world around them while fighting each other, or even while fighting among themselves. Earthquakes, storms, riots . . . The human collateral damage might be regretted, but it wouldn't be considered important. The Library was gambling for tremendously high stakes here. This could go brilliantly right, or it could go catastrophically wrong.

"Are we dressed adequately for the world we're about to enter?" she asked, changing the subject. "We don't want to look too out of place."

"I'd have told you if there was a problem," Bradamant said. "Fashion's jumped about ten years, and corsets and bustles are appropriate for fashionable clothing. For ladies," she added hastily, as Vale raised an eyebrow. "But you can get by on what you're currently wearing. You'll just look a little unfashionable. Vale should be fine. The buttons and collar are a little off, but gentlemen's clothing is much the same. And I'll arrange for a local establishment to deliver something ready-made to the hotel, in case you need to go out incognito."

Irene sighed and nodded. She could think of nothing positive about bustles and corsets, except possibly that one could hide things underneath them. But fashion was fashion, and if they needed to go round Paris asking questions, then they would have to look unexceptional.

"That should be sufficient," Vale agreed. "In addition, I will need an excuse to persuade the local police to cooperate with me. I fear my reputation will mean nothing to them in this world."

"That's been dealt with," Bradamant answered. "We're setting up a cover for you as an expert on anarchists, visiting from England."

"Anarchists?" Irene said. "I know we're dealing with royalty here, but why would—"

"No, it's a current problem in this Paris," Bradamant said. "It's been in all the papers. I'm not sure it's a serious threat, but there's been enough talk that we can use it. As long as Vale avoids any reporters trying to interview him on the subject, we should be fine."

Vale nodded in grudging agreement. "Very well, then. We'll start with the scene of the crime."

Bradamant hesitated. "I'd been assuming you'd want to speak to the leading Librarians at the conference first, so that you could get an overall top-down viewpoint, and a briefing on the personalities involved?"

Vale jerked his head in negation. "While I will certainly require interviews with everyone concerned, the most important thing is to see the victim and his circumstances. Has the body been left untouched?"

"As much as possible," Bradamant said. "He's currently at the Paris Morgue." She saw the judgemental look in Vale's eye and sighed. "It happened in the middle of a busy hotel, and we had to cope with the human staff as well as the conference participants. We couldn't just lock the place and tell everyone they couldn't go in!"

"It would have been much more helpful if you had," Vale said flatly. "Kindly take us there as fast as possible."

Bradamant looked as if she would have liked to argue the point, then nodded understandingly. "Of course," she said. "Just a moment."

She reached into the folds of her wrap and drew out a piece of paper: Irene was close enough to see words written in the Language, but not close enough to read them. Bradamant laid the paper against the sealed Library door, and said, **"Open."**

Something chimed, like a bell tolling very far away. The chains fell loose, and the seal crumbled from the door. Bradamant grabbed the heavy iron handle and dragged the door open with effort.

Irene was the first through, with Vale a step behind her.

The room on the other side was elegant and gracious, even in the moonlight that slanted in through the long rectangular windows. It breathed with the scent of old books and wax polish: the dark volumes that filled the shelves promised countless secrets, and Irene itched just to reach out and touch them.

Vale paused a moment, gathering himself, then gave a sharp

nod as Bradamant closed the door behind them, as though steadying himself in this new reality. "You said this exit point was in the Bibliothèque nationale? Will there be watchmen?"

"I paid the watchman off earlier," Bradamant said. "He shouldn't be an issue. And we're at the older branch of the Bibliothèque nationale, off rue Vivienne, north of the Louvre and the river Seine. These days they call it the Richelieu Library."

Vale nodded again. "And the site of the crime?"

"Le Meurice. That's the hotel where most of the Librarians are staying, and where we're holding the meetings. It's quite close to here—south towards the river and then west along the rue de Rivoli."

"Where's everyone else staying, if they're not staying there?" Irene asked.

"The dragons are at the Ritz, and the Fae are at the Grand Hôtel du Louvre," Bradamant said.

Vale frowned. "Didn't they turn that place into a department store?"

"Maybe in your world," Bradamant said, "but not here. Now, please come along—if you *want* to get a look at the crime scene before Paris starts waking up and all the factions expect you to visit them first."

"I am hardly the one delaying us," Vale said, somewhat unfairly. "Lead the way."

Walking through a library—any library—as they made their way to the exterior had its usual comforting, balancing effect on Irene. It was a reassurance that such places existed and that they would continue, even if she herself was as temporary as any other human.

However, she couldn't help noticing that the weather was several degrees colder than Vale's world had been. She expected cold weather in winter, but this was *bitter*, even indoors. She rubbed her hands together.

Bradamant noticed the gesture. "I should warn you," she said. "Ao Ji has wintry tendencies. That is, when he loses his temper, it gets cold. He wasn't in the best of moods before—there was a blizzard on the night of the murder—and when the body was actually discovered, well . . . The other dragons may have said that he was exercising severe self-control, but it didn't feel like it to *me*."

"I hope His Majesty will manage to control his temper while being questioned, or you'll have wasted my time," Vale commented.

Bradamant winced. She speeded up, her heels rapping on the floor as she led the way out of the library.

"Why are you trying to annoy her?" Irene said softly as they followed.

"Annoy her?" Vale raised an eyebrow. "I am merely stating my priorities. I cannot conduct an investigation if half the suspects stand on their royal privilege and refuse to answer my questions."

"I know that," Irene agreed, "and you know that, and Bradamant knows that too. And we both know each other well enough by now to know that you didn't *have* to phrase that last comment in the way you did. You've met Kai's other uncle. You know what his anger is like. So why did you provoke her?"

"Because you are far too trusting, Winters," Vale said. "I want to know what Madam Bradamant isn't telling us and hasn't told us yet."

Irene chewed that over mentally for a few paces. "Bradamant isn't stupid," she argued, her voice still quiet. "She wouldn't deliberately hide information from you if she knew you'd need it. She realizes just how important—how *dangerous*—this whole situation is."

"What if she'd been ordered to?" Vale demanded.

He had a point there. Irene sighed. "I don't have an answer to that. But I do believe the Library wants an answer to what's happened. Why else would they call you in?"

"*An* answer, certainly," Vale agreed. "But the truth? That might be a very dangerous commodity."

There was a cab waiting in the road outside the Richelieu Library's back entrance. It had clearly been there for hours: the driver was warming his hands in his armpits and cursing the weather, and the horses breathed great clouds of steam out into the cold air. Rime sparkled on the cobblestones and windowsills in the moonlight. The streets were quiet and empty: maybe because this was one of the more policed areas of Paris, or possibly because the usual nightlife had been driven inside by the cold. With the streets empty and snowy, Paris had a sort of agelessness, even if parts of its architecture might date it to within decades or centuries, such as the wide Napoleonic boulevards. But without the actual humans filling the streets, it could be the Paris of any timeline. It could be immortal.

Vale stared out of the window as the buildings jolted by, his face set in forbidding lines that discouraged conversation.

"I don't see why we shouldn't stop off at the morgue first, to see the victim. We could both contrive to get us in," Irene suggested to Bradamant. "And it's on our way too. If we've examined the body, it should make it easier for them to brief us on the situation."

Bradamant shrugged. "I agree with what you're saying, and I

understand why Vale wants to see the body and the scene of the crime before he does anything else. It's just that the instructions I was given were to bring Vale and you directly for a briefing—before anything else." She pulled her coat more tightly closed, shivering. "You of all people should understand what it's like to be juggling multiple sets of instructions."

"Will they still be awake at this hour of the morning?"

Bradamant snorted. "How could they possibly sleep, at a time like this?"

The cab turned into the rue de Rivoli. Irene could smell the Tuileries Garden to their left and the river Seine beyond, a distant waft of growing things and salt and sewage. "Have any of the dragons said whether the river here has a spirit?" she asked.

"No," Bradamant said, "but if it has, it's keeping a very low profile."

A few minutes later, the cab came to a halt in front of the pale frontage of a large hotel, washed white by the moonlight and the street lamps. This was a side street rather than the wide rue de Rivoli, and as such it had shadows and side alleys. Above the covered entrance, Irene could read the hotel's name carved in stone. Rectangular windows dotted the frontage, as regular as postage stamps, fringed by long iron-railed balconies and retreating up to a roof six or seven storeys above. It looked very graceful, but it didn't look particularly secure. Again, there were no humans around—guests, passers-by, or otherwise. The only living thing that Irene could see was a cat, curled up in a crevice and only visible when the light caught its eyes.

As Bradamant walked round to pay the driver, Irene took the opportunity to ask Vale, "What's bothering you?"

"What indeed." Vale poked at an innocent paving stone with

his stick. It was an electrifiable cane, Irene knew, not just an affectation. "Besides the threat to the innocents of this world? The possibility of a war? The likelihood of it expanding further than I can conceive? What could *possibly* be bothering me, Winters?"

"All of which you've dealt with before," Irene said mildly. "The stakes are high, but they're hardly new. Between the two of us, Vale, what *is* bothering you?"

Vale looked down the empty street. Another cab came rattling along it, the horses stepping briskly, the shades of the cab windows drawn against observers. "Petty things like that," he said, indicating the cab with his stick. "In my world, it would be ether-powered. Here? They still have horses. They do not have zeppelins. But they do have automobiles. From what Madam Bradamant has said, they have mass communication to a degree which my world cannot even conceive. There may be other differences, ones which I can't imagine, because I simply don't know *enough*. How am I supposed to *work* when I am unaware of the basic functioning mechanisms of a place like this? In London—my own London—I know every street, every alley, every building, every custom. In the Paris of my own world, I would at least have a basic understanding of the city. But here . . ." He trailed off. "I am a stranger. I am possibly an *incompetent* stranger, and I may be more of a danger than a benefit to this investigation."

"I'm not going to argue all of those points with you," Irene said slowly. "Some of them are valid. But the Library will have researched this world before it tried to hold a peace conference here—they must have dossiers about the sort of thing you'd need to know. That may be one of the reasons they wanted to speak with you before you started the investigation. And in terms of the *personalities* involved, you've had as much involvement with dragons and Fae as most Librarians. If not more. And ultimately . . ." She frowned. "Whoever did this, they still had to obey the laws of physics. That hasn't changed. A stabbing is still a stabbing."

"Trite but accurate," Vale said. His momentary doubt was gone, sheathed under a smooth surface of professionalism as Bradamant approached. "So let us get the formalities over as soon as possible, and proceed to the scene of the crime."

The hotel was half-asleep at this hour of the morning. While a couple of wakeful clerks manned the main desk in the marble-tiled foyer, the corridors were empty and silent, and the large dining rooms and function rooms they passed were closed and still. Irene knew that behind the scenes the hotel laundries would be busy, the kitchens would be preparing for a new day, and the servants would still be awake and ready to spring into action at the touch of a bell. But here in the public areas of the hotel, one could believe that the entire building was comatose. It was quiet enough that their footsteps, as they walked through it, seemed an offence against some rule.

"The room where he was found is on the ground floor," Bradamant explained as she led the way, "on the side facing the rue de Rivoli. It does have accessible windows, but they were all locked shut."

"Which wouldn't stop a Librarian from ordering the locks open or shut," Vale commented.

Bradamant sighed. "Yes, and everyone knew that. Which didn't help. Though I think that someone with wires or threads could do some sort of trick, which could lock it from the other side? I don't know. Irene here was always the one who preferred crime fiction."

"*Detective* fiction," Irene corrected her.

"Whatever. Would it be possible?"

"It might be," Vale agreed. "But it would leave traces. You say there had been a blizzard that night. Were there any marks in the snow?"

"As far as anyone can tell, he was killed while the blizzard was still ongoing. The snow covered up any tracks, I'm afraid."

Vale nodded, unsurprised. They'd come to a pause in front of a particular door. "This is the room?"

"It is," Bradamant said. "The Salon Pompadour. It's the hotel's main banqueting room, and the hotel management are desperate to get it cleaned. To be honest, I think part of the reason they're willing to hush this up is that they don't want to admit that there was a murder in that particular room. There are limits to how much scandal and publicity is good for a hotel. But *first* I need to let Kostchei know you're here and take you upstairs for a word with the elders." She was sounding a little plaintive by this point.

Vale nodded in agreement as he went down on his knees and squinted at the door's lock. "Hmm."

"I've got the key," Bradamant said helpfully. "And about speaking to my superiors—"

"Give it to Winters," Vale instructed, bringing out a lens from an inner pocket to examine the lock more closely. "And I will need to know how many keys to this room exist, and who holds them."

Bradamant hesitated a moment, then passed Irene the key as if she'd been meaning to do it all along. She looked at Irene and Vale, both focused on the door now, threw up her hands, and exited down the corridor in a swirl of skirts and tapping of heels.

"If I undertake a case, then I do so on my terms, not those of my client," Vale noted, not looking up. "And any evidence here must be my priority. This lock shows no signs of interference. No scratches or other marks of a lockpick. Let me see the key." He brought it to his nose to stare at it. "A straightforward design: any locksmith could duplicate it. Hmm."

He rose to his feet and turned the key in the door, swinging it open. No lamps were lit in the room beyond. But enough street-lamp light filtered through the gauze-curtained windows to show the chairs shoved back against the walls and the dark stain on the floor.

"Stay back, Winters," Vale instructed before Irene could even consider stepping into the room. "Now, where would this place have its light controls . . . ah yes." He slid his hand inside and to the right of the door and flipped switches.

The chandeliers lit up in a burst of white light, throwing the dark stain on the floor into sharp relief. Everything else in the room sparkled—white walls and ceiling, white tablecloth on the long table at the centre, white-painted wood on the fragile-looking chairs, mirrored windows along one side of the room, crystals on the chandeliers, glasses set ready along the table, and gilt everywhere—but the dried blood marred it. It spread across the tiled floor and onto the edge of the Persian carpet in the middle of the room in an irregular blob. It wasn't quite the size or shape of a human body, but it was uncomfortably suggestive. A portrait of a woman in the court dress of a few centuries ago looked down from the wall, her painted expression unmoved at the scene of violence.

Irene indicated the portrait. "Before you ask, no, I can't get her to talk."

"A pity," Vale said. "A witness would have been useful."

He stepped into the room, looking around keenly, his eyes moving to the mirrored windows. It was impossible to see outside through them: the street light had come through the circular rose windows set higher in the wall, part of the overall decoration. "Yes. Interesting. Winters, would you be kind enough to do something for me?"

"Of course," Irene said.

"Go and question the staff while I examine this room. Make yourself agreeable. I need to know who has access to this room, who holds the keys, whether anything strange was seen, what the circumstances of the discovery were—you know my methods." His mouth quirked in a thin smile. "Besides, it will give your superiors the opportunity to brief you while I am not present."

Irene sighed. "I can't argue with you on that last point. Good luck."

"Luck is all very well," Vale said, moving forward to the bloodstain, "but I would rather have some facts."

CHAPTER 4

Irene turned a corner and very nearly walked into the group of men and women coming in the opposite direction. They moved as silently as sharks, in neat formation behind their leader. And when he saw Irene, he held up a hand, which paused them in their tracks.

Irene stopped too, taken aback by the near collision, and then hesitated further when she realized the man in the front was a dragon. Like all the dragons in human form she'd met so far, he was easy to identify: there was something about his face and build that went beyond human ideals and into the realm of perfect statuary or art. The others behind him were humans, but oddly matched in their features and heights: two men, two women, all of whom looked similar enough to be brothers and sisters. The men were in evening dress despite the early hour, and the women were in sober dark skirts and matching jackets. They all stood with a casual posture that could easily shift into violence.

The dragon's brows drew together as he looked at Irene. "I believe I know you," he said. "Are you the Librarian who goes by the name of Irene Winters?"

"I am, sir," Irene replied. "But you have the advantage of me."

He was as gilt and ivory as the hotel decorations—and while Irene had a better memory for books than for faces, she was sure she'd have remembered him. His eyes were an only barely human shade of amber, his hair was as yellow as the gilding, and his skin was pale enough that it nearly matched his white collar and cuffs. "My name is Duan Zheng. I am here to bring you to my lord Ao Ji, King of the Western Ocean, so that he can give you your orders. Is the detective with you too?"

"He's present, but he's examining the scene of the crime," Irene said. She wasn't entirely sure she liked the phrase *your orders*. "And I need to speak to my superiors first. If you could wait for a few moments—"

"Delay is unacceptable," Duan Zheng cut in. "I realize that you may not be aware of proper court etiquette, but you should have come to attend on His Majesty at once. The detective should do the same. You said that he was in the Salon Pompadour?"

"I've only just arrived in this world," Irene said. She had to defuse this before they could interrupt Vale mid-investigation, or give Ao Ji any more reason to be annoyed. Fortunately, the dragon sense of hierarchy usually included some acceptance of other people's hierarchies as well. "I came directly here to report to my own superiors, and Vale needed to examine the scene of the crime at once. I apologise if this was inconvenient to His Majesty."

"Your apology is accepted," Duan Zheng said graciously. "You will now accompany us." He gestured again, and the two women in the group following him moved forward to flank Irene. "We will collect the detective and be on our way."

"I'm afraid I wasn't clear," Irene said, trying to ignore the feeling that the women looked ready to pick her up by her elbows and drag her away. "I haven't yet reported to my superiors. I need to do that before I do anything else. And Vale should not be interrupted while he is working."

Duan Zheng tilted his head, puzzled. "Are you refusing to come with us?" He sounded genuinely surprised.

"Of course not." A prickle of nerves worked its way down Irene's back. Just how dangerous was the situation, if the dragons were sending armed scouting parties into neutral territory and demanding private interviews with the investigative team? And were the Fae doing the same? Could Irene expect a matching group to emerge from the other end of the corridor at any moment? "Naturally we will want full information on the situation from His Majesty Ao Ji, in order to find and capture the person who committed this atrocious crime. I'm very glad that we met like this." That seemed to mollify Duan Zheng a little. "But I'm sure that you understand that I need to check with the Librarians in charge here before I leave the hotel."

Duan Zheng shrugged, his shoulders rippling with the motion. He was more heavily built than some of the other dragons Irene had met. She wondered what his position was in Ao Ji's entourage. Intelligence operative? Guard leader? Enforcer? "They will understand that you had no choice," he said. "My lord's command is absolute. The same goes for the detective. Now—"

"No." Irene surprised herself by the strength of her refusal. She took a step forward, moving into Duan Zheng's personal space. "With all due respect, sir"—the traditional signal that one was about to be very disrespectful—"you don't commission the greatest detective in London and then tell him how to do his job. Either Vale is an expert and deserves the right to conduct this investiga-

tion as he sees fit, or he isn't, and you shouldn't have requested his services in the first place."

"He is a tradesman," Duan Zheng said, with a sneer that suggested he personally preferred the second option. "He will do as he is ordered."

"He is a nobleman in his own country," Irene countered. "And he's a scholar, not a tradesman. I will be perfectly ready to come with you in five minutes, but I insist that *he* be allowed to work by his own methods."

Duan Zheng's nostrils flared. The two men in his squad—yes, Irene decided that was the best term for it—moved to flank him. "You, on the other hand, are a junior servant of the Library of no particular rank or importance. You feel you have the right to stand here and make demands of me?"

Irene stared him in the eye. She couldn't back down now. She'd be weakening her own position in his eyes and in the eyes of the entire dragon contingent. The Library *had* to maintain independence—even if they were the weakest of the three factions present, they weren't subordinate to anyone. "I'm not making demands," she said, keeping her voice neutral. There had to be some way to de-escalate this. "I'm informing you that I have orders to report to my superiors."

Duan Zheng snorted. "If you are trying to force my hand, you have succeeded. Restrain her—"

"Hold." It was a woman's voice, coming from the corridor behind him. "Duan Zheng, if I may?"

Duan Zheng tensed, pressing his lips together hard enough that they turned white. Then he stepped back. "Mu Dan. Thank you for joining us."

The woman stepped forward into Irene's line of sight. She was another dragon. Her mahogany-dark hair was braided up round her face, and gem-headed hairpins glittered in it like a scattering of stars. She was still in an outer coat and hat, unlike Duan Zheng and his squad. And both were deep crimson, the same colour as her leather boots. "You must be Irene Winters," she said, and offered Irene her gloved hand. "Permit me to introduce myself. I am Mu Dan, and I will be assisting you in this investigation."

Irene shook hands politely, very aware of how close this had come to violence. The polite formalities seemed almost ridiculous, given Duan Zheng's looming presence at her shoulder. "Pleased to meet you. I regret the circumstances."

"Yes, we all do," Mu Dan agreed. "But Duan Zheng is quite correct that you should attend His Majesty Ao Ji as soon as possible. However, I see your point on reporting to your superiors. Would five minutes be enough?" Her smile was friendly but didn't invite discussion. "Duan Zheng can then escort you across to His Majesty's hotel. Meanwhile I will introduce myself to the detective and make my own observations of the crime scene. Fae representatives are also here, looking to speak with Miss Winters and the detective. But I will explain to them that we have priority."

"I suppose that will be acceptable," Duan Zheng said ungraciously. His attitude towards Mu Dan wasn't exactly *rude,* but it lacked any semblance of deference. "And you can bring the detective with you as soon as he has finished his . . . observations."

"He may be a while," Irene pointed out.

"So may I," Mu Dan said. "Rest assured that he'll be safe in my keeping. I'll see you later, Miss Winters." With a nod to Duan Zheng, she walked past them, towards the Salon Pompadour.

Duan Zheng tracked her with his eyes for a moment, then made an effort and pulled his attention back to Irene. "I will escort you to your superiors," he said. "Then when they've finished with you, I can take you to my lord without any *further* delay."

"What an excellent idea," Irene agreed warmly.

The human escorts fell into place behind them as Duan Zheng led the way through the hotel at a brisk pace. He didn't seem inclined to make conversation, and his silence was thorough enough that Irene didn't try to ask any questions.

He came to a stop outside a gilded door on the first floor and rapped his knuckles on it. "Your superiors are in here, I believe. I will wait outside." The words *don't make me wait long* hung in the air.

"Who is that?" a male voice called from inside.

"Irene Winters!" Irene answered. Caution made her add, "And Duan Zheng, in service to His Majesty Ao Ji."

"Come in, Irene." That voice Irene did recognize—it was her mentor Coppelia, who must have left the Library for this occasion. "Alone, if you please."

Irene opened the door and gasped at the wave of hot air that breathed over her. She hastily closed the door behind her before Duan Zheng could do more than peer in over her shoulder, and just as hastily unbuttoned her coat. It felt as if she'd just walked into a sauna. The thick velvet curtains had been drawn and overlapped to cover the windows as hermetically as possible. A large pile of logs blazed in the fireplace, in addition to the discreet radiators that Irene could see in the corners of the room. On top of that, two of the three people in the room were huddled in armchairs, with additional shawls draped over their shoulders.

It was Coppelia whom Irene focused on. It had been months since last she'd seen her mentor. Against the cream velvet upholstery and decorations, Coppelia's face seemed drained of its normal colour, a shade of dead brown marble rather than living oak. New lines were marked around her mouth, and she reached both hands—the living flesh one and the artificial clockwork one—towards the fire to warm them. "Irene," she said, her voice hoarse with the edge of a cough. "It's good to see you."

Irene bit her lip for a moment before she could reply. She was aware that Coppelia was fragile. Old Librarians *were*. She knew it was stupid, but even so she wanted to scold the older woman for putting herself at risk, for leaving the Library and sitting around in winter weather that would only make her rheumatism worse. For making Irene worry about her. "I wish the circumstances were better," she said. "Tell me what I can do to help."

She glanced at the other two in the room. The man in the second chair, Kostchei, was another senior Librarian: he had pulled a velvet smoking cap over his bald head, and while he still glared with the same ferocity she remembered, the tassel on the cap dangled rakishly over one ear and dampened the effect. His hands were folded together in his lap, his knuckles swollen and his veins showing blue through the wrinkled skin.

Both of them, here outside the Library, huddled up against the cold, looked . . . diminished. Weak. Old. Irene wasn't accustomed to thinking of them in this way. The elder Librarians had always been her superiors, and while she might have been frustrated with them, or distrusted them, or even occasionally cursed them, she had never quite thought of them as *old* human beings. The Library had kept them ageless—immortal unless they chose to leave it and let the natural flow of time resume. They'd made themselves vulnerable by stepping outside and into an alternate world like this one.

It was her job to make their risk worth it.

Kostchei snorted. "You want to know what you can do to help?

If you haven't got the intelligence to see what needs doing, then you're not the person we want for the job."

Irene's sympathy for him evaporated. "Well, obviously I need to find the murderer and resolve the situation without letting a war get started," she snapped. "I meant *besides* that. You know, in my copious free time. And we need to make this conversation fast. Duan Zheng wants to take me to see Ao Ji as soon as possible."

Coppelia wheezed a thin laugh, almost a cackle. "Those are two of the main problems, yes. I'm glad to see you're keeping your sense of proportion and not getting carried away by daydreams of helping a great detective solve a murder."

"The situation's too serious to indulge childhood fantasies," Irene said, and tried to mean it sincerely. A younger version of her would have thought this was the greatest adventure ever, combining her job as a Librarian with working alongside Vale. But the stakes were too high for her to treat it like a game. "And if those are two of the main problems, what's the third?"

"Finding out what Ren Shun meant when he talked about a book," Kostchei grated. "The situation at the moment is that *nobody* knows what he meant, and apparently Ao Ji was the only person he spoke to about it. Unless one of the other dragons knows but isn't talking. There are representatives from two other courts in Ao Ji's entourage—Li Ming from the King of the Northern Ocean, and Mei Feng from the Queen of the Southern Lands."

"Either of whom is far more diplomatic than Ao Ji is," the stranger standing behind Kostchei's chair commented. "Which makes it a pity that he's now planning to conduct the negotiations himself. You've met Li Ming, haven't you?"

"I have," Irene agreed cautiously. The dragon in question was very polished, very political, and very dangerous. And powerful.

He wasn't just a representative of the King of the Northern Ocean: he was said king's trusted liegeman and right hand. The last time they'd met, Irene had rejected his well-meant protection in favour of recklessness, so she hoped he didn't bear grudges. "Though we weren't on the best of terms last time we parted . . . Oh drat."

"A problem?" Coppelia asked.

"Um, purely as a matter of coincidence and with absolutely no personal interference or suggestion from me, Kai might be about to drop by to visit his uncle," Irene said. She wasn't speaking in the Language, so she could lie as much as she wanted—and she could tell from their faces that both senior Librarians knew she'd sent Kai herself. "I'm sure it won't hurt our interests to have Kai there and speaking in the Library's favour, but I'm not certain how he and Li Ming will interact. Given our past encounters."

"Well, won't that be interesting," Coppelia said with a sigh. "Do your best to look innocent, child, or at least make it look plausibly deniable if you're caught asking him questions in corners."

"How many other Librarians are on-site?" Irene asked.

"Half a dozen at this hotel," the stranger said, "and a couple more at each of the other two hotels, acting as liaisons. Most of us are of senior rank: it would have been considered an insult for anyone lower-grade to attend in a significant role. Though there are a couple of juniors assisting." He raised a hand in greeting. "I'm Prutkov, by the way. Sorry not to have introduced myself earlier."

"We haven't time for courtesies," Kostchei growled. "Listen, girl. We're trusting you to find the *right* solution to this. One which doesn't make matters worse. What you report to us in private is one thing, but what you tell the dragons or the Fae had better not light any fuses. Do you understand me?"

Irene felt the pit yawning in front of her. "You want a cover-up," she said.

"I *want* the truth," Kostchei answered. "I may *need* a cover-up. The two are different things. You realize what's at stake here, girl?"

"I'm not stupid," Irene said. "I understand that we can't afford this peace conference to break down. I think Vale might even agree to it, if necessary—he understands how dangerous the dragons and the Fae might be to humanity. And to his world in particular. But I'm concerned, from my own experience, that if we base this treaty on a lie, then at some point it's going to crack."

Coppelia worked her hands together, the flesh one polishing the wooden one. "That's a valid objection. Don't glare at her like that, Kostchei. Our juniors shouldn't be punished for recognizing possible risks."

"No," Kostchei muttered, "but they'll damn well regret it if they don't go ahead and get the job done anyhow. Come on, girl. Pull yourself together. You're supposed to be good at this sort of thing. Ideally it'll turn out to have been a murder for some private motive, one that doesn't involve anyone present."

Irene considered possible responses to that suggestion. Eventually she said, "That one isn't going to hold water."

"Then find something that will!" Kostchei slapped his knee with a sound like a pistol shot. "Prutkov! You said you'd been getting the witness statements, boy?"

"Yes, sir," Prutkov said. He was hardly a boy: his hair was black, grey at the temples, and age had marked lines of humour on his face. He nodded to where a thick folder lay on a side table. "We'll give them to Mr. Vale when he *finally* gets here. Where is he now?"

"Examining the scene of the crime," Irene said. "I know you wanted him to see you first . . . but please be reasonable." She'd noted the thundercloud frown growing on Kostchei's face. "He's the expert. And he'll be wanting to see the body next. Bradamant said it was at the morgue?"

"At the Paris Morgue," Prutkov said. "I know, I know, you're supposed to keep it on the spot, but bribes only go *so* far with the local police, and at least we've paid enough that it'll be undisturbed there. You can take Mr. Vale there after you've seen Ao Ji. Inspector Maillon is assigned to the case, but at the moment he thinks anarchists are responsible."

"Why are we pushing the anarchists as culprits?" Irene asked. "Bradamant's already explained, but couldn't we have claimed something less politically dangerous, like a serial killer or lone assassin or something?"

"There are plenty of anarchists around," Prutkov said, "or at least the newspapers say there are. And the concept of 'serial killers' isn't as well-known at this place and time. If it means the inspector's not looking at us, then that's one less headache."

Irene nodded. "Okay. So." She raised her fingers and ticked items off. "Investigate murder. Find murderer. Find acceptable solution. Persuade other investigators to go along with it. Find out what Ren Shun meant when he talked about a book. Ensure peace treaty." It sounded ridiculous to be counting off tasks as if she was making a to-do list, but it helped her keep it in some sort of proportion and not panic at the scope of what lay ahead. "Is there anything else I should know?"

"There is one thing," Coppelia said. This time it was her turn to sound guilty. "I'm not trying to put additional pressure on you, Irene, but I think that you should know about it. Part of the arrangements, when we were setting this up, was that we should provide hostages."

"Hostages?"

"Yes," Kostchei said, clearly impatient. "It was necessary to maintain the balance of trust. A number of senior Librarians are currently guests of the dragon or Fae courts. If this all goes wrong, then not only are we all dead, in which case we probably won't care about the situation any further, but so are they. And for your information, girl, your parents are among those hostages. They're at one of the dragon courts. So keep your sense of proportion, and remember what's important here." He leaned forward to fix her with his eyes, and his cap didn't seem remotely silly any longer. "We must have an answer that everyone will accept. I don't care about your ethics. I care that the job gets done."

This new revelation lay like a lump of ice in Irene's stomach. She felt very detached from the room around her. "Spare me the theatrics," she said. "Of course I'll do the job. And *thank you*"—she emphasised the words bitterly—"for giving me that to worry about as well as everything else."

"Better that you hear it from us than from someone else," Coppelia said quietly.

There was a hard rap on the door. "Are you ready to accompany us, Miss Winters?" came Duan Zheng's voice.

"Come back for another briefing later," Coppelia said quickly, as Prutkov moved across to pass Irene a heavy purse. "That's for expenses. And, Irene . . ." She hesitated. "This peace conference was kept quiet because we were afraid some Librarians couldn't be trusted with the information. The murder could prove that we might have been right. Be very careful."

CHAPTER 5

The sky was stained with red as they arrived at the Ritz hotel: it was dawn, and Paris was already fully awake. The streets, previously so quiet and atmospheric, were now full of traffic, with new-style motor cars jostling for space with both horse-drawn carriages and bicycles. Even in the refined surroundings of the Ritz hotel, the noises of morning Paris drifted through the windows and faintly insinuated themselves through the walls. The shrill parping of motor horns, the clatter of hooves and creak of wheels on stone, the sound of voices . . .

Irene stared at a closed door, flanked by Duan Zheng's bodyguards, and pondered the universal human—and apparently draconic too—constant of *hurry up and wait*. She'd been rushed here the moment that she stepped out of her conference with the elder Librarians, but now she could only sit and wait for the dragon king to have time to see her. At least she'd been allowed to sit. It gave her time to brood over exactly what she'd say to her parents when she saw them again.

Finally—*finally*—the door opened, and a human servant appeared. He bowed to Duan Zheng, then (rather to Irene's surprise) to Irene herself, and said, "His Majesty will receive the Librarian now."

Cold air brushed Irene's bare skin as she entered the suite. It was like the first moment of walking outside on a snowy morning, before one has had time to get used to the briskness of the air: it caught in her throat and burned against her cheeks. She tried not to shiver too obviously. Instead she curtseyed to the dragon in the centre of the room, giving him a full measure of respect, and took advantage of the moment to steady herself.

As with other dragon monarchs, the room was full of his power. It was as still as a frozen lake, as ominous as the dark of the moon: Irene felt the Library brand across her shoulders blaze up in response, in a burn that was almost comforting.

"You may rise and address me," Ao Ji said. His light tenor voice might almost have been friendly, but Irene could hear the ice beneath it. "You are the Librarian who calls herself Irene Winters?"

"I am, Your Majesty," Irene said, drawing herself upright.

Ao Ji was wrapped in a heavy white silk robe that matched his skin, hair, and scales: although he was in humanoid form, he had not bothered to conceal his draconic nature. His eyes were vivid ruby, as bright as blood, and the claws on his fingers glittered like diamonds. Scale-patterns traced across his skin like ferns or frost, more intricate than the embroideries on his robe. His hair was the same snow-white as his skin, caught back in a long braid that bared the two small horns on his forehead. Only his eyes and mouth were a dash of colour against the white. He was paler than the elegant gold-framed white panelling on the walls, but he made it look cheap by comparison: the suite was impossibly luxurious, but next to him, it seemed barely fit for use.

He considered Irene with those unnerving red eyes and took a sip of tea from the cup he held in his right hand. Steam coiled up from it in the cold air. "Where is the detective whom you were to bring with you?"

"He is examining the scene of the crime, Your Majesty," Irene said. Had Ao Ji never been faced with a murder like this? Possibly not. Possibly he didn't even read crime fiction. "He felt it his duty to do so as soon as possible."

"I would have brought him too, Your Majesty, but Mu Dan said I should let him finish," Duan Zheng said from behind Irene's shoulder. "If she instructed me wrongly—"

Ao Ji shook his head, cutting Duan Zheng off. "Mu Dan is an acclaimed investigator. If she says it is the proper procedure, then we may trust her. You, however, Irene Winters, have little to recommend you."

Irene weighed proper courtesy, and the urgent need to keep Ao Ji in a good mood, against what she thought she could get away with. "Then may I ask why Your Majesty has accepted me as an investigator in this case?"

Ao Ji's expression didn't change. "The other Librarians have even less to commend them. You are a petty and venal crew, barely aware of your obligations, untrustworthy and unreliable."

He seemed to want some sort of answer to that. "I regret that we have displeased Your Majesty," Irene murmured.

"You at least have a proper sense of filial duty to your parents," Ao Ji went on. Was that *approval* in his voice? "I am told that you are obedient to your superiors and that you have risked your life to protect my nephew from his own foolishness."

Is this all because Kai's been saying nice things about me? No, that can't be right. Ao Ji had already approved me as the Library representative before Kai could have reached him. "I am honoured by Your Majesty's words," Irene replied. "I hope that I can serve both the Library and you in this matter by finding out who committed this terrible murder."

The liquid in Ao Ji's cup froze with an audible crack as the temperature dropped. "Yes," Ao Ji said, his voice suddenly harsh, bitter with personal grief. "You do well to remind me of our priorities. Ren Shun's murderer must be found and brought to judgement. All those who are involved in this crime will pay for it. You will seek out the murderer, however well they are hidden and however highly they may be placed." His eyes were frozen rubies fixed on her face. The cold swell of his power hung over her like a glacier. "Even if it is the Fae delegation. Even if one of your fellow Librarians is to blame. I will not suffer the truth to be hidden from me."

Irene breathed deeply. The icy air bit at her lungs. She took that pain and used it, forcing herself to remain standing rather than curtsey or fall to her knees, making herself return his gaze rather than look down like a servant. "Your Majesty," she said, hearing her own words sound thin and shallow against Ao Ji's power, "the Library wants peace. We are sincere in supporting this peace conference. We are the enemy of whoever has committed this crime, wherever they may be. I speak with the full support of my superiors. We will find the truth."

I hope, she thought in the silence of her mind, where Ao Ji couldn't hear her.

Slowly the chill ebbed away. Ao Ji put his teacup down on a

side table and nodded. "I will hold you to your word," he said. "Now. Tell me what your next steps will be."

"The first steps in an investigation of this nature are to examine the body of the deceased and the scene of the crime," Irene said. "We will also need to know the victim's actions on the night he was murdered, and what everybody else was doing at that time. I would be grateful if you could tell me what you know about Lord Ren Shun's actions and motivations that night, Your Majesty."

Ao Ji folded his hands in his lap. "The two of us, and others of my retinue, had dined together here at this hotel in the early evening. I had noticed that he was troubled, and when we were alone I asked him what disturbed him."

Irene nodded encouragingly.

Ao Ji looked away from Irene, towards one of the huge windows, as if he could stare into the past. "You must understand that Ren Shun often heard things that I did not. One of his functions was to bring these pieces of information to me."

Spymaster. Right. "I understand, Your Majesty," Irene said.

"He told me that he had overheard two people speaking at the neutral hotel. He could not be certain of their identity, but they had agreed that the negotiations were proceeding as they desired. One of them used the phrase . . ." He paused, recollecting. "*Everything is playing out as we wanted.* Yes. That was it. And the other had said that when it was all done, would they get the book? And the first one said yes. They said that the peace conference wasn't truly important—that the really significant thing was the book."

Irene swallowed. She had to admit that wording of that nature did rather point to Librarians. "I can see why a statement like that would have troubled him, Your Majesty," she agreed. A thought struck her. "But he didn't recognize either of the speakers?"

"No," Ao Ji said. "Though he did say that they were whispering; he could have failed to recognize a voice he would have known under normal circumstances. He was not certain of their gender, either."

Irene nodded. "And after he had told you this, Your Majesty?"

"I was disturbed." A veil of cloud was building across the sky outside the window: thin, shredding wisps slowly melding together into dark cumulus masses. But was it an echo of Ao Ji's mood and power, or just coincidence? "It was a new factor in the deliberations. I had expected treachery from the Fae, of course, but not from the Library."

"Given that he didn't recognize the speakers, is it possible that the whole business was a fake, meant to incriminate the Library?" Irene offered.

There was an echoing silence. Ao Ji extended his hand. Without a word, one of his servants placed a fresh teacup in it.

It seemed that idea wasn't going anywhere—until and unless Irene could get some evidence to back it up. "Do you know what he did next, Your Majesty?"

"Sadly not." The clouds outside drew together, shadowing the Parisian square beyond the window. "He said that he would make further investigations later. I retired for the night. He must have left the hotel . . . but I do not know when. Our last conversation ended shortly after eleven o'clock—I recall that the clock in his rooms struck the hour while we were speaking."

Irene nodded. "Thank you, Your Majesty. I appreciate the information. We will need to check with the other possible witnesses in this hotel to find out when he left it."

Ao Ji frowned, but he didn't actually contradict her. "Duan Zheng," he said. "How should this be arranged?"

Duan Zheng bowed. "My lord, I believe the two Librarians assigned to you have already been taking statements from members of your retinue, their servants, and from the hotel staff here. That should suffice."

"Thank you very much," Irene said. She gave Duan Zheng her most charming smile. "That will make it much easier for us to know who to ask for more information."

"Why should you need more information than that?" Duan Zheng demanded. "The murder took place at Le Meurice, not here."

Irene wasn't sure whether he was genuinely that ignorant about criminal investigations or simply being obstructive on general principles. "If it did take place at Le Meurice," she said, "then it may be relevant what time he left here, and when he could have arrived there. It's too late now to be certain how long the body was dead before it was found—"

The temperature dipped. She felt cold air clutch at her throat like a hand. Ao Ji's expression drew into lines of anger.

"Your Majesty, I mean no disrespect," she said quickly. "No insult was intended to Lord Ren Shun's memory. It's just that certain vocabulary is commonly used in these cases."

"Maybe," Ao Ji grated, "but this is not a *common* case. You will remember that."

"As Your Majesty says," Irene said. This was not the time or place to moralise about there being thousands of other murder victims, questioning what made this one special, et cetera. This was the time and place to say *yes, sir* and avoid being thrown off the investigation. Or frozen to death. "But I hope you can see why we may need to establish exactly when Lord Ren Shun left this hotel, and if anyone knows where he went after that."

"To Le Meurice, surely," Duan Zheng said, "since he was killed there."

Irene thought back to that outline on the floor. There had been blood, but had there been *enough* blood? Could Ren Shun have been killed somewhere else and then moved there? It would be easier to move a dead body than manhandle a living dragon. Come to think of it, there were certain other things that might happen if one attacked a dragon . . . "Your Majesty," she said, "may I ask a question?"

"Of course," Ao Ji said.

"I've noticed that many dragons have some sort of elemental affinity," Irene said. She'd also found out that some of them—weaker ones—*didn't,* and were rather touchy on the subject. So she needed to phrase this carefully until she knew which type Duan Zheng, right behind her, was. "And they can call their element to support them if they are fighting—floods, for example, or earthquakes. Did Lord Ren Shun have a power of that type?"

Ao Ji fixed her with his gaze again. "His nature was rain and water. But he was stabbed in the back. He was murdered by treachery. He would have had no time to resist."

Irene made a mental note to see if there had been any unexpected surges in the Seine that night, and nodded. "Thank you, Your Majesty. That may be relevant."

There was a knock at the suite door. One of the human servants who stood silently and anonymously around the suite moved to answer it. He returned with a tray on which lay a couple of notes. "Your Majesty, there is a message for you, and one for Miss Winters."

Ao Ji put down his teacup to rip the envelope open and extract the letter inside. "It is from Mu Dan," he said after a moment. "She is escorting the detective to examine Ren Shun's remains, and will bring him here as soon as possible afterwards."

Duan Zheng snorted. "Her grasp of priorities leaves something to be desired, my lord."

"She has reasons." The clouds beyond the window drew in again, massing darkly above Paris. "She fears there may be Fae interference. I imagine she is correct. Their malice and insanity are habitual. They will seize whatever advantage they can gain."

Irene ripped open her own envelope: she'd recognized Vale's handwriting on the front. *Winters,* her letter ran, *I've gone to the Paris Morgue with Mu Dan to examine the corpse. Kindly join us as soon as possible, and bring any witness statements that you've obtained. Make my excuses to the dragon king in whatever language you think he'll find least objectionable: I'll question him later when I have the time. Vale.*

"Is your letter relevant?" Ao Ji enquired.

"Vale presents his apologies, Your Majesty," Irene embroidered. "He hopes to attend on you as soon as possible, but he felt that it was a matter of urgency to investigate the deceased first. He asks that I join him."

"Then I will release you to do so," Ao Ji said. "I will expect you to report soon."

As Irene murmured polite agreement, there was another knock at the door. A servant checked and reported, "Your breakfast has arrived, Your Majesty."

Ao Ji frowned slightly. His body shimmered, and then with hardly a breath's pause, a normal human was sitting in his chair. Well, relatively normal—his hair and skin were still bone-white, his eyes were red, and his face was still inhumanly perfect. But the scales and the horns were gone, and his fingernails were no more than normal human length. He might draw glances for his coloration, but he wouldn't do so for any non-human abnormalities. "They may enter," he said.

The door clicked open. Two hotel staff, their uniforms freshly pressed and their brass buttons shining, came in with trays, while a third behind them pushed a trolley weighed down with covered dishes and fringed with linen drapes. Irene moved out of their way, tucking Vale's note into her handbag. She could smell some of the dishes—fresh bread, some sort of fish risotto, bacon, cinnamon, coffee—and her stomach clenched, reminding her that she hadn't eaten since last night. Perhaps she could grab something on the way out of the hotel . . .

"Wait," Duan Zheng said suddenly. He stepped forward to grasp the arm of one of the two tray carriers. "Who are you and what is your purpose here?"

The question hung in the air for a moment. Then both men dropped their trays, reaching into their jackets and pulling out guns.

The third man grabbed a heavy pistol from under a linen drape and levelled it at Ao Ji. "Death to the bourgeoisie!" he shouted, his finger tightening on the trigger.

Irene tackled him.

It was a very inelegant action, but it worked. His shot went wild, hitting something solid—not a person, she thought, there hadn't been a scream—and the two of them went rolling across the floor together. A gust of air like the dead of winter given physical form shrieked across the room above them, and there was a sound like breaking wood, and the crash of a door being thrown open. Irene ignored it, focusing on subduing the man beneath her. He hadn't been expecting to fight a woman, and at first he tried to simply throw her off by superior force.

That was the only mistake he had time to make. She elbowed him in the side of the throat, then forced him face-down and got her knee in the small of his back, twisting his arms behind him while he was gasping for breath.

When she had a moment to look up and around, the two other men had both been downed. In fact, they were lying on the floor with their limbs and necks at angles that suggested they would never be moving again.

"This one too?" Duan Zheng said, indicating Irene's prisoner with the toe of a well-polished shoe.

Irene realized what permission he was asking for from Ao Ji. "No, wait!" she said. "We need answers."

Then she realized that Kai was in the room as well.

CHAPTER 6

"My lord uncle!" Kai exclaimed. "Are you all right?"

Ao Ji snorted. "Do you think that these humans could seriously threaten *me*?"

"Well, no," Kai admitted, "but where there is one enemy there might be others."

"Which is why we can't kill this man yet," Irene said, seizing the opportunity. "He might be affiliated with whoever killed Lord Ren Shun."

"A very good point," Duan Zheng said. "We must put him to the question."

"And we'll need to somehow explain this to the police," Irene added reluctantly.

"What is there to explain?" Ao Ji asked. "They assaulted me. I slew them. Personal self-defence is acceptable by the local legal code."

"I think Miss Winters means that we want to avoid attracting further attention to the summit, my lord uncle," Kai said. "It will be inconvenient if we are forced to go elsewhere."

Irene noted Kai's extreme level of formality, on a par with the time they'd been on trial before the Queen of the Southern Lands. Apparently Ao Ji's rigidity extended to even his own family. "If I may make a suggestion, Your Majesty?"

"Speak," Ao Ji commanded.

"It will be difficult to transport two dead bodies out of this hotel without being noticed. But we could shift the scene of the assault to one of your attendants' rooms and say he was the one attacked. That will mean you won't be personally involved, Your Majesty. And in the meantime we can find out why this person was trying to kill you."

"It's workable, Your Majesty," Duan Zheng said. "But we'll need to do it before any of the hotel staff come to investigate the gunshot."

"See to it," Ao Ji said. "Li Ming or Mei Feng can be the suggested victim."

The assassin underneath Irene chose that moment to try to struggle free, and she had to yank his arms up behind his back again. "Oppressors of the people," he snarled. "Escaping the law by falsifying evidence!"

"*You* just tried to shoot us, and you're accusing *us* of breaking the law?" Irene demanded.

"I serve a higher law! A society as unjust as this one must be changed by any and every means necessary."

Behind her, Irene was conscious of Duan Zheng handling the crowd of dragons and servants who were trying to enter the suite, drawn by the gunshot. She could hear him drafting servants to carry the dead bodies and arrange the faked assault. But her attention was on the man she was restraining. She'd heard that sort of language before . . . "Are you an anarchist?" she asked.

"Yes!"

Genuine anarchists? This was unexpected. Irene really hoped that mentioning anarchists hadn't actually pulled them into the situation. After all, the Fae caused real life to fall into story forms, and the unfolding events made for powerful drama . . . "And why did you attack us here?"

He glared in Ao Ji's direction. "All monarchs shall *perish*. The people of your homeland would have rejoiced and blossomed into liberty, returning to their natural state under—"

"Kai," Ao Ji said. "Restrain him. Librarian, step back. I would not have you harmed unnecessarily."

Irene let Kai take over her grip on the man's arms and rose to her feet, backing away. The other bodies had been dragged out of the room, and one of the servants was busy brushing tracks and other traces of the fight from the carpet. *At least I won't have to deal with the police trying to arrest Ao Ji. That's one less thing to worry about.*

Ao Ji set down his teacup and stood. He paced across towards the helpless anarchist, cold air ebbing and flowing around him in an almost visible haze of frost. "You are a revolutionary," he said. "You have attempted violence against me. Both these things are worthy of death. But if you confess everything you know, I may be merciful."

His will descended on the room like bitter, crushing frost, like the heart of winter given definition. Irene felt it even at a distance and without its being specifically directed at her: the impulse to submit, to obey, to beg for mercy. Her Library brand across her shoulders flared up again in response, aching like a fresh burn. The human servants in the room fell to their knees, bowing their heads and shivering.

The anarchist squirmed on the carpet, struggling in a desperate attempt to escape from that icy majesty, that absolute power and contempt. "No," he gasped, the words congealing in his mouth. "No, stop, please, in God's name—"

"I thought you revolutionaries were all atheists." Ao Ji came to a stop in front of the anarchist. "You need not fear the divine. Fear me instead. Tell me who is behind you."

The words fell through the air, implacable, impossible to refuse.

The anarchist shuddered. "The—the Theatre—" he began.

Then his back arched in Kai's grip, and blood ran from the corners of his mouth as his eyes glazed over. His breathing abruptly stopped, leaving the suite in silence.

Ao Ji turned away with a small noise of disapproval. The coldness bled out of the air, returning it to something nearer normal room temperature. "Inconvenient," he said. "He broke before we could learn more."

"What happened?" Irene asked. She'd seen deaths before, and she had no particular reason to grieve for a man who'd been ready to kill everyone in the room. But at the same time, watching a man's "questioning" lead to death—whether the "questioning" was physical or mental—was an experience she would rather not have had.

"He attempted to resist me." Ao Ji seated himself. "But beyond that, he had been influenced by one of the Fae. When he was compelled by both that power and my own, his mind broke and his heart stopped."

The urge to see this as a metaphor for humanity, caught between the dragons and the Fae, was highly tempting. Irene put the thought aside for later brooding and went down on her knees beside the body. "Roll him over, please, Kai," she instructed.

"What are you doing?" Ao Ji asked curiously.

"Checking for clues," Irene said, going through the corpse's pockets. "Evidence of identity, Métro tickets, anything like that—er, has the Métro been built here yet?"

"It's in progress," Kai said.

Irene would have liked to ask Kai more about what was currently going on at the hotel and around his uncle, but that might cause Ao Ji to have inconvenient (and accurate) suspicions about their collusion. She just nodded and unbuttoned the anarchist's uniform jacket. "Hmm," she said.

"You have discovered something?" Ao Ji enquired.

"His undershirt is dirty," Irene said, indicating it. "It's dirty enough that it would have fouled his jacket too if he'd been wearing it for more than an hour or two. His shoes are scuffed and worn: they don't match the uniform. I'd conclude that he and his friends sneaked into the hotel, stole the uniforms, and took advantage of breakfast delivery to enter your room, Your Majesty." She finished patting the man down. Her hands tingled with cold. "A coin purse, a packet of cigarettes, and a flick-knife. No papers. With your permission, Your Majesty, I'll take these items in case Vale can deduce more from them than I can."

"Granted," Ao Ji said. He glanced at a servant. "Have Duan Zheng place this corpse with the other ones. Will there be anything else, Librarian?"

Irene decided that the dragons could probably handle the cover-up when the police got here. She needed to get on with the investigation—and if she delayed here much longer, Vale might have left the morgue by the time she arrived. "No, Your Majesty.

Though if someone could take me to the Librarians here who are collecting statements, I would be most grateful."

"Kai, see to it." Ao Ji settled back in his chair. "And have someone fetch me the newspaper."

"At once, my lord uncle," Kai said with a bow.

As he and Irene left the suite, Duan Zheng came striding up, trailed by two of his servants. "Did the man provide any useful information?" he demanded. He seemed to already know that the third anarchist was dead.

"He mentioned a theatre," Irene said. "Nothing more than that, I'm afraid. Does that mean anything to you, sir?"

"Absolutely nothing," Duan Zheng said bitterly. "No Fae conspiracies that I've heard of by that name, no other conspiracies either—and from what I hear of this licentious modern Paris, there are hundreds of theatres in the city." He glanced at the door. "I can't leave His Majesty unguarded. Your Highness, kindly report to me when you've finished doing whatever you're doing with the Librarian here. I'm sure I can put you to good use."

"Of course," Kai said, taking Irene's arm and escorting her down the corridor.

Once they were out of earshot, he took a deep breath and his shoulders slumped. "Walk slowly?" he suggested hopefully.

"Did he mean for *you* to take me to the Librarians here?" Irene asked quietly. "Your uncle, that is. Or are you supposed to be just handing me over to a servant, to get those statements?"

"No, he meant me to see to it." Kai didn't meet her eyes. "I'm supposed to be getting information out of you."

"That's not going to be very successful, given how little I know," Irene noted. "I've hardly had time to discover any interesting clues yet."

"I think my uncle believes that you personally are innocent." Kai shrugged. "He doesn't necessarily believe your superiors are innocent. And let's not go into the potential for guilt of every single Librarian out there. My uncle is wary. He is a monarch. He has reason to be careful."

Irene would have liked to add *your uncle is paranoid,* but that would have been rude. Besides, it wasn't paranoia if everyone really was out to get you. And when you were a dragon king whose closest servant had just been murdered in the middle of a peace conference, and there was evidence of Librarian duplicity floating around, then it was no more than justifiable caution.

Possible evidence of Librarian duplicity, she reminded herself firmly.

"All right," she said. "After all, my superiors are certain to tell me to get information out of you. Turnabout is fair play. I'm not going to take offence." She squeezed his arm reassuringly. "Is there anything we need to cover in private before we run out of corridor?"

Kai looked as if he'd have liked to smile, but he couldn't quite manage it. "The mood is bad," he said. "Most of the courtiers here believe—or say they believe—that the murder is a deliberate provocation to try to stop the talks, so they aren't going to back out of the conference. But that doesn't make anyone feel any safer."

"What does your uncle believe?"

Kai frowned. "I can't be certain. He hasn't told me. He wants answers. He doesn't want to be questioned. But I am sure he thinks the Fae are somehow behind it—whether it's the ones here at the conference or other ones behind the scenes."

"How did he react to your arrival here?"

"Better than I'd dared hope," Kai admitted. "He considers me young and frivolous, so usually I escape his notice. But he seemed actually pleased to see me. I'm wondering if he thinks that my father sent me—though of course if he had, he wouldn't admit it."

"Your father wouldn't admit it if he had sent you, or your uncle wouldn't admit it if he suspected it?" Irene asked, trying to disentangle the pronouns.

"The second," Kai said. "Though if my father had wanted to send a secret representative to these talks, he certainly wouldn't choose me. I'm far too inexperienced, and my mother is of low rank."

"I'm not sure that you can really call yourself inexperienced any more," Irene said thoughtfully. "In fact, I'd bet good money that you've had more experience dealing with Fae and Librarians than a lot of dragon nobles and royalty. Has it occurred to you how valuable that may be in the current situation?"

Kai snorted, sounding very much like his uncle for a moment. "Most of those nobles would tell you there's only one way to deal with Fae."

"Most of those nobles may have to change their habits. If we *can* get a peace treaty signed and sealed, then everything's going to change. Not all at once, but . . ." Irene had never actually considered such a possible future before. It was almost frightening. "Perhaps your uncle's already thinking about that, and he sees you as part of that change."

Kai pondered that for a few steps. "It's a nice idea," he said reluctantly, "but it doesn't feel like what I know of my uncle."

"Has he given you any particular tasks?"

"Besides getting information out of you?"

"Besides that."

"I think he'd have liked to add me to the investigation team, but then the Fae would have insisted on adding a second person as well, and so would the Librarians, and it would have started to get ridiculous." Kai shrugged. "Of course, if I just happen to meet up with you and Vale later, we can share more information. Will you be at dinner?" he asked hopefully.

"In what context?"

"There's a grand dinner tonight in Le Meurice. Everyone's going to be attending. And then it's the opera tomorrow night. All parties are supposed to be *interacting*." Kai's tone of contempt suggested that any interaction on his part would be with extreme prejudice and from a distance.

Something Irene had been wondering about earlier came back to her. "Kai, you can usually tell how much order or chaos is in a given world. This place is supposed to be as neutral as possible. Has this changed at all?"

Kai frowned. "Have you ever seen the sort of marbled dye work where someone's poured different colours of dye over the surface of a pool of water, then used a tool to draw lines through the colours till they're all mixed together in a pattern?"

"No, but I think I can visualise what you mean. So this Paris is sort of currently . . . mixed-up? For want of a better term?"

"That's the best I can manage," Kai admitted. "Some areas are more strongly affected than others, because the people there are intensifying the effect—this hotel's very order-heavy at the moment, and that would be spreading across Paris if it wasn't for the Fae in their hotel. And vice versa."

Irene considered theories. "If there *was* someone here from either the Fae or dragon side, not part of the delegations but someone else—someone powerful, trying to sabotage negotiations—would they be affecting things? Would you be able to tell?"

"I have no idea. Probably not unless I actually ran into them. But I haven't been able to leave the hotel yet."

"Well, if you do, let me know. And how many flights of stairs are we going up here, anyhow? Don't tell me that your uncle's parked his assigned Librarians in the attic."

"No, just the sixth floor." Kai led her along the hallway and knocked on one of the doors. "What did you expect?"

"I'm not sure what I expected," Irene said. "But I would think that if his Librarians were up here last night, then neither of them will have any idea about what was going on elsewhere in the hotel."

"If that was a bet, you'd win it," a woman said, opening the door. Her iron-grey hair was pulled back into a tight bun, streaked with white, and she'd bundled a thick tartan shawl round her stocky shoulders, lurid against the dark green of her dress. "You must be Irene Winters. Do come in. We won't be a moment, Your Highness." She shut the door in Kai's face before he could try to insert a foot.

"That's rather harsh," Irene said. "And yes, I'm Irene Winters. But we haven't been introduced . . ."

"I'm Sarashina," the woman said. "And I've nothing particular against Kai out there, but if he has any political sense whatever, then he knows we need to talk in private. That's Rongomai over there." She nodded to a young man who'd fallen asleep sprawled on the sofa, draped like a sagging tent with multiple blankets. "He's been running around the hotel all night, so I'm letting him have a few minutes' rest before he leaps back into action."

"Collecting statements?"

"Exactly. We can't expect the nobles to come up *here*, after all, can we?" The morning light fell through the window and across

Sarashina's face, bringing out the lines and shadows of weariness. She held herself stiffly upright with the posture of a woman who would have to be knocked down rather than allow herself to relax. "And you're here to pick them up. And to pick our brains."

"Have a seat," Irene suggested, taking one herself. The gilt-and-velvet chairs were more solid than they seemed. "We need to be fast. I don't want to get Kai in trouble for taking too long to escort me, and I have to meet up with Vale at the morgue as soon as possible. What do I need to know?"

"Right, the detective." Sarashina sat down with a sigh. "Basically, we don't know much. This morning—no, it was yesterday morning now, I suppose . . . sorry, I haven't had much sleep. Everyone got woken up early by His Frosty Majesty having a snit fit about where Ren Shun had got to and why he wasn't there with the coffee and the newspaper and the day's agenda. Then just as everyone was really starting to panic, word came over from Le Meurice that they'd found his dead body there. Cue panic. Cue accusations. Cue Lord Icicle down on the first floor declaring that the whole thing was a Fae plot and could anyone give him a good reason not to destroy their entire lying delegation."

Irene winced. "I know this is just between these four walls, but I wish you wouldn't keep on nicknaming him like that."

"It's a defence mechanism," Sarashina said. "Have you ever had to share a hotel with a dragon king for a few days? No? Then don't criticise me. Anyhow, there was an immediate high-level conference at Le Meurice, and everyone spent most of the day trying to thrash out how to investigate it and who should do it. While, you know, lying to the police about it. Not that we were there. Kostchei passed the word that Rongomai and I were to get statements from everyone in this hotel while people still remembered what was going on." She covered a yawn. "Including the hotel staff. And the human servants. And the dragons themselves. You want the bad news? Every single dragon swears that they stayed here in the hotel all night. Absolutely nobody knows where Ren Shun went. And nobody knows what he was up to."

"You're not the only one with bad news," Irene said. "According to Ao Ji, Ren Shun heard an interesting conversation the day before he was murdered. A conversation that *could* be understood to implicate Librarians in a conspiracy to manipulate the talks."

Sarashina stared at her for a moment. "I assume there's no other evidence corroborating this," she said, "on the grounds that, you know, we're all still *alive*."

Irene nodded. "Clearly it was an attempt to frame us," she said firmly.

"Well, of course!" Sarashina agreed. "How incompetent do they think we *are*?"

"Does it sound like something the Fae delegation might be involved in? I haven't met any of them—yet." Hopefully they wouldn't be insulted by her visiting the dragon delegation first. She had to go *somewhere* first.

"Definitely not," Sarashina said. "The Fae Princess is genuinely in favour of a peace treaty. It's the archetype she's compelled to follow—you know how Fae are. She couldn't do anything *else* and be who she is. I don't think she *could* do anything that would hinder the negotiations. As for the Cardinal, he might be up to something . . . actually, he probably is up to something. That's in *his* nature. But whatever it is, if it's him, it would have to be cunning and devious and intelligent."

"Oh dear," Irene said. "One of those." She'd met a Fae who fell into the scheming archetype before. It hadn't been a pleasant experience for anyone involved. Not for Kai, who'd been kidnapped; not for Irene, who had been severely endangered; and least of all for the Fae himself, because Irene had killed him.

"Even so, if he was up to something, it couldn't be *that* blatant, as that would be stupid. And he's not stupid. Hmm. What else do I need to tell you? The Librarians over at their hotel are Blaise and Medea. Do you know either of them?"

"I think I remember a Medea who was just starting as a student when I went out as a journeyman," Irene said, racking her brains, "but we never interacted. I only remember her name."

"You probably won't have time to sit down and catch up. Our Librarians will have collected statements at their end, but I'm not sure what more they can add . . ." Sarashina shrugged. "I suppose this is what we've hired a detective for. Stand back and let the experts work, I always say."

"My life is painfully full of learning experiences where I've had to be an expert at short notice," Irene said. "I look forward to being able to sit down for a few years, at some point, and try to forget them. But you're right, time is short, I should concentrate on the statements. Very well." She mentally cracked her knuckles. "You've given me your opinion on the current situation—I'm assuming there's an overview in with the statements?"

She realized that she was taking charge of the conversation and questioning Sarashina—a more experienced Librarian and an older woman—as if she had the right to do so. But, the thought struck her, she *did* have that right here. She needed to be able to question everyone. Even other Librarians.

Sarashina nodded, not choosing or not wanting to challenge Irene's authority. "Rongomai's and my thoughts are included, in detail.

They're in the briefcase lining, just in case anyone—such as Duan Zheng—wants to see the statements before you leave the hotel."

"What position does Duan Zheng hold?" Irene asked. "He carries himself like the head of security."

"You're right," Sarashina said. "Except that with Ren Shun out of it, he's having to fill *his* position too. Personal secretary, spymaster, right-hand man, sounding-board, et cetera. That's probably why he's not making much fuss about Prince Kai showing up—it means that Duan Zheng can avoid the personal secretarial duties, at least. He's a little stressed at the moment. Don't push him."

"Thanks for the warning."

"My comments on everyone else are in my notes." Sarashina rose and stretched, rubbing the small of her back. "Damn, they never tell you when you're younger how much you're going to ache once you get older . . . Good luck, Irene. For all our sakes."

"One last question. How secure would you say this hotel is, in terms of spies?"

"Hopeless," Sarashina admitted. "Private conversations inside bedrooms are probably safe enough, but anywhere out in a public room or corridor, where a servant could hear you? Or someone disguised as a servant, or another guest? You have to assume it could be compromised. Still, the other hotels have the same problem. Everyone's in the same boat. The peace conference's security was supposed to be based on mutual trust—and on nobody else knowing it was happening until everything was signed and sealed."

And that trust is melting away like snow in summer, Irene reflected.

Kai was waiting at the end of the corridor, staring out of a window at the cloud-streaked sky. "Ready to go?" he asked.

Irene nodded. "Sorry you had to wait out here," she said, feeling a need to apologise for Sarashina's behaviour.

But he just shrugged. "My uncle would understand that she needed to brief you privately. And it's not as if he expects me to listen at the keyhole."

"Of course not," Irene agreed. "That's what the servants are for." She was certain that Ao Ji wouldn't object to the Librarians being spied on. There was probably some unspoken list of what sort of spying was suitable for each rank in dragon society. Princes attempted to cajole secrets from their acquaintances, bodyguards threatened witnesses and removed the evidence, servants listened at keyholes . . .

Kai drew her aside just before they reached the hotel's main entrance hall. "Make sure Vale understands how important this is," he said quietly. "People *liked* Ren Shun. A lot of his friends will have a personal issue in finding out what happened. They'll hold grudges."

"I'll tell him," Irene said, with a sinking feeling. *One more variable to juggle . . .* "And be careful yourself. If someone's trying to sink the peace treaty by killing important people, then you're a possible target. And I put you here," she said ruefully.

Kai smiled. "You think you could have kept me away? You're not in charge of me any longer, Irene."

"Maybe not," she conceded, "but I still expect you to hit the ground if I shout for you to take cover."

"Ah, but that's not taking orders. That's just common sense."

"And you will be careful?" She saw his growing frown. "Kai, someone's just tried to assassinate your uncle. In his *own rooms*. I don't think we could have much better proof that nowhere's safe. And it's not as if you'll always be by the Seine, with plenty of water to hand and able to summon the spirit of the river for help." Kai's personal elemental affinity was for water, as Irene knew from past experience.

"Paris has an excellent sewer system," Kai said, "and the water down there is still flowing, even if it's not exactly pleasant-smelling. I checked. Trust me, Irene. I learned from you."

"That's partly why I'm worried," Irene admitted ruefully.

He kissed her hand and escorted her to a cab.

"Where to, madam?" the driver enquired.

"The Paris Morgue," Irene said. "As fast as possible, please."

"Don't worry, madam," the driver said, directing his horses out into the flow of traffic. "Nobody there's going to get up and run away."

"Let's hope not," Irene said.

After all, dragons and Fae possibly signing a peace treaty was already one impossible thing before breakfast. Why not a few more while she was at it?

CHAPTER 7

The Paris Morgue lay behind the great Notre-Dame cathedral on the Île de la Cité, in the middle of the Seine. It was a monument to the secular processes of death, built in the shadow of a cathedral that celebrated the Resurrection and the Life. And that was one of those ironies that occurred in any great city, when space runs out and buildings are forced to rub inappropriate shoulders. As Irene dismounted from the cab and paid the driver, it was difficult for her to judge whether the streaming crowds were more interested in religion or in gawping at corpses.

Ogling the dead seemed a very odd sort of attraction to her. Yet gendarmes outside the morgue's three-arched marble entrance held back the crowd, corralling them into a queue that filed through the leftmost arch, then out again through the rightmost arch; the central door of the three stayed closed. Above it, words gleamed coldly in the morning light, given an extra sparkle by the frost: *LIBERTÉ! ÉGALITÉ! FRATERNITÉ!* Street vendors serviced the crowds, offering food and newspapers.

All the classes of society seemed present, from elegant men and women about town in top hats and well-cut overcoats or furs and capes and muffs, to the middle and working classes in more practical—and more patched—clothing. The only similarity was that everyone had bundled themselves up against the cold. The wind snaked viciously along the Seine as if it was following the water, and the people waiting for admission clapped their hands together and shifted from foot to foot, unwilling to stand still in the biting air.

Irene joined the queue, caution urging her to blend in rather than shove to the front and persuade the gendarme there to let her jump the line. Her clothing was unfashionable—the skirt too full, the jacket too stiffly cut, the waist not tight enough—but not enough to make her dangerously obvious. Especially given the wide cross-section of society waiting to get into the morgue and view the corpses there. So she waited in line and listened to the gossip around her. Nothing particularly unusual—politics, anarchists, the price of bread, the new bicycle fad, an upcoming balloon ascension, the ballet at the Paris Opéra, the new play by Maurey at the Grand Guignol . . .

When she was waved into the morgue, the mingled smell of ammonia and lye caught at her throat and made her cough. She wasn't the only visitor doing so. Some were already hurrying over to a stall in the corner of the large room to buy throat pastilles and cigarettes. But most of the crowd were more morbidly interested in the morgue's main attraction.

The corpses.

Personally, Irene would rather spend her time with a good

book. But on either side of the large central hall, behind thick glass windows, lay tilted slabs with bodies displayed on them—some naked, with their clothing hung behind them, others still clad. In the dense cold of the building, even harsher than the winter frosts outside, the dead lay still and serene behind glass, their flesh as pale and unchanging as marble. The bystanders stared at them, discussing them, nobody bothering to lower their voices in respect. Parents held up their children to look at the anonymous dead. After all, the theoretical purpose of this display was to identify these bodies—every bystander, young or old, was only doing their civic duty by scrutinising them in detail, by speculating on who they might be and what brought them to this place . . .

At least Irene could be sure that Ren Shun wouldn't be on display with these other bodies. He was, after all, an *identified* corpse.

She needed to find Vale and Mu Dan: they must be deeper inside the morgue. More gendarmes were guarding the doorways that led beyond the main central hall. She approached one of them hopefully. "Excuse me, monsieur—I am here to see the English detective."

Her target looked blank. His companion, on the other hand, brightened. "Ah! You mean the one from Scotland Yard?"

"The very same," Irene agreed. After all, it would be straining probability for there to be *two* English detectives wandering around the morgue at the moment. "Did he tell you that I would be coming?"

"Indeed, madam. He said that a lady would be joining him shortly." The gendarme lowered his voice. "Your name, if you please?"

"Irene Winters," Irene said quietly. Nobody except the gendarmes seemed to be in earshot, but how could one be sure?

The gendarme nodded and turned to his colleague. "Yves, I'll escort this lady—I'll only be a moment."

Further inside the morgue, away from the public display room, the temperature became slightly more tolerable. Other people passed them in the corridors—gendarmes, labourers with heavy aprons, young men carrying textbooks and discussing medicine, an elderly lady with a mop and bucket—but nobody looked twice at them.

The gendarme led the way up a flight of stairs and paused to glance in an open doorway. Irene looked over his shoulder: it was a small lecture theatre with a marble table in the middle, sited to catch the light from the two large windows. "The hall for dissections, madam," the gendarme explained. "Ah! We have him."

Vale and Mu Dan looked up from their conversation. "Your colleague, monsieur!" the gendarme announced, as though he'd just fetched Irene from the other side of Paris in person.

"Ah, Winters," Vale said, not getting up from his seat. "You took your time."

"Things happened," Irene said briefly, "most of which are relevant. Excuse me a moment." She pressed a coin into the gendarme's hand with a smile and closed the door on him. "Is this place secure?"

Mu Dan shrugged. She snapped shut the notebook she was holding and tucked it into her jacket. "I believe so. What has happened?"

"An attempt to assassinate His Majesty Ao Ji," Irene said. She put down her briefcase with relief. A hotel's worth of statements was *heavy*. "Unsuccessful. Three men, apparently anarchists. Two of them died in the assault, and the third one had a heart attack or stroke or something while Ao Ji was questioning him. Ao Ji said that he was under Fae influence. I have his possessions for you to examine, Vale." She considered whether to mention Kai and decided to keep her mouth shut until she knew a little more about Mu Dan.

"We have made some progress," Vale volunteered. He nodded towards a set of cabinet doors on the opposite wall. "Mu Dan and I have examined Lord Ren Shun's body. And we concur with the local coroner—he was killed by a knife thrust from behind, directly to the heart. His assailant was approximately the same height as him. There are no signs of drugs in his system, and no head injuries or bruises on his wrists. Or any other injuries at all, which is interesting. I would conclude that he was taken by surprise and had no chance to resist."

"As would I," Mu Dan said firmly. "Though of course one cannot judge what mental effects he may have been subjected to."

"Please," Vale said, with a wave of his hand. "You have been telling me for the last half-hour that only weaker dragons can be affected by Fae manipulation in that way."

"There may be exceptions," Mu Dan said. "And if a truly powerful Fae was involved—"

This was clearly an ongoing argument that had already been through several iterations. "Perhaps I'd better tell you what happened," Irene cut in hastily. She fished out the anarchist's possessions from her purse and deposited them on the desk in front of Vale, as she quickly ran through Ao Ji's statement and the brawl.

Both Mu Dan and Vale listened with sharp interest. The room seemed to grow quieter as Irene reached the part about exactly what Ren Shun had heard.

"Are you certain about this?" Mu Dan finally asked.

"I'm certain Ao Ji told me that that was what Ren Shun had told him," Irene replied.

"Cautious phrasing," the dragon mused. "Are you a lawyer as well as a Librarian, Miss Winters?"

"No," Irene said pleasantly. "I just feel that at the moment, given the possible consequences if anyone jumps to the wrong conclusions, we need to be very clear about the distinction between facts and hearsay. And you can call me Irene, if you like."

Mu Dan blinked, a little taken aback. "Thank you. I . . . take your point. I have no wish to trigger a disaster. But if we can't trust His Majesty's word, then who can we trust?"

"I'm not questioning His Majesty's word," Irene said quickly. This was a minefield. She didn't want to say something that would accidentally insult either Ao Ji or Mu Dan. "I'm just noting for the record that it would be really nice to have some more information about what Ren Shun heard, and from a more direct source."

Vale had been quiet, sorting through the anarchist's possessions and holding them up to examine them. "Actually, Winters, there *is* something we had not yet shared with you."

Irene stiffened. "What?" she demanded.

"A note from Ren Shun's inner waistcoat pocket. Mu Dan has it. Unfortunately it is in Greek—apart from one English word, *hell*—and has been stained by both blood and water. My Greek dates back to schoolroom days, and Mu Dan has none at all, so we have not yet made a great deal of sense of it."

"You might have said something *earlier*," Irene snapped.

"The assassination attempt was more urgent," Mu Dan said soothingly. "One must prioritise. Can you read Greek?"

"I can," Irene said, extending her hand hopefully. "And while we're at it, was Ren Shun killed where he was found, or was the body moved?"

"Moved," Vale said. "It was clear enough from the lack of blood in the room. He was deposited there after his death. The stains on his clothing suggest that the body was brought into the hotel during the blizzard that night: snow was trapped in the folds of his coat and shirt and influenced the flow of blood from the wound as it melted."

"That does make it look more like an attempt to incriminate the Librarians and damage the negotiations," Irene said.

Mu Dan tilted her head thoughtfully. "I suppose some prejudice on your part is only natural."

The mixture of worry and anger that had been fermenting inside Irene for several hours finally came to a boil. "Yes," she said, her hand falling to her side. Her voice was cold. "I suppose it is. After all, I'm only looking at a situation where my organisation, my *family*, may be accused by both sides of trying to sabotage peace negotiations on a worldwide scale. Is *worldwide* the right word? Forgive me if I don't actually have a convenient word for *affecting multiple worlds from one end of the universe to the other.* I don't normally deal with situations on this scale. It's entirely plausible that a mere human like myself might be *worried* by this sort of thing. And I suppose it's quite reasonable that I might be swayed by *personal emotions* in a situation where my parents are currently hostages and could be killed if the Library is blamed for this."

She took a step towards Mu Dan. "I am going to cooperate in every way possible to find out who did commit this murder, and to stop a war happening. But please excuse me if I have a certain . . . *natural prejudice* . . . about hoping that the Library is innocent."

Mu Dan blinked. Her eyelids flickered like a snake's. "Your parents," she said. "Forgive me. I will not say that I spoke unjustly, but I did speak harshly. I offer you an unqualified apology."

Irene reined in her temper. A genuine apology from a dragon was rare. Dragons did not back down, and especially not to anyone else who wasn't a dragon. Mu Dan had come halfway to meet her by giving her an unqualified apology. It was Irene's duty as a Librarian—and an adult—to respond. "I accept your apology," she said. "I will try to control my prejudice. We all will need to, I think. I hope the Fae member of our team will do the same, when they join us."

Mu Dan sniffed, but managed to control her own prejudice and refrained from actually saying anything rude out loud. "*When* they get round to contacting us."

"If we must be fair to whoever it is, we have hardly been easy to find," Vale said. He put down the last of the coins from the anarchist's purse. "Our next stop should probably be the Grand Hôtel du Louvre. That is where the Fae delegation is staying, I believe?"

Mu Dan shifted her weight uncomfortably. "You might have a better reception if you attended without me," she said. "But on the other hand, I would not like to be derelict in my duty."

And on the third hand, Irene reflected, *the Grand Hôtel is going to be heavily weighted towards chaos. And as a creature of order you'll be uncomfortable—at the very least—the moment you walk through the door.*

"This investigation of ours is going to be awkward whatever we do," she said. "Are we going to leave the Fae representative outside the Ritz if we go back there to question any of the dragon delegation? Or are we going to leave you outside the Grand Hôtel du Louvre whenever we visit the Fae? Just how far are we prepared to go in making concessions? And how far *should* we go?"

Vale sat back. "My opinion, Winters, is that we should make absolutely no concessions at all. They have hired me to conduct an investigation. That investigation will be on *my* terms. And if neither side is prepared to tolerate the presence of the other's investigator, then I question the ultimate validity of this peace treaty."

"You may have a point," Mu Dan admitted. She changed the subject. "Have you learned anything from the assassin's possessions?"

"Very little," Vale said regretfully. "Certain peculiarities of his teeth, given that he was in the habit of chewing his pocket change. His flick-knife was well-cared-for, and also well-used, suggesting frequent violence. Possibly one of the local street gangs—the Apaches, as they're called."

"Native Americans?" Mu Dan asked. "I haven't been able to do more than scan this world's history, but I hadn't expected to find them here in Paris . . ."

"The term is used to refer to the entire criminal subculture here," Vale said. "That at least is the same as my world. Burglars, pickpockets, ruffians, and especially the street gangs. I am not sure of the derivation; no doubt Winters can research the matter if you are curious. In this case, it merely indicates that he is a recognized and violent inhabitant of the Paris streets. Sadly, it is not an indicator to a specific gang. If I may continue?"

Mu Dan nodded.

"His cigarettes are a brand that I am not personally familiar with." That point clearly irritated Vale. "But from the packet I would assume they are local to Paris—to *this* Paris—and cheap. I will be able to learn more from the bodies when they are brought here for autopsy. The local police may be able to identify them.

Incidentally, Winters, should I be concerned about how they died? Are there likely to be awkward questions?"

"It should come down to physical trauma while attempting murder," Irene said. "And a heart attack or stroke for the one whose possessions you have there. Any irregularities about body temperature will probably have faded by the time they are examined." She felt a certain regret (though not quite guilt) that the deaths had occurred at all. Humans drawn into battles between dragons and Fae rarely fared well.

Irene pulled herself away from brooding. The best way to stop any further deaths—and to keep her parents safe—was to find out what was going on and ensure the peace deal went ahead.

A half-remembered guide to problem-solving flickered through her head. *Write down the problem. Think very hard. Write down the answer.* Not very helpful.

A fist crashed hard on the door—then, without even a pause for reply, the person on the other side shoved it open.

A bulky gendarme shoved his way in, followed by three of his fellows. They were more neatly dressed than the one who'd guided Irene earlier: the brass buttons on their tunics and the insignia on their caps flashed brightly, and their trousers were creased to perfection. Unfortunately, they also seemed a great deal less friendly than their fellow. "You're the English detective?" the one in the lead demanded.

Vale rose to his feet. "I am. I'm working with Inspector Maillon on the murder at Le Meurice."

"It's Inspector Maillon himself who's sent us to fetch you along for an interview," the gendarme said. He chewed on his moustache for a moment, his gaze assessing Irene and Mu Dan. "And we'll bring your little chickens along as well. I imagine he'll want a word with them too."

Mu Dan tilted her head at the vulgarity, her eyes hot with anger. "I arrived in Paris *after* this murder took place, so there is nothing I can tell Inspector Maillon about it. I am staying at the Ritz. If Inspector Maillon wishes to speak with me, he may call upon me there."

The gendarme snorted. "Perhaps you haven't heard, madam, but Paris is a republic these days. We don't have time for this sort of high-flown behaviour. If you won't come along willingly, you'll be put under arrest." He turned to his comrade. "Albert, the handcuffs, if you please!"

Well, that escalated rapidly. Irene would normally have used the Language to convince the gendarmes that they had some sort of signed and sealed permission to leave—but that effect would eventually wear off and only arouse more suspicion in the long run. "I'm sure my friend didn't mean it in that way," she said quickly. "There's no need to take such measures."

"I'm in charge here, madam," the gendarme snarled. "I'll take whatever measures I consider necessary." Behind him, his fellow policemen squared their shoulders, and one of them—Albert, presumably—pulled a heavy pair of handcuffs from inside his tunic. "You, madam . . ." he said, pointing at Mu Dan. "Your wrists, *now.* We do not tolerate disrespect to the police."

"That would be quite true," Vale said, "but there is one point I feel I should mention."

"And what is that?" the gendarme demanded.

"You're all impostors." His fist took the gendarme on the point of the jaw, sending the other man staggering backwards, his arms pinwheeling as he tried to regain his balance and his eyes glazed over.

With a roar the other three gendarmes charged at Vale, drawing their truncheons. Vale caught his cane up from the desk and retreated backwards, stabbing it into one man's stomach and then cracking a second across the forehead with it. "Winters, we want to question these men!" he called.

That sounded like an excellent idea. **"Uniform caps, cover your wearers' eyes!"** Irene ordered in the Language. **"Truncheons, split!"**

The three men cornering Vale were abruptly weaponless, as their truncheons shivered apart in their hands, and inconvenienced by their uniform caps obscuring their vision.

Mu Dan grabbed the fake gendarme who'd been addressed as "Albert" by the scruff of his neck, her lips drawn back in a snarl, and literally lifted him off his feet before tossing him across the room. He hit the wall with a crash, shaking his head as he slid down to sprawl on the floor and his set of handcuffs tinkled to the ground beside him.

The first gendarme—the commander of this little kidnap squad, Irene assumed—had managed to refocus his eyes. He grabbed a whistle from his belt and blew on it. The resulting squeal tore through the air, loud enough to be audible rooms away. "Assistance!" he shouted. "Criminals! Assault! *Anarchists!*"

Heavy feet came trampling down the corridor outside, and more gendarmes burst into the room, looking around for targets, and—naturally—fixed on the non-gendarmes in the room. Time moved with the slowness of panic as Irene backed away towards the wall, holding up her empty hands in an attempt to demonstrate how harmless she was. Although she'd managed to affect this many people's minds with the Language—with some difficulty, admittedly—she couldn't do *anything* too public with the Language here. It might have consequences all the way from getting them arrested to wrecking the entire peace conference.

Vale shouted something, but it was lost in the confusion and yelling. More gendarmes were closing in on him. Mu Dan had retreated towards the wall, apparently unwilling to engage in fisticuffs with half of the police of Paris, but with no other convenient tools to handle the matter. The first kidnapper had edged over to his unconscious friend and was dragging him upright. Liquid ran out onto the floor from where a bottle in the man's tunic had broken. Irene could smell it from several paces away. Chloroform.

A combination of fear and anger ignited in her brain and gave her an idea. She didn't know the word in the Language for ammonia, but . . . **"Gas stink, intensify a dozen times,"** she shouted.

Her words were lost in the general clamour, disregarded by the gendarmes and the kidnappers—but the air heard her. She barely had enough time to pull up her coat to cover her mouth.

The stink was like acid—it cut through any attempts to ignore it, burning the nasal passages and lungs worse than swallowed salt water. Combatants on both sides stopped fighting, bending over to cough and clutch at their throats.

The impostors made a break for the door, shoving past choking and confused gendarmes and out into the corridor. Irene cast around for help, but Vale was trapped by the crowd on the other side of the room, and Mu Dan was coughing even worse than the average gendarme, tears streaming down her face. No assistance would be coming from either of them.

Irene thrust her way through the mob of gendarmes, following the impostors' trail. "Stop!" she shouted after them, breaking into a run as she made it out into the corridor and the population density shifted from impossibly packed to merely crowded. "Stop there, you impostors! Thieves! Murderers!"

The still-coughing kidnappers didn't slow down, and sadly nobody tried to stop the gendarme impersonators on Irene's behalf. She caught up her skirts and speeded up, dodging a group of students and two more gendarmes who were trying to work out what was going on. "Excuse me," she gasped as she swerved past the old lady cleaning the morgue corridors, barely avoiding getting tangled up in her mop and bucket. Trampling feet behind her indicated that she was being followed too. Good, additional gendarmerie might be useful. The chase was leading towards the back of the building. Dare she hope that she'd managed to corner the kidnappers?

Sadly, no. There was a back door. Irene stumbled through it just in time to see the last of the kidnappers vanishing down a narrow stairway a short distance down the road, which seemed to lead into the bowels of the earth. She grabbed one of the gendarmes who'd managed to catch up with her by his sleeve. "Where does that go?" she demanded.

"To the sewers," he coughed.

Irene was prepared to chase armed attackers along the street, but common sense urged her not to go plunging into the unknown sewers of Paris. Especially when the kidnappers might have regrouped and be waiting for her. "Damn," she muttered.

"There are regular tours, if madam wishes to see the sewers?" another gendarme piped up hopefully.

The first one sighed. "Jacques, shut your mouth. Madam, would you kindly accompany us back inside? There are a few questions we would like you to answer."

"That will not be necessary," a new voice said from behind them.

Irene turned to see Vale and Mu Dan, in the company of a gendarme with significantly more braid on his cap and tunic than the regular variety. His moustache was also notable for its vigour and ferocity, spreading out over his cheeks and into his sideburns like a grey tidal wave.

"I am Inspector Maillon," the new arrival said. He clicked his heels together, took Irene's hand and kissed it in a pro forma sort of way, then turned back to Vale. "Your associate is brave, but most unwise . . . To go chasing after *anarchists* as though they were a pack of ducklings. We have had too many disappearances of young women lately."

"She was overcome by righteous anger," Vale said soothingly. "I am certain she would never be so reckless normally. Now, about this new anarchist incident at the Ritz—I understand the bodies are being brought straight here for autopsy?"

Inspector Maillon nodded with enthusiasm. "How fortunate to have you on hand! I was most impressed by your testimonials. Together, I am sure we shall root out this nest of infamy."

Vale nodded. "If you will allow me a moment with my colleague here?"

He drew Irene to one side, together with Mu Dan. "I believe I can be of more immediate use here, where I can examine the bodies and have access to the inspector's records," he said quietly. "Madam Bradamant gave me some false identification papers to explain my presence and accredit me as a representative of Scotland Yard. I'll take your documents to review as well, Winters. In the meantime, I suggest you go on to the Fae hotel, find out what they have to say, and collect their representative. I'll join you as soon as possible."

Mu Dan was already nodding, but Irene shook her head. "I'm not convinced this is a good idea," she said. "What if this group tries to kidnap you again?"

"I think it more likely that Mu Dan here was their target," Vale said. "And forgive me, madam, but you are certainly the most distinctive of the three of us."

Mu Dan twitched a shrug, and the diamond-headed pins in her hair flashed. "That may be true, but now they know who you are too. If you're assaulted when I should have been with you—"

Vale glared at them both in irritation. "Do the two of you wish to wrap me in cotton wool? It would appear that nowhere in this city is safe. We can hardly go round in a trio all day. I am forewarned now, Winters. I will not be taken by surprise again. And *I* was not the one attempting to pursue four attackers single-handedly."

Irene realized that he wasn't going to give way on this point. "Very well," she said. "I suggest we meet up at Le Meurice—it's neutral ground. You'll just have to pay your courtesy call to Ao Ji after we've discussed the situation."

"Agreed," Vale said, and walked back to Inspector Maillon before Mu Dan could argue the point.

Irene turned to Mu Dan. "It seems the Grand Hôtel du Louvre is our next stop. I hope they're ready for us."

"Are *you* taking leadership of this investigation, Irene?" Mu Dan enquired warily.

"Inasmuch as someone has to," Irene said, "yes. Yes, I am."

CHAPTER 8

"The traffic is abominable," Mu Dan complained, looking out of the carriage window. "One would have thought that with such wide boulevards, there would be less congestion. It might have been quicker to walk."

The streets were full of a mixture of vehicles: horse-drawn carriages like the one they were sitting in, horse-drawn carts stacked with bales of goods, and even the occasional horse-drawn double-decker omnibus—but also a few very primitive motor cars. And bicycles. Bicycles darted in and out of the rest of the traffic, ridden by both men and women, with the women even daring to wear trousers: minnows in the stream of vehicles, but still moving faster than the larger fish. The pavements weren't quite so full, but they were studded with stalls and kiosks, and every second café had tables and chairs spilling out to impede passers-by. Even in the current wintry temperature, there were people sitting around nursing cups of coffee, or glasses of something stronger, and smoking cigarettes.

"It could be worse," Irene said. "We could be in New York. I think we must have hit the mid-morning rush hour." And she had a sneaking suspicion that their driver wasn't even trying to go fast. He probably thought they were a couple of tourists who'd appreciate a chance to see as much of Paris as possible.

But at least he wasn't trying to kidnap them.

Irene decided to take advantage of the opportunity. This was as close to privacy as they were going to get. "We should talk," she said. "If we're going to work together and trust one another, then some information sharing is probably a good idea."

Mu Dan turned away from the window to face Irene. "You're a great deal more businesslike than I'd expected."

"I know that one never hears anything good by asking this question—but what *did* you expect?"

Mu Dan looked a little embarrassed. "Given the number of exploits on your record, I'd expected someone a little more Fae-like. I apologise for the insult, but given what you've managed to achieve, I didn't think you'd be so practical."

"Practicality is a great help when it comes to getting things achieved," Irene retorted. "If I were going on a heroic quest, I'd probably start off by making a list of things I'd need on the journey. Including some books to read during the dull bits."

Mu Dan chuckled. "Any particular genre?"

"My personal preference is detective fiction, but I read widely," Irene said. "Yours?"

"Dystopias," Mu Dan said. "I find crime fiction tends to be too close to real life for me."

"Are you an investigator by profession, then? I didn't realize that dragon society had such things. And I apologise if that's insulting in any way. I just don't know much about dragon society."

"I am a judge-investigator," Mu Dan agreed, "but I don't usually investigate *dragons*. I'm more often called in to examine a situation among the human hierarchies who serve the dragons. You probably know that we govern worlds? Well, my kind don't exactly handle all the minutiae of the job in person. That would be ridiculous. Impossible, really. Humans handle the day-to-day business, and then—" She indicated a pyramid with her hands. "Then dragons handle those humans. But from time to time, something gets complicated. Conspiracies. Treason. Rebellions. And in those cases, the nobles may choose to call in an independent investigator to find out the truth."

"You say the nobles," Irene commented. "Not the monarchs?"

"Oh, I'm hardly high-ranking enough for *that*."

Something Irene had half noticed earlier came into focus. "You know," she said, "usually when a dragon introduces themselves, they give their name, and they add 'in service to so-and-so.' Is there some reason why you didn't do that earlier?"

"You *are* sharp," Mu Dan said, sounding genuinely pleased—rather than, as Irene had feared, annoyed. "And you're quite right. I'm not in service to anyone."

"How is that possible in dragon society?"

"By being very good at one's job," Mu Dan said, "and avoiding political debts. My family—Green River, for your information—is less than happy about it, but . . ." She shrugged. "They still find ways to make use of me."

Irene knew that family, or clan, was one axis of dragon society, with the other being the royalty and their courts. It would be easy for a dragon to become caught between those two loyalties. The freedom of having only *one* allegiance might be very tempting to some dragons—except for the way that it might leave them alone and unprotected. Mu Dan was certainly unusual. "Patronage can be a very awkward thing," she suggested neutrally. "Once you're in it, you often can't get out of it again."

"And is the Library free of that sort of thing? A pure meritocracy?"

Irene would have liked to say that it was—but that wouldn't have been the entire picture. "It tries," she finally said, "but it does make a difference who you've worked with, or who your tutors were. But let's change the subject before we get too pessimistic about it all. Do you have that note you mentioned earlier? The one in Greek?"

"I do." Mu Dan reached into her reticule and passed over a folded piece of paper. "Be careful with it. Vale will want to examine it again once he has access to better equipment."

"Hopefully Bradamant's setting that up. She knows the sort of thing he needs."

Irene unfolded the paper. It was, to her amateur glance, good-quality writing paper—the sort that a high-ranking dragon might use, or that an expensive hotel would supply. "Well, it is Greek," she judged. "But the bloodstains don't help."

"It was in his breast pocket," Mu Dan noted. "His blood pooled under him as he lay dead. We're lucky it's readable at all."

"Fair enough." Irene raised the paper closer to her eyes to squint at where the bloodstain had run across some of the text. "Do we know if Lord Ren Shun wrote Greek at all?"

"We don't know," Mu Dan said. "And that's an important question."

Irene nodded. "It says . . . Herodotus. The . . . *The Myths.*"

"Yes, that was what Vale thought," Mu Dan confirmed. "But the only work of Herodotus that he knew was the man's *Histories.*"

Irene frowned. "Of course—some books are written in several alternate worlds, but others aren't written in more than one . . ." She'd never heard of anything else by Herodotus either, though. His *Histories,* written in the fifth century BC, about the origins of the Greco-Persian Wars, were famous enough to have won him the title of the Father of History. But the Library didn't collect history—it collected fiction. If this note did refer to another book by Herodotus, then just how rare was that book? And what might a Librarian do to get hold of it? "I need to check the Library records, or talk with a Librarian who knows more about Greek literature than I do. The rest of the script . . ." She frowned at it, trying to make out the writing underneath the smudges of blood.

And then her stomach sank as she realized what the first part of the remaining writing was. Transcription of a letter and a set of numbers—Beta-001. *B-001. The classification which the Library would use to designate a particular alternate world. But that means . . .*

"Yes?" Mu Dan enquired in the gap left by Irene's silence.

Irene had hoped to avoid serious decisions about loyalty and trust until much later in the investigation, if she had to make any at all. Now she was faced with one, with no way to ask any of the more senior Librarians for advice. And if she claimed ignorance now but told Mu Dan the truth later, then Mu Dan would always know that Irene had lied to her at this point. Which was not the sort of thing that built trust.

If she told Mu Dan what the writing said, Irene might be incriminating the Library in this murder. But if she lied to Mu Dan, then Irene herself would be withholding information from the investigation, and that could damage the dragon faction's trust in the Library. And the writing *might* not even be a Library designation. It could be pure coincidence.

Decisions, decisions.

Irene made her mind up. "This part says 'Beta-001,'" she reported. "That could be a Library designation for a particular world."

Mu Dan drew back from her, eyes glinting with a red that had nothing to do with the light outside the carriage. "Are you serious?" she demanded.

"Note that I said *could be,*" Irene backtracked. "Not *is.* And this doesn't contradict my theory that someone could be framing the Library. It might even reinforce it."

Mu Dan nodded slowly. "I agree that having a note incriminating the Library, found in the victim's pocket, could be a little too blatant to be real. But sometimes . . ." She picked her words carefully. "Sometimes the obvious answer is the true answer."

"Can we class it as a noted fact and get on with the investigation for the moment?" Irene suggested.

"Does the numbering mean anything?" Mu Dan asked, probing a point that Irene had been rather hoping she'd avoid. "I don't know how your system works, but does the 'one' mean that it was the first world of its type investigated?"

"I think it does," Irene said uncomfortably. "And I really do need to ask my superiors for more information about this. It's either a huge genuine clue or a huge fake, but either way we need more actual data before we can hypothesise."

"That's reasonable," Mu Dan agreed. "Is there any more?"

"Well, you don't need me to translate 'hell' there." Irene indicated the word in question without actually touching the paper, relieved to have changed the subject. "And then more numbers—thirty-nine, two, seventeen. Does it mean anything to you?"

Mu Dan shook her head. "No. Vale said he might have an idea, but he wanted to make enquiries first—something about making sure that a particular place existed in this world as well as his own. He's very adaptable for a human."

"He's an equal partner in this investigation," Irene said. "I thought you and he were getting on quite well earlier." A little pang of jealousy surprised her, and she realized that she wished *she'd* been there rather than Mu Dan.

"I was pleasantly surprised." Mu Dan gave a sudden charming smile. "You have no idea how many times I've been asked to work with someone's pet scientist or judge! They can be so inflexible, so dogmatic . . . and sometimes so *stupid*. Your Vale is a true delight. I'd be tempted to keep him—if he wasn't under your protection, of course. We may actually manage to get something done now."

And there, Irene reflected, one had a neat encapsulation of the ultimate position of mortals in the eyes of dragons. *I'd be tempted to keep him.* Mu Dan was certainly polite, and she might even make exceptions for unusual cases, but ultimately she had the same biases as any other dragon. Humans were tools. Mortals would never have the same authority as dragons.

Irene dragged her mind away from a contemplation of institutional prejudice and was reminded of something she'd wondered about. "May I ask a possibly personal question?"

"You may certainly ask," Mu Dan said.

"There are legends of dragons in many different cultures. Chinese, Japanese, Korean, Persian, the classic Western gold-hoarding sort—even stories of similar creatures like wyverns. And yet every single dragon I've met so far, or even heard of, has had a Chinese name. I don't want to pry, but I am curious."

Mu Dan's expression was guarded, but not actually offended or forbidding. "I'm not that old myself, and I'm not a scholar of history. But I will say that the monarchs set the style for the rest of my kin. If there were other matters in the past which have been—erased, shall we say?—then I don't know about them. I don't think I can say more than that."

"That's a very reasonable answer, and I appreciate it," Irene said. She politely ignored the fact that *I can't say more than that* could be understood in several ways without actually being a lie. "I ask partly because I may need to know more about dragons before this is over."

"Given my trade, I can hardly object to that."

The final question in Irene's mind was one that might be taken the wrong way. She'd offended with badly phrased questions before. And the source of a dragon's power seemed a private matter. "In the interests of our mutual defence, may I ask if you have an affinity with any particular element?"

"Earth," Mu Dan said. "And what lies beneath it. I'm not as strong as some, but with time and the situation in my favour, I can be of some use. But you've already demonstrated that you're fast with that Language of yours. I think that between the two of us, we should be quite . . . effective. Also in the interests of mutual protection, may I ask exactly how far your Language will go? Can you command the knife which committed this murder to fly to the murderer's hand, or make the dead speak to us? Is there some sort of ultimate word for life or death?"

"I could tell a knife to return to its user's hand, if we had it," Irene said. "But we don't have the knife that committed this murder—and if the murderer had any sense, they'd throw it into the Seine."

"And the rest?"

"The Language has limits," Irene said. She wondered how much of a temptation it would be, if she *could* simply tell someone to die.

"It works much better on things than on people. I can't order someone to sleep, or kill them with just a word." She smiled, just a little. "Does that make you feel safer with me?"

The carriage came to a stop, and the driver rapped on the roof with the butt of his whip. "Here you are, ladies—the Grand Hôtel du Louvre."

They scrambled out, and Irene looked up at the hotel's frontage as Mu Dan paid the driver. The hotel was massive, a four-story castle in creamy gold stone. It ran right along the length of the street, and a flock of carriages were gathered in front of it, waiting for customers. Shopfronts were nestled in a long succession of archways, their contents looking suitably expensive for the sort of customer the hotel served.

And, interestingly, there was no frost on the building—not even in the shadowed crevices of the stonework. Very curious.

Mu Dan frowned, rubbing her forehead as the carriage rattled away. "This is going to be unpleasant," she said with resignation.

"I can't feel anything myself," Irene said hesitantly. She knew that she could expect her Library brand to react to a high-chaos environment, but it wasn't doing so . . . well, not yet, anyhow. "Is the Fae influence here bad enough to make you unwell?"

Mu Dan hesitated. "Probably not. Just unhappy. Would you care to take the lead? Truce or no truce, I think you'll be more welcome here than I will."

"We can but try," Irene said, and led the way into the foyer.

Now that it was late morning rather than the middle of the night, her unfashionable clothing and short hair attracted glances. Mu Dan was more appropriately dressed—or at least, more *expensively* dressed—and thus a more normal customer for a location like this.

The atrium was huge, however, and they were easily lost in the crowd as they worked their way towards the hotel front desk. Above, a vast glass ceiling in geometrical patterns leaked light into the room below, assisted by the dangling glass-globe lamps. Marble stairways ran up the wall in sinuous curves to join the balcony that surrounded the room and provided a convenient viewing point for idle spectators, who leaned on the iron railings and gossiped.

They were halfway to the front desk when Irene spotted something she'd half been expecting. A couple of the idlers drooping over the balcony were pointing at the two of them and discussing them with sudden animation.

"Don't look too obviously," Irene murmured, "but I think we've just been spotted."

"Where?" Mu Dan followed the jerk of Irene's head towards that part of the balcony. "Ah. Who do you think they are?"

"Well, they're either Fae who've recognized you as a dragon, or they're more of the kidnappers from earlier," Irene said judiciously. "Shall we go and find out?" She didn't want to leave Vale operating on his own any longer than necessary. The situation was just too dangerous.

"It would save time," Mu Dan agreed.

The two men were at the head of the stairs by the time Irene and Mu Dan reached them: they'd realized that they were being approached and had obligingly come to meet the two women. Their approach argued that they were indeed Fae, or servants of the Fae, rather than opportunistic anarchists.

The man in the lead spoke first. He and his companion were both in grey, businesslike in good-quality suits, but his cravat was green while his companion's was purple. He addressed himself to Mu Dan. "Kindly explain yourself."

Ice entered Mu Dan's voice. "Who are you, that I should explain myself to *you*?"

"A whole lot of things, madam," Green said, "but primarily *not* a dragon. Certain rules of conduct were agreed. You're on the verge of breaking them."

Before Mu Dan could state her credentials in tones that would have suited a declaration of war, Irene stepped forward. "Excuse me, gentlemen," she said. "I am a Librarian. My name is Irene Winters. This lady, Mu Dan, is accompanying me, and we are here as part of the agreed investigation into Lord Ren Shun's murder. I would appreciate your cooperation."

Green and Purple paused and exchanged glances. Green finally said, "You can prove this?"

Irene wished that she'd been given some sort of safe conduct to wave in their faces. Unfortunately all she had was her Library brand, and she didn't intend to strip off in a public place so they could see her bare shoulders. "We're here to collect the Fae member of the investigative team," she said. "I wasn't told that identification would be required. I assumed that everyone here had been fully briefed."

Another pause for Green and Purple to look at each other blankly. Fortunately Mu Dan kept her mouth shut and didn't make the situation worse.

"Why not take us to see someone higher up?" Irene suggested, growing impatient. "Such as the Cardinal?"

"You want to see the Cardinal?" Green stammered.

"Why shouldn't I want to see the Cardinal?"

"Because he's the *Cardinal*," Green said, in tones that suggested Irene shouldn't have needed to ask. His previous poise had slipped. "He's not to be disturbed. He's busy. People who intrude on his time have horrible things happen to them."

Purple drew one thumb across his throat in a significant gesture.

Irene resigned herself to having apparently run into the very bottom scrapings of the barrel when it came to Fae representatives. *Please,* she prayed to any deity who might exist, *let the Fae who's on the investigative team be someone else. Anyone else.* "Good point," she said patiently. "So why don't you take us to see the Cardinal's secretary, or his bodyguard, or his second in command, or whoever the appropriate person is?"

"Oh, *right,*" Green said. "You should have said so earlier. Come along with us, please."

He led the way through the swirling throng, with Purple at the rear of the group—not, Irene reflected, that she or Mu Dan had any intention of running away. She glanced sideways at Mu Dan, just in time to catch the other woman wiping sweat from her forehead.

"Are you all right?" Irene asked quietly. The chatter of the crowd would stop Green or Purple from hearing her. She tried to extend her own perceptions, to see if she could feel any aura of chaos in this place. But there wasn't enough—at least, not yet—to even make her Library brand tingle. The Fae presence in this hotel was apparently keeping itself well under wraps.

"Tolerable, for the moment," Mu Dan answered. "Have you noticed the temperature?"

It took a moment for Irene to catch her drift. "Yes," she said in surprise. "It's almost warm in here." Maybe it wasn't so much that the Fae were exerting themselves to enforce their own reality, but rather that they were keeping out Ao Ji's influence. Whatever the reason, Irene was grateful for a respite from the winter cold.

Green led the way deeper into the hotel, past several normal-looking servants and hotel porters who grew tense as the group approached, then relaxed again at a casual sign from Purple. They passed frescos that rose from floor to ceiling and then spread out onto the ceiling, and drooping chandeliers almost too ornate to support their own weight. The whole place breathed wealth and good taste, though in a different way from the dramatic gold and white of Le Meurice, or the themed colours and rich luxury of the Ritz. Irene could only hope that it would improve the mood of the Fae delegation.

But as they ventured farther in, Irene began to feel the power of the Fae who were staying here. It was like being in the proverbial boiling frog's saucepan. One moment there was nothing to worry about, and everything was fine—and then somehow, imperceptibly, they had entered a zone of high chaos. Its influence was strong enough to make her Library brand itch and burn, without Irene being quite aware of when the transition had taken place. She stole another glance sideways. Mu Dan had a feverish colour to her cheeks, and her forehead was lined as if she was clenching it against a headache, but she wasn't slowing down.

Green knocked on a random-looking door, then thrust it open. "Librarian and a dragon to see you," he announced.

"Show them in," a voice came from inside.

And Irene suddenly realized that she knew that voice.

She stepped quickly into the room, half eager to see if her hypothesis was true, and half wanting to know the worst as soon as possible—because if it was who she thought it was, that person might have a significant grudge against her.

The woman inside had been sitting behind a desk covered with stacks of paper, but she rose as they entered. Her hair was pinned back in a neat bun, and while her features were attractive, they were so bland that it would have been hard to describe her afterwards. While her pearl grey dress was well-made and appropriate to the period, it was styled for the wearer to blend unobtrusively into the background rather than thrust herself forward. It could have been a textbook illustration for a secretary's outfit. Matching silk gloves sheathed her hands. "Clarice!" she said, stepping forward and offering her hand. "Or should I say Irene?"

"It had probably better be Irene for the moment," Irene answered, shaking the other woman's hand. She could feel hard moulded plastic and metal through the silk glove. "Sterrington. It's been a while."

It had been several months since the incident when Kai had been kidnapped and Irene had needed to impersonate a junior Fae in order to rescue him. She'd made several acquaintances on that excursion, and Sterrington had been one of them. Of course, Sterrington had signed up with the other side that time and had helped hunt Irene across Venice. And had nearly got her hand blown off in the process.

Irene really hoped that Sterrington *wasn't* the sort of Fae who held grudges. She'd seemed the sort of person who saw things in terms of profit and loss, last time. A true . . . businesswoman. Hopefully that hadn't changed.

"You know each other?" Mu Dan enquired. She didn't sound pleased.

"We have met," Irene admitted. "Mu Dan, please allow me to introduce Sterrington. Sterrington, this is Mu Dan, who's the dragon representative on the investigative team." Technically she should be introducing the lower-ranking person to the higher-ranking one first, but she had no idea who outranked whom in the current situation. Possibly as the Librarian on the investigative team she outranked everyone. Now wasn't that a frightening thought?

Neither of the other two tried to shake hands. "Good morning," Mu Dan said.

"Good morning," Sterrington replied.

"Of course, we met previously in a great hurry," Irene said, trying to bridge the gaping hole in the conversation. "We didn't get time to do much more than exchange names. I'm sorry that things ended up so—ah—inconveniently for you, Sterrington." That was true enough: Irene had absolutely no qualms about what had happened to Sterrington's patrons, but she could sympathise with Sterrington herself.

"Oh, don't worry about it. It's just one of those things that happen in the course of business." Sterrington sat back down again, seeming genuinely unconcerned, as if the previous affair had been no more important than closing a bank account or failing to show up for a lunch appointment. "Now, won't you pull up a chair and let me know how I can help you today?"

There was one additional chair, besides the one that Sterrington was occupying. Irene and Mu Dan looked at each other.

"Let me be brief," Irene said, gesturing Mu Dan towards the chair. She wasn't sure she trusted Sterrington, but she didn't need trust to work with her. "We're here to investigate Lord Ren Shun's death. We'd like to join up with the Fae representative on our team. I'd also like to meet the Librarians—the ones staying here—so that I can get their statements. And anyone else, if they've information to give us about the murder. And if *you* know anything about it yourself, this would be a wonderful time to share."

Sterrington picked up a fountain pen and toyed with it thoughtfully. "Of course, I am naturally eager to give you all cooperation possible. Not only because of the investigation, but because of how grateful I am for everything you've done for me."

"I *beg* your pardon?" Irene said.

"After your little escapade, I was able to use the information I had to leverage my position." Sterrington's smile actually looked genuine. "I made myself extremely valuable to a number of people in high places. It allowed me to get this replacement made." She flexed her gloved right hand. "And I've managed to advance my career much higher and much faster than I'd planned. The positives far outweigh the negatives. In fact, if you'd consider doing a wash-up session at some point with me later to discuss it further . . ."

Irene didn't need to look at Mu Dan—now seated—to guess what this was doing to Irene's credibility in her eyes. No dragon would be enthusiastic about trusting a Librarian when Fae were running round saying how much they appreciated the Librarian and wanted to work with her. Sterrington was deliberately torpedoing Irene's position. And Irene couldn't let her continue.

So she smiled in return. "I'm delighted you've done so well for yourself. Would you consider that you owe me a favour?"

The pen in Sterrington's hand stopped moving mid-twiddle. "Well, you know," Sterrington said, "I'm not sure I'd go *that* far."

If a Fae admitted they owed a favour, then they'd *have* to pay it at some later point.

"Oh?" Irene said blandly. "But you were just saying how grateful you were, and how helpful I'd been."

"Not to the point of a favour," Sterrington said flatly, all her effusiveness gone.

"It's a good idea to get this sort of thing in proportion before any of us start misjudging the situation," Irene said, letting her own smile fade. "We're not hostile to each other. That's good. Let's keep it that way. And in the meantime—the Fae team member, the Librarians, the statements, and any other information?"

"All in progress," Sterrington said. She put down the pen. "The Fae member of your investigative team is being briefed on the situation. Incidentally, where's your human detective?"

"He's looking into an attempt by someone to kidnap us."

"Well, clearly *we* weren't involved in that," Sterrington said quickly. "Can you give me any further details?"

Mu Dan finally spoke. "So that you can keep us sitting here even longer? I think not. We are an active team, not some sort of moribund committee."

"That's far too harsh! Not all committees are moribund."

"Mu Dan still has a point," Irene said. If they needed to play good cop, bad cop to get past Sterrington, then Irene would go along with it. At least she got to be good cop. "Sterrington, you know how urgent the situation is. It's not efficient for us to be sitting here and waiting. If we have to leave and come back later, then we can certainly do that."

Sterrington frowned. "I'm not *trying* to be inconvenient. The situation's complex."

"Then perhaps you could explain it?" Irene suggested.

"Your Fae team member is receiving his briefing from the Princess herself," Sterrington said. "I can't break in on that. And your Librarians are playing chess with the Cardinal. I don't want to intrude there either. Neither situation will be helped by interruptions."

"Nor will it be helped by us sitting here and waiting." Irene leaned forward, placing her hands on the edge of the desk. "I appreciate that you need a *good* excuse. Here's one. Just earlier this morning, before breakfast, someone attempted to assassinate His Majesty Ao Ji. Someone who may have been under Fae influence. He was stopped, of course, but don't you think that we should make absolutely sure that nobody's going to try the same thing here?"

Sterrington opened her mouth—and then shut it again, clearly working through the political implications. "You should have said this earlier."

Irene shrugged. "So far this morning we've had an attempted assassination and an attempted kidnapping. And it's not even mid-day. Can we *please* get things moving?"

Sterrington came to a conclusion. "The Cardinal will need to know about this, even if it means interrupting his chess." She rose to her feet. "Follow me."

CHAPTER 9

The drapes in the Cardinal's suite were a charcoal velvet so dark that they were nearly black. The window looked out over an inner garden somewhere inside the hotel, a distant sunlit landscape of pale winter bark and gravel paths. But inside the suite, the shadow was deeper and more intense than any lack of light. It clung to the corners of the room and smothered the colours of the walls and carpet. It veiled sight and muffled sound.

The strange thing was that in spite of all the darkness, Irene could still *see* perfectly well. The two men seated at the centre of the room playing chess were distinct, not obscured or hidden. The shadow was more metaphysical than real, and it centred around one of the chess-players. The Cardinal. Irene realized that the other player must be one of the Librarians she'd come to see, but it was difficult to look at him—not because of any quality of *his,* but because the Cardinal drew attention like a lodestone.

Chaos welled deeply in the room, intense enough to make

Irene's Library brand ache painfully. She squared her shoulders and waited. Each breath of Mu Dan's hissed as if it came between gritted teeth.

"My lord," Sterrington said, stepping forward and curtseying. "The Librarian Irene Winters and the dragon representative Mu Dan are here to see you."

The Cardinal turned away from the chess table—and on the other side of the board, the Librarian caved forward with a sigh of relief, his shoulders hunched as he stared at the pieces. The shadows seemed to retreat a little, as if sunlight had touched the room and brought a smile to the Cardinal's face. "My dear young people," he said. "What a pleasure to see you. I've heard many good things about you, and I know that I can have confidence in your work."

Irene deliberately bit her tongue. The pain cut through the courtesy, the friendliness, the sheer *plausibility* of the Cardinal's words, like a pinch when one is on the edge of falling asleep. But a deeper fear ran beneath the pain: she heard the echoes of another man in the Cardinal's speech, saw shadows of him in the Cardinal's face. Lord Guantes. The Fae who'd kidnapped Kai and tried to force a war. A manipulator, a Fae who'd played with humans just as the Cardinal here was playing with chess pieces. The man whom she'd killed, and who'd very nearly broken her will before that. For a moment her throat was dry, and she couldn't find any words—appropriate or otherwise.

"We appreciate your gracious attitude," Mu Dan said, covering for Irene's hesitation. Her tone was polite but strained. "We apologise for having interrupted your game. There have been certain developments of which you may need to know."

Mu Dan continued with a summary of the day's events so far—*so far,* Irene thought uncomfortably—while Irene regained her mental balance. Guilt gnawed at her. She knew that she should be taking a more active part in the conversation. Lord Guantes was dead. She'd *killed* him. She couldn't let the past control her like this.

She did notice that Mu Dan hadn't mentioned what was written on the paper that had been in Ren Shun's pocket, eliding it into the general category of *ongoing investigations*. That suited Irene too. She wanted to discuss it with her own superiors before anyone else investigated it further.

Mu Dan faltered to a stop. "I think that is all. But you see how urgent the situation is."

"Of course," the Cardinal said, and again his tone was steeped in paternal concern. "I believe you did absolutely the right thing in bringing this to me directly. I'll have our security raised here, and I'll notify the Princess as soon as possible. Thank you for letting me know, my lady. I appreciate that."

Mu Dan's nod of acknowledgement was very cautious, as though she didn't trust her own judgement.

"Now if you don't mind, I'd like a private word with Irene Winters. If the rest of you would wait outside, I'm sure that we'll only be a moment."

Irene's hard-won calm began to fray at the seams. There was no good way to refuse this. She couldn't even think of any bad ways, short of running out of the room screaming. "Of course," she said, her voice automatically polite. "I am at Your Eminence's service."

"Do be seated," the Cardinal said, as the others shuffled out of the room. He gestured at the chair that the other Librarian had been occupying a moment ago. "And really, 'Your Eminence'? I'm not sure I deserve the honour."

Irene let herself down onto the chair, wishing she had an excuse to stay standing. It was too easy to relax when sitting down.

"Well, you are referred to as 'the Cardinal,' sir," she replied. "I apologise if I'm using the wrong form of address."

The Cardinal made a graceful gesture with one hand. A heavy ring flashed dark red in the sunlight. "Sincere respect is good enough. I won't stand on trifles."

Irene tried to focus on his face. Once before she'd met—well, been in the presence of—a very powerful Fae, and his appearance had flickered between different images like the frames of an old movie, strobing from one archetypal form to another. The Cardinal was more settled: he was definitely male, and elderly, and his hair was white. Or grey. Or salt-and-pepper. And he was bearded, or he wasn't, or possibly just moustached, and he was wearing a business suit, or maybe priestly robes, or . . .

With an effort she folded her hands in her lap: it would have been too easy, and too obviously a demonstration of nerves, to fiddle with the chess pieces. "Would it be possible for you to control your power, sir? It isn't conducive to meaningful conversation. Not on my part, at least."

"Naturally." Her perspective of the Cardinal settled, like a television set's image coming into focus, and abruptly the man sitting opposite her was no stranger than any other human being. *Far less strange than a dragon,* something whispered at the back of her mind. *Far closer to what I am . . .*

"Thank you," Irene said gratefully. "Now how may I assist you, sir?"

The Cardinal stroked his goatee. It was the same shade of greying brown as his hair. His robes were dark and vaguely ecclesiastical. "I believe we have an acquaintance in common."

"Do you mean Sterrington?"

"A servant and dependant. Hardly an acquaintance yet. No, I was thinking of an older acquaintance, a former pupil of mine. When you met him, he was calling himself Lord Guantes."

Irene's stomach lurched and dropped. It took all her composure to keep her face bland and her voice even. She remembered a moment in Venice when she'd almost lost control and agreed to serve Lord Guantes—and betray every oath she'd sworn. Only Vale's intervention had saved her. "He seems to have been on a different political side to you, Your Eminence, if you are in favour of peace. He was attempting to start a war."

"You will notice that I said *former* pupil." The Cardinal shook his head sadly. "It's such a shame when an apprentice whom one trusted, who seemed to have truly understood the principles of power and manipulation . . . falls. Or rather, fails."

"Would you have wanted him to succeed?" Irene ventured.

The Cardinal considered. "On the whole, no. I prefer a more stable game." He tapped the chess-board meaningfully. "Games of strategy which rely on agreed rules and which avoid all semblance of luck are far more to my taste than cards or dice. I like to know where all the pieces are. I like to know what's *possible* in a game. I don't appreciate being surprised. Would you agree, Miss Winters?"

A headache pressed across Irene's forehead like an overly tight bandage, trying to worm its way into her temples and behind her eyes. Her mouth opened to agree.

She pinched herself, her fingers biting into her palm. "To an extent," she jerked out. "I work in situations where random events happen. I can't *forbid* them to happen. I can only make allowances for them and deal with them when they occur."

"Interesting." He leaned back, regarding her. "So you accept your status as a piece, rather than a player."

"That's not what I said," Irene disagreed.

"On the other hand, it's what I understood. Please don't feel upset. I think it's important to actually *understand* what you are. That was Lord Guantes's error—well, one of them. He failed to see the full scope of the board, and he involved himself in direct action."

Irene decided she might as well be hung for a sheep as for a lamb. "If *you* see the full scope of the board, sir, then can you tell me who killed Lord Ren Shun?"

"I can tell you whom I suspect," the Cardinal answered imperturbably. "Not quite the same thing, but it will have to do for the moment."

For a moment Irene was elated. Then caution kicked in. It might be just another case of pointing fingers at the other side. "And that is?"

The Cardinal leaned forward. "Have you ever heard of the Blood Countess?"

The words hung in the air like a dark prophecy. Shadows seemed to congeal in the corners of the room. The hotel's heat receded, and a chill ran down Irene's spine.

She pulled herself together. "Historically . . . I've heard of Countess Erzsébet Báthory, or Elizabeth Báthory, who was known by that name. In some worlds, at least." It went without saying that history did not always progress in the same way in all worlds. "The lady had a bad reputation. But in terms of immediate problems, she hasn't been one of them. And I'm not sure I'd want her to be."

"Sometimes we must all face things that go against our natural inclinations. I could not possibly allow you to leave, Miss Winters . . ." He paused before adding, "Without warning you about her."

Irene's pulse, which had jumped mid-sentence, slowed again as he finished speaking. *Is he deliberately trying to terrorise me, in the nicest and most affable way possible?* Sadly, the answer was probably *yes*. It was the sort of person—the sort of Fae—that he was. The more powerful Fae couldn't step outside their archetype—or, arguably, stereotype. It would be nearly impossible for him to have a conversation with anyone without it turning into a complex power game. And she had so much to lose.

"Are you implying that she wasn't a human being?"

"The original woman was," the Cardinal said judiciously. "But the legend is not. Legends and folklore and stories survive human beings. They persist. And those of my kind can fill the impression that they make in human minds. The lady who goes by the title of the Blood Countess lives up to her legend. The torture, the executions, the bathing in blood, the devil worship . . . When I heard a rumour that she was coming to Paris in order to disrupt the peace talks, I'm sure that you can understand how concerned I was."

Irene mentally flicked through what she knew about Erzsébet Báthory. Unfortunately, the few facts she remembered were more gory folklore than genuine history . . . though from what the Cardinal was saying, gory folklore might be a better guide to this Fae than whatever the true story had been. Sixteenth-century Hungarian countess. Reputedly tortured hundreds of maids and young women to death and bathed in their blood to preserve her youth. Brought to trial, sentenced, and walled up for the remainder of her life. This was *not* an encouraging résumé. "She's opposed to peace?"

The Cardinal smiled. "You're quite right. She prefers an unsettled situation, because it gives her that much more opportunity to indulge her appetites. A dubious woman. She's even supposed to have negotiated with your Alberich."

"I see." Irene had nothing particular against devil worship, but the rest of the list sounded damning enough on its own. And anyone who'd dealt with Alberich—the Library's first and worst traitor—was someone to be avoided with extreme prejudice. "Er, exactly *when* did you hear she was coming here, sir?"

"Barely a day or two ago," the Cardinal said, in tones that denied all possibility of contradiction. "And of course, it was only a *rumour.* I didn't want to cause unnecessary alarm by suggesting that one of my own kind had somehow discovered our highly secret meeting. And that she might want to disrupt it by any means necessary. Just think of the consequences if the rumour had turned out to be false. The negotiations might have been permanently set back."

Irene opened her mouth to say *As opposed to someone being murdered and the negotiations definitely being set back?* Then she shut her mouth again. He was telling her too much. Spymasters and manipulators didn't give people the facts this easily. Either he was lying and this was all a false trail, or he was setting her up to take action as his pawn. Neither option appealed.

"What a difficult situation, sir," she said, trying to sound sympathetic. Or credulous. Or at least neutral. "I can agree that if she is here in Paris, then she's an obvious suspect." Inspector Maillon's words echoed at the back of her mind. *We have had too many disappearances of young women lately . . .* "Do you have any further information?"

"Unfortunately my lines of investigation are limited while I remain in this world." He moved his hand again. The light on his ring flashed and caught Irene's eye, and she had to force herself to look away. "Many of my agents have already died to bring me this information. When the Blood Countess takes action, she is ruthless. She leaves nobody alive who might be *able* to provide information. If she is somewhere here in Paris, then she will be well hidden." He paused for thought. "She is often associated with an elderly woman, her old nurse and teacher. That might be a valid avenue for you to explore."

Irene was ready to seize on the flimsiest thread of evidence, but even for her this was a little thin. She decided to try a direct approach. It might be more efficient than attempting to match an archetype of manipulators at his own game. "Your Eminence, you've given me all this information, but you could previously have shared it when the murder was first discovered. I grant you that the Blood Countess may be responsible, but why tell *me*? And why here and now?"

"Don't you want a personal victory?" the Cardinal asked softly. "Wouldn't it be useful for you to be able to solve this case and obtain the peace you desire? I know your history, Miss Winters. That's such an evocative name, isn't it? I believe you might even deserve it. I almost feel that the two of us ought to have a history, as master to agent. Or perhaps that should be a future."

Irene's mouth was dry. She knew the Dumas stories about the Three Musketeers just as well as the Cardinal did—how Milady de Winter had been one of Cardinal Richelieu's most efficient (and erratic) agents, and how she'd ended up dead. Irene had absolutely no desire to link herself with this Cardinal in that way. It wasn't even *her* fault she'd ended up with the pseudonym *Winters*—Kai was to blame for that, months ago, picking aliases for the pair of them at short notice.

"I'm already sworn elsewhere, sir," she answered. "And while I do want peace, yes, it's for everyone's sake and not just mine."

"Really." The Cardinal's tone suggested that he didn't believe her. "The stories that I've heard about you suggest that you have very personal motives for peace and alliances."

"The Library is neutral," Irene said quickly.

"Neutrality can involve alliances with both sides simultaneously. Balance is a wonderful thing, Miss Winters. Checks and balances, rewards and threats . . ."

"My parents are already hostages to these negotiations." Again Irene felt the shadow of fear brush over her. Were they safe? What would happen to them if, any gods forbid, the dragons took offence or the attempt at a treaty failed? "I don't require any further encouragement."

"Your parents?" the Cardinal said thoughtfully. "I had heard a different story . . ." He trailed off suggestively.

"My parents in every way that matters." Irene heard the ice in her own voice. She had questions about her parentage, and how she'd been adopted, and why her "parents" had lied to her. But that was the *point*—they were still her parents, they had raised her, and they had loved her. Genetics were not important. Affection and protection were the truly important things.

He nodded slowly. "As I said earlier, I think it's very important to truly understand yourself. And I see that you do. Let's look at matters from another viewpoint, then, Miss Winters. You acknowledge that I have a high personal investment in the outcome of these negotiations?"

"I'd say that was obvious, sir," Irene answered cautiously.

"So." He leaned forward. The shadows drew further in around the two of them. Irene's Library brand ached like a fresh burn at the swell of his power. "Consider my reaction if they fail. I would have suffered a personal loss in terms of reputation and resources. I would need to take very definite steps to amend this. I will not waste my time threatening physical destruction in the way that my potential partners in this treaty would. I will be more *productive*."

They were together in the darkness now, a thousand miles from anywhere else, from promised safety or hope of rescue. The daylight beyond the windowpanes was very far away. Irene might as well have been in some oubliette, forgotten by the rest of the world, with nothing to hold on to but the Cardinal's voice and the gleam of his eyes and ring.

I am your only hope of safety, his presence said on a level deeper than conscious thought. It was subtler than Lord Guantes's attempts at domination had ever been, and more compelling. *I am the fear of what might happen to you, and the promise of everything you desire. I punish those who fail me, but I protect my own.*

"Librarians are valuable assets." His voice was as patient as time itself, and as inexorable. "There are levers which can be used to compel them. The safety of the worlds they love. The welfare of their friends. Fear for themselves. I promise you that I will *collect* Librarians, Miss Winters, in order to redress my losses should I fail. I am very well-informed. I will find them, wherever they try to hide. And you will be the jewel of my collection. The first among my agents. My protégée. My demonstration to everyone who would oppose me that I do not take losses lightly."

The air was so thick inside the room that it seemed to curdle inside Irene's lungs, and she had to struggle to breathe. The last flicker of light burned on the chess-board between them: the white pieces and squares were as pale as bone, and the black ones as dark as the void.

"No," she said.

"No?"

"The game is still in play." She forced herself to look away from his ring, to raise her eyes and meet his. "If you try to break me here and now, you will ruin the investigation. That will derail the peace talks.

You need me as myself—not as your agent or pawn. If the dragons think that you've compromised me, they won't trust anything I discover." Her logic was a light and a wall against the currents of fear that webbed the room like a spider's nest. She held on to it, setting brick on brick with every word she spoke. "I understand your warning and I accept it. You wanted to make me afraid? You have succeeded, Your Eminence. You have absolutely succeeded. But we both know you're going to let me walk out of this room untouched."

The Cardinal smiled. It was paternal, understanding, a blessing against the cruelty of the world. It was also the expression of a man who knew that he was in control of the situation and who was appreciating her quick wits rather than in any way losing a battle. "I do so enjoy talking to young people like yourself. It gives me hope for the future. And bearing in mind what we've just said, Miss Winters, do you understand why I can't go round warning everyone about the Blood Countess?"

It fell into place in Irene's mind. "Because if you tell them, they will assume it's just another Fae ploy. But if I discover it independently and can prove it, then the dragons will trust my findings." This depended on the other side being paranoid and untrusting . . . and the logic was contorted and devious. Which was, Irene reflected, only to be expected from the Cardinal.

"Yes."

The darkness receded, and the chaos and power ebbed from the room. Once more they were two human beings sitting across a chess-board from each other.

Or, Irene reflected, two entities that looked human. The Cardinal certainly wasn't human. But she herself was—wasn't she? How far could a person change and still remain human?

She pulled herself away from philosophical digressions—or

maundering distractions, depending on how useful one considered such trains of thought—and bowed her head. "Thank you for your advice, Your Eminence. I appreciate your time and attention." *And I hope to avoid it for the rest of my life, if at all possible.* "If you will excuse me, I'll collect the rest of the team and the witness statements and be on my way."

"Of course." He waved towards the door. "Please forgive me if I don't accompany you. An old man like myself enjoys the chance to sit down. And ask Sterrington to join me, if you would be so kind."

"Certainly, sir," Irene said.

She didn't quite flee the room, but she was conscious of overwhelming relief when she shut the door behind her.

Mu Dan grabbed her arm, and Irene flinched before she could catch herself. "Don't do that!" she demanded.

Mu Dan didn't let go. She had a briefcase in her other hand. "I've got the statements," she said. "We need to get out of here—now."

"Why?" Irene could understand if Mu Dan was unhappy in the high-chaos atmosphere, but there were questions she still needed to ask the people in this hotel. "Look, if you have to leave, then I can stay a little longer . . ."

"No, *now*," Mu Dan insisted. Her fingers bit into Irene's forearm with draconic strength, and she started to tow her down the corridor. "I'll explain in a moment, but we can't afford to be caught—"

"Ah, just in time." The voice from the far end of the corridor was far too familiar. "My favourite little mouse, and her newest friend."

Mu Dan hissed in annoyance.

The man standing there would have made a perfect illustration for any scandalous magazine of the period. His elegant suit was in the same shade of grey as Sterrington's dress earlier, but it somehow suggested libertine excess—an implication Irene knew was very well justified. His pale hair was tied back from his face in a loose tail, ensuring that all onlookers could fully appreciate his handsome face, and an overly familiar smile lingered on his lips. "How lucky that I caught you. A few minutes more and I might have missed you entirely."

"Lord Silver," Irene said flatly. She didn't add *what a pleasure to see you,* even though it would have been the polite thing to do. In fact, she really wanted him to understand how little of a pleasure it was. As he was the most powerful Fae in Vale's London, she'd had dealings with him before, and they'd never been comfortable. His deserved reputation as a notorious rake and rogue didn't help either. And while he held the rank of ambassador from Liechtenstein, according to Vale he was actually the country's main spy in England. "I hadn't expected to see you here."

"I'm sure you hadn't." He sauntered towards them, top hat swinging in his hand. "But fortunately we'll be seeing a great deal of each other in the near future."

"We will?" A horrifying suspicion abruptly solidified. "Don't tell me—"

Silver smiled sweetly. "I'm the Fae representative of the investigative team. This *will* be interesting, won't it?"

CHAPTER 10

Irene looked around the table, and for a moment she allowed herself the luxury of imagining that she could walk away from the current situation. She was good at stealing books. She was good at *reading* books. She was by no stretch of the imagination *remotely* qualified to organise this team and handle diplomacy.

Unfortunately, it seemed that everyone else was even less qualified or interested than she was. Vale and Mu Dan were going through the piles of witness statements. Silver was sprawling in his chair, nursing a cocktail. And lines of demarcation had been very visibly drawn across the table by means of deposited documents and glasses—this side for work, that side for drinking. The afternoon sun slanted in through the window and made the glasses sparkle prettily.

Irene resigned herself to reality. "Perhaps now we're all in the same place, we might sum up our findings," she suggested. Said same place being Le Meurice—the theoretically neutral ground, and the logical headquarters for the investigative team.

"You go first, little mouse," Silver said with a wave of his glass. Liquid sloshed and nearly spilled. Irene could smell mixed brandy and absinthe. "I've barely dipped my toes in the waters so far."

"Yes, you might as well, Winters," Vale muttered, barely looking up from the documents. "I assure you that I am paying attention."

"I suppose some sharing of information might be useful," Mu Dan agreed. Her tone suggested that the operative word there was *some,* and that if Silver expected full disclosure, then he would be waiting till the next ice age.

Which, given the current weather and temperature, might not be that far away. Ao Ji must be in a bad mood. *Did he have any others?* Irene wondered gloomily.

Focus, she reminded herself. "Everyone at this table knows each other, I think?"

"Two of you I know already," Silver said helpfully, raising his glass in Mu Dan's direction, "but the judge-investigator over there is comparatively new to me. I look forward to finding out about her in full and interesting detail."

"Our current task is more important than our personal circumstances," Mu Dan said primly. "Rest assured that I have no interest in your own debauches."

Before Silver could respond, Irene rapped a knuckle on the table. "Please," she said, as they both turned to look at her. "Can we—at least for the moment—agree that solving this murder is more important than our personal feelings about each other? No, not *more* important. It's the *most* important thing. Otherwise the peace negotiations are finished." She had to find a way to get some genuine cooperation out of them. She tried to think of channels of persuasion. "Lady Mu Dan, I know you want to find the person who murdered your compatriot. Lord Silver, I know from our past history that you would prefer peace to war. Myself . . . the Library has put its reputation at stake here, and my parents are hostages for the safety of this deal. I have *everything* to lose."

Silver shrugged. "Much as I would like to meet your parents someday, my dear Irene, the welfare of the Library is hardly my main concern. And while I do prefer peace to war, I'm no fanatic—"

"What will the Cardinal do if you fail him?" Irene cut in. "To be precise, what will he do to *you*?"

Silver's mouth twisted as if he'd bitten into a lemon, and for a moment his glass trembled in his hand. "Now, there you may have a point."

Irene decided not to push it further. She didn't need to actively humiliate him, however entertaining it might have been, and however much he'd have done it to her if their situations had been reversed. "Our position, then—the basic facts. Lord Ren Shun was murdered. An assassination attempt was made on His Majesty Ao Ji. Finally, someone attempted to kidnap us—that is, myself, Vale, and Mu Dan here—while we were visiting the morgue."

"Agreed so far," Mu Dan said thoughtfully. "Do you think these points are connected?"

"Logically there could be some connection between the murder and the assault on *us*, but is the attack on Ao Ji linked to it as well? Or is someone being opportunistic?"

"Why are you all looking at me?" Silver complained.

"You're the best authority we've got on Fae motives and actions," Irene said briskly. "*If* it was Fae . . ."

Mu Dan drew in air sharply between her teeth. It wasn't quite a hiss, but that term would do until a better example came along. "Are you suggesting that *dragons* might have been behind it?"

"It seems unlikely—" Irene started.

"It is impossible," Mu Dan snapped. Her glare across the table at Silver suggested that while she might consider the possibility while talking to Irene alone, she certainly wouldn't accept it in front of a Fae. "And you already said that His Majesty smelled Fae interference on the mind of that assassin. Why are you raising issues where none exist?"

"I'm considering all the possible viewpoints so that we can say we've considered them," Irene answered. "If we can definitely say that no dragons could possibly have been involved, then good, marvellous, fantastic! Then we can sign that and put a bow on it and hand it over, and for the record, I have no problem with that. But we'll have people from all three factions looking over our findings as if . . ." She hunted for an example. "As if our lives are at stake. And maybe they are . . . And I'm throwing the Librarians into the big suspicion pot while we're at it. By all means let's try to work out how and why they might have tried to assassinate Ao Ji. Maybe it was just a fake assassination in order to get him to trust me, because they knew I'd try to stop it? Have you thought about that?"

"Yes," Mu Dan said.

"Oh."

"But having met you, I can't imagine you being knowingly involved in an operation like that," Mu Dan added. She probably thought she was being reassuring.

Irene, who was fairly sure that she could be knowingly involved in an operation like that, without a moment's qualm, simply nodded. "All right, then. I concede that given His Majesty detected

Fae influence on the anarchist, there was a Fae involved somewhere. However, this doesn't rule out the possibility of someone *else,* be it dragon or Librarian, cooperating with that Fae. Though if everyone's cooperating that well in order to mess up the peace talks, I don't know why they can't just all agree we can get on and sign the treaty in the first place . . ." She became aware that she was wandering from the subject. "And now we're going to get onto some more specific areas which are high-security. Excuse me a moment." She shifted to the Language. **"All electronic or magical listening or transmitting devices within range of my voice, explode."**

Nothing happened.

Vale frowned. "Do you feel that was strictly necessary, Winters? I understand that this world hasn't yet invented anything capable of such achievements. And magic doesn't work here. Or so I'm told."

"There's nothing to stop someone bringing a device across from another world where it *has* been invented," Irene said. She'd had an unpleasant encounter with a Taser a few months back, in a situation where she'd had no reason to expect it. "And as for magic, I'd rather be safe than sorry."

Silver leaned forward, his eyes narrowed. "The fact that you're going to such extremes is very interesting, my little mouse. It suggests you have something really juicy to share with us."

"Several things so far," Irene said. "Plus anything else that anyone else at this table wants to mention. I'll start with the Fae side. Lord Silver, have you ever heard of a person known as the Blood Countess?"

Silver went very still. It was like watching a feline—a particularly elegant one, of course—freeze mid-step while considering a new variable that had entered the situation, and making up its mind whether to run away, ignore it, or push it off a table. "If I say yes," he ventured, "do I incriminate myself in any way?"

"Cooperation," Irene said wearily. "Please."

"I know *of* her." Silver's emphasis was very definite. "I have absolutely no desire to go anywhere near the lady. Her amusements are far more drastic than mine. She's wasteful. She's dangerous. And before the judge-investigator can ask, yes—she's more powerful than I am."

"Is this some sort of reference to Countess Elizabeth Báthory?" Vale asked. "Or Erzsébet, or however one pronounces it properly? I thought it had been established that most of the testimony at her trial was unreliable, and that while her personal character may have been less than ideal . . ."

Silver was shaking his head. "Detective, I appreciate your zeal for accuracy, but the lady in question is more than fact. She is a story. The Fae who has adopted her archetype has used all the worst possible variants of that story—yes, before you interrupt me, I do mean all of them at once, even if this involves some logical inconsistencies—and she is *real*. She enjoys situations of war and disorder, because it gives her more opportunity to indulge her tastes."

"So do you all," Mu Dan noted.

"No. Actually, we don't. May I point out the current states of the worlds to you? Are we all at war with each other? Are the spheres in a constant state of battle and havoc?" Silver paused. "Well, perhaps a little. These things do happen. But there are just as many of us who prefer a peaceful environment. The Cardinal likes it that way because he can get his fingers into more games. The Princess likes it that way because it's in her nature to be a sweet, kind, gentle, virtuous, noble, peace-loving . . ." He broke off the string of adjectives with an effort. "Forgive me. I'm still suffering from an interview with her this morning. And I like it that way because I can enjoy myself. I admit my amusements may occasionally be a *little* questionable, but at least I don't bleed virgins to death in order to fill my bathtub."

"Point taken," Irene said hastily. The Cardinal's earlier statements seemed to be confirmed. "So if we were to be told that the Blood Countess is here, and is interfering with the negotiations, what would your reaction be?"

"Leave the city," Silver said without hesitation.

Mu Dan bit back something that might have been a chuckle.

Irene wished she had a drink. It might help. "I mean, how plausible do you find such an idea?"

"Ah. You should be more precise, my little mouse." Silver seemed to be recovering his equilibrium. "That's an interesting way of putting it. I'd say that if she *did* know the negotiations were taking place, then it's entirely plausible that she might try to interfere. Who told you about her in the first place?"

"The Cardinal," Irene answered.

"And yet he didn't tell anyone else," Mu Dan said thoughtfully.

"His position was that if he told everyone, nobody would believe him—and people would assume he was just trying to pin the murder on a notorious bogeyman," Irene explained. "He wanted me to find proof that she was here, in order to convince everyone. And yes, I realize this doesn't mean he was telling the truth."

"Couldn't you force him to swear to tell the truth?" Vale suggested.

Silver put down his glass. "Detective, that might work on someone of *my* level of power. But pledges need to have equal validity."

"Which means what, precisely?"

"That if you want someone of the Cardinal's level of power to promise to tell you the truth, you had better have something of equal value to offer in return. Do I really need to go into detail?"

The flicker of expression that passed across Vale's face suggested that several possibilities had come to mind, none of them good. "I appreciate the warning," he said. "So on a wider note, we have no way to be certain that he—or the Princess—is telling the truth."

"Well, the Princess is prone to being truthful," Silver said thoughtfully. "She could lie, but it would only be under very specific circumstances. Protecting a loved one, for instance."

"So if the Blood Countess was here in Paris," Irene said, trying to drag the conversation back to the original topic, "where would we look for her?"

Silver shrugged. "Some hideout where she can command her minions to bring her victims. I've hardly had the chance to explore this Paris yet."

"But if it *was* her men who tried to assassinate His Majesty," Mu Dan started, then raised her hand to stop Irene from interrupting. "And yes, I realize that's an assumption, but it is at least possible. In that case, we know there's a theatre involved from what the assassin let slip."

"That's something," Silver agreed grudgingly. "Assuming it *is* connected. But there are a couple of thousand theatres in Paris—counting the cubiculum ones, of course. Those are very small and mostly involve the aesthetic portrayal of a female actress on stage in the process of losing her clothing. Surprised in the bath, trying to climb over a wall, assaulted by a flea, maybe you know the sort of thing . . ."

Mu Dan and Irene exchanged looks. "It's probably not *those* ones," Irene said firmly.

"Now, if we were back in my usual haunts, in the detective's world, I could simply look them up in the index that I keep," Silver said wistfully. "But here—I can't necessarily be sure what's where or how interesting it is."

"It's an avenue of investigation," Irene said. "And besides that, we have another clue. One that isn't yet public knowledge."

Mu Dan brought out the paper that had been found in Ren Shun's pocket, and Irene provided a translation. Then she turned to Vale. "Mu Dan said that you'd had an idea about the reference to hell in that note?"

"Indeed." Vale steepled his fingers. "Have you ever heard of the Cabaret de L'Enfer, Winters? I'm sure Silver has."

"The name doesn't ring any bells," Irene admitted. She mentally translated from French to English: Cabaret de L'Enfer, the Cabaret of Hell. "Is it well-known?"

"It's famous," Silver said. "And yes, I'm sure it exists in this world. It's in Montmartre, in the Pigalle—in the neighbourhood of the Moulin Rouge. A marvellous place. The doorman dressed as Mephisto, the waiters all dressed as devils, some magical tricks and illusions to amuse the guests, and of course the drinks are splendid. Yes, if we have to make a tour of the Paris nightspots, I would certainly recommend it." He was frowning, though, as if something else was teasing at his memory, and he cast a sideways glance at Irene. She ignored it with the ease of practice.

"What are the numbers, though?" Mu Dan asked. "A date and time? A recognition signal, or some sort of code?"

"The numbers are thirty-nine, two, seventeen," Irene said. "They don't really fit a date or time. I suppose it could be a question-and-response recognition signal, but if so, then there's no way of knowing who it's supposed to be given to. Unless maybe it refers to a table at the Cabaret de L'Enfer?"

"Unlikely," Silver said. "I don't think the place can manage thirty-nine tables, and certainly not thirty-nine places at a table. We might need to send in some bait and see who tries the signal on them."

"Your willingness to volunteer is noted," Irene said drily. "But still. It's a lead."

"There are other avenues," Vale cut in, turning to Mu Dan. "For instance, we have yet to consider Ren Shun himself. What sort of a person was he? And might anyone have had a grudge against him?"

Mu Dan tapped a fingernail on the table as she thought, picking her words carefully. "He was one of those whom almost everyone liked," she finally said, "and he had to be. Monarchs are always difficult to deal with, so it is often necessary for their first ministers and their closest servants to be more—shall we say approachable? Now, I'm not saying that Lord Ren Shun was everyone's best friend, but he was easy to deal with. He didn't try to abuse his position. But equally he didn't try to pretend everyone had his advantages or was on the same level that he was. You must know people like that: those who claim that there's no need for societal change because naturally everyone rises to their *proper* position, and the ones trapped at the bottom must *deserve* to be there."

"His Majesty Ao Ji struck me as that sort of person, to be honest," Irene said carefully.

Mu Dan shrugged, a sharp, unhappy movement. "Royalty generally is that sort of person. Why should they object to a system which is so very much to their advantage?"

Silver opened his mouth to say something, then visibly changed his mind and sipped his drink instead.

"He sounds unusually generous of spirit—" Vale began.

"For a dragon?" Mu Dan interrupted harshly.

"For an aristocrat, I was going to say." Vale leaned back in his chair. "Did this make him any enemies?"

"Ah." Mu Dan hesitated, and this time she glanced at Irene. "Not an *enemy* as such, but there is a person with whom he was not on the best of terms."

"Someone I know?" Irene asked.

"Lord Li Ming, in service to His Majesty Ao Shun."

Irene blinked. "Li Ming? Really?"

"You seem surprised," Mu Dan noted. "Why?"

"Li Ming's always seemed . . . well, I wouldn't use *nice*, but certainly rational, polite, and practical—not the sort who might hold a grudge with such passion it could lead to murder . . ." *Although he was very, very good at making sure Ao Shun's wishes were carried out,* Irene remembered. "I can't see why he'd be on bad terms with another dragon whom you've described as approachable, generous, and helpful."

"Family matters," Mu Dan said briefly.

Irene cast around for how to approach this tactfully, then gave up. "Forgive me, but is this a case of it being inappropriate for you to say anything more than that, or is it just that you don't *know* any more than that?"

For a moment Mu Dan was silent. Irene wondered if the dragon was making the same sort of calculation that Irene herself had done earlier, about just how far she could trust her fellow investigators and what she should tell them. Finally she said, "I heard something of a public disagreement when they last met. But I think there may be something besides that. *Think,* don't *know,* and it would be a very bad idea for any of us to make unsupported suggestions about it in public."

Irene made a mental note to check Library sources, and Silver's abstracted look suggested similar thoughts. "That's reasonable," she said.

"And since we're examining all sides, what do you make of the Library reference on that paper?" Mu Dan said pleasantly. "Or the reference to Herodotus's *Myths*?"

"I don't know," Irene admitted. "I need to ask some questions about if there actually is such a book. I told you about it in the first place. I'm not trying to *hide* it." *Well, not much,* she thought. *And if it is out there, and it is unique, then I'd rather like to read it myself before handing it over to anyone.* "But I would appreciate it if we could keep some of the details of our investigation between ourselves till we know a little more."

"Keeping secrets, Miss Winters?" Silver had shifted from his usual disparaging *little mouse* to Irene's name. That meant he was being serious. "I can entirely understand that. But I'm surprised that you're publicly asking us to go along with it."

"I'm trying to avoid starting a panic," Irene said. "Or possibly avoid starting a hare—until we're ready to do so. If the Blood Countess *is* behind what's going on, for example, how will she react if she finds out we know about her?"

"You're suggesting that someone among the delegations is a traitor," Mu Dan said thoughtfully. "And it could be from any delegation."

"There are a lot of ways of compromising someone," Irene said. "Blackmail. Threats to someone they care about." She knew a little too much about *that* option. "Suborning their servants, going through their waste-paper bins, claiming that you're actually a higher-ranking secret agent on their side—someone could even have been persuaded to bring in electronic devices. Though I admit it seems inappropriate for someone who's playing the role of a sadistic medieval countess. Telling His Majesty Ao Ji, or the Cardinal, or my direct superior is one thing. But spreading around some of this other information . . . can you all see my point?"

"I do *enjoy* you when you're like this," Silver commented. His lazy smile suggested other methods of enjoyment as well, and Irene stiffened her shoulders to resist the fantasies that went with it. Just because his archetype of the libertine seducer was generally non-violent didn't mean that he wasn't dangerous. "Edged, intelligent, stimulating . . ."

Irene repressed the urge to knock the glass out of his hand and shake him. "Stay on point, please, Lord Silver. We don't have all day to enjoy each other's company."

"Oh, I agree." He considered her from under lowered eyelids. "It makes perfect sense. And I've never liked sharing secrets, anyhow. Now, what is the next item of interest which lurks upon your lips?"

"This one is more of a hypothesis than a definite fact," Irene said carefully, keeping half an eye on Mu Dan. If anyone at this table was likely to know about the point she was about to raise—or be irritated by it—then it would be her. "I understand that there was another recent dragon assassination. Minister Zhao, in service to Ya Yu—the Queen of the Southern Lands."

Vale stiffened. "Isn't that what touched off your recent assignment?" he asked. "Strongrock mentioned it."

"Touched off, yes, as in igniting a trail of gunpowder," Irene agreed. "I'm wondering how relevant it may be."

Silver shrugged. "The name means nothing to me. How should it be relevant?"

"I'm theorising. I admit I don't know anything about Minister Zhao's murder, apart from the fact that it happened. But two murders in such a short period of time? Coincidence, or could they be linked? Ya Yu has an interest in this peace treaty—Mei Feng's here, and I think she's the queen's most trusted servant." Irene thought about the timing of her recent mission, rescuing another Librarian who'd been dragged into a contest for power in the dragon courts. "And Ya Yu was very eager to fill the assassinated Minister Zhao's post *before* this peace conference took place. Is it possible that the minister's death was also someone's attempt to sabotage the conference—before it even happened?"

There was silence around the table. Eventually Mu Dan spoke. "Irene, I'm not saying that you're wrong. I find this chain of logic very interesting, and there might even be reason to believe it. But the evidence about Minister Zhao's death will be under seal. We are unlikely to obtain it simply by asking."

"Mei Feng is at the Ritz," Irene said thoughtfully. "I'm sure she could give us any information we need."

"If she has it," Vale pointed out. "The investigations must have been exhaustive. If they had a suspect, or any proof, wouldn't they have acted on it by now?"

"But what if they wanted to avoid an outright rift with the Fae?" Silver suggested. "Let's theorise—no, let's *guess*—that they found out one of my kind committed the assassination. But in that case, saying so publicly would rouse public opinion and inflame any hostilities. It'd be even harder to negotiate peace under those circumstances. Her Majesty might have hushed the whole thing up to avoid that."

"Possible," Mu Dan admitted. "Let *me* speak to Mei Feng. I can present our thoughts on the subject. She will be able to tell us if our direction here is valid or if the matter has already been resolved and kept silent."

"If it was the Countess there as well, she's unlikely to have been subtle about it," Silver noted.

Mu Dan nodded. "I'll see to it."

Silver finished his glass. "Since you're giving orders, my little mouse, what would you like me to do?"

"I think you're the one of us here who knows Paris best," Irene said, after a moment's thought. She glanced to Vale and Mu Dan, and they both nodded in agreement. "If you can find any trace of the Blood Countess in the city, or any follow-up on this 'theatre' that was mentioned, that would be extremely helpful."

"I can but try," Silver said. He set down his glass and rose to his feet. "I imagine we'll meet again this evening."

"Won't you be busy?" Vale asked acerbically.

"You haven't heard?" Silver raised an eyebrow, enjoying the moment. "We're all to attend the dinner tonight. It *will* be interesting."

He swept towards the door, pausing by Irene's chair to bend and brush a kiss against her cheek as she flushed and tried to pull away.

It wasn't quite the distraction it would normally have been. The usual heat of his presence was lessened, as though deliberately, and he murmured in her ear, "We'll speak later. Privately. You know why."

She didn't even have time to swallow, or demand answers, before he was out of the door.

"I'm at a loss as to why *he* is the Fae representative on this investigation," Mu Dan said with a sniff. "Someone more academic or experienced would have been far more useful."

Irene pulled herself together. She very deliberately didn't rub the spot on her cheek where Silver's lips had brushed her skin. "Maybe it's because he knows Paris?" she suggested. But Mu Dan's question nagged at her. There must be Fae out there whose archetypes tended towards investigation. Why hadn't one of *them* been called in?

"He is at least a known quantity." Vale stacked the documents in a pile. "Winters, I need to search Ren Shun's rooms and question some of the hotel staff. Mu Dan has her own direction of investigation. We can meet this evening and compare notes, if no prior crisis intervenes."

Mu Dan nodded. "Hopefully there will be time to discuss our findings before this obligatory dinner. What will you be doing, Irene?"

"Going through the statements," Irene said, "and asking my own questions here, now that I can actually spend more than five minutes with my own superiors. I'll find out what that Herodotus reference means, and if that Beta-001 *is* a world designation. If we absolutely have to attend this evening's dinner, I'll certainly be kept busy beforehand."

She spared a wistful thought for whatever Kai was up to—and hoped that she hadn't dropped him into a nest of vipers.

CHAPTER 11

The knock on the door brought Irene's head up from her papers. "Enter!" she called hopefully. She wasn't quite wishing for another murder to get away from correlating statements, but it was a close thing.

Prutkov entered, closing the door behind him with barely a click. With a sigh of relief he took a seat opposite Irene. "I'm sure you've been wanting a word," he said.

"Yes," Irene said. She saw no need to dance around the subject. "Very badly. But I was told that Coppelia and Kostchei were both in meetings, and I didn't know who else I should report to."

"Easy enough," Prutkov said. He settled back in his chair comfortably. "Gods, it's good not to be roasting or freezing—I admire our elders, but they've got rheumatism and I haven't. And you report to me."

"You do realize that I've never actually met you before today?" Irene said.

"In the presence of Coppelia and Kostchei, both of whom treated me as a trusted and reliable Librarian and underling," Prutkov said. He didn't lose his smile.

Irene sat back and considered him. He could have been anywhere between forty and a well-preserved sixty, though that told her absolutely nothing about his real age. One didn't age inside the Library. Years could pass. Centuries. He had a comfortable air of experience, like a well-travelled uncle, but his clothing was bland, giving her no hints about his personality. His only clear trace of individuality was in his accessories: his heavy, opalescent Tiffany-glass cuff-links and tie-pin. Not expensive enough for ostentation, but certainly a personal choice. She had no way to read his motivations—but, as he said, he had been there earlier with her superiors and was clearly working with them. Why *should* she be suspicious?

"Understood," she said. "Please don't be offended. I seem to be running into a number of Librarians whom I've never met before. It shouldn't be that strange, given that there are hundreds of us—there's no way we could meet all our brothers and sisters. But ” She shrugged. "It still feels a little odd. As if there are political currents in the background, which I'd never seen between *us* before."

Prutkov's shrug matched her own. "Trust, but verify. It's a sensible principle to live by. At least you're not asking me to take my shirt off so you can see my Library brand."

"As you said, Coppelia and Kostchei proved you're one of us."

"Ah yes. Just another of the Library orphans."

There was enough *meaning* to his tone that Irene couldn't miss the reference. She'd only recently found out that she was adopted, and that the two Librarians whom she'd believed to be her parents . . . weren't. She was still coming to terms with it. Even if other Librarians had parents outside the Library and had left them behind years ago, at least they knew who those parents *were*.

"You're well-informed," she remarked.

"I was Melusine's star pupil."

"Was?" Irene said, noting the past tense.

"She suggested that I find another career route. She felt that I was too secretive. And let's be honest, there was a lack of career progression. Melusine is at the top of her personal little pyramid of power, and has no intention of moving."

Irene could understand that. Melusine, the Library's wheelchair-using head of Security, was unlikely to relinquish her position. What did concern Irene was Melusine's referring to someone *else* as too secretive. That was a serious case of the pot calling the kettle black. And if it was true, Irene should be careful about what Prutkov said—or rather, what he *didn't* say.

"So you're head of security on this particular job?" she asked.

"Exactly." Prutkov seemed pleased that she'd put it together so fast. "Kostchei and Coppelia are in charge, of course"—was there something a little too emphatic about that *of course*?—"but I'm overseeing the details and practicalities. This world allows technology, which opens certain interesting avenues, and we've taken some advantage of this. Though *of course* we're not wiretapping any meetings ourselves." He again laid a certain degree of stress on *of course,* implying the complete opposite. "So if you have any questions, I'll be glad to help."

"Thank you. But I'm not sure whether it's more urgent for me to tell you what we've discovered or to ask you *a lot* of questions."

Prutkov wiped his forehead theatrically. "You've just convinced me that you *are* the right person for this job, Irene. Most Librarians would have gone straight to the second option without even considering the first one."

"First things first, then," Irene said, feeling a private glow of pleasure. It was nice to have common sense on her part *appreciated,* not just taken for granted. "This is what we've found out so far . . ."

Half an hour later, Irene sat back in her chair and finished her cup of coffee. It had gone cold. Prutkov had debriefed her thoroughly and had actually raised some new questions in her own mind. "I realize that us splitting up wasn't necessarily the safest option," she said. "But it seemed the most efficient one, and everyone knows to be careful now."

"Besides, if you're all separated, it might draw out some more kidnappers, which would be a very useful source of information," Prutkov agreed. "I approve. Good work. Your turn to ask questions, I think. Then we can get down to the question of what to do next."

"One thing that particularly worries me is the B-001 reference," Irene said. "That bit of paper in Ren Shun's pocket was clearly a Library designation . . ."

Prutkov frowned. "I think you're right in your earlier supposition. It's a sophisticated attempt to frame us. A number of dragons and Fae know about our system of classifying worlds. It would be easy to guess that a low number would sound important. Perhaps it's a pity that you told the others—but at least it shows our honest intentions. I'll pass that reference and the title to some of our researchers back at the Library, and they'll see if they can find anything relevant. For what it's worth, I have heard of a book by Herodotus with that name. It was a collection of myths and fables. But it's only shown up in a few worlds and is extremely rare. You can share that with your team, if you think that would help. But I don't think that it's significant enough to have bribed a Librarian. Not even if there was a worst-case scenario and we had a Librarian whose particular mania was Herodotus."

Irene nodded, mostly reassured—even if she was still a little tantalised at the thought of getting her hands on a nearly unique book. *Just a normal human impulse,* she tried to reassure herself. *One doesn't even have to be a Librarian to feel that way . . .*

She pulled herself together. "All right, then. Practicalities. How many Librarians are currently in Paris, what sort of a response force can I count on if I need to take action, and do we have reserves that we can bring in via the Library?"

Prutkov's expression of pleased approval withered and dried on his face, like a time-lapse photograph of a flower losing its colour and freshness. "Now, don't you think that's a more *aggressive* approach than we really need to be considering here? You're supposed to be leading an investigative team, not some sort of . . ." He looked for the most appropriate words. "Some sort of *strike force.*"

"If an extremely aggressive war-minded Fae with a habit of torture and assassination has set up shop in Paris, we're going to need a strike force," Irene pointed out. "Especially if she's going to be proactive about it." *Rather more proactive than we're being,* she couldn't help feeling. "We can't risk having any more of the diplomats killed. And I'd rather not be killed or kidnapped myself."

"I don't think you're quite looking at the full picture here," Prutkov said thoughtfully. "Certainly what you're describing would be unfortunate, but on the positive side, it would definitely put the blame where it deserves to be put. And don't you think that a joint effort from both sides would be more thematic here, rather than a Library triumph? More symbolic of what we're trying to achieve?"

"Compared to the risk of more murders—and having either

side walk out of the negotiations?" Irene asked rhetorically. "No. That is, I agree that a joint task force to wipe out a warmongering interfering Fae—assuming she *exists*, and this isn't all a red herring—would be splendidly symbolic. But I'm not convinced leaving the investigative team to just get on with it is a justifiable risk. Not to mention the possibility that someone on one side or the other is feeding the Countess—or some other suspect—information. There could be someone else out there tied to this murder after all. There could be *any number* of suspicious parties out there. But if our culprit is her and she knows she's been found out, she'll probably flee. Or set an ambush. Neither would be good. I think we'd do better if we could bring in our own people—as many as we need—investigate thoroughly, and then present the result as a fait accompli."

"What you say is all very valid, but the final judgement doesn't rest with you." Prutkov smiled reassuringly. "Don't worry. The situation is under high-level review, and I can tell you that the Blood Countess is exactly the sort of suspect we'd hoped you'd dig up. I knew it was the right decision to bring you in on the case."

Irene experienced—not for the first time in her career—the dizzying sensation of safe ground dropping away behind her and leaving her with her back to a precipice. "Just how much autonomy do I have here?" she demanded.

"You obey the Library, don't you? Which means that you're under my command. Unless you actually want me to go and get it in writing from Kostchei or Coppelia. That may take a little longer, but I assure you the orders will be the same."

"I'm not trying to dispute your authority," Irene said firmly. It was quite true. If—or when—the time came that she had to dispute his authority, it wouldn't be a case of *trying*. "I apologise if it sounded that way. But I am concerned about the consequences if this goes sour."

"Are you afraid that you'd be left to take the blame?"

"I have a great many other things to be afraid of before we even get to that point. My parents, for instance." She saw Prutkov's expression change and held up a hand to stop him. "Yes, I *know* I'm adopted, but that doesn't change the way I feel about them. And what about the other Librarians who are hostages? Or the greater risk to the Library? And to this world?"

Prutkov leaned towards her, and his voice lowered to a murmur. "Irene, would it surprise you to know that we have arrangements to pull the hostages out of danger if things do go off track? We don't want to lose our Librarians any more than you do."

A weight that she hadn't fully been able to express seemed to lift from Irene's heart. She felt like slumping forward in relief. "That's very good news," she breathed.

"Don't tell anyone," Prutkov warned her. "Don't even speak about it to other Librarians. Part of the reason the dragons and Fae are working with us here is that we've been willing to give them hostages. If they thought it was just an empty gesture on our part . . ." His grimace made it clear how little all their lives would be worth.

Irene nodded. "Point taken. I'll keep my mouth shut. Besides, even if you have set this up, it's not as if they're *safe*."

"No," Prutkov agreed. "No, you're quite right." He hesitated, then seemed to come to a decision. "And you deserve to know the rest of why I can't just pull in assistance for you. Do you have any idea of the current number of active Librarians in the field?"

"No," Irene admitted. "I'd assumed that there were a few thousand of us."

Certainty drained from her as Prutkov slowly shook his head. "At least a thousand?" she guessed.

"There are perhaps five hundred Librarians who are currently active in the field and able to handle dangerous or violent situations," Prutkov said. "And of those Librarians, perhaps a couple of hundred have connections to either the dragons or the Fae that could render them compromised. I'm not saying that they're unreliable, but I am saying that they can't be trusted with information about this peace conference. The *only* way that we've been able to make this work is by keeping information about it to an absolute minimum. Even from our own people. The dragons and the Fae are doing the same—that's why there are so few of them here. I can't just wave my hand and arrange a dozen competent Librarians to back you up. The ones who are really good at their job, like yourself, are going to be in the middle of their own high-risk projects. It would take them days to disengage and get here."

"There can't be that few of us," Irene said, horrified. "When I've been to the Library recently, I've seen plenty of people . . ."

"Students," Prutkov said. "Or retired elders. Or people who've suffered injuries, like Melusine, severe enough to stop them working in the field. Don't get me wrong, I don't want to criticize the capabilities of our brothers and sisters who've been handicapped in the line of duty. But being in a wheelchair, however high-tech it may be, makes it a great deal harder to steal books. One has to be reasonable about these things. And this isn't information which we can allow to get out. This has to be kept secret. Even from those we consider our friends. If the dragons or the Fae suspected that we were weak . . ."

He tilted his head, gauging her reaction. "The question now, of course, is what we do about it."

Irene herself wasn't quite sure how she felt. She'd never thought about the total numbers of Librarians. She'd always vaguely assumed it was along the lines of *not enough, but we manage,* and let it go at that. Like many hasty past judgements, this approach was now showing its flaws. "I've noticed that a number of Librarians aren't keen on recruiting or mentoring," she said. She herself had always been more enthusiastic about the *stealing books and reading them* part of her job. She'd never asked for Kai as an apprentice—however much she'd grown to appreciate him.

"Yes," Prutkov agreed. "We don't select for those character traits. We select for obsessive tendencies and high levels of skill. The problem is that we can't go on doing that. And that's just the tip of the iceberg. Things are changing."

His voice settled into a persuasive cadence. This was clearly a speech he'd made before. "Even before Alberich's attack, the number of Librarians was declining. The deaths and injuries which he caused cost us over a hundred more. And now we may be heading into a situation where we will be effectively unnecessary."

"Are you sure that's the right word for it?"

"What else would you call it, if the dragons and Fae will each be keeping to their ends of reality? The balance of worlds won't be under threat any more. We won't need to steal books to stabilise them."

Irene felt that this was far too simplistic a view of the situation. Signing a peace treaty might be an important step forward in terms of preventing outright war, but it wouldn't stop the intrinsic conflict between the two sides. Not to mention that only *some* of them would be signing it.

But Prutkov clearly wanted her to agree to this point, and she wanted to find out where he was going with the argument. "I see what you mean," she said, letting herself frown. "You're thinking of a possible future where both sides could claim that things are balanced, and the Library isn't needed. That they don't need us Librarians. A future where dragons and Fae might even be able to join forces to metaphorically divide us up and share out the profits. So to speak."

"Yes," Prutkov said. He didn't try to disagree with her, which seriously worried Irene. "Yes, we could consider that the worst possible future. And there are other alternatives which aren't a lot better. Irene, the Library is outnumbered and outgunned. We need to think about different future strategies. We need to be willing to change."

"I've heard other Librarians saying that we need to change," Irene said carefully. She wanted to keep him talking, but outright agreement with everything he said would look suspicious.

Something inside her twisted unpleasantly at the thought that she was handling a Librarian—one of her *own*—in the same way that she'd flatter and lie to an enemy for information.

But what the hell was Prutkov up to? She had to *know*.

"Anyone in particular?" Prutkov asked casually. "I thought you stayed out of politics."

"Penemue. It was a few months ago." Irene shrugged. "She tried approaching me, but the moment she heard I was on probation she backed off. Perhaps she didn't consider me useful enough. She was making noises about more democratic representation and consultation and that sort of thing. But it was in the middle of Alberich attacking the Library. An oncoming car crash isn't the moment to argue about who's driving the car."

"Penemue has too simplistic a view of the situation, but she's not entirely wrong," Prutkov said. "She's just wrong about what needs doing, how to do it, and who should be doing it."

"From where I'm standing, I can't see that leaves much scope for her being right." Irene had the sense of picking her way through a minefield. She'd assumed that Prutkov had wanted this talk with her so that she could tell *him* any important facts in private. Now she suspected that the privacy was for his benefit; he didn't want anyone hearing what he was telling *her*.

"She's right that something needs to be *done*!" Prutkov brought the flat of his hand down on the table in a gesture that reminded Irene of Kostchei. "We have to change. We can't afford to become unnecessary. And fortunately for us, there is a space that's just waiting to be occupied."

"Go on," Irene said slowly. "I'm interested."

"The dragons and the Fae are never going to be *that* close. Even if their cultures permitted it, they can't tolerate each other's worlds." Prutkov conveniently ignored the fact that earlier he'd been suggesting they could ally closely enough to dispose of the Library. "There's a place for us in the middle. We're seeing the start of it now. We're the deal makers, the peacekeepers. We can have a real *influence* over them this way." He looked Irene straight in the eyes. "Have you ever wondered what our ultimate purpose might be?"

"I never actually thought of it in those terms," Irene said. "I was always busy with what was directly in front of me."

"Then you should be thinking further ahead," Prutkov scolded her, as if he were her teacher. "Scope. Potential. Look up and plan for the future. Maybe we were meant to keep the peace by holding the reins on both sides. If they trust us, then we can persuade them separately to work with us. We can use this opportunity, Irene. We can use *them*. I've seen the records of your work with Kai while he was your apprentice. I know you understand what I mean." He leaned forward with the air of one sharing an intimacy. "Both sides are bound by their nature. We're human. We can be *more* than that. The Library can grow. It can keep the peace rather than just steal books around the edges of creation. But for that to happen, they have to depend on us. They have to trust us. They have to *need* us."

Irene could actually feel her blood running cold. Her hands tightened in her lap. Had Prutkov spent all his time in the Library? Had he never actually *met* a powerful dragon or Fae? Did he think that they were always as amenable to reason as they were being at the moment? Was he, she wondered in mental language that threatened to lapse into profanity, completely incompetent?

"This is playing with fire," she said. Caution urged her to soften her language and apply some flattery. "I appreciate what you're saying. I'm very flattered that you see me as part of the Library's future. But what you're suggesting is a huge gamble. Leaving aside any questions of morality . . ." And she had quite a few such questions, come to think of it. When people started talking about *using* other people, they were usually envisaging a power structure with themselves at the top. That was not what she wanted for the Library. It had *never* been what she wanted for the Library. But she made herself continue the sentence. "I have a lot of concerns about this idea's practicality."

Prutkov frowned. "You're uncertain. I can understand that. But I want you with me, Irene. You've demonstrated you're part of the Library's future. I don't want you to be left behind . . ."

"I'm cautious," Irene said. She could hear the double meaning behind his words. She'd been offered the carrot: the flip side was the stick, the threat of being left out of his plans. "I've always found it a good strategy. The current situation is highly volatile, and I'm in the middle of it. Am I expendable?"

"Why are you asking me that question?"

"Because everyone *else* is." Irene wanted to steer the discussion away from *join me in committing something which sounds awfully like treason* before he asked for her commitment one way or another. "Or rather, the rest of the investigative team seem to be people their superiors can live without. The Cardinal's got a grudge against Lord Silver and would probably be glad to see him destroyed. Mu Dan's not in service to anyone, so Ao Ji can write her off without any consequences. This does not reassure me. Being in the middle of such a group makes me feel that there's a target on *my* back too. And I worry about who might have put it there."

"There are a lot of good reasons why you were asked to head up the team," Prutkov said calmly. "None of them mean that you're in any way expendable. I'm not denying it's a high-risk assignment, but you know that already. Any Librarian who's in the middle of this is in danger. You, me, Coppelia, Kostchei, Bradamant . . . That reminds me, I'll be assigning Bradamant to assist you in some areas. I've told her to make sure that you and Vale have suitable clothing for tonight and in general. Not just fashionable gear, but styled to make sure you can run or fight if there's trouble."

"That'll be useful," Irene said, glad to have one problem less to worry about. She didn't *want* to spend her time at a political dinner tonight, but if she had to go, then she preferred to be dressed properly. "I'll be sure to thank her later. Is there any chance I could have her help now, with these statements?"

"Not right this minute, but I'll send her down later if she's available." Prutkov hesitated, as though turning something over in his mind. "I know that she's had some past irregularities in her record, and she hasn't your experience in dealing with dragons, but I think she could manage quite well under your supervision. What do you think?"

And here was another carrot, designed to appeal to Irene's worst instincts. *A chance to be supervising your previous mentor, who made your life extremely unpleasant.* She knew just how Bradamant would feel about this too. That would, after all, be part of the appeal, if Irene was the sort of person to enjoy that kind of payback . . .

She wasn't. Was she?

"I look forward to working with her," she said neutrally. "But Bradamant's an experienced operative. I'm sure she won't need any supervision from me."

"Then let's just say that I'll make sure she knows she has to follow your orders in an emergency." Prutkov smiled at Irene encouragingly. "You need to trust your judgement more. Once we've identified the Blood Countess's current hideout, we can coordinate an assault with everyone involved and resolve this situation to our mutual benefit."

Irene wondered just whom *we* and *our* referred to. The three factions present? Or just Prutkov and herself, in a private little conspiracy? And she was concerned by his eagerness to pin everything on the Countess as the obvious culprit. Where was the evidence? "There are still a lot of unresolved factors between now and then," she pointed out. "We don't have any significant proof that it is her—or that she's here at all. We need more information. And what about Minister Zhao's murder—might it be connected too?"

"I'll do my best to investigate at my end," Prutkov promised, with an undertone that made her remember he'd been Melusine's pupil. "I'll put enquiries in train. But I expect you to do the same on yours. I understand that Lord Silver's taken a personal interest in you in the past. If it got him talking, I don't suppose you could . . ." He raised an eyebrow, letting the statement trail off suggestively.

"Absolutely not," Irene said firmly and quickly.

"I would have thought you'd be professional about it." Prutkov actually managed to sound disappointed in her.

"I am not stupid enough to hop into bed with a Fae whose personal archetype is 'libertine seducer,'" Irene said fervently. "That is asking for trouble. That is about as sensible as playing chess with the Cardinal. There is absolutely no point in challenging someone in the area where they're particularly talented. All you do is lose."

"Well, I hope you'll see what you can get out of Prince Kai," Prutkov said with a shrug. "We need to know what his uncle's thinking. I trust you not to let any personal feelings get in the way there. You've shown that you can keep him under control. Do whatever it takes."

He pushed back from the table, preparing to rise. "Any last questions?"

Irene bit back some of what was boiling in her mouth, but she couldn't entirely control herself. This man—this *Librarian*—was supposed to be on her side. "Just how far do you expect me to go?"

Prutkov blinked, his expression pleasantly bemused, as though he couldn't quite see her point. "Irene, you've stolen for the Library. You've killed people. When I tell you to do whatever it takes, I mean precisely that. I'm a little surprised that you're taking all this so personally. I thought that you were a professional."

"I have standards," Irene said, unable to suppress the cold fury in her voice.

"And you have orders too," Prutkov said. "Remember what all this is *for*. Remember what's at stake." He pushed to his feet. "I'll get back to you with any information I've collected later. Do keep me informed, won't you?"

Irene didn't rise to her feet as he left the room. It would have suggested a level of respect that she couldn't remotely say she felt.

The stacks of paper sat in front of her, waiting for her to get back to them. Plenty of data on comings and goings, but none of it what she *needed*.

Irene had always felt she could rely on her superiors in the Library. She'd believed that if they were to sacrifice her, then it would be reluctantly and for a good reason. She'd never met one whom she so outright distrusted. She'd disliked Bradamant—she'd been afraid that Bradamant would use her—but she'd never doubted that Bradamant truly believed in and served the Library. Prutkov, on the other hand . . .

If the Library's future is at stake here, do I really want it to be what Prutkov wants to make it?

But with all the possible consequences, can I risk failure?

She didn't have any answers.

CHAPTER 12

Irene twitched aside the curtain of her room and peered down into the street below. The veil of snowflakes blurred her vision, but she could see the line of carriages and motor cars dropping off guests below.

"You're wasting your time," Bradamant said from her armchair. "The top people on either side will be the last to arrive. You know how this sort of thing works."

"Of course," Irene said, controlling her irritation. She shivered in the cold air that filtered around the edges of the window but was unwilling to turn away and close the curtain. "And I know that Duan Zheng and Sterrington were both conducting security sweeps just now. For all I know, they're still doing it." She shuddered, and it wasn't just from the cold. "When I think of all the things that could go wrong . . ."

"Hopefully not cyborg alligators this time," Bradamant said with a frown.

"Yes, I suppose we can be grateful that this world doesn't go in for that sort of technology." Irene gave up on trying to recognize any of the guests from their umbrellas or evening coats and let the curtain drop shut. "I'd rather be downstairs and helping with the security checks."

"So you've said repeatedly. There is such a thing as cramping other people's style and making them nervous by leaning over their shoulders, Irene. Even if you are leading the investigative team."

"Coordinating," Irene corrected her. She wanted that point to be absolutely clear. "Why don't we go on down anyhow? Better to be early than late."

Bradamant raised one perfectly shaped eyebrow. "Aren't you going to tell me how well you have it under control?"

Irene attempted to gauge how much of the other woman's mood was genuine irritation and how much was habitual sarcasm. "Didn't we agree to at least *try* to cooperate with each other?"

Bradamant put down her newspaper and rose to her feet, a reply clearly on the tip of her tongue. Then she seemed to deflate and sighed, just a little. "Irene, I realize you haven't yet had this personal experience yourself, but it is just a *little* difficult to cope with watching other people promoted over your head and catapulted into positions that—to be entirely honest—you're not sure they're competent to manage. Allow me a moment of annoyance. I promise you that I'll be all smiles downstairs."

"You are not reassuring me that I can rely on you," Irene said. "It may be the new form of honesty to confess to all this personal . . . annoyance, and then say you'll be my very best friend in front of witnesses. But it doesn't leave me feeling comfortable."

"Your comfort is hardly my concern," Bradamant said with a splendid shrug. Her white shoulders and neck were beautiful in the lamplight—the sort of thing that would have been poetically described as swan-like. And both she and Irene were in the latest fashion for evening dresses, which meant bared shoulders and a nearly bared bosom, tight waists over tight-boned corsets, and long skirts with trains that required careful management. Irene was in dark green watered silk, Bradamant in glittering beaded black. Irene rather regretted that they hadn't been in time for the previous fashion, which had involved much heavier layers of fabric and highly defensive bodices, not to mention puffed sleeves and shoulders that could have hidden an arsenal. She wasn't particularly body-shy, but in a situation like this, any degree of cover would have been welcome—however illusory.

Especially with Silver or Kai present. Prutkov's words from earlier still rankled, lying like a thorn in her mind and causing her to flinch mentally whenever she considered them.

"If my comfort is irrelevant, then what is your concern?" she asked, dragging herself away from that unwelcome thought.

"Helping you," Bradamant said. "Solving this murder. Stopping a war. I can provide you with a list if you've forgotten. Since I've been assigned to help you." This time there was no doubt about her annoyance; her words had a sting to them.

Irene cast around for some way to soothe the other Librarian's temper. *Damn Prutkov. I didn't want this.* "Look," she said, "we've known each other for a few years now. I know you don't have the world's highest opinion of me—" She held up a hand to stop Bradamant before any witty remarks could be hammered into the conversation. "But really, do you think I have the political ability or interest to try to deliberately engineer any of this? Be reasonable. I'm out of touch with other Librarians, I'm not interested in the

Library power structure, I'm not trying to raise my position. I'm *happy* being a Librarian-in-Residence."

"With fringe benefits," Bradamant put in slyly. But a frown was ghosting across her features. "I'll admit . . . you may have a point. I could accuse you of a lot of things, but trying to play the system isn't one of them."

"When you've quite finished damning me with faint praise . . ." Irene muttered. She very much wanted to ask Bradamant for her opinion of Prutkov. But now she found herself beset by a brand-new emotion—paranoia. How might Prutkov react if that sort of question were reported back to him? He hadn't actually done anything *wrong*, after all. Merely having personal opinions on the future of the Library wasn't itself a crime.

Irene would have liked to curse. She had enough things to worry about, without adding paranoia to the list. "Let's go down," she said. "If Vale's arrived, I'd like the chance to speak to him before we're all seated."

With a nod of agreement, Bradamant followed her out into the corridor and down the stairs. Irene felt the metaphysical confusion in the air around her, the mixture of order and chaos from the presence of the two delegations, and shivered with a sensation that had nothing to do with the cold.

The dinner had been hastily relocated from the Salon Pompadour to the Salon Tuileries, on the grounds that it would be asking a bit much of the dragon delegation to socialise in the room where Ren Shun's body had been found. (In fact, for all Irene knew, they still hadn't managed to clean the outline of the body off the floor.) It was sensible, but it also complicated an already complex occasion. Dragons and Fae were being encouraged in as soon as they arrived, but the corridors were still full of people taking the opportunity to exchange a few words—and, Irene suspected, not wanting to have to go into the Salon Tuileries and endure both sides staring at each other. Human servants from both sides swirled and eddied, valets and maids and bodyguards, trying to avoid being banished too far from the presence of their superiors.

"Please move along, *if* you don't mind—oh, it's you." Irene turned to see the Librarian Sarashina just behind her. Unlike when Irene had last seen her, in the dragon hotel, she looked smartly formal in a black kimono whose starkness was relieved only by five small white family crests and a patterned gold brocade obi. "Will you help me clear the corridor? The hotel's made a couple of reception rooms available for everyone who's not actually dining. And they're both packed. Gods help us if there's a fire alarm."

"Do you have to be so pessimistic?" Bradamant muttered. She clearly knew the other woman. "And if you're here, is Ao Ji here already?"

"No such luck. I think he and the Princess are engaged in an unofficial game of Who Can Show They're More Important by Arriving Last, not that either of them would admit it." Sarashina turned to Irene. "Your friend Vale is here—he went into the Salon Pompadour to check something."

"Thank you," Irene said gratefully, and escaped before she could be drafted into crowd control.

The Salon Pompadour was hushed, insulated from the hubbub in the corridors by the thick doors and the heavy curtains. Vale was on his knees, examining the outline on the floor—it *was* still there—and he'd turned on all the lights for maximum illumination. "Anything new, Winters?" he commented as she closed the door behind her.

"No new attempts at murder or kidnapping, if that's what you mean," Irene said drily. "And I see you've survived His Majesty's attention."

"He had very little time for me," Vale said. "Fortunately I had very little to ask him—for the moment, at any rate. I may have more questions later."

Irene stood there, looking down at him. "I wish I could be more help," she finally said.

That was the very least of it. When she'd been younger, she'd loved detective fiction, and she'd imagined herself assisting great detectives at their work—providing the crucial piece of evidence or making the vital deduction. And now here she was, in the middle of a murder investigation, and unable to do more than stand around and talk politics while Vale did the actual *work*.

It was a bitter pill to swallow; all the more so because a childish part of her was whining that Irene was missing out on the good bits. Sometimes Irene wished that she could edit out the pettier parts of her personality. And this was not some sort of game. It was deadly serious.

"Don't denigrate yourself, Winters," Vale advised. "At the moment, you're doing precisely what I need."

"Which is?"

"What was that phrase Strongrock uses? Ah yes, running interference." Vale straightened and rose, brushing dust off his knees. Someone had provided him with immaculate evening dress: he'd blend in perfectly with all the other gentlemen in black and white. "I would find it impossible to conduct an investigation with dignitaries from both sides constantly demanding attention and answers. You are absolutely vital to this situation in which we find ourselves. Furthermore, you have a degree of authority over Lord

Silver and Lady Mu Dan which I lack. Don't criticise yourself for the lack of faculties which you have never possessed."

Irene had just begun to congratulate herself on doing something useful and doing it well, when the last sentence punctured her self-esteem. "We should get ready to go in to dinner," she said flatly. "The principals will be arriving at any minute."

"I look forward to observing them. Oh, for your information, Strongrock and I investigated that Cabaret de L'Enfer place earlier this evening, following up on that note in Ren Shun's pocket."

"Why didn't you take me?" Irene demanded, feeling rather left out.

"You were analysing the statements," Vale said blandly. "And too large a group would have attracted attention. Have no fear, Winters, you missed nothing. Strongrock reported a higher-than-usual level of chaos, and apparently an elderly fortune-teller had been frequenting the place of late, claiming to be a witch, but there was nothing more to find. No secret cellars. No murders. Nothing except some rather poorly costumed gentlemen in red velvet, and highly priced drinks. Strongrock was rather disappointed."

"Even so," Irene muttered. She had a sneaking suspicion that the men had been trying to protect her by avoiding taking her along. *She* was not the person round here who needed protection. But if she tried to raise the point, they'd only deny it. Reluctantly she decided to let it go. "One last thing, Vale . . ."

"Yes?" he asked, offering her his arm.

"Be careful with Prutkov," Irene said, taking it. "I'm not saying that he's unreliable, but I think he sees personal advantage in this whole business."

"I hardly needed a warning to be aware of *that,*" Vale commented, making Irene wonder what Prutkov had already said to him. But then they were out of the Salon Pompadour and in the mass of people flooding into the Salon Tuileries, and there was no more time for private talk.

The Salon Tuileries was another fantasia in gold and crystal and white: the multiple chandeliers sparkled too brightly for comfortable viewing. Reflections in the mirrors filled the room to the bursting point with elegant strangers, and groups of small tables stretched the length of the room. It didn't surprise Irene to see that the Librarians were filling out the central section, with dragons on one side and Fae on the other. The peace conference might be moving forward, but it was difficult to imagine it going so well that Fae and dragons were willing to sit at the same tables.

The air was thick enough to choke on. It wasn't just the heat and tension of several dozen people in the same room, or even the mixture of scents—perfumes, tobacco, and hints of the forthcoming dinner—but the sensation of mingled power, as heavy and close as a steam-room. It was, Irene found herself imagining, like being in a bathtub with hot water coming in from one side and ice-cold water from the other in a hundred tiny jets. Her Library brand tingled with the sting of power. But at the same time, there was something stimulating about being in the middle of it all. It was like a microcosm of the universe, with order at one end and chaos at the other, but confined to a single room.

She glanced under her eyelashes at Vale to see how he was holding up—he was, after all, human. Possibly the only non-Librarian human in the room, other than the waiters and servants. Certainly the only mortal who had any chance of affecting the outcome of this conference. "Are you all right?" she murmured.

"Nothing to signify," Vale answered, which from him probably meant that he had a pounding headache but could cope with it. "Tell me, is there likely to be any risk from this dinner?"

"There are people from all three groups in the kitchens checking the food," Irene said. She and Vale found their seats—they were both at the lower end of the central group of tables, conveniently next to each other—and sat down. The room was full of quiet conversations. They would not be overheard. "I don't think there's a risk of poison."

"Not so much that: I was considering risks from the sort of thing you call metaphysics." Vale's gaze roved across the people present—the dragons, as perfect in their human forms as statues, and the Fae, like illustrations in a story she had yet to read. And the Librarians in the middle, far more ordinary than either side, unmistakably human, ageing, and imperfect. Different skin tones and hair colours among the guests made the whole affair seem highly multiracial and multicultural—which it was, Irene reflected. Though not in the way that a local Parisian onlooker might have guessed. "Given what you've said in the past about chaos and order—is it safe to have so many people from both ends of the compass in close proximity?"

"Precautions have been taken," Irene said. "This whole hotel's been seeded with writings from the Language that affirm stability and balance. They're helping defuse any possible build-up of power or any untoward reactions. Bradamant told me. We couldn't go round actively writing the Language on the walls, of course. The hotel staff would complain. But we could write it on pieces of paper and hide them everywhere. This hotel is probably the most stable spot in Paris at the moment. Possibly in this entire world."

"What would happen if one were to place such things around Lord Silver's home in my own world?" Vale asked thoughtfully. "Purely out of scientific interest, of course."

"He'd probably just have a servant remove or deface them," Irene said regretfully. "What is written can be erased, alas."

Then there was a murmur from the doors at both ends of the room, and abruptly everyone was silent and rising to their feet. The tension twisted another notch higher in Irene's stomach as power came walking into the room on human feet, from both doors at the same time. Everyone sank into curtseys and bows as if moving to the directions of an unseen conductor. Cold air washed around Irene's shoulders from her right—from where Ao Ji had entered the room, she didn't need to look to check—but on her left the air seemed to grow softer and warmer, as if touched by spring and modulating into summer.

She didn't try to look directly at the new arrivals. Instead she glanced at one of the mirrors opposite. Curiosity made her try to see the Princess first, and she wondered—just a little—if what was in the mirror was a true reflection of reality. Because the reflection was difficult enough to endure.

The Princess shone, even in the bright room, like a diamond among mere crystals, or the sun among stars. It wasn't a visible brightness—she was that much more intensely *there*. Everyone else seemed to fade into the background in comparison. Getting a clear visual impression of her was even harder than seeing the Cardinal clearly. Her hair might have been any colour from blonde to raven-black to ice-white or flame-red, and her skin any shade from spotless ebony to rosy-cheeked or snow pale. The only clear thing about the Princess was her beauty and—Irene hated to admit it, but it came washing over her in waves—the genuine *niceness* of the Fae woman. She was sweet, she was innocent, she was heartfelt, she was sincere, and it was all *true*. She was the sort of maiden who would stop to help old women without a second thought. She'd probably spend seven years keeping her mouth shut and spinning nettles in order to save her brothers—as the fairy tale went—or any other relative. Any toads coming near her would turn into roses and diamonds on the spot.

Irene dragged her mind away from such vagaries and forced herself to take a mental and emotional step back and to look *around* the Princess as well as directly *at* her. She was being escorted by the Cardinal, in plain black robes that were a stark contrast to her gorgeous dress—*as bright as the moon and stars*, Irene's mind filled in from old stories, even if she wasn't quite clear what colour or style it was.

At the other end of the room, Ao Ji stalked across to his seat. He was in full ceremonial dress of the sort that Irene had seen once before on his brother, robes of embroidered white brocade sashed and cuffed in scarlet that matched his eyes. Kai was a step behind him, in Parisian evening dress, head lowered and clearly present as an attendant rather than any sort of equal family member. The cold gust of wind that followed them left ice crystals on the mirrors and raised goose bumps on the naked shoulders of women.

The dragon king and the Fae Princess reached their seats at the same moment. Both seated themselves simultaneously.

In a rustle of skirts and tail-coats, the assembled guests followed suit. Waiters circulated silently, filling glasses with champagne. The bubble of liquid was for a moment the only sound in the room.

Then Kostchei rose to his feet. "Most noble guests," he began, his voice rough, human, and old. "We have come together at this time . . ."

Irene mentally tuned him out as she surveyed the room, free for the moment from the twin lenses of power. The two other Librarians at her table were her age or younger—she recognized one of them from this morning, Rongomai, Sarashina's assistant, and she guessed that the other might be his matching number from the Fae hotel. She could see Sterrington among the Fae across the room, in long gloves that concealed her hands and arms, and Green and Purple (she had to try to find out their names at some point) were near her, with Silver charming the woman next to him. On the dragon side, Duan Zheng was seated conveniently close to Ao Ji's table—for security purposes, probably—and at the same table as Mu Dan. Both Li Ming and Mei Feng were actually at Ao Ji's table. Li Ming was in male dress, matching his chosen gender, while Mei Feng was in an amethyst gown that draped her in clouds of deep purple silk. Kostchei, Coppelia, and Prutkov were all together at what must be the head Librarian table in the centre of the room.

Everything seemed to be under control. She tried not to phrase the thought too clearly to herself, afraid that it might somehow invite disaster, but for the moment nothing was actually going wrong . . .

Kostchei came to the end of his speech—a bland peroration on the virtues of peace, and praise for everyone present, presumably censored for content due to the local waiters—and there was applause. There was quite a lot of applause. As the clapping of hands rang through the room, Irene wondered if the problem was that nobody wanted to be the first person to *stop* applauding.

Thankfully the waiters settled the matter by moving in with plates and bowls. As Irene lowered her hands and reached for her champagne, she turned to the woman at the table whom she didn't know. Her vivid red hair—dyed?—was up in a high knot, contrasting with the plain grey-blue of her dress and gloves. "I'm sorry that we haven't been introduced yet," Irene started.

"Oh, don't worry about it," the woman said. "My name's Medea. I'm currently working under Blaise—he's the Library liaison at the Fae hotel, but you probably worked that out already—and he said that if I saw you before he did, I was to thank you."

"Why?"

"You saved him from yet another chess game with the Cardinal by coming in when you did. It's not that he dislikes chess, quite the contrary—but with the Cardinal?" Medea shuddered and adjusted her gold-framed glasses. "Games with him are so *meaningful.* I'm glad to be beneath his notice."

"I wish I was," Irene muttered. But a bowl of soup with a very appealing smell had been slid in front of her, and practical considerations of hunger were overtaking metaphysical worries about Fae influence. "Have you and Rongomai met Vale yet?"

"I've interviewed Mr. Rongomai, but I haven't had the chance to question Madam Medea here yet," Vale said. "Since we're seated at the same table, I am glad to have the opportunity. Unless there are any more speeches, of course."

"Ten to one that we have a speech after each course," Rongomai said, "and twenty to one that everyone makes a speech over coffee and brandy."

Irene picked up her spoon. "There are worse things in life than enduring after-dinner speeches. I'm fairly sure even the Fae couldn't weaponise them."

A waiter materialised at her shoulder. "Miss Winters?" he murmured.

"Yes, that would be me," Irene said, putting her spoon down. "May I help you?"

"A minor issue outside, if you would be so kind."

"Should I come?" Vale asked, ripping a roll in half.

"Only Miss Winters was asked for," the waiter explained. "Mr. Prutkov's instructions."

"I'll be as quick as possible," Irene said, rising to her feet. So much for everything being under control. She should have known that she was tempting fate.

One of Duan Zheng's human servants was waiting outside the Salon Tuileries, in evening dress that was more businesslike than ornamental. Duan Zheng himself was no doubt guarding Ao Ji in person. "Miss Winters? I apologise for calling you away, but we have a problem and would be grateful for your assistance."

"How can I help?" Irene said, getting to the point. In spite of the potential trouble, and the fact that she was escaping probable hours of tedium, a little part of her mind couldn't help thinking wistfully of that cooling plate of soup sitting at her place. She was *hungry.*

The man looked relieved. "It is possible—not certain, you understand, but possible—that there may be poison in some of the food. Mr. Prutkov said that you should be called if there was any sort of danger or emergency. I hope that you can help us . . ."

CHAPTER 13

Poison. The thought banished all other minor irritations with its potential for disaster. "Yes, of course you did the right thing to call me," Irene said quickly. "Where is this food, and what is it?"

"We have it in the kitchens," the man answered. "It's a dish of apples, sent from the Grand Hôtel du Louvre—or at least, that was what the messenger said."

"Is he still here?"

"No, he left after making the delivery. Unfortunately it was to the hotel staff, not my people, so they didn't detain him."

Irene nodded. "Lead me to the kitchen and the apples. And can you have Vale fetched as well?"

The man pursed his lips. "Your superior Prutkov said that if anyone besides you was to be called, it might cause a disturbance. People will worry."

"People will worry anyhow," Irene muttered. She could see his point, but she didn't like it—but she wasn't ready to outright challenge Prutkov. Not yet, anyhow. "Very well. Show me the situation. And what should I call you?"

He blinked for a moment. "My name is Hsien, Miss Winters."

His personal name, Irene assumed. "And your family name?" she asked as she followed him.

"Unimportant." His tone shut down any possibility of further questions on that subject. "The kitchen is down this way, and through here—ah, here we are."

Sound and smells and heat washed over Irene as she stepped into the long room. It was clearly a place where people *worked,* as opposed to the gold-and-white perfection of the parts of the hotel to which guests were confined. Men and women in starched white clothing—how nice to see an equal division of labour—were bending over counter-tops and stove ranges, too busy to pay any attention to her. Knives flashed and thudded against chopping boards as meat and vegetables were reduced to their component parts. There was no casual conversation, only the quick back-and-forth of questions and responses. The place was full of complete and partly assembled dishes, raw and cooked meats and fish and vegetables, dishes being frantically scrubbed in the sinks. Room and people hummed with activity, as tightly wound as an overcranked musical box, running to its own inner melody and trembling with leashed energy. Saucepans and frying pans hissed at intervals along the flat tops of the ranges, and heat came gushing out every time one of the cooks opened a door along the side.

In one shadowy corner of the room Irene noted an out-of-place small bowl of fish heads on the floor, next to a basket with a blanket in it. No sign of its occupant, however—it had probably been chased out of the kitchen while the meal was in progress.

"Over there," Hsien said, directing Irene to the end of one of the long tables. One of Hsien's fellow bodyguards was watching a carefully plated dish of apples as though it was an unexploded bomb. The crate from which it had been extracted sat on the floor next to it, and Irene made a mental note to see that it was saved for Vale's later attention. "What do you need to do?" Hsien asked.

Irene inspected the apples. They were beautiful specimens, dark red and glossy. She didn't recognize the variety, but then she wasn't sure what varieties were current in France at this point anyhow. They glistened on the white porcelain platter as though to say, *Bite me.* "I assume there was no card or letter with them?"

"Only a verbal direction that they were for 'the lady from the Grand Hôtel du Louvre,'" Hsien answered.

"And do we have any proof that they're actually poisoned?" Irene paused, considering how naive that must sound. "Well, apart from all the other suspicious circumstances surrounding their delivery."

"Anonymously delivered, untraceable, and unnaturally attractive?" Hsien shrugged. "I admit I have no actual proof, but . . ."

Irene nodded. "All right. I'll need a pair of tongs, a clean bowl, and a small plate."

Hsien nodded to his colleague, who promptly collected the items from nearby workbenches, ignoring the glares of the cooks. "What do you propose to do?"

"Try a test." Irene used the tongs to place one of the apples on the plate—the glossiest—then returned the others to their holding crate. "Please move this crate out of earshot. I'm going to use the Language to check this one for poison, as a random sample. If it comes up positive, then we can analyse the others later in more detail. Is this satisfactory?"

Hsien's brows twitched. He seemed mildly surprised to be asked for an opinion at all, but he nodded. "That seems logical. I bow to your leadership."

"Good." Irene glanced at the chefs. Nobody was watching them. She waited for Hsien to get the other apples out of range, then lifted the bowl towards the glistening apple. It was difficult to choose her words without knowing what the poison was—or if there was a poison at all—but she did her best. **"Let any substance which is not a natural part of this apple, which has been added with the intent to make it poisonous or harmful, leave the fruit and enter this bowl that I am holding."**

She wasn't entirely sure whether or not she wanted something to happen. The situation would be a great deal easier if the whole thing was a false alarm.

But then a tendril of black liquid came spiralling out of the apple, sliding through the air and into the bowl she was holding. The apple deliquesced, crumpling in on itself and dissolving into a bag of mush inside its skin. The sound of the viscous liquid collecting in the bottom of the bowl was inaudible against the greater noise of food preparation. All the chefs had their attention on their work. Only Irene and Hsien saw the poison leave the fruit and form a seething black puddle of ooze.

"Can you identify it?" Hsien demanded intently.

"No," Irene admitted. She was grateful that they'd caught this, but the brief moment of relief was overshadowed by the definite knowledge that a poisoner was at large. Even if it was someone outside the hotel, with an urge towards dramatics. Come to think of it, poisoned apples formed part of a very specific fairy story . . . A question for Silver later, perhaps.

"I think we'd better quarantine the remaining apples and this poison for Vale to examine later, and keep up all current precautions," she said, focusing on the situation at hand. "This is almost too obvious. I wonder if it's meant to induce false reassurance and make us *think* we have everything under control. I'm assuming you and the Fae security people have the hotel and this kitchen well secured?"

"Of course," Hsien said without a moment's hesitation. "And we are watching their people too. In case of betrayal."

Just as they're no doubt watching you for the same reason. "Good," Irene said. She looked around the room, wondering how secure it *was*. "How many ways into this room are there?"

Hsien indicated several doors as he spoke. "That's the cold room over there. That archway at the far end goes down a flight of stairs to the wine cellars. And that one on the left is the storeroom, which has a tradesmen's door leading directly outside, which they bring supplies in through—but we have a guard out there already. It's the only one that I can say definitely wasn't used by any assassins."

Irene nodded, getting an idea of the geography. "And I take it there are no other exits from the cold room or the wine cellars?"

"Precisely," Hsien agreed. "We have a sealed area. Any coming and going has to be through the main doors that we came through. I had Wei watching that: only waiters and chefs and hotel staff have been that way."

And you and all the other security people, of course, Irene thought. Another possibility to take into account. "Are you having any problems with the humans working with the Fae? Any difficulties in cooperating with them?"

Hsien hesitated, looking as if he wished he *had* something concrete to complain about, then shrugged. "They know their job, and they're as concerned for their masters as we are for ours. We can work with them. If there is any trouble, it won't be *us* causing it."

"Right." Irene passed him the bowl of poison. "I'd better go back to the dinner before anyone suspects something wrong. Call me if you need me."

After all, with one assassination attempt already so far this evening, there were bound to be more to come . . .

Back at her table, they'd already finished the fish course and had reached the entrees. A waiter, too well-trained to comment on her reappearance, doled out filet mignon onto her plate. Vale gave her an inquisitive look. And he wasn't the only one. A good half of the people in the elegant room were glancing in her direction, though some were better at concealing it than others. Kai was apparently devoting his full attention to conversation with his uncle, but Irene saw his eyes flick to her in one of the mirrors.

"Anything serious?" Medea enquired. "A problem of some sort?"

"Nothing important," Irene answered, knowing even a whisper might be overheard.

However, she'd borrowed pencil and paper from Hsien outside and had taken a moment to write a summary of the situation. She passed the folded note to Vale under the table and had a blessed few mouthfuls of filet mignon while he surreptitiously read it. "I hope I didn't miss anything in here?"

"People are just enjoying the food and wine, I think," Rongomai answered. "Is the new plan to get everyone so drunk that they haven't the will to fight? I think I read somewhere—Egyptian mythology, was it? The myth of Bast or Sekhmet or one of those lion or cat goddesses . . . conspirators got the goddess drunk on ale mixed with red dye, which she'd thought was blood? Or was that Hathor?"

"No, Sekhmet," Medea corrected him. "Do dragons drink blood?"

"Not that I've ever noticed," Irene said, "but I try not to provoke them."

Next to her, Vale had gone tense, like a hound on point. He forced himself to relax, tucking the note away in a pocket. "I would agree that it's nothing important," he said to Irene, indicating the note. "I cannot think of any other steps I would have taken. I will inspect the items later."

Part of Irene wanted to say damn the consequences and drag him out to have a look at the situation now, even if it panicked the rest of the room. But her sense of danger warned her just how fragile the temporary peace was. It was a miracle that they'd managed to get dragons and Fae in the same room and eating together. Even if they were at separate tables. They couldn't risk straining the truce by suggesting—no, confirming—that a poisoner was on the loose.

She nodded to Vale, then turned to Rongomai. "Might I ask where you got those facial tattoos?" she said. "They're very striking, but they must occasionally be a little inconvenient."

"That's the polite way of putting it," Rongomai said cheerfully. He sliced into his vegetable dish. "My supervisor threw a fit when he saw them. Pointed out how recognizable they'd make me, as if I hadn't already realized that myself. Such a pity."

"Are you saying that you had them done deliberately so you wouldn't have to do undercover work?" Medea asked.

"Well, it wasn't the primary motivation, but I'd definitely call it a fringe benefit," Rongomai said.

"Excuse me, Miss Winters." One of Hsien's people was at Irene's shoulder again. "If you would accompany us for a moment . . ."

With a sigh Irene put down her knife and fork, leaving her half-finished filet mignon behind, and followed him out of the room, conscious of all the eyes on her as she left.

"What is it this time?" she demanded of Hsien, once the door was safely shut behind them. "Another poison attempt?"

"No, something else this time." Her earlier performance seemed to have given her some credibility in Hsien's eyes. He was speaking to her like a colleague now, rather than with his earlier wariness. "There's been another crate delivered—from the Ritz, this time. Or again, that's where it's *supposed* to be from. The men delivering it left after it had been signed for. And before we could question them. At least we didn't bring it inside this time."

"I think you'd better have someone waiting at the door in case anyone else tries to make anonymous deliveries and then leave before they can be interrogated," Irene suggested. But possibilities were speeding through her mind, each more horrifying than the last. "More poison? Wild animals? Spiders? A bomb?"

"They claimed it was a cake." Hsien shrugged. "We haven't uncrated it yet."

"All right." Irene wished that Librarian powers included X-ray vision. "I think we can agree that it's highly unlikely that this is going to be a genuine cake, correct?"

"Your logic agrees with mine. I'm reluctant to open it in case we trigger something, but if it has a timed mechanism inside . . ."

"Yes. We need to get it open now. Can someone find me a cape or a coat of some sort?"

A few minutes later, they were outside in the Tuileries Garden, across the road from the hotel, with the snow drifting gently down around them and glinting in momentary flakes of brilliance in the gleam of the garden lanterns. The other member of their current group had introduced herself as Erda and was the head of the Fae security group. She was a stranger to Irene, with Nordic golden hair and a Valkyrie's muscular shoulders and arms.

They stood at a safe distance from the crate. It was about three feet across, covered with various requests to handle it with care, and it could have contained anything. Like everything else in this weather, it was acquiring a coating of snow. *Ao Ji must still be in a bad mood. A pity—everything else seems to be going quite well.* Irene's borrowed cape was little use against the cold, and she could feel her silk slippers growing damp as the snow melted under her feet, but she almost welcomed the physical sensations. They distracted her from all the potential reasons to be afraid.

Deliberately she listed them to herself, naming her fears and then pushing them to one side to focus on the current emergency. *My parents are hostages. The Cardinal in the Fae delegation has promised me a fate worse than death—yes, definitely worse than death—if I fail. Ao Ji will not only retaliate against my parents, but also against me and all the Librarians here and all of Paris if we can't find the murderer. Vale's at risk from all sides if things get worse. Someone—possibly the Blood Countess, possibly someone entirely unknown—apparently wants to poison everyone. And my current supervisor is an arrogant idiot who thinks he can manipulate the situation.*

"What do we do now?" Erda asked.

Irene had reluctantly come to the conclusion that the security teams on both sides were headed by people who were fine within the scope of their job but who needed firm direction when it came to anything unusual. "Please stay back: don't do anything unless I tell you to, unless the circumstances demand immediate action."

Another reason to be grateful for the cold and the snow: nobody except the desperate was wandering through the Tuileries Garden on a night like this, and none of those were nearby either.

Irene mentally cracked her knuckles and chose her words. **"Without activating any interior mechanisms or triggers, fastenings of the crate in front of me come undone, and planks fall apart to reveal what lies within."**

The planks slowly, silently fell apart into the snow, like the segments of a puzzle box, revealing a large pale object semi-concealed by layers of muslin.

"No snakes," Erda said with satisfaction. "I hate snakes."

"They might be concealed inside," Hsien said. "Cobras, perhaps—waiting to leap out the moment the cake was opened. That would be a very Fae trick."

Erda gave him a sideways glare that was perceptible even through the snow.

"Gentleman, lady," Irene said wearily, "do you mind? Let's get this sorted out before anything else can happen." *And before I die of hunger,* she thought. The taste of that half-eaten filet mignon still lingered wistfully in her mouth.

Both sides fell silent and chose to stare at the muslin-shrouded object rather than each other.

"Muslin wrapping the object in front of me, unwind and fall to the ground," Irene continued.

The fabric fell away in folds as if unseen hands were reverently displaying its contents. Beneath it was a cake.

It was a very impressive cake. It almost shone with its own radiance. It was a confection of spun sugar and royal icing designed to look like some royal palace, ornamented with sugar jewels and a sash of chocolate-stained profiteroles that begged to be devoured. (Or perhaps that was just Irene's hunger talking. It was hard to tell.) Crystallised rose and violet petals traced an intricate pattern across the top, surrounded by curls of carefully sculpted icing and pallid towers of sugar. A faint aroma of oranges—cointreau?—hung round it, perceptible even from the distance where Irene and the others stood. The falling snowflakes around it were the perfect touch.

"Someone put a lot of effort into that," Irene said. "Do you think it's possible to trace whoever made it?"

"We can try," Erda said. She reached into her cape and pulled out an anachronistic electronic camera, then strolled around the cake, taking photos from different angles. The flash glared mercilessly, and Irene had to look away.

"I'll get these printed out back at our hotel," Erda explained, putting the camera away again. "We can explain the photos as a new printing technique. I'll make sure you and Mr. Vale get copies."

"Thank you," Irene said gratefully. Using anachronistic technology in an alternate world was always risky; she tended not to rely on it, because without the physical infrastructure to handle repairs, or the ability to recharge items, it could become more trouble than it was worth. But this would be useful. Craftsmanship like this cake had to be recognizable.

She sniffed again. Perhaps it was her imagination, but there seemed to be something other than the smell of oranges in the air. And the natural scents from the garden and the Seine, of course, but the bitter cold and frost cut down on both of those to some extent. "Can you smell anything?" she asked the others.

Frowns and shrugs. "Perhaps," Erda suggested. "I'm not sure."

"You suspect gas?" Hsien asked.

"It'd be a logical trap."

"Then allow me to spring it." He reached inside his jacket—getting the same sort of reaction from Erda as his earlier twitch in response to her camera—and withdrew a knife, tossing it at the cake. The blade spun through the air and thudded solidly between two profiteroles, slicing through the icing and into the interior.

The vapour that came spilling out was a malicious, foul yellow-green under the garden lanterns, and the outright stench made them all retreat. The gas flowed over the ground towards them, billowing in nightmarish waves.

Irene had never actually been under gas attack before, but memories of chlorine-cleaned swimming pools told her what the gas had to be. **"Toxic vapour, return to the cake and remain inside!"** she ordered hastily.

"Reseal the icing?" Erda suggested, as the gas flowed backwards again, leaving a seared trail in the icing around the hole.

"That'd only be temporary. We need to dispose of that stuff." The Language worked on gas, but only temporarily: gas wouldn't stay where it was put unless there was some better way to seal it in. Better to defuse the whole thing, if that was possible. Irene racked her brains for memories of chemistry lessons at school. Chlorine reacted with almost everything, she remembered that much. "Everyone stay well back in case this goes wrong, please—"

The speed with which everyone backed even farther away was gratifying. It was nice to have people pay attention to her orders.

"Snow on the ground around the cake, melt," she said. **"Poisonous vapour"**—she wished she knew what the word in the Language for *chlorine* was—**"emerge from the cake and dissolve in the water."**

Once again the gas flowed outwards, with more of the cake drooping and dissolving in its wake, but at the same time the surrounding snow collapsed in on itself, dissolving into water. Fortunately the ground was frozen hard enough that the water couldn't immediately trickle away. The gas fluxed and shifted, moving like a living thing as it snaked into the growing puddles, which heaved and bubbled as the chemicals reacted.

"If I'd tried to do this at school, they'd have made me use a fume cupboard," Irene said absently. This was taking more energy than she'd expected. She folded her arms, fingers digging into her forearms as she focused. Frozen ground vegetation wilted and turned yellow as the liquid hydrochloric acid ate into it. Holes formed in the ground as the acid trickled farther down. Some moles were going to get a nasty shock. The cake gave up the ghost, collapsing in on itself in a heaving yellow-smeared morass of spoiled icing, profiteroles crumbling and sugar towers tumbling down.

"You did this sort of thing at school regularly?" Hsien asked. Irene wasn't sure if his tone was one of shock or jealousy.

"Well, occasionally. With test tubes and so on. Not with the Language, and not with cake." Irene watched the last of the gas dissolve into the water. Fragments of glass protruded from the remains of the cake. "I think the gas must have been in thin glass containers inside the cake structure. The moment someone stuck a knife in there . . ."

"You are probably correct," Hsien said. "Fortunately it wouldn't have been a danger to my lords, but even so . . ."

Fury counterbalanced Irene's weariness and hunger. This wasn't just a plan to spoil the alliance and cause who knew how many deaths in the process: this was a murder attempt that would have hit the hotel staff first and foremost. It would have been a waiter or chef who cut the cake open, and waiters who were gathered around to distribute it when the gas came pouring out. It would have been ordinary innocent humans who would have suffered.

She wasn't sure whether or not she liked Hsien and Erda, but she *really* didn't like whoever was behind this. Whether it was the

Blood Countess or some *other* totally unexpected villain hiding in Paris. Or some devious machination by the Cardinal. Or . . . whatever. There were too many possibilities and not enough *facts*.

"We'd better get back to the hotel," she said. "Can someone else guard the evidence till Vale's had a chance to examine it, then dispose of it?"

"I'll have some of my people do it," Erda said. She looked at the surrounding damage. "We don't want to be blamed for this. The gardeners will probably think that wholesale poisoning would have been better than damaging these grounds."

Irene nodded, brushing snow off her hair and shoulders as they turned back to the hotel. And, really, Erda had put the basic problem in a nutshell. Everyone here viewed damage to their own particular interest as more significant than damage to anyone else's. Whatever the scale of the damage.

"Wait," Hsien said, holding out an arm to bar Irene's way.

A shadow covered the pavement around the hotel. At first it might have been simple darkness, but as the three of them stood there, it moved, sliding over the paving like water. Dozens—no, hundreds—of little eyes glinted in the darkness, tiny and feral, catching the light from the street lamps.

The carpet of rats rippled across the road towards them, slowly enough to make the blood crawl and to allow a full understanding of the situation. They were moving to encircle them.

CHAPTER 14

Irene found herself retreating, step by step, unwilling to take her eyes away from the rats. She'd never tried outracing rodents before, but she wasn't sure she'd win. Especially not in thin slippers and a full-length dress. And there was something about the rats that made it impossible to look away: there was a *presence* that united them, that bound them together and looked out of their eyes at their targets. It wasn't a remotely healthy presence; it conjured unpleasant squirming thoughts of blood and darkness. She could taste chaos on the air, more potent than sewage, more poisonous than chlorine.

"Perhaps if we could reach the Seine . . ." Hsien suggested quietly.

A little wave of movement ran across the rats, as though they could perfectly well hear and understand him. They scuttled faster.

A desperate plan came together in Irene's head. She grabbed Erda's arm—half to get her attention, but the other half to keep her where she was. The rats had to be in just the right position for this to work. "Could it be the Blood Countess commanding them?" she demanded.

"It's her." Erda was keeping her composure, but her eyes were wide with fear and her arm was tense under Irene's hand. Of the three of them, she probably had the best idea of what they were facing, and she was clearly horrified. "Who *else* would it be? It's exactly the sort of thing that she'd do. They say she sealed people up in a dungeon once, for rats to eat."

"Tell me *what* she is!" Irene gave Erda's arm a shake. "I need to know!"

"The witch-queen," Erda whispered, "the demon-summoner, the crone who washes her skin in the blood of maidens, the lady of the dungeons, the . . ."

The rats had slowed their pace to a crawl again, spreading out across the road in a broad, rippling wave of rancid fur, eyes, and teeth. *Just as I thought,* Irene reflected drily. *No powerful Fae is ever going to miss out on the chance of hearing someone else talk about them.*

But it put them where she wanted them. Almost all of them on the road.

"Street, hold the rats!" she shouted at the top of her voice, forcing the words out as fast as she could.

The rats burst into movement as Irene's words in the Language seared the air, scurrying towards them, but she was—just—in time. Stone flowed as if it were water, clasping tiny clawed legs and writhing bodies. A hideous screeching chorus broke out as the creatures squirmed and tugged at the stones that now held them.

One of the rats had made it across the road in time, and it raced towards them. Hsien's knife pinned it to the ground. "I'm impressed,

Miss Winters," the dragon's servant said. "I hadn't realized—Miss Winters?"

Irene was sagging with the effort of multiple Language uses in a short time. She leaned against Erda, grateful for the other woman's support. "Let me get my breath," she muttered. "Anyone got some aspirin?"

But something was prodding at her mind besides the oncoming pain of a headache. Something was wrong here. No, not exactly *wrong*; but she was *missing* something.

Erda made a noise of shock and disgust. "I'm not sure we have the time," she said.

Irene forced herself to look up. The rats were actually gnawing at their own trapped limbs, trying to bite through the flesh in order to pull themselves free. Her stomach twisted with nausea. "That's . . . repulsive."

"*She* controls them," Erda snapped, pulling herself together. "And they may be infected with diseases. We can't let them bite us. Time to retreat—"

"No," Irene said quickly, trying to focus. Her head ached. She could try to sink the rats farther into the pavement, but that might knock her out. They had chaotic power invested in them; she'd be fighting that as well as the nature of reality. Her first attempt had been hard enough; she wasn't sure she would succeed with a second one. "Let's circle round them and get back into the hotel. They can't get in there."

"Are you sure?" Hsien asked. He had a new knife between his fingers now.

"If they could, why would they bother being out here chasing us?" Irene reached down to gather up her dress to run. "Damn these slippers—"

"I'll take her," Erda said to Hsien. "You guard us." She grabbed Irene and easily slung her over one shoulder, not bothering to ask Irene's opinion first.

"Now," Hsien agreed. The two of them began to run, heading sideways down the pavement and towards the hotel entrance.

Irene jolted along on Erda's shoulder, trying to control her growing feelings of nausea. A fireman's lift might be a more efficient way of carrying a passenger than sweeping them up in your arms, but it was much less pleasant. And it gave her a view of the rats ripping themselves out of the stone, leaving bone and flesh trapped behind, dragging themselves after Erda and Hsien with bloody mouths and mad little eyes.

She really, *really* hoped that she was right about the hotel being safe.

Erda gathered up her skirts with her free hand and took a long running leap over a swirling mass of rats. She nearly stumbled as she fell, but Hsien caught her elbow and steadied her. There were yells of encouragement from ahead of them, but Irene couldn't see what was happening. The rats were moving again, faster now, flooding towards them and leaving trails of blood on the stone and snow.

And then Erda and Hsien were stumbling into the hotel reception area, and hotel staff were gathering round them with murmurs of shock and horror, offering assistance. Erda let Irene slide off her shoulder, setting her on the floor again, and someone pushed a glass of brandy into Irene's hand. Irene tossed it back before the thought of poison even crossed her mind. It helped her steady herself. She glanced towards the hotel doors: they were safely shut. The rats weren't trying to enter.

The hotel staff offered apologies, swearing that such a thing had never happened before, that the police would certainly do something about it, or the fire brigade, or someone at any rate. Irene made a mental note that another Librarian might need to go out there later and use the Language to smooth down the street's surface, before anyone asked awkward questions.

But now that she was out of immediate danger and had a moment to think, her feeling that she was missing something had clarified. "Hsien," she said quietly, pulling the man aside, and beckoning Erda. "Erda. Would it be fair to say that all the threats so far this evening have been—well, not *safe*, but manageable? Things that we could handle, if we devoted sufficient time and attention to them?"

Erda frowned. "I'm not sure we could have handled them as well without your assistance, but you may be right. Why?"

"We're being diverted," Irene said savagely. "Managed. Distracted. Our attention's being kept focused on minor threats while our enemy is up to something else. Something more serious." She glanced between the two of them, but neither of them disagreed; they were both nodding slowly.

"What do you think she's trying?" Hsien asked. He didn't need to explain who *she* was. Mu Dan must have passed on their suspicions about the Blood Countess.

"We need to be prepared for something large and wholesale, just in case." Irene said. "But I'm not sure . . ."

She frowned, trying to make the pieces whirling round in her mind come together into a recognizable shape. The rats, buzzing with chaotic power and malice, but unable to enter the hotel. But why? Because of the Library wards? But the Fae delegation had been able to come and go without any problems. Was there some *other* reason why the rats hadn't tried to get in? *The witch-queen,*

Erda had called her. The Blood Countess was a Fae, and Irene knew that powerful Fae could infuse their power into dramatically appropriate animals.

Yet what had the rats actually *done*? Well, they'd attracted everyone's attention to *outside* the hotel . . .

Her eyes opened wide in shock. She recalled the empty cat's basket in the kitchen. The cat being traditionally a witch's familiar . . . The archway leading down to the wine cellars. And the fact that with the anarchists, an enemy had already proven that they could use the Paris sewers to move around underground . . .

"The threat might be down in the wine cellars," she said, very softly. "Whatever it is. I don't know, but I have to check. I'm about to disregard Prutkov's instructions. I need Vale, and Mu Dan and Silver, or if you can't get them, someone else *competent* from both sides, and I need them now." Besides, the political back of her mind pointed out, in addition to the straightforward physical and metaphysical assistance, having witnesses from both sides might be very useful in the near future—if Irene found what she was afraid she might find downstairs. "As fast as possible. I'll be down in the wine cellars."

"Alone?" Hsien demanded.

"We have no *time*." Irene shrugged off her cape and tossed it to Hsien, brushing snow from her hair. "I'll take along some of your people if we meet them on the way, but we have to search the place *now*—and if there's nothing in the cellars, then we'll go through the rest of the hotel. We've gone past the point of worrying about disturbing supper. If I'm wrong, then I'll take the blame for it. *Now*, please!"

She put authority into her voice, and they responded, heading off at a run for the dining room. Irene herself caught up the skirts of her gown and ran for the kitchens, leaving a trail of wet footprints behind her. If she was right and the Countess had a bigger scheme ready to trigger, then it wasn't a matter of *if* she'd do it—it was a case of *when*.

The kitchen was still quiet. Well, technically it wasn't quiet, it was a hive of activity with a constant buzz of noise. It would be more accurate to say that it wasn't a scene of bloody murder or any other sort of violent disruption. Asparagus was being chopped, squabs were in the final stages of being roasted, and foie gras was being carefully positioned on artfully decorated plates.

"Madam, is something the matter?" Hsien's assistant demanded. She'd been keeping an eye on the cooks, but Irene's entry had been hasty enough to signal that something was wrong.

"Has anyone been down to the wine cellars?" Irene asked quietly.

"No, madam. All the wines for the dinner were removed earlier, and there has been no need yet to fetch extra bottles." The woman flicked a glance at the archway. "Is there some reason . . ."

"There may be. What lighting do they have down there?"

"Electric, madam, like the rest of the hotel."

"Good. We need to investigate down there urgently. Can you be spared from supervising here, or do you need to stay on guard?"

The woman hesitated. Irene suddenly realized how dubious she must look: she'd shown up here alone, without Hsien to back her, and she was demanding that the woman leave her assigned post to accompany her. "It's all right," she said. "Keep an eye on things up here. I'm going down there. Send Hsien and anyone else down after me as soon as they arrive."

The woman nodded, clearly relieved. "I will do that, madam."

As Irene passed the cat basket, she glanced at it. It was still empty, except for a scattering of black hairs on the blanket.

The archway yawned in front of Irene. She flicked the light switch, then began to descend the stone stairs in the sudden glare of light. The stonework was older than the new gilding and woodwork upstairs; it belonged to a Paris that disregarded time and was built to last. The air down here was colder than in the main hotel, stroking along her skin in icy draughts and raising goose bumps on her bare shoulders and arms.

The short stairway led into a sequence of long cellars that were lined with racks of bottles and heavy barrels. Despite the best attempts at ventilation, there was a tang to the air: the memory of wine and brandy, port and liquors, and echoes of all the alcohol that had sweated out of barrels or through corks.

Irene sniffed again. She could feel it now. It had been drowned out by all the Library's own safety wardings and by the great presences at the banquet above, but now that she was down here and in close proximity to it, she could tell it was present. It wasn't a scent or a touch or a physical sense, but she was aware of it, and her Library brand tingled in response. Something—someone—that belonged to chaos was down here in the cellars with her.

And if whoever it was had noticed the lights being turned on and heard Irene's steps on the stairs, then that person knew that they were about to have company.

The place was silent. Nothing moved. Nothing dripped.

Now, if I were a threat, what would I be . . . ? The first answer that came to mind was a bomb. And if a bomber was trying to catch the maximum number of dinner guests, then the bomb would be located beneath the Salon Tuileries. Irene mentally oriented herself and headed for that part of the cellars.

Then the lights went out.

Irene weighed her options: turn the lights on again with the

Language and force a confrontation, or try to navigate this place in pitch darkness with an enemy hunting for her?

Something brushed against her leg from behind.

Irene bit back a gasp of shock, jumping forward. That settled it. Open confrontation was preferable to trying to dodge someone who could clearly see in the dark. **"Lights, turn on!"** she commanded.

The lights came on again, but they were dimmer now, like half-burned torches, throwing shadows at every angle. There was no sign of whatever had brushed against her leg. Silence filled the air: hungry, expectant silence.

Two clocks ticked down in Irene's head. One of them was the time until her reinforcements arrived. The other was the time until the theoretical bomb went off—or whatever else might be down here.

If the Countess—or whoever the enemy was—*had* been directing the rats, then she'd seen Irene outside. Acting innocent would do Irene no good. She might as well gamble for high stakes.

Before she could let herself realize how bad an idea it was, she called out, "Blood Countess? Milady? I request an audience."

There was still no sound, but the lights began to flicker off one by one behind Irene and to either side, leaving only a single corridor of illumination ahead of her. The invitation was clear.

Irene followed the lit path, collecting a bottle of brandy from one of the racks that she passed. She felt more comfortable with a solid object in her hand that could serve as a weapon. The lights went out once she had passed them, and darkness drew in behind her. A barely audible scuff on the floor made her glance to her left: a dust-smeared tabby cat slid out from behind a rack of bottles to pad beside her. More cats emerged from the shadows, squirming out from under barrels or spilling down from the higher racks.

They moved around her in a silent escort, herding her forward, brushing against her dress and glancing up at her with unreadable bright eyes.

Irene came to the archway of the final cellar and paused there, looking into the room ahead of her. A draught tugged at her dress and curled around her shoulders, making her shiver. Realization cut in: there must be an opening of some sort in the wall of this cellar, if the air was moving. It might be a gap into the sewers or into some other building's cellar next door or across the street. But from this angle, all she could see was more stacks of bottles . . .

Then light flared redly at the end of the room, and Irene saw the woman standing there.

Her hair might have been gold under sunlight, but in this dim light, under the glowing bulbs, it was burnished copper, braided up and surmounted with a crimson coif. She was in the stiff formal clothing of the sixteenth century, with a huge white lace ruff and puffed white sleeves, crimson full skirts, and laced bodice. The only parts of her skin that showed were her hands and face. She was very beautiful. Nobody could possibly have disagreed. But something about the extreme pallor and purity of her skin was unhealthy; it made Irene think of lilies and fungi grown on graves and nourished on corpses. Like Irene, the woman was surrounded by an entourage of cats. They pressed against her legs, their mouths open in silent purring, as if she were as intoxicating as catnip.

She was impressive, and Irene would have been more impressed if the day hadn't been an utter cavalcade of people doing their damnedest to impress her. Between dragon kings and Fae nobility, she was worn-out, and her capacity for awe and terror was nearly exhausted. Nearly, but not quite; she had enough left to be sensibly afraid.

"Madam," she said, and dipped a curtsey. The important thing was to play for time. Or perhaps—maybe—even manage to negotiate a truce? It was probably wishful thinking, but she'd never know if she didn't *try*. "Do I have the honour to address Countess Elizabeth Báthory de Ecsed?"

The woman seemed vaguely amused. "You do. But if you already knew who I was, then why did you come sauntering down here so very bravely?"

"To speak to you, of course," Irene lied. "And I just followed the cats."

"They say I once cast a spell to summon a cloud filled with ninety cats to torment my enemies." The Countess gestured at the animals surrounding her. "That may be an exaggeration. But I've always found them to be my friends."

Irene raised the bottle in her hand. "May I offer you a drink, perhaps?"

"I never drink . . . brandy." The Countess pursed her lips, mildly irritated at herself. "Dear me, how hard it is to avoid cliché! But I'm certainly not going to accept any food or gifts that you offer me."

"Then why are you here?"

"You know perfectly well." The air smelled of blood and dust. "I am here to bring ruin upon this pitiful attempt at peace."

"What I don't understand," Irene said, walking closer, "is why." Her throat was dry with fear. She could feel just how powerful this Fae woman was: every step towards her was like walking into a cobra's reach, safe only so long as the snake chose not to strike.

The Countess shook her head, and her hair fell free of its coif and braids, flying out around her face like a lion's mane. Her face remained unmoved, as perfect as a mask. "Do you know what it is like to be part of a cycle?" she asked.

Irene blinked. "I beg your pardon?"

"I am Elizabeth Báthory." The Countess ran her hands through her hair, smoothing it back. Her dress was changing, shifting to a younger woman's clothing, less ornate and with a smaller ruff. For a moment her skin seemed natural rather than cold alabaster. "I am her as she was when she was young and innocent, marrying an older man who went off to the wars. I am her when she grew older and had to rule the estate with a rod of iron. I could tolerate no disloyalty, no dissent. I was cruel because rulers *were* cruel, maiden. I am the Elizabeth who was falsely accused and who died in darkness, immured in my own castle, with day upon day to learn to hate the world beyond those walls. And I am also the Elizabeth who was truthfully accused, and who bathed in the blood of virgins to be young again, and who grew old and withered without that blood. I am the witch-queen and the torturer, the owner of the iron maiden of Nuremberg. I am all these things at once. Do you understand me?"

Irene wasn't entirely sure she *understood*, but she was developing some nervous theories about what happened to Fae who had to embody contrasting parts of one archetype at the same time. Insanity might be the least of it. "Madam," she said, "I appreciate all this, but I do not see why you should want war rather than peace."

The Countess's eyes were deep dark brown, the same shade as old dried blood on white cloth. "There is no truth to peace," she said. "Peace is at best a brief interlude between hostilities. The treaties which might be signed here are no more than lies. The field of battle is more honest. What you are trying to build here won't last, and you will be blamed for it when it falls apart. Name yourself."

"No," Irene said. She had to force herself to refuse; the Countess's words came with an impulse to obey, with a tang of fear and promised pain. She took a step closer. The drift of cats around her feet merged with the mass surrounding the Countess.

"You are walking into my hands," the Countess said. "Are you waiting for your friends to arrive and save you? They will be lost in these cellars for a century if I will it so." This time her smile was edged and pointed, full of a lust for the suffering of others. This was a woman who could bleed her victims to death and bathe in their blood. "You speak like a heroine. We shall see if you can suffer like one."

Her words held such a promise of pain that for a moment Irene was trapped, frozen where she stood. Then an unexpected recognition cut through the fear and gave her words. "I thought we were trying to avoid cliché."

The Countess raised a mocking eyebrow.

"That's from *The Mysteries of Udolpho,*" Irene pointed out. "If you're going to threaten me, please be original about it."

The air seemed to congeal around Irene, as tight as a noose around her throat. "Don't mock me," the Countess said very softly, each word a sharpened knife. The colour drained from her skin, and her clothing darkened to black: now she was as pale as ice in a morgue, in a dead-black dress that blended with the shadows. "Little Librarian, down here with me in the darkness, all alone . . . have you no respect? Have you no humility? Have you no fear? I promise you, I give you my word, that I will be more *original* than you can possibly imagine."

It is probably not a good idea to taunt the Blood Countess, Irene reminded herself, lowering her eyes. "Forgive me," she murmured. "I am a Librarian. Books are our business."

But something additional had caught her attention. While the Countess was changing her aspect and appearance as the Cardinal had earlier, or like another powerful Fae Irene had once seen, there was something translucent about her. She was just a fraction . . . unreal. The scent of blood that suffused the cellar was centred on her, but it wasn't coming *from* her. She wore no perfume. It was as if she was a hologram, or a projection.

And there were no doors in the wall behind her; Irene could see that, even in the dim light. Apart from the entrance that Irene had used, this cellar had no openings large enough to admit a human being.

But now that Irene was actually *looking*, she could see that there was a small recent opening in the wall to one side, at floor level, barely a foot high. The scatter of bricks around it suggested that it had been broken open from the other side. It was far too small for a woman.

But it was big enough for a cat.

And the cats pressing around Irene's legs, rubbing against her, eyes catching the light as they stared at her, were real enough.

"It's true that it has been a while since I played with a Librarian," the Countess mused. "It will be interesting to see if you still break as easily."

Irene's half-formed plan jumped from *maybe* to *immediate*. The Countess sounded like a woman unwilling to waste any more time before getting to the *disembowelling* stage of the conversation. "Now I'm the one who wants the drink," Irene said. She raised her bottle. **"Cork of the bottle of brandy in my hand, come out."**

The cork popped out as though the bottle of brandy had been a shaken bottle of champagne, bouncing off the ceiling to land somewhere in a corner.

"You will find that isn't as good a painkiller as you might hope," the Countess said. She'd tensed for a moment as Irene used the Language, then relaxed again, as the words had become clear.

"We shall see," Irene said. She raised the bottle. "But the thing that I'm wondering at the moment is . . ."

"Yes?" the Countess enquired.

Irene tipped the brandy out over the felines, swinging the bottle so that the alcohol sprayed out in an arc. "**Brandy, cleanse these cats of chaos influence!**" she ordered.

The cats shrieked as the liquid hit them. It would have been more efficient—more symbolic—to use pure water as an agent, but under the circumstances Irene could only hope that brandy would work. It was a logical chain of reasoning; the cats were the only things that could have gotten in and out of here, and the cats were somehow acting as an agent for the Countess to project her will into this place. So theoretically, if Irene could somehow *break* that link, then the Countess would no longer be able to access the hotel. It was all perfectly solid logic, and Irene desperately hoped that it was correct.

The sound of the cats screaming was almost worse than human voices in pain. Their desperate noises *weren't* human; they were creatures that didn't understand what had been done to them, or why Irene's actions hurt them so much. They rolled on the floor, snarling and scratching at each other, and something rose from their bodies—something like lightning, or fox-fire, or the first flare of light in an incandescent bulb. It flowed towards the Countess and through her, flaring in her eyes.

Irene found herself staggering, wanting to collapse to her knees, as the huge drain of her words in the Language hit her. She was deliberately opposing herself to an ancient and powerful force of chaos that very much wanted to keep things as they were. The

Countess flickered in and out of existence like the juddering images in a roll of film, trying to maintain her presence.

Irene swayed but held herself upright. *I have too many people depending on me to let her win.* It was a promise to herself, a self-set binding on her own will that was as real as anything the Language could do. The thought of everyone sitting up above her, unaware of what was going on, drove her to take a step forward, and she dashed the last of the brandy in the Countess's face. **"Creature of chaos, leave this building!"**

The Countess froze, abruptly as flat and two-dimensional as a painting. Her face was a mask of anger, as white and dead as bone.

Darkness closed around Irene as the last of the lights went out.

CHAPTER 15

Irene sank to her knees in exhaustion, dropping the empty bottle. She knew that she was still conscious—at least, she thought she was conscious. How could one tell whether one was conscious or unconscious just by thinking about it?

She pulled herself together, breathing deeply and trying to stop her head from spinning. Being in the darkness like this made it worse: there was nothing visual to hold on to. The cats were still there—she felt warm fur against her hand when she reached out—but they'd stopped that awful shrieking. They were lying sprawled on the ground like worn-out rags, barely moving.

Priorities. What was most important? She needed to close that gap in the wall. **"Bricks which come from the hole in the wall, rise back into place and seal it again."**

The sound of bricks grinding against each other ran through her head like an earthquake. She honestly considered throwing up. The only reason that she hadn't realized how bad her headache was had been the comparative silence. Her nose was bleeding, and she couldn't even be sure when it had started.

She pinched the bridge of her nose hard. That was what they'd taught her at school in first aid. Or was it supposed to be lying back with an ice pack on your nose and stuff it with cotton wool?

Focus, she told herself harshly. **"Lights, on,"** she tried.

Nothing happened.

Well, that was a nuisance. The combined influence of the Language and chaotic power must have blown a fuse somewhere, and even the Language couldn't turn a light on if the light was physically incapable of turning on. She pulled herself upright and slid a foot forward, trying to avoid trampling on semi-conscious cats as she felt around for a wall.

"Winters!" came a call from the distance.

That was Vale's voice. Irene breathed a great sigh of relief, coupled with just a fraction of annoyance that he couldn't have gotten here five minutes earlier. "Over here!" she called back, then winced and put her hand to her head again.

She could hear multiple people approaching, not just Vale—hurried steps, the swish of skirts. Light broke through the darkness, and Irene shielded her eyes at the sudden glare from hand-held lamps.

"Are you all right, Winters?" Vale demanded.

"Passable," Irene answered. "The Countess came off worse. But she's gone from here now. I think. I drove her out." She looked around the room in the lamplight. No signs of explosives. No big piles of dynamite. Nothing obvious. "Did you pass anything odd on your way in here?"

Mu Dan looked over Vale's shoulder, scrutinising the room with flared nostrils. "This place stinks of chaos," she opined. "As well as brandy. And why are there cats everywhere?"

"The Countess was somehow using them to manifest." Irene picked her way across the living carpet of felines. "Let's not kill them. Please. I don't think it was their fault."

"Can you guarantee that they are safe now?" Mu Dan asked. "We can't afford to take chances."

"How interesting." Silver stepped from behind Vale and raised the lamp that he was holding to inspect the floor. He stirred one cat with the toe of a mirror-polished shoe: much to Irene's regret, it didn't lash out at him. "This place has certainly been the focus of power, but otherwise we seem to be a *little* lacking in evidence."

"Well, I apologise for not having the lady in iron chains waiting for your inspection—" Irene bit her lip and stopped before she could get any further. There was no time for this. "I came down here because I thought whoever was causing trouble was trying to decoy all our attention outwards—which meant that they didn't want us looking inwards and down here. I found the Countess in this room, together with a whole mob of cats. You can see the cats. And there was a hole in the wall, a cat-sized one, but I've blocked it now. But I'm afraid that she's planted some sort of bomb here in the cellars, or done *something* which is going to be . . . bad." *Bad* was far too minor a word for the current situation, but it would just have to do. "So we'd better search these cellars. Now."

Silver frowned and checked his watch.

"You have an appointment?" Mu Dan needled him.

"No," Silver said. "But it is five minutes to midnight. If I was the sort of person who wanted to be needlessly dramatic . . ."

A chill wormed its way down Irene's spine. Because of *course* a lunatic warmongering bloodthirsty Fae would set off explosives at midnight. What could possibly be more appropriate? "We have to hurry," she said urgently.

Vale nodded. Without needing to be prompted, the four of them separated, Silver and Mu Dan running ahead to check the cellars on either side. Irene stumbled along behind Vale, looking to left and right in the light of his lamp. "How long till they fix the lights?" she asked.

"Uncertain," Vale said crisply. "It took a great deal of persuasion for them to let us come down here with lamps. Speaking of which, Winters, I apologise for the delay—"

"Here!" Mu Dan called, from ahead and to the right. Vale broke off and jolted into a run; Irene followed.

Mu Dan pointed mutely into the small side wine cellar she'd found. Tangles of wires ran from various points in the stacks of wine bottles—and behind them—to a central nexus, where they were wrapped around a clock-hand dial. The second hand was moving silently, barely visible behind the network of fuses.

"Stand back," Vale said, assuming charge. "Winters, can you do something about the light conditions?"

Irene couldn't turn the lights on—but she might be able to upgrade the lamps that everyone was holding. "Give me your lamp," she said, reaching out for it. **"Lamp which I am holding, increase your light until you are lighting up your surroundings as brightly as noon."**

The lamp burned more and more brightly, bringing the old cellar timbers and bricks into focus and casting everyone's shadows into harsh relief against the walls and floor.

"Hold it up," Vale said. He frowned. "Yes, I thought so. Stay back, all of you. Winters, keep me illuminated. Don't use the Language." He stepped carefully over a wire Irene hadn't even noticed that ran across the cellar entrance, then dropped to his knees next to the dial and its surrounding fuses. Reaching into his jacket, he withdrew a small flat case the size of a manicure kit. But the tools inside were lockpicks, not nail files or clippers.

"Should we clear the hotel while he's working?" Mu Dan asked. She was in sleek dark crimson silk, with a diamond collar that matched her hairpins. "If this goes wrong—"

"We've only got a minute and a half anyhow," Silver said from behind Irene. "We'd never manage it in time."

"You're very calm about it," Irene commented.

"My dear little mouse . . ." She hated that epithet from him. It was so *diminutive* in every way. "I trust the detective here to be able to do his job. It's in his nature, after all. Besides, I honestly can't see myself dying like this. Would you like to know how I do visualise myself dying?"

"No," Irene and Mu Dan said simultaneously.

Irene couldn't take her eyes off the clock dial and the second hand slowly creeping around it. The second hand was one of the sort that made little shuddering jumps forward rather than moving slowly. Second after second was counted off.

"I can stop the clock—" she offered.

"If I'd wanted that I'd have asked for it," Vale said, not looking up. He chose another pick and slid it behind the clock. They were all quiet enough that the tiny sounds of metal against metal were audible. "Underneath a hotel full of Librarians? She'll have booby-trapped it against what you can do."

Irene knew that was true. She'd encountered that sort of trap before—and the fact that the Countess had wired the entrance already demonstrated that she was capable of thinking that way. But if it got down to five seconds and Vale hadn't defused the timer, was it worth the risk?

Her mouth was dry. She swallowed, trying to clear her throat. Ten seconds. Nine. Eight.

She could still smell the odour of blood from earlier. Her lamp blazed pitilessly bright, stripping away comforting shadows. Each second seemed to stretch out longer and longer. Seven. Six. Five.

If she didn't stop the clock with the Language now, then this whole hotel could go up in the explosion. People would *die*.

Irene bit her lip hard enough to hurt. She trusted Vale.

Four. Three.

The second hand stopped.

Vale sat back on his heels and began to put his implements away. "A nasty little piece," he said calmly. "One of the more complex that I've seen. Can you go into a little more detail about your encounter with this Countess, Winters?"

Irene ran briefly through a description of the meeting. It was a relief to finally know who the enemy was. "But why would she put the bomb here?" she asked. "It's not that close to the Salon Tuileries."

"No," Mu Dan said thoughtfully. "But I think it's beneath the Salon Pompadour."

"Which raises interesting questions about how much the Countess knows about tonight's dinner." Vale rose. "We should return upstairs, I think."

Irene saw that Mu Dan was frowning. "Is something the matter?" she asked.

"It's a pity," Mu Dan said carefully, "a very great pity that we couldn't actually see this Countess of yours ourselves."

A sudden uncertainty gripped Irene. She realized that she'd been subconsciously congratulating herself on the fact that not only had they seen off the Countess and defused her bomb, but they now had actual proof of her existence. "I beg your pardon?" she said, hoping against hope that she was misunderstanding Mu Dan.

"I'm not trying to be awkward," Mu Dan clarified. "I agree that this place reeks of chaos."

"Could we be just a *little* less prejudiced in our verbs here?" Silver suggested. But his manner was restrained, and his objection clearly more for the sake of snideness than a genuine contradiction.

Mu Dan paused to glare at him before continuing. "I concede some sort of chaotic interference down here. Possibly Fae. But we have no proof beyond your word that this theoretical Countess set the bomb. And as for evidence of what you'd been up to down here—well, we found you in the middle of a pile of drunken cats!"

"They weren't drunk, they were just soaked in alcohol—" Irene started hotly, then realized that she was arguing on the wrong front. A sense of betrayal was making itself keenly felt. "All right, I admit that doesn't actually sound much better. But why are you trying to disprove what I've told you?"

Mu Dan glanced between Silver and Vale, as if hoping that one of them would supply the answer instead of her. Neither of them spoke. She turned back to Irene. "Because it's in your interest—in the Library's interest—to have some third party trying to sabotage things. And so far we have no actual proof otherwise—"

"You mean besides the attempt to kidnap you earlier today?" Irene snapped. "Or the chlorine gas in the cake delivered to the hotel? Or the rats outside?"

Mu Dan's face might have been carved from stone, but her eyes were hot with anger. "I am an impartial judge-investigator. These events happened, but where is your proof of some evil genius behind them all?"

"Are you saying," Irene asked very carefully, biting down on the urge to scream in the other woman's face, "no, wait, forgive me—are you *suggesting* that we might have set all this up in order to provide fake evidence that the Countess exists and is here?"

"I am saying," Mu Dan replied, an equal anger and restraint audible in her voice, "that at the moment we can't prove or report otherwise."

Irene was drawing in her breath to say precisely what she thought of that, when Mu Dan's choice of words raised a red flag. Perhaps Irene wasn't the only one having to cope with unreasonable management on this job. "Report," she said carefully. "Hmm."

There was a momentary glint of relief in Mu Dan's eyes. "I'm not saying that I wouldn't *like* such proof, you understand."

"What about you?" Irene turned to Silver. "Do you have any thoughts on the subject that you would care to share with us?"

"Manners, manners," Silver murmured. "Just because you've had a near-death experience with a powerful kindred of mine down here in the cellars, all on your own, and you didn't even get to drink any of the brandy yourself, does *not* mean that you get to take it out on me. It's my superior's official position that the Countess exists, but he acknowledges—no, let's go the full stretch, he positively *insists* that we get outright proof of it. And that would be more proof than just your testimony, a lingering odour of chaos, and a lot of cats."

"We are omitting something here," Vale said thoughtfully. "Winters has always assured me that Librarians can bind themselves in their Language to speak the truth. Surely that makes her testimony as reliable as I believe it to be?"

Irene was about to thank Vale for his support, but then she saw the possible flaw. "Let me guess," she said, resigned. "Certain people—certain high-ranking people, whom we can't actually name because they wouldn't want to be quoted on this—are going to say that the problem with this is that it all relies on 'the Librarian's say' in the first place. Or that I could have somehow been fooled and that I'm honestly telling the truth, but that I'm wrong about what I saw. Or *something.* And nothing is going to be acceptable here except for proof so big and obvious that you could sink the *Titanic* with it."

Vale didn't bother asking what the *Titanic* was. He was better at prioritising than Irene. "Well, then," he said briskly, "we had better find this proof. Starting by tracing the dynamite in the morning, and any other evidence which may have come to light—did you say something about a cake and chlorine, Winters?"

"Yes," Irene said. She was dragging herself back from the verge of despair. This was a temporary roadblock, not a total burning of bridges. "Erda on the Fae security team has photographs. We should be able to trace it. And the poisoned apples too."

"You should have said so earlier," Mu Dan chided Irene, as they headed back to the stairway. "When will I be able to inspect them?"

"Hopefully as soon as she's got them developed," Irene said. "I think she'll need to go back to their hotel for that."

The kitchen was still active, though it had moved to the dessert stage, and waiters were carrying through bowls of peaches swimming in jelly. Irene's stomach rumbled, reminding her that she had so far managed to avoid almost every course. "Do you suppose we can sneak back in with nobody noticing us?" she asked hopefully.

"Ah! Monsieur Vale!" It was Inspector Maillon, melting snow

dripping from his cape, followed by a couple of gendarmes, with Prutkov, Duan Zheng, and Sterrington right behind *them*, and the whole procession backed up by a couple of waiters desperately trying to usher them out of the kitchen. "We have had another outbreak of this vile anarchist behaviour! I would not normally call a man away from his dinner, but your hotel was en route to the scene of the crime—and this may be connected with the earlier assault upon you."

"What's happened?" Vale asked.

The chopping of knives and sloshing of jelly and pouring of alcohol had quietened enough for the entire kitchen to listen to the conversation. Inspector Maillon's words were audible throughout the room. "An explosion at the Richelieu Library, sir! At the stroke of midnight. Minor, no serious destruction, but still an appalling act of vandalism and anarchy! I am on my way there at once, and I thought to invite you to accompany me as well."

Irene felt the colour leave her face. She put the lamp down on the nearest flat surface before she dropped it. She'd failed even worse than she'd thought she had. The Countess must have had a double-pronged attack ready to go, and Irene had only guessed at half of it. She'd *failed*.

In the background she was half-conscious of intense discussion, then Vale shouldered in front of her. "Winters, I need to—Winters, are you all right?"

With what felt like an effort big enough to shake Paris, she pulled herself together. "We're going to investigate the explosion?"

Vale lowered his voice. "To be precise, Winters, *I* am going—the inspector and this whole world seem to think it inappropriate to drag ladies into such a situation. I will be taking Silver as well: he assures me he can locate any signs of Fae interference. I fear you and Mu Dan will have to deal with things here. I'll let you know what we discover in the morning."

Irene thought of protesting. Then she looked across at Inspector Maillon and gauged the level of his gender-based prejudice. It wavered somewhere between bristling moustache and indignant eyebrows. Irene might be able to insist on coming along, but it would take valuable time, and the inspector's willingness to cooperate might dim in the face of what he considered unreasonable demands. She'd just have to sneak in later. "I'll be here," she said with an effort. "Good luck."

With a nod, Vale was gone, and the whole group of them were sweeping—or, more accurately, being swept by the principal chef, who'd had quite enough of them all—out into the corridor. Irene glanced wistfully after Vale and Silver, who were vanishing together with the inspector and his gendarmes, but then found herself being backed against the wall by Prutkov. "Irene," he said. "Kindly explain what's going on. And why you have been calling people away from the formal dinner, in spite of my specific instructions otherwise."

Irene would have preferred to be giving her report to him in private, rather than in front of other people from both sides, but at least it distracted her from thoughts of the Richelieu Library in ruins. She clung to the inspector's description of it as *minor* like a talisman, and ran through the evening's events so far as quickly as possible.

Prutkov's lips tightened as she went on. "I see," he finally said. He turned to Duan Zheng and to Sterrington. "I must ask you to accept my apologies for the situation, and for the lack of any clear evidence about what has taken place. Clearly our response to this whole threat was inadequate. We will review the situation and are prepared to have another Librarian take charge of the investigation, if your representatives would rather work with someone else." *Someone who hasn't fouled up and demonstrated her incompetence,* his tone made clear.

Irene had been blamed for situations and hung out to take the blame before, but rarely quite so publicly. A dozen different responses boiled in her mouth and tried to force their way out, from the childish *that's not fair!* to the more adult *there was no way anyone could have predicted this!* to the blame-shifting *you yourself refused to give me any further assistance.* She quite literally tasted bile in her mouth as she kept her mouth shut and swallowed. Contradicting Prutkov in public would only weaken the Library's position. Dragons would see it as improper behaviour. Fae would see it as showing a potential weakness they could exploit. Either way, saying anything at all would be a mistake. She knew that. She was—oh, how she hated that term right now—*professional* enough to keep her mouth shut.

Though if she had been capable of telepathy at that precise moment, Prutkov's head would have boiled from the inside and exploded.

Duan Zheng and Sterrington glanced at each other measuringly. Irene guessed that they were weighing up the chance of getting any advantage in the negotiations from the current situation. And of course, there was the possibility that they were each waiting for the other to begin, so that they could disagree with them.

And who would the Library put in Irene's place? Bradamant, maybe, or someone else brought in from outside. Irene folded her hands meekly behind her back and began revolving plans to get back in on the investigation. Vale would talk to her, wouldn't he? He'd *better.* Normally she might have sat back and assumed the

Library knew best what they were doing, and that someone better than Irene would be taking the job . . .

It surprised her to find that for once, she didn't believe that. Irene *was* the person on the spot. She had contacts on both sides. The rest of the team were prepared to work with her. And the Countess now knew about her and considered her a personal enemy—which in this case practically guaranteed that Irene would be a target. This was, in a way, good, inasmuch as being hunted by a bloodthirsty torturing cat-loving sadist could ever be considered good. It gave them a lead.

And her parents were at stake.

Irene *couldn't* let them take her off the case. But as the seconds ticked by and fear congealed inside her, she knew that it was entirely possible.

Sterrington was the first to speak. "We see no reason to ask for a change in the Library's representation on the investigative team."

"Nor do we," Duan Zheng said. He glared sidelong at Sterrington, as though annoyed at having the same opinion as a Fae. "Mu Dan, accompany me; my lord will expect a report."

The corridor emptied, leaving Prutkov and Irene alone. "Mm," he said. "That went about as well as could be expected."

"It did?" Irene said. She reminded herself that they were still in a public corridor and that they might be overheard, and that giving Prutkov her free and full opinion on proper treatment and leadership of subordinates who'd just had the sort of evening she'd suffered through was not a good idea. Just a very tempting one. "I'm glad to hear it."

He patted her shoulder. "Well, of course we weren't going to take you off the case. But I'm sure you understand I had to make the offer."

It would have been comforting to believe him. It would have been reassuring. But Irene trusted him just as much as she trusted thin ice to hold her weight. One false step and she'd be going under while he murmured sad nothings about her failure. "Of course," she agreed, matching her tone to his. "It was an awkward situation."

"I'm glad you understand." He smiled at her, his eyes like blank glass. "Now, if you'll excuse me, I need to make sure things are under control . . ."

And he was heading back towards the Salon Tuileries.

Irene looked down at herself. Dust and cat hairs smeared her skirts at knee-height and below. Her evening slippers felt as if they were in rags. Her gloves were dirtied and torn. She could still smell the echoes of blood and chlorine. A ferocious headache was twisting behind her temples. She was absolutely not fit company for a polite evening's state dinner. And she was exhausted.

The stairs up to her bedroom seemed to take forever. Weariness had settled into her bones, and she was reminded with every step just how little sleep she'd gotten the night before. *I'm not twenty years old any more,* she thought sourly, *and given the way things are going, I'm not even sure I'm going to live to see another birthday . . .*

She slammed the bedroom door behind her and kicked her slippers off, sending them tumbling across the room. The petty violence made her feel a little better. She peeled her gloves off, shivering as the cool air ran up her arms, and wondered about the possibility of a bath.

There was a knock at the door.

Irene opened it to find Kai standing there. He had a tray in one hand, and even with the cover over it she could smell hot soup and fresh bread. "May I come in?" he asked.

Irene hesitated, though her stomach clenched, reminding her just how hungry she was. "I'm fairly sure that your uncle will be very unhappy if he finds out that you're acting as a waiter." She knew she was making excuses—possibly even stupid excuses—but she had been through quite enough this evening already. The situation was fragile enough as it was.

Kai lowered his voice. "I've spoken with Duan Zheng. I know what happened tonight." Raw anger showed in his voice, and his eyes were briefly dragon-red, like rubies with a flame behind them. "I should have been there too!"

Irene took a deep breath, biting back the urge to agree with him. "When we agreed to have you come and find your uncle, we both knew that would mean working with him rather than necessarily working with me. The point is getting the treaty signed. Right?"

"Irene."

"Yes?" She tried to raise an eyebrow coolly, but she'd never been very good at that.

"Look me in the eyes and tell me in the Language that you didn't want me there."

"Kai." Irene counted silently to five. She wasn't sure she could have reached ten. And she couldn't look him in the eyes. "Let me make something clear to you. An evening when I have been facing off rats, poison gases, evil Fae, and useless, selfish management is *not* the evening to be asking me emotionally revealing questions about our relationship."

There was another silence, and Irene wondered if Kai was employing his own private version of mentally counting to five. But then his expression cleared, and he said, "You have a point. And I have something for you." He offered the tray.

"Aren't you coming in?" Irene would have liked to talk with him, if nothing else.

Kai coughed. "Well, to be entirely frank with you . . . I *have* had it suggested that I should seduce you in order to get more information out of you. And as you said, it's been a difficult evening for you. I wouldn't want to make it worse."

"Really?" Irene found her spirits lifting. "Well, just for the record, I've been told to seduce you as well."

Kai frowned. "That sort of order shames whoever gave it to you."

Irene was tempted to agree. "But what about you?"

"That was just a suggestion," Kai said. "That's quite different."

"Well, I'm not obeying orders," Irene said, and took the tray from him, stepping aside so he could enter. Her headache was vanishing. So was her exhaustion. What she wanted, right now, was to be with someone whom she could trust. Kai might be ordered to act against her. She could accept that. But he was honest. He wasn't lying to her. And she desperately needed—no, *wanted*—to share that with him, for just one night. For their own reasons, between the two of them, and for no other motive than that. "I'm off the clock for the rest of the evening. That's been made quite clear to me. What happens next is just between the two of us as private individuals."

"But what about tomorrow?" Kai objected, taking a hopeful step forward.

"Tomorrow is another day," Irene said.

She beckoned him in and locked the door behind him.

CHAPTER 16

Irene's dreams had been as peaceful as the snow falling outside: unformed and indistinct, but quiet and unthreatening, free for the moment from fear and desperation and worry. When she opened her eyes, trying to work out why she'd woken up, the only noises were the crackling of the fire and Kai's breathing next to her in the bed.

Then the thunder came again, tearing away her last shreds of sleepiness. Someone was rapping on the bedroom door. Actually, rapping was too minor a word for it. Someone with absolutely no concern for sleepers in this bedroom—or neighbouring bedrooms, or possibly the entire corridor—was pounding on the door.

"Winters!" It was Vale's voice. "Winters, are you awake in there?"

"I certainly am now," Irene muttered, staggering out of bed. Pale greyness outlined the window, leaking around the edges of the thick curtains. She flipped the light switch and blinked in the sudden illumination; the ormolu clock on the mantelpiece said it was seven o'clock in the morning. She shook her head, pulling herself together, and looked round for her dressing gown. "Yes!" she called, more loudly. "Give me a moment . . ."

Kai had come awake and was sitting up in the bed, his black hair ruffled but his composure untouched. "Should I be found here?" he asked softly.

"I have news about that explosion," Vale explained through the door. "Lord Silver's with me. May we join you?"

That settled Kai's question without Irene even having to reply. It would be bad enough putting up with Silver's verbal barbs on the subject of whom Irene might choose to share her bed. But outright confirming to him that she was sleeping with one of the dragon delegation, when he might report it to the Cardinal . . .

Irene pointed at Kai, then towards the bathroom. "Just a moment, please," she called to Vale, wrapping her dressing gown round her. She was still shivering with cold—now that she was out of bed, the wintry temperature was much more noticeable, and her dressing gown was the lacy peignoir variety rather than the heavy flannel type. She dragged the counterpane off the bed to drape it over her shoulders as well.

Kai slipped out of the bed and caught up his clothing from the chair where he'd left it. He touched Irene's hand for a moment—an acknowledgement, and a wish that they had time for more—and glided into the suite's bathroom, closing the door behind him.

Irene stumbled across to the door, handling her multiple layers with some difficulty, and opened it. Vale and Silver were standing in the corridor. They were both still in last night's evening dress. Vale looked a bit raw around the edges; he had the air of a man who could certainly do with sleep but was far too busy to bother with it for the moment, and would simply make up the difference later. She'd seen him stay awake for two or three days on end and then catch up on his sleep as a lump sum once the current case was over. She rather envied him that talent.

Silver, on the other hand, looked in the prime of life, his eyes sparkling and his hat cocked jauntily. No doubt given his usual schedule—rise mid-afternoon, then stay out partying and debauching until the early hours of the morning—this was nothing unusual for him. Or perhaps his ebullience was simply due to getting to see her in a lacy dressing gown. She tugged the counterpane tighter round her.

Vale strode in without bothering to wait for a formal invitation, and dropped onto one of the flimsy chairs. Silver followed, settling himself with more grace. "Rather cold in here," he commented. "I hope that you found some way to keep yourself warm last night."

Well, that level of innuendo settled any questions about whether or not Silver knew about Kai's presence. Irene ignored his comment and knelt to poke up the fire. "You said you had information about the explosion," she remarked over her shoulder in Vale's direction.

"I do," Vale agreed. He slipped off his gloves and rubbed his hands together. "I'll say this for the current weather—anyone out on the streets last night or this morning has a reason to be there. Unfortunately, this has resulted in rather fewer witnesses than usual, or so Inspector Maillon informs me."

"Fewer than usual?" Irene took the remaining chair, huddling under the counterpane. She would have liked to get some clothes on, but this information was more urgent, and Vale in this current mood would barely notice if she was naked and painted with woad, other than to check her decorations for relevance to the current case. "Paris nightlife, I suppose?"

"Sadly curtailed at the moment," Silver agreed.

Vale nodded. "We do have witnesses to *when* the explosions took place—yes, explosions, Winters, and kindly don't interrupt me with questions, I'll get to that point in a moment. Small charges were laid at various rooms in the Richelieu Library, most of them dealing with matters of the *ancien régime*: histories, lineage, whatever. One of the other rooms was the one which we arrived through when we came to this world, which is now unfortunately past saving. Of course, to Inspector Maillon this only supports the anarchist theory, though he did remark to me that he found the activity almost too obvious."

Irene rubbed at her forehead. "Which it probably is. Given that it's an attack on a library, rather than anywhere more significant in terms of royalty or authority, can we assume that this is someone just using the anarchist movement to cover their strikes against the peace conference? Rather than genuine anarchist activity? Though if the inspector's noticing that something's off-key, then we may have even more problems. I'd rather not cope with the Paris gendarmerie as well as everything else."

"The inspector will probably be satisfied with the current story so long as no other compelling motive presents itself. And while we cannot be certain, the balance of probability seems to me to lean towards this attack being linked to the conference." Vale leaned forward. "Which brings us to the next point. Why? Why set off explosives in the Richelieu Library, rather than at some more useful location? Granted, the Countess did *try* to blow up this hotel, but if her primary motivation was to assault the dragon delegation, would it not have made more sense to attack the Ritz? I think you may need to reassess her priorities, Winters. The evidence suggests that she is targeting the facilitators of this potential alliance just as much as the participants. Are your superiors well-guarded?"

Irene rejected the immediate thrust of fear, forcing herself to think practically. "I believe so," she said slowly. "Besides Prutkov and Bradamant, there are half a dozen other Librarians currently in this hotel. They've been taking precautions." Though there were very few precautions one could take against an assassin who didn't care whether or not they survived, as long as they completed their mission. The thought chilled her more than the icy air. She withdrew from it into logical analysis. "But attacking the Richelieu Library isn't really very . . ." She looked for words. "*Effective.* Even if it did break the direct Traverse between this world and the Library, it wouldn't stop Librarians from being able to force a connection and get there from some other collection of books here in this world. I'm sure there are other libraries in Paris which could do the job. Either the Countess is very poorly informed—"

"Which is possible," Vale interrupted. "She might have thought that she was cutting you off from escape."

Irene nodded, acknowledging his point. "Or she thought that we'd all be haunting the place like bats, rather than sleeping in our hotel rooms. Though her spying efforts argue against that. Cancel that theory." She frowned, thinking about it. "Or it's another diversion."

"From what?" Vale demanded.

"I don't know. And that worries me."

Silver had been watching them both thoughtfully. Now he spoke. "I'd appreciate a private word with Miss Winters."

The fact that he was addressing her by her name, rather than some irritating epithet, was almost as disturbing as the fact that he wanted a *private word* with her. "I don't think I have anything to say that I'm not willing to share with Vale," Irene said carefully.

"I think you do." Silver's golden eyes glittered, for a moment as inhuman as any dragon's gaze, as he considered her. "Detective, you have my word that I don't intend any harm to Miss Winters. But all of us have our own private loyalties, don't we? I'd like to discuss a little point with her out of your hearing. She can make up her mind whether or not she wants to tell you about it afterwards."

Vale frowned. "Your choice, Winters," he said, dropping the decision in Irene's lap.

"You can go and wait in the bathroom with Prince Kai," Silver suggested helpfully. "Compare notes, if you like. Tell him what you noticed during the night's events that you haven't told me yet."

Vale shot him a look of pure dislike. "I assure you that I have not been concealing matters from *you* in particular. If I have been silent about some of my thoughts, it is because I require more information first."

"A shame that can't be said for everyone in this . . . hotel," Silver murmured. "Well, Miss Winters? Your decision?"

Irene would have liked the chance to think about it first—and, preferably, be fully dressed. But this was obviously related to Silver's earlier comment, yesterday, that they'd "talk later." Later had arrived. And she wanted to know what he was thinking. Reluctantly she nodded. "As you wish, Lord Silver. I apologise, Vale—hopefully this won't take long."

Vale rose. "I trust you won't be forcing your attentions on Winters," he said coldly to Silver.

"For a situation where everyone's talking about trusting each other, you both have remarkably little trust to spare for me," Silver said. He leaned back on his chair—though, Irene noted, he took care that the flimsy piece of furniture wouldn't give way and drop him ungracefully on the floor. "I'll try to be brief. Though that may depend on Miss Winters."

Vale snorted and retired to the bathroom.

Irene pulled the counterpane around her again. She was grateful for anything that shielded her from Silver's eyes. They were remarkably speaking, and right now they were conveying a message that he'd like to see her naked. "Well?" she asked.

"I should be asking you that." Silver permitted himself a languid smile. "For once, Miss Winters, I think I have *you* at *my* mercy, rather than the other way round."

Irene's throat was dry. "I don't understand you."

"You want to pretend ignorance? Understandable. You don't want to be in a situation where you have to outright admit what you've said to anyone else." Silver's smile sharpened. "I can understand that. You can bind yourself to speak the truth in your Language, while I can bind myself by my name and power. Really, Miss Winters—my little mouse—we have so much in common."

Irene should have known the polite nomenclature wouldn't last. In a way, it made things easier: she could simply be irritated, and use that to ward off softer thoughts about his eyes, or his skin, or his lips . . . damn it, he was getting to her even in spite of everything she knew about him. "I'm going to guess that you think you have some evidence about me or the Library that I don't want shared," she suggested.

"How very hypothetical. But yes." He had lowered his voice enough that it wouldn't be easily audible through the bathroom door. No doubt Kai and Vale were doing their best to listen. "Something along those lines. I can understand your wish to keep silent. The question is, how much are you prepared to give to keep *me* silent?"

Irene's heart sank. She'd been operating throughout on the principle that the Library was innocent of Ren Shun's death. But if Silver knew something that proved otherwise, then . . .

Her mind ran frantically through possible alternatives, and every single one came up with the same answer. She had no options. The Library was at stake. Her parents' lives were at stake. Silver had her trapped, and every passing second saw his smile widen as he enjoyed her silence.

He could be lying. This could all be a huge bluff. But she believed him when he said that he wanted the treaty signed. The Cardinal—and the Princess—had him boxed in on that side. Whatever else he might be up to, he wasn't trying to personally torpedo the negotiations.

Perhaps she could use that. "Will the Cardinal be pleased with you if you share this information publicly?" she asked.

Silver shrugged. "He certainly wouldn't. But there are all sorts of people I can tell about it without making things *public*. Including the Cardinal himself. I haven't told him *yet*. And let's be reasonable, my little mouse. Information can be released in many ways. Some are more damaging than others."

Irene could feel the metaphorical wall at her back. She was running out of manoeuvring room. She swallowed, gathering her thoughts. Silver held all the cards. He obviously thought that what he knew was significant enough that she'd have to make a deal with him. But what *could* be that damaging . . .

. . . and why did he assume that she already knew what it was?

"Let's assume that I'm prepared to agree," she said carefully. "But I have a condition."

Silver reached across to take her hand. His fingers stroked the underside of her wrist, as possessively as if he already owned her. "Very good, little mouse. Then it just comes down to negotiating the price."

Irene set her teeth, trying to ignore the pull of his presence. It urged her to believe that she was warm and comfortable, as soft as moulded wax and ready to relax into his arms. She took a deep breath of the cold air. *The temperature is freezing cold. This man is not a friend.*

"What *is* the secret?" she asked.

Silver's eyes narrowed, and his fingers tightened around her wrist. "Don't try to be funny."

"I'm not." Irene saw that she had thrown him off balance, and it helped her regain her own stability. "I accept that you have—or that you believe you have—information. I am prepared to negotiate. But I'm being quite honest here when I tell you that I don't know what the information is."

Kai and Vale probably had their ears plastered against the bathroom door. She wondered how long it would be before they decided that she needed protection whether she wanted it or not.

"Little mouse," Silver said, rising to stand over her, "I know from experience that you're extremely good at bluffing. That isn't going to work here. I want a decision from you."

Irene broke her hand free from his clasp and rose to her feet to look him in the eye. She left the counterpane on the chair. The cold air helped her focus, kept her mind clear and untangled from the heated interests of the body. "You don't believe me? I'll convince you. **I swear to you in the Language that I don't know what this piece of information of yours is.**"

Her words hung in the room like the chord of an organ. Silver took a step away from her, swaying back like a leopard. For a moment, almost too fast to be perceived, his face was full of indecision, and then he was all calm and grace again, but Irene had seen his uncertainty. It had been the expression of a cat trying to claim that he hadn't been going for the cream in the first place, after being found in the middle of shattered crockery and a destroyed kitchen.

A dainty knock came from the corridor.

Irene stalked across to the door and opened it. "Yes?" she demanded.

Mu Dan was standing there, fully dressed, fresh snow crusted on her hat and coat. "Ah, good," she said. "I'm glad you're already up. May I come in?"

"Certainly," Irene said. She decided that her best move at the moment was to keep Silver off balance. Throwing a dragon into the mix would certainly help.

Silver dropped back down into his chair and draped his arm across his face theatrically as Mu Dan stepped into the room. "These constant interruptions . . ."

Mu Dan frowned. "Really, Irene. Receiving a visitor like this, and in this state of dress—are you sure that you should be behaving in such a way?"

"I've got chaperones," Irene said, banging the door shut. She decided that there was no point in concealing things any longer. Silver already knew, and as for Mu Dan . . . well, Kai had said he'd been told to seduce Irene. Ao Ji wouldn't object if he'd succeeded. "Vale, Kai, you might as well come out of there now."

Vale was the first to emerge from the bathroom, with Kai a step behind him. Both of them scowled in Silver's direction. Silver very obviously ignored them.

Mu Dan's brows rose higher as she took in the gathering. "I wasn't aware that we were having a full meeting of the investigative team now. Or that His Highness"—she nodded to Kai—"would be present."

"Miss Winters is so enticing that we just can't stay away from her," Silver informed the ceiling.

"Have you finished your private conversation with Winters?" Vale enquired. "Then perhaps we can continue."

"For the moment," Silver said.

"I don't think so," Irene contradicted. She walked across to look down at him. "I think Lord Silver is about to share some valuable information with all of us."

Silence filled the room, spreading like ink in water. Finally Silver said, "Are you quite sure about this?"

Mu Dan's interruption had given Irene the chance to get her mind in order. And the thought that had come most prominently to her attention was that any attempt to cover things up was going to make things worse. She could certainly make a temporary bargain with Silver to cover this up—whatever *this* was. (It would be very embarrassing if *this* turned out to be something as petty as Kostchei being a vegetarian, or Coppelia using whale-oil on her clockwork joints.) She could sacrifice her own dignity or personal life if she had to.

But the moment that this piece of information came out via other means—whether through Silver or Irene or some other misdemeanour by the culprit—and people found out that Irene had tried to cover it up, then the Library would lose its credibility. At the moment the Library had to be open, public, and thoroughly non-secretive.

Irene could only pray that *this* secret would be manageable . . .

and that the people in the room with her would react in a more rational way than, say, dragon kings or Fae cardinals.

"We're a team," she said. "We're here to find out the truth. If you happen to know something relevant to the case, Lord Silver, then I would like you to share it with us. Whoever it incriminates."

"Fine. Very well." Silver flicked a glance around the room. "I would just like to point out, before this goes any further, that I offered Miss Winters the chance to discuss this in private first. I am not *trying* to cause trouble for her Library or impede the negotiations. And is it fair that the prince here should be listening?" His gesture indicated Kai's general area of the room. "Do I get to bring in more of my own kind, if we're adding more dragons to this . . . *team*?"

Kai was distinctly pale. It wasn't just the cold: whatever he was thinking had caused him to lose his colour. "Lord Silver"—he emphasised the *lord*—"has a point. And I'm prepared to leave the room, if you all wish me to. However, given that I already know that there's some sort of secret here to which Lord Silver is privy, and that it involves the Library, I'm not sure that having me leave at this point will make things much better. If I know what it is, that might at least mitigate the damage."

Assuming it's insignificant, Irene thought numbly. *Because if it is significant, then you'll be bound to share it with your uncle, and then who knows which way the cards may fall . . .* She wished that she could rewind the last half-hour of her life and somehow wipe Silver out of it.

"Lord Silver," she said. "I'll overlook your private discussion about this fact with me, if you'll overlook Kai's presence while we thrash this out. Deal?"

Silver's eyes glinted, and Irene had the impression that he was making a mental note for some future bill that she'd have to pay. With interest. But he nodded. "Very well. Deal. Here's what I was thinking."

He straightened up in the chair, no longer stressing the back to the breaking-point, and leaned forward in an imitation—conscious or not—of one of Vale's characteristic poses. "There is another hell in Paris besides the Cabaret de L'Enfer. And after all, Ren Shun's note only mentioned 'hell'—he never implied the cabaret connection. This hell—this *enfer*—is a place where one might reasonably think one could find books too—so it seems far more relevant. To me, at least, much though I prefer cabarets . . . We can't forget that Ren Shun overheard a conversation about a book the night before he died, one that apparently could be more important than the conference itself. But I digress. I'll be honest . . . no, *astonishingly* honest with you. When my little mouse here didn't mention it, I assumed she had a good reason for keeping her mouth shut, and due to my charitable and generous nature I decided to play along."

Irene searched her memories desperately. She couldn't think of anything that matched Silver's train of thought. "I'm sorry," she finally admitted—to the room, rather than to Silver. "I don't know what you're thinking of. I really don't."

"Your tastes in literature must be more limited than I'd thought," Silver said with relish. His eyes strayed to the unmade bed for a moment, and Irene felt herself flush with embarrassment. "But to the point. There is an area within the Richelieu Library known as the Enfer. And yes, detective, before you raise the issue—it was one of the places targeted in last night's bombing. Or should that be this morning? One loses track."

Irene's growing indignation got the better of her and took the reins. "How on *earth* could you know something about *any library in Paris* that I don't?"

"A question I asked myself," Silver murmured, "and the reason why I kept silent."

"Of course I know it was one of the places targeted in last night's bombing," Vale said calmly. His restraint was so carefully honed that the anger behind his words was obvious. "Did you really think that I hadn't checked the records, Lord Silver? I was going to raise the matter myself—but you insisted on speaking with Winters in private first."

Silver looked at Vale sidelong. "Ah. So it's not a case of you finding out, wanting to discuss it in private with Winters, and hoping that *I* hadn't realized it? How suspicious of me to think that you might have your own motives."

"I would find you more tolerable if I thought *you* had any motive besides blackmailing her for your personal gratification," Vale snapped. "This is hardly the first time, either."

Irene realized with alarm that the fragile peace was about to shatter. Vale and Silver would need only a moment's push to be at each other's throats. Kai would unhesitatingly side with Vale, in defence of Irene's honour; Mu Dan would be only too glad to join any faction against Silver. She had to get them back on the subject, fast.

"So what is the Enfer?" she demanded of Silver, stepping between him and Vale. "What books are stored there?"

"Erotica and pornography," Silver said with relish. "Only rare or valuable pieces, you understand. And other banned books, though they're not as interesting. One needs special authorisation to enter. I have visiting permission for the area in your own world." He smirked. "But my point, Miss Winters, is that even if you didn't know about it—which I admit is possible—are you confident that your superiors wouldn't? If they knew there was a library in Paris called Hell, and it might be related to the note in Ren Shun's pocket, why didn't they share that information with *you*?"

CHAPTER 17

Throughout Irene's life—and during the last year or two in particular—she had been growing more and more habituated to a key principle. *Don't waste time arguing against the impossible; accept it and find a solution.*

For a moment she wondered if Prutkov could have been as ignorant of the facts as she was. But she rejected the thought: he was Melusine's apprentice, and he was one of the people *organising* this peace conference. He would know as much as possible about this Paris—and about its libraries.

Which meant he'd lied to her.

No. He'd not *just* lied to her—that might be understandable in the line of duty. He'd lied to her when having that lie discovered would leave the Library even more endangered than it had been before. Irene could—barely—tolerate being used. But she would not accept being used *badly*.

A thread of fear ran down her spine at the thought of what

might be going on here. Prutkov being secretive was the *good* explanation. The alternatives were much worse. "All right," she said. "I take your point. Clearly I need to discuss this with my supervisor. Will you all let me look into this?" *Before you tell your superiors that the Library's untrustworthy,* she meant, and they all knew it. "It's possible that I'm just a victim of lack of communications, from someone who didn't think that I . . . *needed to know.*"

"I think we can agree to that," Vale said.

"Speak for yourself," Mu Dan said, a snort implicit in her voice. "This is either incompetence on the Library's part or deliberate malice. You can't expect me to keep silent about it."

Irene wished for the counterpane back. Her feet were aching with the cold. She saw Kai open his mouth to speak, and she cut in before Mu Dan could reject it as personal partiality. "But can I ask you to keep silent until I've investigated? Do you believe that I'm sincere, at least?"

"Anyone can *seem* sincere," Mu Dan countered. She pointed a finger at Silver. "*He* seems sincere."

"Do you accept, on the evidence so far, that I'm acting in good faith—and that I honestly didn't know about this Enfer business?"

Mu Dan considered, then shrugged. "Yes, I do. But, Irene, consider my position. I can't conceal secrets from His Majesty Ao Ji."

Irene noticed the interesting hierarchy indicated there. Not *my lord* or *my superior,* but just *His Majesty*. This was an avenue she could work with. "You're an *independent* judge-investigator," she countered, turning Mu Dan's earlier words back against her. "I'm sure there have been times when you've held back from immediate prosecution in order to confirm the full facts of a case. Let's be honest." She looked round at the room. "If anyone tries to take this to my superiors here and now, those same superiors are going to put the blame on me. They'll say I was ignorant, or I misunderstood, or something. They might take me off the case—and then you'd have to work with someone who might not be as . . . sincere."

It would have been nice if they'd disagreed. But they didn't.

"We do unfortunately live in a world of politics," Mu Dan finally said. "Very well, I agree, on the understanding that you'll share your results as soon as you have them. And what about His Highness here?" She indicated Kai. "What will you say to your uncle?"

The edge to Mu Dan's voice suggested a personal dimension, possibly even a grudge towards her fellow dragon, and Irene noted that down for later investigation.

But Kai merely shrugged. "As various people have pointed out, I'm not a member of this investigative group, and thus I am under no obligation to report its findings. Regarding my obligations to my uncle . . . I'm making a personal judgement that allowing Irene to investigate will be the most productive course of action. Is that acceptable?"

Mu Dan nodded curtly and the tension in the room went down a notch. She turned to Vale. "So what did you find out about last night?"

Irene retrieved her counterpane while Vale recounted last night's investigation, with occasional input from Silver. It boiled down to the fact that yes, there had been explosions; yes, there had been anarchist slogans daubed on the walls; and yes, there were currently no clues. Or should that be no, there were currently no clues? It was difficult to be sure of the proper grammar when everyone was gloomily agreeing on the absence of evidence. At least the immediate animosity had been defused.

"There's something I've been thinking about," she said. "I don't know how long they had to do it, but I'm assuming that representatives of all three sides gathered as much information about this Paris as possible—before the conference started. Nobody was going to jump into these waters unprepared."

Silver frowned. "True, but unfortunately the Cardinal isn't sharing anything that significant or useful."

"Yes," Irene agreed. "I can accept that. But who was doing the investigation on the dragon side?"

"Ren Shun," Mu Dan said. "It would have been one of his duties, naturally."

"But he wouldn't do it himself, would he?"

Mu Dan tilted her head thoughtfully. She'd taken one of the chairs and was sitting in it as primly as an etiquette illustration. "No. He would have his agents do that. You think that I should press for access to his servants and private records?"

Vale nodded. "Winters is right. Perhaps while he was researching this location and the peace conference participants, Ren Shun stumbled across something which caused his murder."

"His Majesty won't like it," Mu Dan said. "He wanted to keep this investigation entirely separate from Ren Shun's private life. But I can see your point. I'll make the request for access."

"You hadn't made it already?" Irene asked, as innocently as possible.

"As a matter of course, yes, but it had been turned down. I'll stress the point."

Irene glanced across the room at Kai and saw that he was looking thoughtful. She knew what was on his mind. Mu Dan was being less than honest or forthcoming here—but Vale, who lacked

Irene's experience with dragons, might not have realized it. "Correct me if I'm wrong," she said, "but I understand that most dragons of Ren Shun's rank would have at least one private servant to see to things that were beneath their master's dignity. Even if Ren Shun was a spymaster, he wouldn't necessarily go out on the town every night to collect reports. That would be what his trusted staff did. Dragon society is very hierarchical. I've come to appreciate that fact recently. And Ren Shun's servants would be particularly loyal to him—and particularly interested in avenging his murder, one hopes. So where *are* they?"

Mu Dan was silent, tapping her fingers on the gilded arm of her chair. When she spoke, she was clearly picking her words with care. "Irene, you've asked me to let you handle your own affairs inside the Library. In return, I formally request that you let me pursue this trail myself. I know that something's wrong. What's that phrase from the play? Something is rotten in the state of Denmark."

"You think there's obstruction at a high level?" Vale said, leaning hawk-like towards her.

"I think there's obstruction at *some* level," Mu Dan returned, "but I need more information. As you've pointed out, we usually have servants. *I* have servants. But right now, I'm isolated here without my staff, and with nobody but you to depend on. This is not a state of affairs which I enjoy."

"Ah, sweet honesty," Silver drawled. "The pin that pops the boil and brings all the inflammation to the surface. Should I confess my suspicions now as well, just to complete the triangle?"

Kai and Vale exchanged glances. "Well," Kai said, "since we're on the subject, you could tell us if it's relevant that the Cabaret de L'Enfer was stinking of chaos and has a witch in its back rooms."

"Don't think you can shock me, princeling. The detective already told me about that." Silver shrugged elaborately. "And *he* said that *you* didn't think it was significant enough to warrant further investigation. So stop pointing fingers. Given that I arrived in Paris at the same time as everyone else—and I can prove it—I don't think *I* should be your prime suspect. But I can certainly try to shake a little more information out of my own kindred, if only to save us from unjust accusations."

"Right," Irene said as firmly as possible, trying to regain control of the situation. "Other immediate trails to follow from last night are the rats and cats, the cake, the apples, the explosives, and the chlorine gas—I'm assuming it wouldn't be *that* easy to get hold of explosives and chlorine gas, even in Paris?"

Silver raised a languid hand. "I'll take the cake—that is, I'll investigate the bakers. And of course I'm still looking into the question of theatres, after that anarchist attack on the dragon king. But alas, I have nothing to show, except for a growing set of entertaining nude studies for my private collection. I'm wondering whether or not we really have a connection here. Are the anarchists linked to the Blood Countess? Or do we have two separate enemy factions? And any number of theatres could theoretically be harbouring the Blood Countess in their basements, attics, or somewhere backstage, but . . ." He shook his head. "No evidence."

"If there is a link and she was hiding out in one of the theatres, wouldn't it be saturated in chaos?" Mu Dan asked. "Wouldn't you be able to recognize such a thing the moment you set foot inside it?"

"Yes, except for two points. The first is that she would be *hiding*. I believe she's muffling her influence in order to go unseen by both sides, otherwise either we or someone else would have found her already. And the second point is that I'm finding Paris rather a mess, to use the vernacular. Have you ever seen one of those weather maps with wavy pressure zone lines all over it?" He waited for Mu Dan's nod. "It resembles something like that. There have been so many powerful ones of my kind—and your kind—wandering around the city that it's frankly impossible for *any* of us to sense her unless we happen to walk directly into her lair. Surely you've noted the same thing yourself, while you've been making the rounds."

"Can you scry for her with the Language, Irene?" Kai asked.

"I doubt it," Irene said reluctantly. "The only times I've managed to do such a thing in the past, I've had a direct connection to the person in question. I've used their blood or had their Library name."

"Could you use the cats from the cellar?" Mu Dan asked. "Put some sort of metaphysical leash on them?"

"I don't know," Irene admitted. "I'll investigate. It's not something I've tried before. And it couldn't be any harder chasing a cat through Paris than it has been tracing some of the people at this conference!"

"Surely you're exaggerating," Kai said.

"I'm not," Irene said. "Really, I'm not. You haven't seen the witness statements, have you? Well, trust me, the concept of 'work ethic' seems rather lacking round here. 'Junket' would be more appropriate. The principals on both sides are the only ones who are doing any real negotiating or have any say in the eventual result. Everyone else is just here as servants or staff or bodyguards, or simply to bulk out the retinue to the same size as the other group. A dozen of the lower-ranking people from both hotels were sneaking out on the night of the murder to hit the theatres and cabarets, even if they tried to claim otherwise. The testimony from the servants and the hotel staff proves it. At least two of the dragons have been spending their spare time art shopping for their private collections. Green and Purple—or Thompson and Thomson, or whatever they call themselves, from the Fae delegation—apparently want to sign up with the Paris police or the Foreign Legion or anywhere that will send them on interesting jobs. Heaven help anyone who *does* sign them up. Even the Cardinal admits to hanging out at rare bookshops. A dozen of the witness statements confess to being in someone else's rooms. Three of them contradict each other. And pretty much every single servant from both sides is refusing to contradict anything their master or mistress says! If we want to find out who killed Ren Shun, we're going to need something more definite than 'if my lord says he was in his room, then of course he was in his room.'"

"An excellent summary, Winters," Vale agreed unhelpfully. "So what are your thoughts?"

Irene looked round the room. Two dragons, one Fae, and two humans. In a way, it was a positive omen for any future peace treaty that they could all be in the same room together, planning a cooperative effort. "I'll look into what my superiors know," she said, "whether or not they think I 'need to know.' And I'll see if the link from the Richelieu Library to the Library is still there or if it's been broken. I'll examine the crime scene there from a Librarian's perspective too. And I'll look into chasing cats. Lord Silver, please add the Cabaret de L'Enfer to your list of places to visit. I'd be interested in your opinion." She waited for his gracious nod before continuing. "Mu Dan, you've told us that you'll investigate Ren Shun's servants and his research. How are you with chlorine gas and explosives? Or poisoned apples?"

"Underinformed," Mu Dan admitted. "I'm used to having the

skilled members of my staff perform those analyses. Perhaps that is something Vale should take to Inspector Maillon?"

Vale nodded. "That I can do, and I've been given the equipment for some scientific analysis. I should have some data and a list of addresses of chlorine suppliers by lunch: the inspector is not overly gifted, but his records are sound. We may be able to track down the agents of the Countess by practical methods, if not by metaphysical ones." The idea clearly pleased him.

"Excellent," Irene said. "And what about a connection between the previous assassination of Minister Zhao and Ren Shun's murder? We'd thought"—well, *she'd* thought, at least—"that Mei Feng might have useful knowledge, since both she and Minister Zhao served the Queen of the Southern Lands."

"I was going to mention that," Mu Dan said. "Vale, Mei Feng will permit you to interview her at your convenience. She will be glad to discuss the matter with you."

Vale's brows rose. "Interesting. And suggestive."

"Of what?" Mu Dan asked, with a trace of irritation. Clearly she'd rather have been the one doing the questioning.

"Anything out of the ordinary is suggestive," Vale said blandly. "Rest assured that I will keep you informed."

"Kai," Irene said hastily, "can we call on your assistance, or does your uncle require you today?"

"My uncle has requested that I attend him as a secretary, and naturally I am glad to oblige," Kai said, in tones that couldn't have been faulted by the highest arbiters of etiquette. But regret showed in his eyes: clearly he would much rather have been out and around Paris, contributing to the investigation.

A memory surfaced at the back of Irene's mind. "Actually, there is something that you could do for me—and I don't think it would conflict with your obligations. Could you set up a meeting for me with Li Ming, seeing as he's your uncle Ao Shun's courtier?"

Mu Dan was motionless under her cape, but Irene had the impression that her shoulders had stiffened. If she'd been a cobra she would have flickered nictitating membranes, and possibly even spread her hood in warning.

"Easy enough," Kai said. "But why Li Ming in particular?"

Interesting: clearly Kai didn't know of any quarrel between Ren Shun and Li Ming, such as Mu Dan had hinted at. And clearly Mu Dan saw no need to share. "I've heard of a possible issue between Li Ming and Ren Shun," Irene said diplomatically. Let everyone assume it was Librarian gossip if necessary. "I don't believe Li Ming is the sort of person to go round committing murder—"

"I assure you he could, my little mouse," Silver said. "Without a second thought."

Irene wondered what caused *that* reaction. "If you will allow me to finish my sentence," she said, "I don't believe he's the sort of person to go round committing murder, then dumping the body where everyone would find it."

Silver tapped a finger against his lips. "Fair point."

Kai didn't actually disagree. Which also said something about Li Ming's reputation among dragons. "I can tell him you want to speak with him," he said. "But we have several conference sessions scheduled, and then it's the opera in the evening. The principals on both sides are attending."

"Which opera?" Vale asked.

"Tannhäuser."

"Hmm. The Paris version, or the Vienna version?"

"The Paris version, I heard," Silver said, "which should mean we get the full ballet in act one—"

"Much as I usually like opera," Irene said through gritted teeth, "at the moment, I'd only take an interest if a masked maniac was about to drop a chandelier on the heads of the audience. Which I hope is not going to happen."

"At least it's not *Siegfried,*" Kai said. "The whole dragon-killing thing could imply *such* an insult . . ." He caught the look in Irene's eye and smiled as he pulled back from his digression. "I should probably be getting back to the Ritz. Irene—Mu Dan, gentlemen—I know that I'm not directly involved in this investigation, but you have my word that I will cooperate in any way possible."

The room felt that much colder with him gone, and Irene wished again that everyone else had turned up a few hours later. For just a little while last night she'd been able to forget the pressures of the investigation and everything that was at stake. Now it was crowding back in on her. And she faced the additional issue that someone higher up in the Library could be guilty of anything from concealing information to active malfeasance.

"We'd better get started," she said. "I apologise for throwing you out of my bedroom, but I need to put some clothes on . . ."

"Of course," Mu Dan said, rising. "I'll be in touch as soon as I have something to report."

"As will I." Vale held the door for the dragon. "Be careful, Winters. Of all of us here, you are the one who's given the Countess personal reason to dislike you. Watch your step."

Irene had been trying *not* to think about that. "Trust me, I will," she said. "I have no intention of complicating matters even further."

Silver was the last to the door, and he paused there for a moment, until Irene was forced to ask, "Is there anything further?"

"Why, yes." Silver's teeth gleamed as he smiled. "Yes, there is, my little mouse."

"And that would be?" Irene supposed it would be too much to expect him to apologise for earlier.

"I'm just musing on the fact that every member of this team is hiding a scandal. Except me, of course. Quite a change from usual."

Irene frowned. "We've already been through that, haven't we?"

"I think we omitted something." His smile was less pleasant now, and more the curled lip of a man who feels himself in control. "Your friend the detective, for instance."

Irene snorted. "That's ridiculous. Vale's about the only person here who isn't hiding something."

"Is he? Tell me, Miss Winters . . ." Silver let the moment draw out. "What do you think the dragons would say if they found out the detective had Fae blood somewhere in his family tree?"

"That is a ridiculous attempt to stir up trouble—" Irene started, knowing that she had to say something, that silence would be an admission of the truth.

"Neither ridiculous nor an attempt," Silver contradicted her. "I'm sure if anyone thought to look, they could find proof."

Irene weighed her options. Silver had hinted at Vale's family bloodline before. She'd ignored it—she honestly didn't *care* about it. But under the current circumstances, with people eager to take offence, this might indeed raise claims of bias about any evidence Vale found.

And then two facts clicked together in her mind, answering a previous question. "Now I know why they brought you in as the Fae representative," she said slowly. "It's not because you're an investigator. It's because they think they can use you to control Vale."

Silver tipped his hat to her. "I couldn't possibly comment. Just remember that *I* didn't tell you that. And I've grown rather fond of you, Miss Winters, so as the detective said—watch your step. I wouldn't want to lose you."

CHAPTER 18

The morning was an exercise in slowly growing frustration. Prutkov was in a meeting, or possibly in several meetings (Irene refused to accept that he was capable of splitting himself into multiple Prutkovs; that was not a Librarian ability), or at any rate he was always somewhere *else*. There were at least four ongoing seminars, meetings, or breakout sessions (that last was Sterrington's influence; she had apparently internalised too much management literature) going on in different parts of the hotel. Irene was constantly being informed that Prutkov was either unavailable or she'd just missed him.

She didn't *want* to think that he was deliberately avoiding her, but . . .

Her mood wasn't improved by the security presence that clogged the corridors, or the mix of chaotic and orderly power that ebbed and fluxed through the hotel—like an ocean tide trying to simultaneously obey two moons. Both Hsien, the dragons' main human servant, and Erda, his matching number on the Fae side, had nodded to her in passing in a friendly way. But they were clearly preoccupied with their own jobs.

And the cats had not survived the night, which ruled out any attempt to find the Countess via enchanted feline. Irene still wasn't exactly sure *how* she could have done it, but it would have been worth trying.

Irene was bitterly conscious that her morning so far had been deeply unproductive. It had just passed eleven o'clock, and people were taking temporary pauses from their meetings and mingling in the hotel corridors or sipping coffee and devouring cakes. And there was *still* no sign of Prutkov. It was as if the man had vanished into thin air.

Reluctantly she came to a decision. If she couldn't find him to ask any questions, then she was simply going to have to be a little more proactive.

Fortunately she already knew where his suite was, so she didn't need to ask anyone. It was always a good idea to avoid asking questions that might raise suspicion later.

His room was on the same corridor as those of Kostchei and Coppelia—both of whom were engaged in the talks downstairs. On the negative side this made them both unavailable for consultation too, but on the positive side they wouldn't interrupt Irene while she was up here. She reassured herself that she wasn't exactly going to break into Prutkov's rooms and search them for evidence of treason. She was just checking Prutkov's room to see if he was here, given that he wasn't elsewhere.

But as it turned out, someone else had beaten her to it.

Irene turned the corner of the corridor, her step silent on the thick carpet, to see a maid kneeling in front of Kostchei's door, peering at the lock. It wasn't even the sort of pose that could have been excused as *trying to polish up the brasswork, ma'am*. It was the sort of assessment that went with judging lockpick size and technique.

Half a dozen reactions flew through Irene's mind, from shock to anger to a certain dry amusement that someone else had gotten there first. But the most significant one was jubilation. A lead!

She walked softly but quickly towards the maid, whose attention was on the lock in front of her. As she advanced down the corridor, she felt chaos prickle against her skin, deepening like a hive's angry buzz as she approached the girl. That settled it. This might not be the Countess herself—it would be very out of character for someone of that status to lower herself to dress as a maid and pick locks—but it was certainly one of her servants.

The girl made a noise of excitement and pulled a hairpin from her neat bun, reaching forward to insert it into the lock.

"I don't think so," Irene said. Her hand closed on the maid's wrist.

The maid dropped her hairpin and looked up at Irene in shock. And at that moment Irene realized although she could *see* the maid, and although the maid was right next to her, she wasn't exactly sure what the maid looked like. There was hair, certainly. It was tied back in a modest style. There was a face—a beautiful, charming, sweet young face, full of girlish modesty and innocent wilfulness, and generally deserving a bookful of romantic poetry to describe it properly. But as for the precise details . . . it was as if someone had delivered the basic notes for a theatrical role to the back of Irene's brain—*maid, young, pretty, innocent*—and left her to decide on the exact details. This wasn't just one of the hotel maids here, empowered or enchanted or whatever. This woman was a very powerful Fae.

The maid jerked upright and kicked at Irene's shins, trying to make a run for it. Irene's hand stayed clamped shut around the maid's wrist. Her current prisoner might be about as safe to hang on to as an enraged tiger, but she had also been about to break into Kostchei's room. And Irene wanted some answers before letting her go. "Please calm down," she said, as soothingly as she could. "I'm not about to hurt you, but I want to know what you're doing here."

"I dropped something and was picking it up?" the maid—the Fae—said hopefully.

"Plausible reasons, please," Irene said patiently. "That wouldn't even have worked when I was eleven years old and still at school."

"I was doing up my shoelace?"

For a moment Irene almost *believed* that. Then the Library brand across her back flared like a sunburn, and the words rearranged themselves in her head from *a plausible reason, let the poor little thing go* to *a blatant lie, pick her up and shake her till the truth comes out*. "Third time lucky . . ." she said through gritted teeth.

Then they both heard the sound of multiple heavy footsteps approaching. The maid's eyes went wide with panic. "Please don't let them catch me, and I promise I'll tell you why!"

This was a Fae formally giving her word. Assurances didn't get much better than this. "Right," Irene said, and dragged her along the corridor to what she was fairly sure was an unused suite. She'd been told that all the rooms surrounding the main Library contingent had been booked and deliberately left empty as a safety measure. She hoped that was correct. **"Lock, open,"** she hissed in the Language. The moment she heard the lock click, she pushed the maid in, stepped in herself, then shut the door behind her and relocked it.

They were only just in time. They heard the footsteps pass by outside—two men, heavy, not bothering to speak, walking in step with each other—and continue down the corridor.

"Very well," Irene said, finally releasing the maid's wrist. "Why?"

The maid rubbed her wrist gingerly, her eyes swimming with tears. "You're not very kind," she whispered. "Are you someone's stepmother?"

"I'm not even someone's mother," Irene said, trying to be firm. It was difficult. Every finer emotion that she possessed was urging her to be nicer to the poor girl in front of her. She was clearly an innocent, someone who'd been caught up in this against her will, someone whose beauty and dignity showed that she was of noble blood . . .

Irene dug her fingernails into her palms and forced herself to actually *look* at the storm of emotions currently washing through her head. What was she thinking? And why was she thinking it? And what sort of Fae would she be having those thoughts about?

The answer froze her in her tracks. "You're the Princess . . ." she whispered. She wanted to swear, but she couldn't bring herself to do it. It seemed *wrong* to use such words in front of royalty. *And if I'm thinking in terms of it being morally wrong rather than politically stupid, then I'm already compromised . . .*

The Princess blushed. "Oh, heavens. You recognize me!"

"More deduction than recognition." The situation was still expanding to reach its potential for full-scale disaster in Irene's mind. Which was worse? For the head of the Fae delegation to be caught breaking into the Library delegation's private rooms (quite unlike one of the Librarians, such as her, doing so, of course) or for Irene to have been manhandling the Princess? "Madam—Your Highness—what on earth are you *doing* up here, and why?"

"I promised I'd tell you," the Princess said reluctantly. "But I must ask you never, never to speak of it to another living soul!"

Irene felt the threads of oath and story forming round her like a strait jacket, trembling against her lips. If she even so much as breathed a half-formed *yes,* then she'd be bound by her own words. The Fae in front of her might look like a teenage maid-of-all-work in plain black dress and white apron and cap, but she was a nexus of chaos. She was a very long way from being human. In her own way, she was just as much a threat as the Cardinal. If Irene let herself be caught up in the Princess's narrative, then she wouldn't be able to drag herself out of that undertow—even with her oath to the Library itself.

She forced herself to think calmly and logically, to step out of the wellspring of emotion that the Princess inspired. *She's an archetype. The innocent princess, disguised as a working girl, heroically venturing into danger. I have to work with that.*

Irene took a careful step back and curtseyed. "Your Highness, do you know who I am?"

"No," the Princess admitted.

Which meant that Irene's role in the story wasn't fixed yet. Good. "I am a Librarian," Irene said firmly, "and I'm sworn to find the murderer of Lord Ren Shun."

"Noble paladin!" the Princess gasped. "Oh, thank heavens that the kindly stars have led us together. Now I *know* I can trust you. But you must beware. Treason is afoot!"

Irene found her usual mental reaction of *you really shouldn't trust me, you know* being drowned out by a wave of optimism. The

Princess was almost *sparkling* through her commoner disguise, her hair as black as the wings of ravens, her eyes as blue as sapphires, her skin as white as snow. She glowed with the full inner beauty of her royal blood and pure soul. A wave of tenderness washed over Irene, much stronger than any lust that Silver could excite, much purer, much more sincere. She wanted to take the woman in front of her into her arms and . . .

Irene mentally forced herself to pull back and remember who and where she was. She'd apparently managed to insert herself into the Princess's narrative as a heroic knight. That was good. That would get the Princess to trust her. The only problem with this was that heroic knights had a tendency to fall in love with the Princess.

"Your Highness, we haven't got much time," she said. "Do your own people know you're here?"

"No. I was afraid they might try to stop me." The Princess looked around nervously, as though a wicked stepmother was about to jump out at her from under the table or behind the curtains.

"How did you get away from all the meetings?"

"I said that I needed to powder my nose, and I slipped away before anyone noticed," the Princess said smugly. "I thought that if I searched the bedrooms of all the important Library officials, I'd be able to find proof which would identify the traitor. But you stopped me." She drooped like a snowdrop, tears showing in her eyes. "Now I may never be able to find out who it is—unless you can help me."

Words along the lines of *of course I'll help you, just tell me what you want me to do* bubbled up in Irene's mouth, begging to be said. She bit her tongue hard. "Your Highness," she said, wincing, "please tell me why you suspect treason, and why you think one of the Library officials is a traitor."

"I just *know*!" She fixed Irene with a vulnerable deep blue gaze. "A woman knows these things. The Countess is working with one of the Librarians, I'm sure of it." She shuddered, genuine fear showing in her eyes. "I can't sleep for thinking about it. Even though she's of my own kind, she's in my nightmares. I know she wants to destroy this peace conference, but it's not just that. She wants the blood of maidens. She wants *me*."

"But the Cardinal—" Irene tried, fighting the urge to take the Princess in her arms and protect her from the cruel world. The more pragmatic part of her mind was noting the Princess's absolute fear and abhorrence of the Countess. *Is she* the *ultimate wicked stepmother? Or at least* an *ultimate wicked stepmother*?

The Princess clasped her hands together. "He's too good, too noble a man to understand the sort of evil that people can do. He'd just laugh at me and pat my head. No, this was the only thing I could do! And now that you understand, you'll help me . . . won't you?"

Irene sourly reflected that this archetypal Princess clearly had the traditional attributes of selfless innocence, courage, purity and sweetness. But she also had another traditional character trait of fairy-tale princesses: the ability to totally misjudge other people and think the best of them while they were plotting to cut out your heart, or poison your apples, or maroon you on a desert island, or whatever. Granted the Cardinal might not be planning to go *that* far, but Irene wouldn't in her wildest imaginings have described him as a pure and noble man who was too good for this world.

On the other hand . . . the Princess was a very powerful Fae, possibly the most powerful Irene had ever met. (*Yet,* the gloomy part of her mind added.) She lived in a cloud of narrative imperative. She'd managed to escape while "powdering her nose" because that was the sort of thing that happened in stories. Irene had come along at exactly the right moment—again, because that was how stories worked. And Irene was now on the verge of agreeing to do anything she said, because that was how people behaved in stories if you were a princess.

But the story could go many different ways from here. It might have a happy ending, where the Princess told Irene exactly what she needed to know to find the putative traitor. Or on the other hand, it might become a dramatic tragedy, if someone came along at exactly the wrong moment and caught them together—

There was a knock on the door.

The Princess opened her mouth to squeak in shock. Irene moved faster than she'd thought was possible and got her hand over the Princess's mouth. Fortunately she didn't have to struggle with any chivalric urges. This was apparently the right thing to do, in narrative terms.

"Nobody in here," someone in the corridor said. "This'll do." A key turned audibly in the lock.

Irene looked round for a hiding place. They'd never make it to the bathroom in time. The nearest—the only—possibility of shelter was behind the heavy gold brocade curtains. She pulled the Princess over and they scurried behind the curtains together, pressing up against the window, which led onto the balcony. Snow outside lashed against the windowpanes, a hissing wind-driven veil of whiteness that blurred the balcony and the traffic in the street below. It also made the glass bitterly cold to the touch.

Chaos wrapped around Irene as she stood shoulder to shoulder with the Princess. Her brand itched and burned across her back like the worst excesses of chickenpox or measles, impossible to ignore.

In the room beyond, the door clicked open. "Dark in here," a strange woman's voice said. "Shall I open the curtains?"

"Just turn the light on, if you must," Prutkov answered. "Don't move anything or leave any traces." It was definitely his voice. Irene froze as she recognized it. She'd wanted to catch up with him and ask some questions, but these weren't the circumstances she'd had in mind.

There was a click as the light went on, then the sound of someone sitting down. "This place stinks of chaos. So what's next on the schedule?"

"Hopefully nothing," Prutkov said. Another creak. Him sitting down too? Irene wasn't going to try peering through the crack where the curtains joined. That was just asking for discovery. "The less you have to do, the better. What's our team been up to?"

"They met in Winters's room, then split up to investigate stuff," the woman reported. "The prince went back to his uncle. Mu Dan is looking into something at the dragons' hotel. The detective's gone to visit the police inspector again. And the Fae's out hunting the Countess and the anarchists in the city. He's going round cake shops at the moment. Borges is following him."

"He's not shadowing the detective?"

"There's too much chance of the detective spotting someone trailing him. The Fae's less observant. Do you think they'll be able to find the Countess?"

"They'd better." Prutkov's voice was distant, as though he was considering multiple options. "We need to locate her fast, before Ao Ji can escalate the situation any further. It was bad enough *be-*

fore Ren Shun's death, but now it's even worse. We're lucky the Cardinal's playing the long game."

"I've been wondering," the woman said tentatively.

"Yes?"

"Who did kill Ren Shun?"

"The Countess, of course," Prutkov said sharply. "That's been agreed."

"Agreed. Right." The woman's voice oozed disbelief.

"Are you trying to be awkward?"

"I'm curious. It's a question *you're* going to have to answer, after all. Why would the Countess kill *Ren Shun,* rather than go for Ao Ji or the Princess?"

"That one's simple," Prutkov said bitterly. "It's because of all the people involved in this mess, removing him did the most damage. He was one of the few people *His Majesty* Ao Ji would actually listen to. Other dragons such as Li Ming and Mei Feng didn't command the same respect. And killing him—like that, in particular—was a mortal insult. It was the most damaging thing she could have done. Short of blowing up this hotel."

And how, Irene wondered behind the curtain, *did the* Countess *know that it would cause the most damage?*

"Yes, I heard you almost got dynamited last night—in a library too. Some people would have called that karmic justice."

"You're being very pushy. Are you trying to make a point?"

"No. We're all in this together. Though you'd better work out a new way for us to stay in touch. Now that they've upped the security here, there's more chance of someone noticing Borges or me when we come in to report."

"That's true," Prutkov admitted. "But physical letters are risky as well. Permanent evidence is a dangerous thing." He hesitated, considering. "For the moment, run silent and don't try to contact me unless you get a lead on where the Countess is, or if Winters's team is about to do something drastic. With a bit of luck, we can wrap this up tomorrow."

"I don't know why you put her on the case in the first place," the woman said with a snort. "The girl's a magnet for trouble."

"It wasn't *my* idea," Prutkov protested. "If it had been my choice, I'd have picked someone a bit more versed in the art of manipulation. But at least she's obviously sincere. That's buying us more time, and at the moment time is what we need to get the treaty agreed. And if we need a scapegoat at some point, her behaviour's dubious enough that she can take the blame."

Well, they do say that eavesdroppers never hear good of themselves, Irene reflected drily. This was all highly informative, and she was delighted to be finding out even more about Prutkov than she'd expected. But she knew that it came at a price—falling in with Fae narrative. Hiding behind curtains like this and hearing top-secret conversations was the sort of thing that happened in stories. And in at least half of those stories, the person eavesdropping was dramatically discovered . . .

Chairs creaked as both the people on the other side of the curtain rose. "Very well," the woman said. "Good luck with wrangling this lot."

"People can be managed," Prutkov said calmly, "and all the individuals we're working with here, whether dragons, Fae, or Librarians, are still just people. You do your job—"

Prompted by some instinct, Irene glanced sideways and saw the Princess screw up her face as she struggled not to sneeze.

Imagination immediately painted a horrifying picture of what would come next. The noisy sneeze. The pause on the other side of the curtain. The ripping away of concealment as Prutkov found them both there. The possible consequences.

Irene silently locked one hand over the Princess's mouth and pinched the bridge of the Fae's nose with her other hand. *Don't sneeze,* she pleaded with her eyes, *just hold it in a little longer, just keep quiet for a moment until they're gone . . .*

"—and I'll do mine," Prutkov finished. "Till later."

Irene listened to the footsteps on the other side of the curtain, the click of the light switch, and the door opening, then closing. The Princess was wriggling in Irene's grasp like a kitten, but she couldn't break free. *Apparently really powerful Fae are vulnerable if it's in line with their own personal archetype. Princesses can be manhandled because that's what happens to princesses. That might be useful for future reference. Though what would the Blood Countess be vulnerable to?* It was something to think about.

The room was silent. With a prayer that the two others really had left and weren't just stealthily lying in wait, Irene released the Princess, who promptly started sneezing loudly enough to shake the curtains.

Irene stumbled out into the room. Staying that close to the Princess had been like being wrapped in a drugged haze, with the brand across her back a heavy weight that she felt with every breath. She still wanted to take the Princess tenderly in her arms, to look deep into her eyes and to swear with every atom of her being that she'd protect her, that she'd keep her safe, that nobody would ever be able to hurt her again, that through knowing her Irene had become a better person, that . . .

As Irene had discovered before, knowing that you were under Fae influence did not necessarily help you break free of it. Physical distraction, however, could help. She took hold of the lobe of her ear and pinched it hard enough that tears came to her eyes.

"I told you there was treason afoot!" the Princess announced triumphantly, her sneezing gone as if she'd never so much as sniffed a grain of dust. "Now we just need to search everyone's rooms to find out who the traitors are."

Irene realized that the Princess hadn't recognized Prutkov's voice, thank goodness, and reoriented her priorities. Forget catching Prutkov. Besides, he obviously wasn't going to answer her questions anyhow. She needed to get the Princess back to the rest of the Fae delegation before she could do anything that might start a war. "Your Highness, leave that to me. I know the people involved. I can find out what's going on."

"Will you?" The Princess somehow caught Irene's hands in her own tender fingers. "Will you swear that you'll find out and report back to me?"

Her innocent gaze caught Irene like a laser cannon focusing its sights, and Irene's words dried up in her throat. It didn't matter that the Princess apparently had the brain of a guinea pig, the standards of a chivalric romance, and the sense of priority of a lemming. When she asked someone to cooperate, and put all her heart and soul behind it, her target couldn't refuse. It wasn't even deliberate malice and control; it would have been easier for Irene to resist if it had been. The Princess wasn't consciously trying to *manipulate* Irene—that wasn't the sort of thing that beautiful fairy-tale princesses did. She just wanted Irene to help her.

Irene shuddered with the effort of trying to say *no*. It wasn't working. Her mouth wanted to say *yes*. Her *heart* wanted to say *yes*. Saying *yes* was the right thing to do, the proper thing to do, the *only* thing that she could do . . .

She tried to look away from the deep, melting blue eyes of the Princess, but she couldn't even focus on anything else, not even the window beyond her and the snow outside. At the back of her mind she tried to frame some sort of logical idea for escape, some way out of this whirlpool of emotion and need.

What she needed was order. And there was none inside this room. But maybe outside, where Ao Ji's temper made the snow dance and the winds howl . . .

"Windows, break." The words twisted on her vocal cords, but the Language gave her strength, and the gasp of surprise from the Princess as the Fae was distracted gave Irene even more freedom. **"Snow, come in!"**

The windows shattered in a crash of glass, and wind and snow came funnelling into the room in a furious blast of pure winter. The air was full of cold, biting whiteness. The Princess cried out in shock, releasing Irene's hands to brush the snow away from her own face and hair, but Irene welcomed the cruel cold. She breathed it in, grateful for its harshness, her mind her own once more.

"Your Highness, here . . ." Irene unlocked the door and pulled it open. The Princess fled out into the corridor, and Irene followed her, taking care to keep a safe distance. "You ought to rejoin your delegation, Your Highness," she suggested. "They'll be worried about you."

"You're right," the Princess agreed. Irene could see how sympathetic she was to even her servants and menials, and her heart was touched . . . damn it, not again. She tried to find strength to hold on a little longer, until the Fae was someone *else's* problem. She focused on her Library brand, on the coldness of the snowflakes melting and streaking her dress with water stains, on anything other than how good and nice and beautiful the Princess was.

"You're a very noble person," the Princess said. She was within Irene's reach again, and Irene wasn't sure she had the strength to fight back this time. "I trust you."

The touch of her hand against Irene's cheek was like fire.

Then she was gone. Irene sagged against the wall, each breath coming hard and making her tremble. Part of her wanted to curl up and weep at the loss of her true love. The rest of her, more sensibly, was trying to point out that not only was the Princess not her true love, but Irene had never *had* a true love in any case. So she didn't even know what it felt like to lose her true love.

At least she didn't have to worry about letting a murder suspect escape. Irene was reasonably sure that of all the people in Paris, the Princess was the *least* likely person to stab someone else from behind. It just wasn't in her character to do such a thing. Prutkov, on the other hand—what was he up to? He wasn't just trying to manoeuvre the Library into a better position. He was playing some entirely separate game of his own.

Too many games. Too many narratives. And all of them wanting Irene to play some different role in them. Was she the Library's agent or the Princess's knight? The Cardinal's spy and assassin or the Countess's victim? Kai's lover? Vale's friend? Where did she ultimately stand in all this?

Steps approached. Irene raised her head and saw Li Ming.

"Miss Winters," he said, taking her in with some surprise. "What *have* you been doing?"

CHAPTER 19

Irene brushed flakes of melting snow from her dress in as unconcerned a manner as she could manage. "Lord Li Ming, how nice to see you. I hope I'm not taking you away from anything important."

"Only the usual round of meetings," Li Ming said. "I take it that you haven't been asked to join any yourself?"

"No," Irene said, grateful that nobody had tried to corral her. "I've been kept busy with this investigation. And as you've probably deduced, that's what I'd like to discuss with you."

"I'm not really surprised." Li Ming glanced along the corridor. "Will here do for a little chat, or would you rather take it elsewhere? And do you require witnesses?"

"What I require is information," Irene said. "I can't promise that what we discuss will remain secret, but I'll be as discreet as possible when it comes to sharing it."

"Then I suggest that we speak in private, and somewhere that we can be reasonably sure we won't be overheard."

A few minutes later, Li Ming was taking a seat in Irene's bedroom. Irene decided not to tell him that it was the same chair Silver had been lounging in earlier. Li Ming had adjusted his clothing to the local fashions but was in his usual light grey, with black cravat and cuff-links. His silver hair stretched down his back in a long braid, every strand perfectly in place. He could have been a moulded statue of marble and silver, if not for the bright focus of his eyes. Irene did wonder for a moment what the local Parisians were making of the fact that this was an apparent woman in a man's clothing—but then again, extravagant foreign visitors could get away with all sorts of violations of custom.

"I had been told you wanted a meeting with me," Li Ming said. He folded one hand over another in his lap. "I appreciate your tact in arranging it privately via His Highness, Prince Kai."

"I see no need to spread rumours unnecessarily," Irene answered. "But when there *are* rumours about a possible connection to this murder, we have to investigate them."

"And you wish to ask me about a rumour?" Li Ming asked politely, as if it was nothing more than a question about how many lumps of sugar he'd like in his tea.

"I think I'd be negligent not to."

"And the rumour is?"

Irene sighed mentally. Clearly she was going to have to work every step of the way in this conversation. "Concerning the fact that you and Lord Ren Shun may have had a disagreement in the past."

Li Ming frowned. "Normally I'd ask who told you that, but I suppose under the current circumstances there may have been a queue of people lining up to inform you. Let me be blunt. Am I a suspect?"

"The main suspect is the Blood Countess, as you probably know," Irene countered. "But it's our duty to review all possible people with the means, opportunity, and motive."

"I see," Li Ming said icily. "And when you've finished interviewing half of Paris, what will be your next step?"

Irene shrugged. "Half of Paris doesn't have any motive at all, unless Lord Ren Shun committed a great many crimes which I haven't yet heard about. And I have great difficulty imagining any normal human subduing a powerful dragon. I cited *means* and *opportunity* first because they significantly lower the number of possible suspects."

"And you believe that I could do it?"

"In purely physical terms . . . my lord, you are a close servant of His Majesty Ao Shun. You are not weak. I've seen you on the verge of launching a snowstorm across London." Irene wondered if Li Ming would react to that, given that they'd nearly been in conflict at the time, but he didn't so much as twitch an eyelash. "So, yes; I believe that you *could* do it. However, I see no reason *why* you'd want to derail the peace negotiations. But I've been told that if we wish to convict the Blood Countess, we need actual proof. And we don't have this, yet, so suspicions can be pointed anywhere. I'll find it much easier to discount you as a suspect if I know why you came under suspicion in the first place."

Snow hissed against the window outside, and the faint noises of traffic drifted past: horse-drawn carriages and carts, motor vehicles, the murmur of human voices. Finally Li Ming asked, "How much do you know about our families?"

"Not a great deal," Irene admitted. "I know that they exist as major political forces inside your society." And she knew she wanted to stay *well away* from the Winter Forest and Black Mountains families, after certain recent events. Even if they'd been ordered not to hold a grudge against Irene by the Queen of the Southern Lands herself, that didn't mean they'd be friendly. Although Li Ming served another dragon royal entirely, and they'd had their differences too . . .

Li Ming remained entirely still. He didn't move his hands or tilt his head in the way that a human might have done. "I believe Prince Kai has chosen not to talk about certain aspects of our society, and you have chosen not to ask him about them. That was wise of you both. It would have cast a shadow over perceptions of your relationship, if you had appeared to be seducing him for information."

"Our relationship has always been a careful one," Irene agreed. *And is probably non-existent if things go badly here. Along with a lot of other things, such as my parents' lives, my liberty, the Library's future . . .* She restrained herself from glancing towards the bed as she thought of Kai, and wondered just how well-informed Li Ming was. Why delude herself? Part of Li Ming's job as personal aide to the Dragon King of the Northern Ocean was to know that sort of thing. "Let me be blunt. After all, neither of us wants people asking why we've vanished for a long private conversation. What am I missing here?"

"You might say that there are two main axes of power in our society," Li Ming said carefully. "There are the monarchs, and then there are the families. One is obligated to one's family. But one is also obligated to one's king or queen. These mutual obligations can create problems."

Irene could recognize a *don't quote me on this, but . . .* speech easily enough. "I'd expect it to be a strictly internal matter, if a dragon finds themselves caught between obligations and duties," she said. "A dragon certainly wouldn't mention it to outsiders, who might try to exploit the situation."

Li Ming's eyes narrowed in satisfaction at her assurance of discretion. His irises were the same pure silver as his hair and eyebrows, and his pupils were startlingly dark in comparison. Like Kai—like many of the other dragons here—his face could have been a classical line painting, all sharp lines and shadows. "Between the two of us," he continued, "Prince Kai escapes a great many potential problems because his mother is not from a distinguished family."

Oh. Irene knew how that could play out in a lot of human societies, and it wasn't always pretty. Kai was an acknowledged prince, but no doubt there were degrees of authority even among princes. And this might explain why a dragon royal might be allowed to run off and do his own thing, rather than settle down to studies or service. "Would this have anything to do with the way that he was allowed to infiltrate the Library, or his occasional lack of duties?" she asked as delicately as she could.

"It might," Li Ming agreed. "And while he is dear to his father, not *all* of his paternal relatives have the same affection for him."

There was a clear warning in Li Ming's eyes and tone. Irene tried to translate whatever the dragon didn't want to say out loud. She knew that Kai's uncle Ao Shun cared for him, but could the same be said of Ao Ji . . . "Between the two of us, is there a problem?"

Li Ming's eyelids flickered. "Well, His Majesty Ao Ji could possibly come to value Prince Kai, for his current hard work and support. But that would certainly be an unexpected turn of events."

In other words, Kai is going to get the short end of the stick, and don't hold your breath hoping for anything better. A painful resignation weighed Irene down. It would have been so nice to believe that Kai's family were wholeheartedly behind him, whatever the circumstances of his birth. Why did they have to be so damned *human* about it? Kai probably considered it just part of how things were, and he'd avoided telling Irene because he knew she'd be angry on his behalf.

And why should she be angry, anyhow? It was how things worked. History told her as much. *Maybe that's why we need a bit of chaos in our lives, so things can happen against probability and outside logic, where a family can love one another even if one of them is lowborn—or adopted . . .*

"Thank you for making that clear to me," she said flatly.

"It's blatantly obvious why and how Prince Kai happened to turn up at this particular moment too," Li Ming added, almost kindly. "But since he is making himself useful, nobody will raise the point."

So much for even semi-plausible deniability over their relationship. "Our aim is to find the murderer," Irene said. "And to get the peace treaty signed. I hope that everyone else here has the same priorities."

"Priorities. Ah yes, the murder. And Ren Shun." Li Ming glanced towards the window a moment, as though looking for words. It seemed that for him, discussing Ren Shun was more uncomfortable than delivering political warnings. "Both Ren Shun and I myself are of the Yellow River family. We share the same father, Lord Shantsu, though he companied with different dragons to bear us."

Irene sorted through her reactions before replying. Gawping at Li Ming and saying, *You're brothers?* would be stupidly rude. Even if it had been her first thought. And why hadn't Mu Dan told her? Didn't she know about it? Or had the other dragon assumed it was public knowledge? "I offer you my condolences on the loss of your brother," she murmured.

"Your courtesy is appreciated," Li Ming said. "I fear that we had not been on speaking terms for several decades now, after a sadly public disagreement at a family gathering."

"Oh?" Irene said, as neutrally as she could.

"We had both taken oaths to our respective kings at that point. I felt my younger brother was not serving his lord as well as his oaths demanded. He took issue with my opinion. The disagreement became public. We have scarcely spoken since that time, except at formal occasions or festivals."

Irene chose her next words carefully. This was important information, but she could sense a simmering slow-flowing resentment and anger beneath Li Ming's glacial surface, as hot and dangerous as lava. Just because a dragon was polite didn't mean that a dragon was safe. "I had a bad experience in America with a dragon who was certainly not serving his master as well as his oaths demanded." In fact, said dragon had cheerfully betrayed his master in the hopes of personal advancement, without a single moment's hesitation. "I'm sure a brother of yours would have done nothing as drastic, but . . ."

The air in the room had become cooler. Irene had enough time to wonder if she'd said too much, and whether she might be the next dead body to turn up, before Li Ming answered.

"How do you serve the Library?" he asked. "As it commands, or for its own good?"

"I'd hope that the two aims were aligned," Irene replied. But she thought of Prutkov's words from earlier. He thought a dragon and Fae truce would render the Library's mission obsolete and that they'd have to rebuild their power base some other way. She still served the Library as a keeper of the balance. She was *not* some sort of power broker.

Li Ming leaned forward, and the cold air swelled around him like an ocean wave. "There are two sorts of servants, Irene Winters: those who are expected to obey without question, and those who are expected to use their intelligence and judgement. Ren Shun would have done *anything* for Ao Ji. He did not understand that for Ao Ji's own sake, there are some things which his servants should never do."

Irene took a deep breath. The air tasted like ice in her mouth. "You think that he might have gone . . . too far." The euphemism was petty, but it could cover such a wide area: fraud, blackmail, treason, murder. "And that some action of his might have resulted in his death?"

Li Ming's eyes flicked shut for a moment, then open again, as quickly as a serpent's. "If you brought me proof that this Fae, this Blood Countess, murdered my brother in order to start a war, then I would welcome that. It would be a better answer than others which come to mind."

"I'm sorry." Honesty was all Irene could offer. "I'm looking hard for that proof. No—let me be more clear. I'm looking for the truth, and I hope the truth will be that proof."

"Who told you about our quarrel?"

"I thought you said that you weren't going to ask," Irene countered.

Li Ming flicked his fingers casually. "Well, if it was Mu Dan, you might remind her that independence is all well and good, but it carries with it a lack of protection."

"Are you threatening her?"

Li Ming's expression was one of mild surprise. "She is already very aware that I think she has burned her bridges. If she goes around reporting private matters, then her family will no doubt want to discuss that with her in private—despite her public lack of affiliation to them. But without a family or a lord, what is she? What authority does she have?"

Irene thought of some of Mu Dan's earlier comments. "The value of her skill and experience?" she suggested.

"That's not the same thing, Miss Winters, and you know it. Consider your own position. Your words—your voice—have no power without the Library behind you. You are, and I say this with the greatest admiration for your abilities, only mortal. I respect your choice to bind yourself to the Library. But doesn't that simply prove that what I'm saying is true?"

Irene knew there should be an answer to that—something about inherent worth, or individual value, or choice. Unfortunately, from Li Ming's perspective, he was simply stating facts. "It may be true that organisations give individuals their power," she answered, "but it's what those individuals do that makes the organisations strong. Without you as an individual, your family would be weaker."

"I think we shall have to agree to disagree," Li Ming said, his smile showing he felt he'd won the argument. "But please be aware that I respect you both as a representative of the Library *and* as an individual. And that I trust your discretion concerning this little talk."

His tone hadn't changed, but there was a flicker of red in his eyes: the true shade of dragon eyes, a sign of emotion or anger. And Irene knew that it was a warning.

"I appreciate your cooperation with the investigation," she said. "Thank you for your help."

Li Ming hesitated for a moment before rising. "There is one last point," he said. "You know of Minister Zhao, I believe?"

"From the Queen of the Southern Lands' court? I wasn't acquainted with him, but I knew he'd been assassinated recently." Irene chose her words carefully. "Given that the Queen of the Southern Lands is involved in this peace effort, his death just before this conference makes me wonder if there's a connection."

Li Ming nodded approvingly. "Indeed. He was one of the nobles who strongly supported peace. Mei Feng is attending instead of him, on behalf of her queen."

This news corroborated her suspicions about Minister Zhao's death. "We wondered whether the Blood Countess might have murdered him too. And Mei Feng has agreed to answer questions from Vale."

"That is a logical deduction. But it grows more complex when one tries to work out how a Fae could reach so far into our territories." Li Ming twitched a shrug. "Minister Zhao was poisoned. The fruit that he ate was never traced, so we don't know who sent it. Mei Feng knows more than I do, as they were part of the same court."

"Why wouldn't Mei Feng talk to Mu Dan about it, given that dragons prefer to keep such matters between themselves?" Irene asked.

"For much the same reason that I didn't talk with my brother," Li Ming said. "Their mothers were sisters. But they themselves have not been fond of each other for a long while now. It is a pity when such strife arises within a family."

He gave Irene a small courteous bow. "Until later, Miss Winters. As I said, I trust your discretion."

Irene made her way downstairs by a separate route from Li Ming's: she had no wish to answer awkward questions. It was about two o'clock in the afternoon: she'd lost time somewhere in her confrontation with the Princess. That was an occasional hazard of dealing with powerful Fae.

She needed some fresh air and some time to think. Wrapping herself up in a fur cape (courtesy of Bradamant's efforts to provide an appropriate wardrobe), Irene stepped outside, under the shelter of a canopy, and looked up at the sky. The snow had eased off to leave grey rolling banks of cloud in sole occupation of the sky, and the wind had calmed to barely a whisper. Drifts of snow filled the crevices of masonry and lay along the windowsills, but the streets and pavements themselves had been kept mostly clear by traffic and pedestrians. Ridges of dirty slush showed here and there, moulded from Paris grime and frozen in place.

She now had almost too *much* information. Prutkov had his own agents in Paris and was setting Irene and her team up to "discover the evil Countess." This wasn't a huge surprise, but it was a depressing confirmation. And did he have anything else going on besides that? The existence of one hidden scheme suggested the possibility of others. The Princess feared there was treachery afoot. Which there probably was. And according to Li Ming, Ren Shun might have done something unethical while following his lord Ao Ji's orders—or while doing what he thought Ao Ji wanted him to do. Which raised new possible questions about why Ren

Shun might have been murdered. Could this have been triggered by the peace conference, by inter-dragon politics, by family matters, or by a combination of the three? Questions had been raised that would involve a lot of research into the dragon's private life, and probably nobody would be prepared to answer them. Plus there was the business of who killed Minister Zhao and whether there was a link between the two deaths. And Irene and her team wouldn't be the only ones looking for a connection there. Mei Feng wasn't stupid. None of the participants in this conference could be described as stupid.

And then there was Herodotus's *Myths*. Assuming it actually existed and that it wasn't just a red herring, a detail dreamed up as part of an elaborate frame job on the Library. If Prutkov was wrong and it *was* significant enough to bribe a Librarian, then what secrets might it hold? How important could it be?

In addition, Mu Dan was Mei Feng's cousin, part of her family, and hadn't wanted to tell anyone. Could their issues have something to do with Mu Dan's independence from her dragon clan?

Irene stared out at nowhere in particular, as a new possibility fell into place. Li Ming had suggested that dragon monarchs and the great families didn't always have the same priorities. Were the kings and queens trying to make an end run round the power structure of the families in order to get this treaty in place? Was that why an independent investigator, like Mu Dan, had been brought in? And was Kai an unfortunate low-born son, or a useful independent playing piece—without inconvenient maternal family connections—sired for later advantage?

She regretted getting Vale and Kai into this. No, that wasn't fair. This sort of situation was Vale's meat and drink; if she'd tried to talk him out of it, he'd have insisted on coming anyhow. However, it was her fault for bringing *Kai* into the situation. If anything happened to him . . .

Instinct made Irene break her chain of thought and pull herself back to the here and now. Someone was watching her.

She let her gaze drift casually across the wide street in front of her, trying to identify the source of her unease. The waiting cab-drivers, perched atop their cabs, warming their hands inside their coats or eating pastries? No, none of them seemed likely. A group of middle-class women hurrying back from lunch to their place of work, their wide-shouldered jackets flapping as they walked briskly, their skirts damp at the hem from snow and slush? No, they were preoccupied with their own business. The newspaper vendor across the street? The gendarme watching the hotel in what he thought was an inconspicuous way?

Or was it the grey cat nearby, sitting like a statuette with her tail tucked around her paws, watching Irene with an unblinking gaze?

Irene weighed the possibilities. Then she turned towards the cat and spread her hand in an open gesture, as if to say, *Your move.*

The cat unwrapped its tail from its paws and stretched, back arching as if it had discovered a dozen extra joints and meant to use them all. It turned and began to walk away from Irene down the pavement. It had gone a dozen steps before it paused and turned back on itself again, mouth opening in a silent beckoning mew.

This was the sort of situation where operatives who went off on their own deserved everything that happened to them. It might be—no, it probably was—nothing but a lure into a trap. But some traps had to be sprung, just to find out who or what was behind them.

Irene crossed to the gendarme, keeping half an eye on the cat. Fortunately it seemed disposed to wait. She reached into her purse and pulled out a five-franc piece, offering it to him. "Please do me a small service," she said. "Please have the note I'm about to write taken into Le Meurice and given to the lady Mu Dan—the hotel staff will find her."

"Of course, madam," the gendarme agreed. It was good money for the job, and he wouldn't have to leave his post for more than a moment. "The note?"

Naturally Irene had pencil and paper in her purse. She pulled them out and scribbled hastily, *Following a beckoning cat down the rue de Rivoli westwards—will try to leave messages or markers if I change direction. Irene.* She folded it and passed it over. "A thousand thanks."

"A small matter," the gendarme said gallantly, clicking his heels together as she turned away.

The cat was still there. Irene wondered if its mistress had been able to see everything she'd just done. She also wished she'd been able to call for more backup. But Vale and Silver were both out, Kai was with his uncle . . . and to be honest, she wasn't sure that she trusted Prutkov any more. Mu Dan was her best option.

A couple of blocks along, the cat turned right, up the wide rue des Pyramides—then left again, and then right again, picking its way along the street with the same careful precision as a normal cat, but barely pausing. Irene managed to leave a couple of messages with street vendors or gendarmes, but she didn't have time for more than a scribbled couple of words. The cat was in no mood for delay. And Irene knew enough of the geography of Paris to be certain that the cat was leading her away from the central district of wide streets and broad avenues and frequent gendarmes, towards the rougher back streets and more shadowed alleys.

This was hardly a surprise. But she couldn't stop now.

All right, technically she *could*, but then she'd never find out what was going on. Besides, she reassured herself, if the Countess had simply wanted her dead, then there were simpler ways to do it.

Empty clothes-lines dangled from the windows of the latest back alley. Not even the most desperate housewife would hang washing outside in the current weather. A group of ragged boys huddled round a can of burning coals, bundled up in multiple layers of tatters and oversized coats. A couple of them called out to Irene as she hurried past, offers to act as a guide or show her the wonders of Paris. She knew that she was out of place here. Her cape, dress, and hat had been intended for the best hotels in Paris, not for this area. This was one of the places where families crowded into the same building, six to a three-storey house, where artists could only afford hired attics, and where even in the middle of winter, the gangs who called themselves Apaches lounged on street corners and sneered. She was an obvious target.

But at least the cat had finally come to a stop. It sat down next to a battered doorway in one of the buildings and began to lick a paw meditatively.

"Thank you," Irene said politely as she drew level with it, slightly out of breath. "That was quite a walk."

The cat ignored her.

The building was old—these were parts of Paris that had endured over centuries, and been added to rather than rebuilt. Grey stone bricks and flaking cement showed underneath the slush, and slate and tile roofs gleamed wetly as the snow melted; they had no insulation to keep the heat inside, and the cold seeped in with every breath. A battered sign that might have depicted a wine bottle hung beside the doorway. She could smell tobacco, sweat, black coffee, beer, and wine. A soft buzz of conversation came from inside, barely audible through the worn, knife-marked planks of the door.

She could feel eyes on her, waiting to see what she'd do next. The Apaches on the nearest street corner were watching her, as uniformed as any military force in their striped jerseys, neckerchiefs, and red sashes. The boys around the can of coals stared at her. Even the cat had finished with its paw and had fixed its wide eyes on her.

Carefully Irene opened the door and stepped inside.

A rush of smoky air greeted her and made her blink. The room was sunken, several steps down from street level, and it was full of people. Men, mostly. They crowded around their tables, nursing pipes and glasses, conversing in a low drone of argot French. The few women who were present were curled up against their male companions, with shawls drawn round their bare shoulders, nursing small glasses of spirits. A couple of servers circulated between the tables and the bar at the far end of the room, but otherwise the place was static, as drowsy as a bear's den in winter. And just as dangerous.

To her left, a cat mewed. Irene glanced across and saw an elderly woman, so wrapped in faded shawls that she was barely more than an outline, seated at a table on her own. A black cat was sprawled on the surface in front of her. There was a single spare chair at the table.

Irene took a moment to review the situation. *Allies non-existent, enemy in front of me, potential foes to either side.*

But she walked across to the spare seat and set one hand on the rough wooden back. "May I join you?"

"I've been hoping that you would," the old woman croaked. Her face was wizened, dry with age, but there was the sense of something corrupt underneath, and her eyes gleamed like a spider's. "I have some questions."

CHAPTER 20

"It would be nice to hope that we can have a free and full exchange of information," Irene said, sitting down. She offered her gloved hand to the cat to sniff. "Should I be assuming there's a third party present?"

"My lady's only watching," the crone said with a rasping chuckle. "She sent me out to do the talking. Poor old Dorotya, her feet aching, her back aching, but never a moment's rest when her beautiful mistress needs fresh blood . . ."

"Fresh blood?" Irene asked blandly. She could feel the coldness of fear slowly oozing up her spine, but she had no intention of showing it.

"Did I say the wrong thing? I mean fresh information. A lady likes to know what's going on, but she can't go traipsing all around the marketplaces and taverns herself, now, can she? No, she says, Katarina, where are you, girl? Katarina, you be a good girl and go out and ask some questions of that nasty little bitch who threw brandy all over me yesterday."

"Katarina?" Irene tried to think where she'd seen the crone's face before. There was something familiar about it.

"Dorotya. Katarina. Maybe Ilona. An old woman like myself loses track of that sort of thing. You'll come to understand it yourself when you're a bit older, dearie, assuming you ever get there." The crone peeled her lips back to bare a gap-toothed smile. "Now, are you going to be sensible?"

"I'm prepared to talk," Irene said carefully. "I can't commit myself to anything more until I know what the stakes are."

Dorotya took a slurping swig from her tankard of beer. "Fair enough, dearie. You are nicely spoken, I must say. I suppose even the gentry can be polite when they've got something to gain by it."

"For what it's worth, my mother and my father were honest working people," Irene said firmly. *So what if they were stealing books? For Librarians, that is honest work.*

Dorotya sniffed noisily. "You can say what you like, dearie, but I know what I see and what my mistress sees, and you're wearing silk and dealing with royalty. In fact . . ." She sniffed again, and there was something more feral to the noise this time. "I can tell you've been keeping exalted company on both sides. Now isn't that interesting?"

Irene suppressed the urge to lean away. "Let's get down to business. What do you want to know?"

"My lady and I want to know who killed a certain dragon," Dorotya said. "We hear you're looking into it yourself, dearie. Perhaps you'd like to tell us all about it."

Irene blinked. This certainly wasn't the question she'd expected. "May I just check which dragon you're talking about?" she temporised. "I mean, so many dragons, so many possible murders."

"Now that's the sort of thing I like to hear." Dorotya cackled approvingly. "That's the spirit, dearie! But you know who I'm talking about. The one that they found stabbed in Le Meurice."

Irene spread her hands. "I arrived just two days ago. I don't know who did it. It wasn't me."

Dorotya put down her tankard and raised a finger. There was a scraping of chairs from behind Irene, and the sound of men rising to their feet.

Irene didn't need Vale's deductive skills to tell her she was in trouble. But there was something *liberating* about this. She was surrounded by known enemies, not politics. And she didn't have anyone to worry about—apart from herself.

She smiled.

"I'm not sure you understand quite how serious your position is, dearie," Dorotya said. "You're in a lot of trouble here. I think you should be grateful for the chance to spill your guts to a nice mother confessor. You wouldn't believe how many young ladies have shared their last words with me."

"I bow to your experience. But I'm rather hoping these won't be my *last* words."

"Well, my little lambkin, I'd say that the ball's in your court on that one."

The approaching feet were right behind Irene now. She restrained her urge to turn around. The impression of nervousness, however accurate it might be, would only weaken her position. Besides, her memory had just come into focus. "I remember where I saw you before," she said. "You were at the morgue." Another piece of memory clicked into place. "You nearly tripped me when I was chasing those fake gendarmes, when they ran for the sewers!"

"Now, with a memory like that, you've got no excuse for not telling me everything." Dorotya nodded to one of the men behind Irene. "If you'd be so kind, my precious?"

A thin braided cord fell across Irene's line of vision, coming to rest against her neck, and the man standing behind her pressed close against her chair, drawing the garrotte tight enough that she could feel it through the fabric of her high collar.

"Now, my sweet," Dorotya said, returning her attention to Irene. "Can you think of any little details that you might possibly have left out? As a favour to me?"

"When you put it that way . . ." Irene was fairly sure that she wasn't in immediately lethal danger *yet*. But that could change with a moment's tightening of the cord around her neck. "Since you were investigating the morgue yourself, I assume you know the dragon was stabbed from behind."

Dorotya nodded. "With a good knife too. None of this modern rubbish. You need a nice sharp piece when you want to be sure you're tickling someone's heart the first time, and not getting caught up on a rib."

Irene sighed. "The problem, Madam Dorotya—and you, milady countess—is that at the moment I'm still investigating." She decided that it wouldn't hurt to share a few of the basic details. "We're aware that the gentleman went out for a walk, alone, on the night of his murder. We know his body was found in Le Meurice the next morning. Unfortunately, we're still trying to trace what happened in between."

"That's all?"

Irene raised a finger to tentatively touch the cord round her throat, testing to see if she'd be ordered to keep her hands on the table, but nobody said anything. That meant she had leeway. "Let me put a card on the table. Your mistress the Countess has been accused of the murder."

"Yes, and that's what she's so annoyed about."

Irene blinked. "I beg your pardon?"

"I know, dearie, I know. You're about to tell me my lady has a teeny tiny little bit of a bad reputation, but that's what makes it so irritating." Dorotya slurped more beer. "You see, when she was brought to trial, that time before, perhaps she had done a few of the things they said she had. But a lot of it she hadn't. They made it all up, they did. Lots of lies to discredit my lovely lady, to get her out of power and lock her up for the rest of her life. You can't trust people in power, dearie. They'll say whatever they want, all the witnesses will be paid to agree, and then you're behind bars till the end of your days. Or worse."

Irene turned this over in her mind. Statements that the Countess had been falsely accused didn't quite square with the threats that Dorotya had been making earlier. But perhaps that was the problem with Fae who had conflicting stories in their archetype. The Countess could be both a bloodthirsty monster *and* a falsely accused martyr. At the same time.

"So if I understand correctly, your mistress has a particular dislike of being accused of crimes she genuinely hasn't committed?" she suggested. "Even if she might, for instance, have been trying to do something fairly similar last night involving bombs, chlorine gas, and poisoned apples?"

She did wonder if the other drinkers were paying attention to their conversation—not to mention the man holding the garrotte—since neither Irene nor Dorotya was keeping her voice down, but nobody was coming over to interfere. At least that meant a lack of interruptions.

"It's the principle of the thing, dearie," Dorotya said firmly. "Perhaps she was having a bit of amusement with bombs last night, but that doesn't mean she was stabbing people in the back two nights before. Even a little wet-behind-the-ears girlie like yourself ought to know that. So I said to her, I said, mistress, why don't you let me go and ask some of those clever young people a few questions? And if they say they don't know anything, well . . ."

"You let them go unharmed, as a token of goodwill?" Irene said, not very hopefully.

"I was thinking more that we help you change your mind, dearie. Hand." The last word was snapped to one of the men behind Irene. He grabbed Irene's right arm at the wrist and elbow and forced it flat on the table palm down.

Irene didn't try to struggle. The cord around her throat tightened there like a warning. "And next?" she asked politely.

"You should be a little more worried, lambkin. Next we try a little trick that the boys here like to play while they're drinking. They take a knife, and they bring it down between their fingers, one, two, three, only sometimes they miss. Don't you Librarians like to be able to write?"

"We do," Irene admitted, "but that's not all we can do."

Dorotya waved an admonitory finger at her. "Now, don't get any ideas about saying something with that magic trick of yours, dearie. The moment you open your mouth, Jehan behind you is going to twist that rope so tight . . ."

Irene closed her eyes for a moment, praying for patience. "We may have a problem here, then. How do you expect me to be able to talk if you're strangling me?"

Dorotya paused. "Well, sweetheart, I was thinking that I'd recognize your mystical powers—"

"I'm afraid not," Irene said apologetically. "It all sounds like normal speech. Just ask your mistress if you don't believe me."

The cat, which had been sitting there and listening all the time, gave a single sharp mew that might have been agreement.

"Well, this is most annoying," Dorotya muttered. "I don't suppose you could write your confession down for me, dearie?"

"I'm right-handed," Irene said, with a nod towards the hand in question, which was still being held immobile on the table. She knew that she should probably be more afraid. There was something about this whole situation that was not only faintly ridiculous, it was simply *human*. "I'm sorry. I know it's inconvenient."

"And how would you know, you smart-mouthed jumped-up little hanger-on?" Dorotya spat.

So much for friendliness and *dearie*. "Well, I was questioning another Librarian less than a month ago," Irene admitted. "We had him tied down on the bed, but even so it wasn't easy."

There were multiple male sniggers from behind her. Dorotya leered unpleasantly. "There we have it, dearie. You're definitely an aristocrat."

Irene sighed. "I should introduce you to an acquaintance of mine. You and he would get on splendidly. But in the meantime, can we come to terms in a way that doesn't involve you cutting my fingers off?"

"What have you got in mind?" Dorotya asked. The cat leaned forward smoothly, its eyes gleaming in the gaslights.

"As your lady has said that she wasn't involved in the murder, I am happy to take her word for it," Irene lied smoothly. "But if you want me to find out who *did* do it, then you need to let me go. Having me vanish here isn't going to be very useful to you."

"And you think you can find out who did it?" Dorotya demanded.

"I can, if you release me," Irene said. "I'm neutral in this, after all. I'm not a dragon."

But the cat snorted and turned its back in a motion that was clear denial.

Dorotya shrugged. "A pity, dearie. Her ladyship says no. It looks as if we're going to have to continue this discussion elsewhere. But don't you worry, a nice well-bred young madam like yourself is always useful—one way or another."

Irene would have tried to argue, but she suddenly smelled chloroform. She would have considered remaining a prisoner if she stayed conscious. She could have found out where they were hiding, after all—but being taken along as an unconscious captive involved too much risk.

Irene had let her left arm drop to her side. Now she moved. She brought her left elbow up behind her, slamming it into the crotch of the man with the garrotte. There was a manly scream. The loop around her throat went loose. She pushed herself backwards, stool going flying, pulling against the man holding her hand to the table. The man who'd been bearing down on her arm hadn't expected her to pull in that direction: he lost his grip, and with a thump and a few splinters Irene dragged herself loose. She rolled as she hit the floor, clumsy in her dress and cape, scything her legs around, and heard a satisfying crack as her booted foot caught the garrotte wielder's ankle. He yelped and folded over, hopping away.

"Grab her," Dorotya shrieked, leaning forward and waving her tankard. "*Incompetents.* Get the bitch!"

Irene pushed up to her feet in a swirl of skirts and a creak of corseting, gauging the situation. The two men she'd assaulted so far were incapacitated but would be threats again very shortly. The third man, to her left, had set down his bottle of chloroform and flexed his hands, clearly about to grab for her. The other occupants of the drinking hole were—unsurprisingly—staying out of it.

There were too many people here for her to affect their perceptions. But perhaps a hostage would be useful?

Irene focused on the man moving towards her. He was adequate but not that good; she sidestepped his rush, moving back towards the table as though it was accidental.

And then she shrugged off her cape and used it to grab the cat, bundling it up in a mass of heavy fabric and fur. It was a risky move—laying unwanted hands on felines was always dangerous, even if they weren't possessed by ancient Fae countesses. It struggled and flailed in her grip, trying to squirm free or maul anything within range, but she had it—for the moment. Finding a replacement cat to possess would hopefully take time, meaning this one was valuable.

"All right," Irene said in the sudden pause. "Everyone stay back, or the cat's going to regret it."

That seized the room's attention in a way that even the brawl hadn't managed. The situation had crossed the line from private intimidation to a public display. Calls of encouragement to both sides filled the room. A few men began to thump their glasses rhythmically on their tables.

The cat in Irene's hands hissed and tried to scratch her, writhing like a snake ridged with razors. She could feel a prickle of chaotic power through her gloves and the cape, as if she was dipping her hands into an electric field, but it wasn't a problem. Yet.

"You think that's a threat, dearie?" Dorotya demanded, levering herself to her feet. "My mistress isn't worried about one little cat!"

"How cruel of your mistress," Irene said. "But since you put it that way . . ."

"Yes?" Dorotya demanded, craning forward.

"Catch."

Irene threw the cat at Dorotya's face. Possessed or not, it reacted on instinct, landing claws first. Irene took advantage of the screaming and confusion, ducked the third man's attempt to grab her again, and ran for the door. Without backup, discretion was the better part of valour.

None of the room's other inhabitants tried to stop her. She didn't blame them—she wouldn't have involved herself either. Irene made it out into the street and extended an ankle as the third man came rushing out after her. He went face-first onto the snowy cobbles.

"Door, seal to your frame," Irene ordered, then turned to the man as he picked himself up out of the slush. "Can we negotiate?"

The man pulled out a flick-knife and snapped it open.

Thumps came from the door as those inside tried to break it down. "Ah well," Irene said, stepping away. Time for a trick that worked better on a single person than a roomful. **"You perceive I'm actually the person who hired you for this job."** She switched back from the Language to English, feeling the start of a headache as the man lowered his knife and looked confused. "Don't worry, everything's under control. Now, where were you planning to take the target?"

The man's face furrowed in a frown. "I don't know, do I? You only just picked us up round the corner. Hadn't told us yet, had you?"

Damn. He doesn't know a thing. "Had you heard of me, before I hired you?" Irene tried.

The man looked shiftier now. "Heard you'd been telling fortunes down at the Cabaret de L'Enfer," he admitted. "And you'd been hiring other men to get work done." Illegal work, clearly. "Jean said he'd been asking around, but nobody knew nothing else about you."

Irene was about to ask another question, but someone whistled, and the man promptly turned and ran, scuttling down the nearest alleyway like a weasel. The few onlookers on the street abruptly found business elsewhere. The banging on the tavern door also stopped, and she could hear the sound of running feet from inside. Running away. They would all be bolting out of the back or down into the sewers. That had been an alarm—the local equivalent of *here come the police*—and now her possible source of information was slipping through her fingers. She'd never catch up with Dorotya now.

But on the other hand, she was alive and safe and knew more than she had half an hour ago.

Irene straightened her hat and cuffs and began to retrace her route, regretting the loss of her cape. She was still considering the implications of what she'd learned when she saw Mu Dan and another woman—one of Hsien's security people—standing on a street corner, having an obvious debate about which way to go next.

"Sorry to have kept you waiting," she said as she approached.

"Where have you *been*?" Mu Dan demanded. She looked as if she was suppressing stronger language.

Perhaps, Irene decided, a bit of apology was in order. "I'm sorry to have left without waiting for you, but I didn't have any choice. I was approached by an agent of the Countess. She wouldn't have talked if you'd been there as well."

"And you're sure you're all right?" Mu Dan asked. "Not contaminated in any way?"

"I'm fine." Irene looked up at the sky. It was still clear, but the late afternoon sun had little warmth to it. "To be brief, the person was an old woman, a Fae linked to the Countess—probably some sort of procurer and servant from her story. She wanted information."

"What did she think we knew that she didn't?" Mu Dan asked. Her voice was cooler now; she'd recovered from her first flare of temper.

"That is a *very* good question. She wanted to know who killed Ren Shun."

The security woman stood next to them, eyeing the ebb and flow of passing traffic, with the disinterested air of an agent who knew that it wasn't her place to listen. Though of course she would. Hsien—and anyone he reported to—would know all about this when they returned to the hotel.

"But . . ." Mu Dan was clearly retracing Irene's own train of thought. Unfortunately, the railway tracks led to the same destination: *if the Countess didn't know who did it, and she didn't do it herself, then who did?* Which resulted in a derailment of the entire current theory and a major explosion of possibilities and unfortunate implications.

"Yes," Irene said, "exactly. It's entirely possible that this whole approach was a deliberate ploy to misinform me, and I was *allowed* to escape. I concede that. But it's difficult to see *why* the Countess's agents would bother lying about Ren Shun's murder, given that she had no qualms about admitting she tried to blow up the hotel last night. Dorotya didn't hide it."

"We still have no evidence that she *didn't* kill Lord Ren Shun," Mu Dan muttered, but her heart wasn't in it. "And we've lost track of Lord Silver too. I left Vale with Mei Feng so she could fill him in about Minister Zhao's murder. But Lord Silver hasn't been seen since this morning."

That was unwelcome news. "It's not just a case of him being over-enthusiastic about his investigations and not having got back to the hotel with a report yet?"

"It could be. You know him better than I do." Mu Dan's tone wasn't quite suggestive, but it was definitely sour. "Or he might be out there making some deals of his own."

"So might I have been," Irene pointed out. "If Silver's in trouble—"

"You're far too trusting," Mu Dan cut in. "You trust beyond all reasonable limits. What does it take to get through to you that he's a Fae? How many times has he tried to seduce or blackmail you in the past? You let yourself walk into a Fae ambush just now—you *admitted* it—why? Because you thought they'd be polite and willing to talk? Do you have any idea how many times I've dug up Fae infiltrations in the past—and had to watch the strongest penalties be enforced on those involved?"

"The world is changing," Irene said quietly. "We're working to make that change happen—so perhaps someday you *can* trust a Fae. I'm aware of what's at stake, but if we succeed, then we're going to have to change as well. If you want to actually create peace, then we *have* to trust each other. No magical bindings, no blackmail, no family authority, just each other's given word. I'm not saying that we have to trust blindly. But automatic mistrust is a luxury we can no longer afford."

"His Majesty Ao Ji is never going to trust a Fae," Mu Dan countered.

"Then how can he ever sign a peace treaty with them? What is he doing here?"

Mu Dan was silent for a moment, thrusting her hands into the folds of her cape. "We're wasting time," she said. "And there's more I haven't told you. I found out what happened to Ren Shun's agents. They're all dead."

Irene blinked at the enormity of the statement. "What, *all* of them?" she said, realizing as she spoke how stupid a question it was.

But Mu Dan didn't snap at her. Perhaps she shared Irene's sense of shock. "I was given their names and descriptions, and I was able to match them to unidentified bodies in the morgue. Most of them, at least. Two were killed by head shots which damaged their faces, but I'm reasonably certain of the identification. Two more were stabbed, three were found with broken necks, and five were drowned."

Irene tried to make sense of this information. "Was someone trying to wipe out all of Ren Shun's agents, just in case they knew something incriminating? But in that case, how did the murderer know who they all *were*?" She tried to imagine how one would go about rolling up an entire network like that. Lure them all to the same place, and then kill them en masse? Follow them to their separate hideouts and dispose of them there? "This doesn't make sense."

"No," Mu Dan agreed. Her lips were pressed tightly together, her face calmly ferocious. "No, it doesn't. So where do we go now?"

"Why didn't you tell me that Li Ming and Ren Shun were brothers?" Irene asked.

Mu Dan blinked, taken aback. "You didn't know? But it's only on their father's side, and they serve—served—in different courts.

And Li Ming was raised by his mother until he declared himself male, so they were never close as children. I'm sorry. It didn't cross my mind to mention it."

Irene would have liked to ask more about dragon family structures, but this wasn't the moment. Mu Dan's answer seemed honest enough. So where indeed were they to go now?

"I think I need to take some questions to the source," Irene said reluctantly. "I don't like to leave Paris now, but it shouldn't take long. I need to go to the Library."

INTERLUDE
Vale and Kai

"I trust you understand why I have requested this interview, under the circumstances," Vale said.

Mei Feng nodded. "You have demonstrated that there may be a connection between Minister Zhao's murder and this latest one—and we all want to bring Lord Ren Shun's assassin to justice." If it was distressing to face questions on her murdered colleague, Minister Zhao, she didn't show it. She was sitting opposite him, as calm as any politician he'd ever questioned. There was little to learn from her appearance: her hair and make-up demonstrated the attention of careful servants, and her clothing, while slightly out of place for his own London, was appropriate for a lady of wealth and rank in this Paris and this time. She was in dark purple silk, with a light green scarf at her throat and emeralds of a matching shade in her bracelets and earrings. Winters had remarked previously that this was a sign of allegiance among the dragons. And that it indicated the woman's immediate superior was a light green shade in her "natural" shape. Winters had also said she believed Mei Feng's personal affinity to be for wind, and any unnatural movements of air might indicate strong emotion.

Winters was a useful source of knowledge.

But Mei Feng herself provided more information than she might have realized. Her left cuff was already marked with a few ink stains, indicating that she was left-handed and that she preferred to make notes herself, rather than leaving it all to servants. The muscles of her arms and shoulders, even though the cut of her dress attempted to conceal them, indicated a dragon with more than the usual amount of upper-body strength. Her height was also impressive, matching Vale's own six feet. (In fact, female dragons in general were about that height, equalling or exceeding their male counterparts. A topic for future research.) And Mei Feng had instructed her servants to check the room for hidden listening devices before their interview, which suggested that she might not want everything she said to be on the record.

"I will begin by asking why you wished to speak with *me*, rather than your cousin—the lady Mu Dan," Vale went on. "I believe she has some sort of investigative rank among your people."

"She does," Mei Feng said. Her voice was high-pitched but not girlish. "However, she is accustomed to investigating crimes among the lower-ranked and human servants. It would be inappropriate for her to question one of Her Majesty's most highly ranked ministers. You are a man of rank in your own world, I'm told. You should understand this."

Vale had very little regard for his own rank, save when it was necessary to use it as a blunt instrument. While he technically held the position of Earl of Leeds, it was a ceremonial title rather than one with any genuine authority, and he had left his family as far behind as possible. Yet if it eased his dealings with these dragons, he would allow them to assume anything they wanted.

"But you are aware that I may discuss what you tell me with her and Winters, if it is necessary to resolve this current case?"

Mei Feng shrugged. "That will be your decision." *And you will be held accountable for it,* her tone implied.

"Thank you for making that clear," Vale said drily. "Now, you say that Minister Zhao was one of the most highly ranked ministers in the Queen of the Southern Lands' court?"

"That's no secret," Mei Feng agreed. "He stood directly below me in rank, with only one or two others on the same level. His death unbalanced the whole court." Her eyes, a clear shade of grey-lilac, darkened at the thought.

"And yet he was replaced by someone comparatively junior, after his death?"

Mei Feng wobbled a hand delicately in the air. "It was an awkward situation. While there were several older and more experienced courtiers who could have taken his place, they were all very well placed where they were, and several outright stated they did not desire the promotion. Her Majesty resolved to—what is the phrase?—bring some new blood into the position. Of course, this did mean that a few of the more onerous duties of the minister could be removed from the portfolio. And certain cliques at court were affected."

Vale leaned forward thoughtfully. "So the queen took advantage of the situation, unwanted as it was, to dilute the minister's power and break up several political cliques? Winters told me of the contest for the position. Was that to set two powerful families at each other's throats, rather than have them potentially interfering with her rule?"

"You said that," Mei Feng said. "It would be inappropriate of me to agree."

"Madam, however important it may be to avoid dangerous statements and slanders, there are going to be certain questions which will require definitive answers."

"I'll do my best to give them," Mei Feng said with a bland smile. "To those questions, at least."

So it was going to be one of *those* interviews, Vale noted resignedly. Still, he was hardly inexperienced on that front. "Very well," he said. "Perhaps you would like to tell me about the death of Minister Zhao, in your own words, and with as much relevant detail as you feel you can share." Facts and methods of murder would tell him more than political implications.

Mei Feng paused, as though marshalling the facts in her mind and deleting the ones she did not wish to reveal. "Minister Zhao was on a tour of duty, you might say. He was visiting a number of worlds under his authority in order to collect information. On one of them—under the peaceful governance of an empire based in Korea—he was found dead mid-afternoon in a local orchard. The autopsy revealed he had been poisoned, via some tainted crystallised fruits. The local staff were questioned, and the evidence examined. The plums had arrived as a present from a junior subordinate of his, Lu Bu. But when Lu Bu was questioned, he knew nothing of the fruits. We have reason to believe he was speaking the truth and that someone counterfeited his name on the package."

"Was Minister Zhao fond of crystallised fruits?" Vale asked thoughtfully.

"They were a favourite delicacy of his," Mei Feng confirmed. "Everyone who knew him knew that."

Vale nodded. "And the poison was definitely in the plums, and not introduced by some other method?"

"Give our investigators *some* credit," Mei Feng said. "We do not employ incompetents. He was definitely poisoned, and the poison was in those fruits."

"What was the poison?"

"Cyanide," Mei Feng answered.

"Sugar and alcohol should have retarded the effect of the cyanide," Vale mused aloud, "but I imagine the proportions of the ingredients would be a factor." He observed the twitch of Mei Feng's face at the unseemly biological information. Clearly a woman who considered herself above such things. "Was someone present at the time, or was his body only discovered later?"

"He had intended to work without interruption," Mei Feng replied. "And while he did have a human secretary with him, he was unavailable for questioning later." She saw the frown growing on Vale's face and amplified her answer. "Minister Zhao had a strong affinity with the earth. When he felt himself afflicted by the poison, he reacted . . . Well, that is, we *assume* he reacted emotionally. There was a minor earthquake as a result. The secretary was among those who died. We consider ourselves lucky to have been able to obtain what evidence we did."

"I suppose I should be grateful my usual investigations are spared that level of destruction," Vale reflected. "Can you be certain that there were no others present?"

Mei Feng hesitated. "We are as certain as we can be, given that it was an isolated country estate with no known visitors, and no Fae could have penetrated so far into our territories."

"And that no strange dragons were observed in the sky . . ." Vale suggested.

"Yes, I was afraid you were going to raise that possibility," Mei Feng said ruefully. "One must consider all alternatives, after all. However unlikely they are."

Vale noted that she had not described it as *impossible*, however. Was this intended to convince him of her impartiality? Or did she seriously consider another dragon might have been involved? "Let us agree on the facts so far," he said. "Minister Zhao was poisoned, by the fruits, in the orchard. The fruits were apparently sent by a trusted subordinate—I assume he was trusted?"

"Lu Bu is reliable, stoic, and lacking in imagination," Mei Feng agreed. "His sole vice is tea, and I cannot see him being corrupted by it."

"Who would have had the opportunity to send such a package, which claimed to be from him?" Vale asked.

"Naturally we questioned the minister's staff and household. That world is close enough to disputed territory that Fae interference would be difficult but not impossible. Or a human agent for the Fae might have been involved. Two of Lu Bu's human servants had recently been involved with new romances or friendships—with people who could not be traced afterwards. Lu Bu's handwriting might have been imitated and his seal stolen. And he regularly sent Minister Zhao gifts of crystallised fruit. It was a noted product of the area, and . . ." Mei Feng shrugged. "Lu Bu was not an original person when it came to gifts."

"All very plausible," Vale said. "Tell me, how common are such assassinations?"

Mei Feng's shoulders stiffened. "Extremely uncommon," she said. The wind outside strengthened a notch, making the fire jump in the fireplace. "The Fae might strike at us, or we at them, in the disputed territories—but not in the heart of our own lands! The affair has caused what I can only describe as paranoia in some of my kindred, who should know better."

"You mistake my meaning," Vale remarked. "I was not referring to assassinations by one side against the other. I meant between dragons."

Mei Feng guarded her expression so carefully that Vale knew she must have expected the question. A more natural reaction would have been anger or shock at his suggestion—especially from a mere human. "It is unheard of," she said. "Such things haven't been known since ancient times."

But you've just described a murder which would have been extremely difficult for a Fae to commit, Vale reflected. *Yet entirely possible—simple, even—for a dragon.* "Then let us discuss something more recent. What were Minister Zhao's political views? Or did his personal life provide any possible motive for his murder?"

"His personal life was rather lacking in interest," Mei Feng said. "The usual sort of mating contracts, children, affairs, whatever. His political life was more . . . vivid. He was a member of the Red Plain family, and naturally he used his political influence to support them whenever possible. And because of his diligence and skills, he had accumulated a large number of portfolios. He was well-respected. And of course, he favoured the peace faction."

"Let me be specific," Vale said. "How much did he support this conference? Was he, perhaps, involved in organising it?"

"Involved, instrumental, and very important." Mei Feng looked slightly smug at having found three matching adjectives. "He stressed to Her Majesty that a truce would in no way weaken the monarchs and it would offer opportunities for diplomatic inroads into disputed territories. One cannot deny that we are somewhat more organised and collaborative than the Fae."

"Somewhat," Vale agreed. What he had seen of the infighting

between dragon families suggested that the cooperation only went so far. "Was he one of the most significant parties in favour of this peace, then?"

Mei Feng opened her mouth to speak, then paused, considering. Finally she said, "He is perhaps—was, rather—the most significant individual who was not one of the monarchs themselves, or one of the monarchs' most favoured counsellors. He was also one of the few who knew that the monarchs were seriously considering a signed truce. Many who talked about such a thing considered it merely supposition, or a vague hypothesis to be worked out over the next century. He knew it was actually a viable proposition. Some people might well have thought removing him would remove any chance of peace. Though he was not one of those with the duty of discussing such a peace with the Library."

"Who was that?" Vale asked, diverted for a moment.

"Tian Shu, a favourite of His Majesty of the Eastern Ocean, opened negotiations there. I am not privy to the full details."

Vale noted the slight twist of discontent to her lips at those words. "Information has been kept strictly rationed throughout this affair," he said. "An interesting approach."

"But necessary," Mei Feng said quickly, springing to the defence. "If Minister Zhao's assassination was connected to Ren Shun's murder—well, we can see the depths to which our enemies would stoop."

"And if it was connected," Vale probed, "who do you think those enemies *are*?"

"Fae, clearly." Mei Feng's voice and eyes were firm and unhesitating. "Some petty faction which is trying to brew open war between our two sides—by murdering some of our most trusted and valued nobles. The news about this 'Blood Countess' explains a great deal."

"And yet Minister Zhao was murdered in your own territory," Vale countered, "using a method which required knowledge of his personal habits and official duties, through your own internal postal service."

Mei Feng's gaze tightened to a full glare, and for a moment she looked as if she would have liked to have him dismissed from the room, the hotel, and the investigation. But her tone was amiable enough. "No doubt these suspicions are necessary on your part. But I submit to you that that information could have been gathered by human spies, dispatched by Fae into our territory. We hope our own investigations will identify them, and soon. Cyanide is a weapon anyone can deploy. Indeed, this Countess apparently did so last night—or at least, some kind of poison? Or so I was told?"

"Aconite," Vale said, "though my analysis so far has been somewhat hasty. And that was directed *against* the Fae delegation."

"The Fae are petty creatures who will even strike against their own kind," Mei Feng said, with an air of generous tolerance. "Still, I suppose we should be grateful that some are civilised enough to restrain themselves and negotiate this truce."

"And what exactly will come after the truce?" Vale asked.

"We see who's prepared to abide by it," Mei Feng said crisply.

"And if some dragons are not?"

"Then they will have directly disobeyed the eight monarchs and will be subject to judgement," Mei Feng said. "A simple enough scenario."

And one which will give the dragon kings and queens official and legal sanction to strengthen their authority over the dragon families, Vale reflected. *Wheels within wheels. And the more political Fae will likewise be able to use any of their own infractions against enemies on their own side. I do believe the benefit of peace to humans in the middle is hardly relevant to either group. What a surprise.*

Still, the humans in the middle *would* benefit too, even if it wasn't a priority for either dragons or Fae. And that would be the Library's gain from the truce—Vale had picked up enough from Winters to understand that—and Vale's own.

He spent another half-hour questioning her, looking for facts or evidence that might relate to the current investigation—rather than theories. But she had no further information of value. Finally he allowed himself to take visible notice of her glances at her watch, the window, and the door. "Thank you for your time, Lady Mei Feng," he said. "You have been of great assistance to me.

"It is my pleasure," she murmured. "I hope that I can trust your discretion about what we have just discussed. I will not bear witness to any wild suppositions."

"Of course," Vale agreed cynically. It would be his own unsupported word, if he used any parts of their conversation later to imply the murderer was a dragon. "But one final question, if I may?"

"Of course," Mei Feng said.

"Who do *you* actually think murdered Lord Ren Shun?"

"This Countess, of course," Mei Feng said. "Any other solution is quite unacceptable."

And there one had it, Vale reflected as she left the room. That was the dragon position. Any other solution was not wrong, but . . . unacceptable.

Strongrock came blowing in with a slam of the door and threw himself down in a chair. "Vale," he said dramatically, "I've found something."

Vale lifted his gaze from the bomb components strewn across the table. "Useful, I trust."

"Would I have bothered you if it wasn't?"

"Probably not," Vale allowed. He carefully lowered the fuse he'd been examining, releasing the tweezers and setting them down next to it, then wiped his hands on a napkin. "What is it?"

Strongrock leaned forward. "I've found something in Ren Shun's papers," he said. "I think it may be relevant to where the Countess is hiding."

He showed signs of strain—the wrinkles between his brows, the tightness of his expression, the over-meticulous care given to his clothing—but Vale was inclined to write those off as due to the stress of playing secretary for his uncle. "Kindly give me the full details," he said.

"My lord uncle had told me to go through Ren Shun's notes for the last few days, to make sure he had the full background on a particular situation," Strongrock began. "While doing that, I found a misfiled report, from when Ren Shun and his people were surveying this Paris—and another linked one from a later time. They identified the Grand Guignol Theatre as a source of concern, and the report noted that it had a higher-than-natural chaos level."

"But not high enough for immediate investigation?" Vale queried.

"It was rated as a low priority," Strongrock said. "Especially if Fae had been visiting and contaminating the place. It'd be the sort of thing that interested them, after all . . . But the second report was actually dated on the day Ren Shun was murdered. The agent, whoever it was, was wondering whether the Fae delegation at their hotel was using the theatre as a secondary base. Perhaps to hide backup or something like that? But if the Countess is the second Fae presence in Paris, that would explain everything."

While his words were very proper, and conveyed sentiments his uncle would have approved, Vale could see the flicker of interest in his eyes. He could sympathise. The Theatre of the Grand Guignol was a fascinating place. Even if a good half of the plays catered to the lowest and most depraved imaginings of the population, with their depictions of blood, torture, madness, and murder, it was still an interesting psychological study of human mentality. And he was rather curious about how they achieved some of their make-up and stage effects.

A piece fell into place in his mind. "If Ren Shun's men investigated and found a higher chaos level than normal," he said, "it is most intriguing that Lord Silver didn't think so."

"Silver's already been there?"

"Winters did assign him to look into theatres," Vale reminded him. "I pried the details out of him last night. He said that he'd called on the Grand Guignol, but a cursory examination had been fruitless, and he'd gone on to cast his net wider. Curious."

"So either he's lying or he's blind," Strongrock declared, leaping ahead of Vale's reasoning in a sadly unsupported way, "or the chaos level there has gone down since Ren Shun had it checked out."

"You know more about such things than I do, Strongrock. How likely is the third possibility?"

Strongrock frowned. "Well, levels could drop naturally, or the fall could be the result of dragons passing nearby. But I wouldn't expect this to happen if Fae were still visiting the theatre—and according to those witness statements Irene examined, some Fae *had* been there."

"An anomaly, then," Vale said with satisfaction. "And in keeping with levels dropping, I would put forward the theory that someone at the Grand Guignol is now attempting to *conceal* their presence—whether it is the Countess or someone else entirely. These reports of yours from Ren Shun—they are reliable?"

"Absolutely," Strongrock said swiftly. Then he paused. "Well, they're certainly *authentic*. I've seen enough of his handwriting over the last couple of days to be sure of that. Whether or not they're accurate might be a different issue."

Vale nodded. He rose from his chair and began to pace. "This agrees with certain details I have already established. Chlorine purchases—explained as for stage effects. The fact that several of the anarchist assailants were apparently devoted Guignolers—and that one of them mentioned a theatre. It requires investigation. Can your uncle spare you for a few hours?"

"That's not a problem," Strongrock said with slightly too much heartiness. "He told me to go and occupy myself elsewhere for the rest of the day. He doesn't need me for the moment. I did try to raise the possibility of the Guignol being a Fae base . . . but he dismissed it. He said, why look for additional imaginary enemies when we already have quite enough." For a moment he caught Ao Ji's tone and disdain. "He said that he felt I was seeing shadows rather than looking at facts, and that I had clearly been spending too much time with . . . my own imagination."

Vale suspected the words had been stronger than that, and more specific, but he was tactful enough not to ask for details. It was, he admitted privately—in an overly sentimental part of his mind—a pity that uncle and nephew didn't get on better. Instead he nodded. "Very good. Then we can get down to work without interruptions. I suggest we scout around the area, which would allow you to determine if there are any overt signs of chaos."

"We might need to approach the theatre more closely, if signs of chaos are hidden," Strongrock said. "Should we bring in the others?"

"Winters and Mu Dan are off on some investigation of their own," Vale said with irritation. He'd returned from a discussion with Inspector Maillon to find Winters had taken off on a scent and Mu Dan had followed her. "And Lord Silver is still hunting bakers and cakes. Besides, I'm not certain that we should bring him in at this stage . . ."

He and Strongrock exchanged glances. They'd both been present that morning when he'd attempted to blackmail Winters. Even if he wasn't working for the Countess, his loyalties could not be entirely trusted.

"And even if Irene was here," Strongrock said slowly, "it could be better if we find some independent proof of the Countess's presence, without her being involved. Not everyone believes—that is, there are some people who claim that the whole 'Countess' thing is a fabrication."

"A fabrication who assembled a bomb, filled a cake with chlorine, organised a kidnap attempt at the Paris Morgue, and sent poisoned apples to the Princess," Vale said drily. "How much evidence of malicious intent do they want?"

"He wants evidence that doesn't depend on Librarian or Fae testimony," Strongrock muttered. "I'd swear to Irene's good faith, but he says that my judgement's suspect."

Vale had to agree with the *he*—Ao Ji, obviously—in that respect. If Winters should ever lie to Strongrock, Strongrock would never doubt her. And doubting factions *could* use this.

Fortunately Vale's own judgement was rather better. And he was certain Winters was telling the truth about what she'd experienced. But he could see the direction of Strongrock's argument.

"We'll need to keep Winters informed, of course," he said. "And this is in the nature of a scouting expedition. We must assume that this Countess may recognize us, so a change of appearance is in order." He glanced at Strongrock's clothing—proper morning dress, suit and cravat. Rather too obvious. "We will simply wander the streets nearby, and your own metaphysical senses should reveal whether we need to investigate further."

"Of course," Strongrock agreed. "We can fetch the others later. But I wish we knew where Irene and Mu Dan were. If we're wrong about the Grand Guignol, they may be walking into danger themselves."

"I think they are quite capable of doing that, whether or not the Countess is hidden at the Grand Guignol," Vale said. "I'll leave a message for Winters . . ."

The streets around the Grand Guignol were busy, and Vale was able to blend into the crowd with ease. He and Strongrock were just one more pair of gentlemen strolling out for an evening's diversion, near anonymous in their hats and battered overcoats. They'd taken care to avoid observation while leaving the hotel, whether by humans or felines. And he was relatively certain that if the Countess or anyone else was present at the theatre, then their approach would be unexpected.

Since he had no way to observe any metaphysical abnormalities, he left that to Strongrock. Instead he observed the city of Paris and its inhabitants. It had been a year or two since last he visited, in his own world—and it reassured him to discover that despite the lack of certain technologies, and the divergences in history, this Paris and these people were much the same. Similar geography, similar men and women, similar police and criminals. It explained why the Librarians were able to function as an organisation. Whatever the world, human beings were still human beings.

A two-tone whistle sounded somewhere in the background, behind the noise of revellers and the sounds of music, and Vale concealed a frown. *That* was far too similar to the sort of communication a gang would use when they'd sighted a target and were signalling to close in. Perhaps he had underestimated the Grand Guignol's level of security—if this was connected. "Do you notice anything unusual?" he remarked to Strongrock, keeping his tone conversational.

Strongrock's eyes swept across their surroundings as if he was doing no more than inspecting the cabarets and entertainment on offer. "That man on the right—the one with the scar on his right cheek—is following us, I think."

"Yes," Vale agreed. "And the one over there on the left, under the black sign, the one with the single glove; he passed us two turnings back. We're being bracketed." The realization was unwelcome.

"Options?"

"Best to retreat and return in force," Vale said with regret. "Take the second right turning. If I remember my local geography correctly, we can fall back to one of the main streets."

"If we do that, we're risking her escaping—if she is based at the theatre," Strongrock pointed out.

Vale grunted in annoyance. "This is not the time or place for heroics."

"My objection's purely strategic."

"If the Countess is here and does evacuate her base, then she'll be off balance and unlikely to stage any immediate attacks. And she may leave evidence behind that we can trace."

They strolled on together, Vale watching the two men now

keeping pace with them on either side of the street. They passed through the crowd like sharks. "Of course, if we are assaulted during our retreat and can take some prisoners, then our little trip would not be entirely wasted," he added.

"Excellent," Strongrock said, brightening. "Oh, did you notice that new pair behind us?"

"Of course," Vale said, a little annoyed. He would hardly have missed such obvious followers. Clearly the men had decided to forgo caution and close in. "Turn right here . . ."

The alley was a narrow one, overhung by the houses on either side, and twisted back on itself before turning towards the main thoroughfare . . .

With an unpleasant shock, Vale saw that the alley was blocked by a wall that had clearly been there for years. As a difference between this world and his own, it was very minor, but it meant he and Strongrock were blocked. Trapped.

The two of them exchanged a glance, before turning to face the group of men now slouching into the alleyway, moving towards them.

Shortly after, they encountered the Fae member of their team.

"How nice to see you both again," Silver said bitterly, as Vale and the unconscious Kai—beaten into unconsciousness and chloroformed to make sure he stayed that way—were chained up in alcoves opposite him.

CHAPTER 21

The passage to *the* Library from the Richelieu Library had been destroyed. That was quite clear. There wasn't enough left of the room it had been in to support a way through.

Fortunately, the rest of the building still contained enough books, enabling Irene to create a temporary connection. She found a remote area where she wouldn't be disturbed by students, guards, or visitors. Then she chose a door and wrote on it in the Language, **THIS DOOR OPENS TO THE LIBRARY.** The connection would only be stable for half an hour or so before it vanished. Hopefully that would be long enough to get some answers.

Swaying a little from the drain in her energy, but unwilling to wait long enough for her head to stop swimming, she grasped the handle. **"Open to the Library,"** she said, and walked through into her true home.

In the large room beyond, heavy bookcases filled with thick leather-bound volumes filled the walls between pillars of crimson marble, and polar bear skins dotted the dark stone floor like icebergs, their white fur mottled with dust. There was a computer outlet in the room, Irene saw with relief: she wouldn't have to go searching for one. Ignoring the books on the shelves, she checked the room's designation and quickly sat down and logged in, composing a hasty email.

She hadn't wanted to do this, but she needed to contact Library Security. They were the only people who could answer some of her questions about Prutkov. Assuming that they were willing to do so.

Melusine,

I request an urgent consultation, based on my investigation into Ren Shun's death. I've established a temporary link to the Library, so please can you arrange a transfer shift down to Security and back, or come to discuss this with me in person. I can't afford to lose my passage back to the world where negotiations are taking place. I'm in Antarctic Literature, world B-23.

Irene

For a moment she debated signing off with *yours sincerely* or *yours faithfully*—or even channel Poe with *for the love of God, Montresor!* But none of those seemed likely to help. She hit the return key and stared at the screen. How long would Melusine take to read it? Was Melusine even available? What if she was having a half-hour nap and Irene didn't get a response by the time she had to return . . .

The computer chimed. Irene checked her incoming email.

Visual connection set-up in progress. Please hold.

A new window appeared on the computer screen, expanding to show a webcam view of Melusine's den. Melusine herself was in her wheelchair, looking much as she had the last time Irene had met her: short-cropped dark blonde hair, battered checked shirt, comparatively young face, centuries-old eyes. Only the rug over her legs had changed, from a weathered tartan specimen to a bilious green one.

"This is not what I wanted to hear," she said without preamble. "This is not the sort of call I wanted to be getting. What do you want a consultation about, and why, and why does it have to be with *me*?"

Irene didn't waste time asking about the visual connection. Possibly the Library's computer system had had an upgrade while she wasn't there, or this was something exclusive to Melusine's position. "You know about Ren Shun's murder," she said. "Did you know that the blame's being put on a particular Fae—the Blood Countess—and we're supposed to be tracking her down?"

"Yes, yes, and yes. What's gone wrong?"

"The Countess *is* in Paris, and she doesn't want a peace treaty signed, but I'm not so sure that she's guilty of killing Ren Shun." There had been something that had rung very true in Dorotya's disclosure of how passionately her mistress disliked being falsely accused. "Also . . ." And here was the bit where Irene could possibly shoot herself in the foot. "I need you to check something for me."

"What?"

"I want to know if anyone was entering or leaving the Library from this world last night."

"Why?"

Irene wistfully imagined being able to bark out questions like that and expect an answer, rather than having to dance around the subject and grease it well with flattery. "Because they shouldn't have been."

"Wait." Melusine pushed her wheelchair back from the computer, moving across to one of the many bookshelves in the background. She could guess what the head of Library Security was checking: the entry and exit logs for that particular portal to the Library. A cold trickle of fear made its way slowly down her back and clenched in her stomach. If her logic was wrong . . .

But Melusine slammed the book closed. "You're right," she said, turning back towards the computer screen. "There's an entry and exit recorded for Borges. He's one of the Librarians seconded to assist Prutkov. Eleven thirty local time, just before midnight. Now tell me what's going on and why this is significant."

Just before midnight, the words chimed at the back of Irene's mind. If it had been just *after* midnight, then Borges might have been trying to reach the Library to report the explosion, or to check that he could still reach the Library from the Paris where the peace conference was taking place. But just *before* midnight?

"Prutkov's up to something on his own account," Irene said, getting the words out before nervousness could stop her.

Melusine's face shuttered. There was no better word for it. Expression drained out of her eyes, and her mouth became a thin line, giving nothing away. She could have been an old photograph, the sort where the camera required several minutes of exposure, and as a result the subject's expression was flat and impassive, drained of life. "You know that's a serious accusation. Explain."

"He's trying to set things up so all sides blame the Countess, to encourage both sides to cooperate. I can understand that, but he also made an approach to me in private. He was trying to sell me the idea that the Library's future depends on us being essential to both sides, ostensibly as peace brokers—but actually as manipulators behind the scenes. As a faction who'd hold the balance of power." A fragment of speech brushed her memory again. "And when discussing the Countess's failed plan to blow up the negotiation hotel, with one of his female agents, the woman called it karmic justice for him."

"Why is that last point relevant?" Melusine was still unreadable, but at least she hadn't immediately called Irene a liar or taken her off the case.

"The note found in Ren Shun's pocket mentioned 'hell'—which is *enfer* in French—and a set of numbers. And the title of a book—*Myths,* by Herodotus. You'll have seen the report." A fraction of a nod from Melusine was confirmation. "And you presumably know the Richelieu Library was bombed last night, breaking our connection to the Library. Which is why I'm on a time limit."

"Yes," Melusine said. "And?"

Irene leaned forward. "I believe Prutkov was behind the bombing. The Enfer, the part of the library where they kept erotica, was one of the areas bombed. I know we get coincidences where there are Fae around, but that's too *much* of a coincidence. Let me theorise here. Someone left that note in Ren Shun's pocket deliberately. They wanted the investigation to follow the trail to the Enfer and to find Herodotus's *Myths* there—just as Ren Shun's note suggested. Combine that with the rumours that Ren Shun had said he'd heard at least one Librarian making a private deal to get hold of rare books? Suspicion would point right at the Library. So I think Prutkov decided to get rid of all the evidence."

"The first part of your theorising holds water," Melusine said slowly. "If someone wanted to sabotage the negotiations using the Library, and the rare book turned up where the paper on Ren Shun indicated it would be—combined with the overheard conversation—then it would be impossible to prove the Library wasn't guilty of *something*. But you haven't given me any proof that Prutkov's involved . . ."

Irene swallowed. Her throat was dry. "The rest of my theory is that Prutkov himself organised that bombing, in order to make us look like victims of the Countess to everyone else—and to hide any evidence that there had ever been a copy of the *Myths* in the Enfer. But if the book's so important, as a Librarian, he wouldn't want to destroy it. But equally he couldn't risk hiding it here in Paris. If I was him . . ." And how easy it was to imagine the chain of events, the tidy concealment of evidence. "I'd have taken it through to the Library itself. Then I'd have come back to set off the explosives—or have my agents do so, such as Borges—during the middle of the diplomatic state dinner when I'd have a perfect alibi. That's why Borges made a transit to the Library just before the bombs went off. He'd been organizing all this. But if Prutkov did this, if he did *any* of this, then he did it without telling *me*."

"You feel you should have been informed?" Melusine demanded. "You think you have some sort of right to know?"

"Yes!" Irene declared, her growing anger finally coming to a boil. She tried to gauge the shadow-play of emotions across Melusine's face. And hoped against hope that Prutkov's instructions hadn't come from the top. "Prutkov's already made it clear to me what *he* thinks the Library's future should be. I disagree. We're not in this to be power-players or manipulators. We're not in this job for the *power*. And anyone who thinks we are is a dangerous liability. I've heard him talking when he didn't think I was there too;

I know he looks on me as a disposable tool. He'd *never* tell me what he's up to behind the scenes. So I'm bringing it to you."

Melusine's fingers tapped against her desk. "I thought we were training you out of running to us with all your problems."

Irene was past the point of being insulted by something that petty. "If he's running this operation and you and Coppelia and Kostchei all know about it, then I'll accept your orders. I'll admit that I was wrong. But if he's doing all this and you don't know—then how far can you trust him to run this vital conference?"

"It's been over twelve hours," Melusine said slowly. "If he'd wanted me to know about this, he'd have got word to me by now. This is far too risky. All of it. Trying to carry off this sort of deception—and under the noses of top-level people from both sides? If Prutkov came up with this idea on his own, he's on the edge of treason. And if he's been subverted by someone like the Cardinal, that's even worse."

"The *edge* of treason?" Irene said.

"You know the old proverb. 'If it does prosper, none dare call it treason' . . . but he will have left evidence behind—we just have to find it. Assuming you're correct."

Irene wasn't quite sure of Melusine's current mood, but there was something uncomfortably brittle about it. "If *I* can deduce or guess at what Prutkov's done—making sure that the Countess is blamed for bombing the Richelieu Library and destroying vital evidence—then someone else can certainly discover it. And if anyone who wants to discredit us finds out about this, and uses the information against us . . . our reputation and our overall mission will be damaged for generations." It struck her that she'd shifted from blaming Prutkov for his morals to blaming him for his incompetence. But that wasn't just it. There was a deeper underlying problem here. "We can't afford to base the peace treaty on lies."

"You're one of the last people I'd have expected to be in favour of abstract truth, rather than practical results."

Irene wondered, not for the first time, exactly *what* was in her Library records. "I can use as many tactful lies as you want, but in a situation like this, where it's absolutely vital that all three sides come to the table honestly and trust each other . . . Blaming the Countess isn't going to work if she's not actually guilty. It'll come out sooner or later. And then the whole peace process will be suspect. And us most of all, if we are the ones who meddled with it. This is not a situation where truth is the best course, it's a situation where truth is the *only* course."

"Go on," Melusine said, tapping on her keyboard. "I can listen and type at the same time. Tell me what you have in mind."

"That's the problem. I don't have any other feasible culprits for the murder. We can't track most of the delegations that night. Half of them could have sneaked out without their servants knowing, and the other half could have had their servants lie about it. Li Ming's the only person with any sort of reported grudge against Ren Shun, his half-brother—but they fell out over Ren Shun's ethics. As a motive for disrupting the peace conference, it isn't convincing. Assuming that he told me the truth. But I think he did." Irene wanted to run her hands through her hair. "And if Ren Shun's murder is linked to Minister Zhao's assassination—which could also have ended the peace process previously—the culprit has to be someone who could reach right into dragon territory. If the Countess *was* responsible for Ren Shun's death, then does she have a dragon ally who's behind Minister Zhao's murder? How many murderers can we actually postulate here, before our theories start getting ridiculous? The only culprit apart from the Countess who would satisfy all parties would be some *other* mysterious warmongering Fae—or dragon; let's be fair—who's currently hanging out in Paris and wants to break up the conference. But we have even *less* evidence of that than we do of the Countess." A thought struck her. "Tell me—I know it's very rare, but is Herodotus's *Myths* as rare as I'm assuming it is? And is it significant if it's from Beta-001?"

"Why do you ask?"

"I'm grasping at straws and looking for any evidence that could conceivably be related to what's going on. If Ren Shun did hear someone discussing the *Myths*, then the book *is* connected to the case."

"That book's not the correct edition," Melusine said. "And the Library reference on that note indicating the book's location is misleading. There *is* a version of that book which has some very interesting information about the past history of dragons. But it's not the one from Beta-001, the location in the note." Her eyes narrowed at the flicker of interest that Irene couldn't help showing in her expression. "And no, you don't need to know which version it is. We already have a Beta-001 version, and there's nothing unusual about that one or the half-dozen versions which exist in other worlds. It's a collection of myths—a very good collection of myths—but it's not something so unique and special that any Librarian, however insane, would destroy this peace conference to get their hands on it. If the note in Ren Shun's pocket had mentioned, well, a specific reference, which I'm not going to give you, then I'd have agreed that was highly significant. But Beta-001? No. Only to a collector or a purist." She checked her watch. "How much time do you have left?"

"Ten minutes if I'm lucky, five minutes if I want to be safe." Thoughts buzzed in Irene's head. If the *Myths* from Beta-001 *wasn't* significant, then why the reference to it? Was it because someone was trying to frame the Library, for both Ren Shun's murder and for general treason and peace conference disruption, and had chosen the reference to Beta-001 by mistake? They might have known that *a* version of the book was significant, but not which one—and so they'd written down a Library world designation at random, hoping that Beta-001 would sound significant enough to any non-Librarian. That would fit with the theory that the Library was being framed. But that didn't fit with anything that the Countess had done so far, or that Irene had learned about her. So if not her—then who?

"Right." Melusine glanced at a second screen out of Irene's view. "I've just had one of my runners check on the room which used to link to your Paris. The copy of Herodotus's *Myths* is there. Or at least, it's *a* copy of the *Myths*. We can't be sure which world it's originally from without more detailed checks, but it's certainly not from the world where the peace negotiations are taking place. It was never written there. The book wasn't very well hidden either, but they probably didn't have time to do better. That part of your theory checks out. But if I pull Prutkov out in the middle of the negotiations, that'll destabilise the talks, and we need more answers." She ran a hand through her short hair. "All right. I'm going to bring in someone with enough authority to handle Prutkov and help you, but it'll take me a few hours."

"Can't you come yourself?" Irene suggested.

"I don't leave the Library," Melusine said. She might as well have said it in the Language, binding herself with an oath: it was a statement of fact that was not going to change, even if the universe itself did. "I can't promise who you'll get, but they'll give you a password to show they're directly from me and you can trust them. Let's make the password . . ." She typed again. "The password is Nevsky. That should be original enough. In the meantime, try to shake some answers out of your friend Vale, even if he doesn't want to share them. He probably knows more than you do. It's his job, after all. And make sure nothing else happens that might derail the talks. Can you do that?"

"I can try."

"Why didn't you take this to Coppelia or Kostchei in the first instance?"

"Because I was afraid Prutkov would find out if I asked for a private conversation with them in Paris. And if it came down to his word or mine without proof, when I wasn't even sure if he'd done something wrong or just been careless . . ." Irene shrugged. "Also, they're being kept busy in meetings all the time."

Melusine nodded. "Probably his work too. All right, you'd better leave while the link still holds. Be careful. I'd like Paris to still be in one piece by the time I can get someone to you."

And she cut the connection before Irene could make any sort of comeback.

Mu Dan seized on Irene the moment that she returned to Le Meurice. "Your bedroom, now," she said grimly. "We have another problem."

Irene let herself be dragged up to her room, her heart sinking. "What is it?" she demanded.

Mu Dan glanced around the room dubiously. "Will we be overheard?"

"Just a moment." Irene switched to the Language. "**Listening**

devices or listening magic, malfunction and stop working." There were no signs of anything happening at that—but then if there weren't any listening devices, there shouldn't be any consequences. "All right, unless there's someone actually with an ear to the door, we're safe. What's happened?"

"Prince Kai has dropped out of sight too—as well as Silver," Mu Dan said. She sat down. If it hadn't been for the corseting under her dress, it would have been a despairing collapse. As it was, the chair creaked with the force of her movement. "And so has Vale. Apparently Prince Kai came to the hotel while we were both away, and met Vale. Then they went out together without telling anyone where they were going. I cannot *believe* that nobody has the sense to leave some sort of message behind them when they go to investigate—"

There was a knock at the door.

"What is it now?" Mu Dan snarled. She looked as if she would like to rip out her hairpins and use them to impale whoever was interrupting.

"Just a moment," Irene said, as calmly as she could. Melusine's words echoed in her memory. *I'd like Paris to still be in one piece by the time I can get someone to you.* She crossed to the door and opened it, to find herself staring at a hotel page. "Yes?"

"Message for you, madam," the page said. He offered her a sealed note on a tray.

Irene recognized Vale's handwriting. Vast relief and hope bloomed inside her. "Thank you," she said, finding a coin for a tip. "Where and when were you given this?"

"Just a couple of hours ago, madam, downstairs. The gentleman said to give the note to you when you came back."

"Was the gentleman doing anything else?"

The page frowned, trying to remember. "He was with another gentleman, madam, though not one staying at this hotel. He asked for you, and when you couldn't be found, he left the note and they both left together."

"Thank you," Irene said, handed over the tip, closed the door, and turned back to Mu Dan. "A note from Vale. Apparently he had some sense after all."

"Well, thank the heavens and earths for that! What does he say?"

Irene broke the seal on the note and opened it. "Winters," she read aloud, "I hope your investigations have been more useful than mine. Strongrock has found information among Ren Shun's papers which suggests the Countess is hiding in the Theatre of the Grand Guignol, and we are going to investigate. Kindly join us there as soon as possible, and bring Mu Dan. And Silver, if you must."

She looked up from the note at Mu Dan. "That's curious."

"Which of the many possible things within is curious?" Mu Dan asked. She looked slightly less ready to explode than earlier—possibly because Vale had remembered to mention her in the note, or possibly because there was a note at all.

"If Kai found information in Ren Shun's papers, which are presumably at the Ritz, then why didn't he tell *you* about it? You were there earlier."

Mu Dan snorted. "You overrate the prince's willingness to speak to me. He would far rather communicate with you."

"Maybe," Irene said. Perhaps it was true that Kai's first reflex had been to tell Irene and Vale, rather than a comparatively new acquaintance. But something still felt wrong about it. She mentally filed the thought for later. "All right. I'm guessing that Vale and Kai haven't actually been absent for that long, and that nobody's raised any alarms yet?"

"You're right. But something's wrong. I can feel it." Mu Dan rose and began to pace angrily back and forth, constrained by the length of the room. "First Lord Silver goes wandering away and doesn't come back, and now those two are off on their own. If you hadn't returned, I wouldn't even have had that note, and then where would we be?"

Irene reread the note thoughtfully, then held it up to the light to see if there were any hidden messages or pinpricks, or any other secret ways of passing information. Nothing was obvious. "I agree," she said. "I know that we shouldn't be worrying on the basis of just an hour or two's absence. But if they *have* found the Countess's lair, then they're walking into danger."

"Much as you were earlier," Mu Dan sniped. "And you didn't have backup either."

Irene sighed. "We don't have time for recriminations. Shall we just agree that hypocrisy is my middle name, and leave the matter there? Besides, I knew that I was walking into a possible ambush. And I had the advantage that she underrated me. I'm only human, after all. She won't underrate Kai. She'll recognize him as a dragon. But he's young." As she put words to her fears, they became firmer and more concrete. "We need to get to the Grand Guignol now."

"Should we take backup?"

Irene hesitated. "I don't know. If it *is* the Countess's hidden base, and she sees us arriving in force, we may spoil Vale and Kai's investigation. Or if they're prisoners, she may use them as hostages."

"And if we go in on our own and get killed as well? Marching in there two at a time for our own executions won't *help* the situation."

"No, it won't," Irene agreed. "But I think we need more information first." She looked at Mu Dan thoughtfully. It would be very hard to disguise the other woman's beauty or forcefulness, or the draconic perfection of her features. "You're a judge-investigator. Your first instinct is to go in at the front door and get answers. I'm not. I'm a Librarian. And a spy. And it's time I focused on that."

CHAPTER 22

Even the vicious weather couldn't douse the nightlife in the Montmartre district of Paris. The place had a gaiety to it, a joie de vivre that even London couldn't match. Throngs of students and partygoers swept from one bar to the next, discarding old hangers-on and collecting new ones with every change of location. Artists' models, courtesans, and dancers orbited around the drinkers in trembling masses of feathers and lace. Those women rarely had to pay for admission to the more private cabarets; their fashionable clothing was the only passport they needed. The vendors on street corners sold roasted nuts and sweets, little cakes and rolls, hot milk and coffee.

Tables spilled out from Montmartre's establishments onto the pavements, filling them from wall to kerb, and pedestrians were forced to crowd down the centre of the streets. The buildings leaned closer to each other here, quite unlike the wide avenues of later-built Paris, and parties spilled into upper stories and even onto the roofs. Stamped rhythms echoed on the floorboards as Irene passed bar after bar.

She didn't make a very convincing young man, but with her short hair and in men's clothing, and a bit of shadowing on her cheeks, in the twilight pall she could pass for one. A borrowed cap was pulled down low, and she slouched in her cheap overcoat, with a muffler wrapped round her neck. Just another citizen of Paris, out for a good time, too poor to be worth professional attention from the ladies of the night or the tourist-fleecers.

She'd passed under the skeletal arms of the Moulin Rouge windmill, interwoven with red electric lights that threw scarlet streaks across the buildings, the snow, and the faces of the revellers below. Flaring gaslights lit the darkness, and panels of light fell into the streets from the open windows and doorways as she passed them. A small hand tried to slide into her pocket, and she knocked it aside without undue violence. Montmartre was just as ready to prey on its visitors as it was to entertain them.

At that moment, Mu Dan was circling around to the theatre's entrance in the rue Chaptal. The plan was for her to hang around ostentatiously near the entrance, making herself visible (though absolutely not getting herself kidnapped or assaulted), while Irene sneaked in through the stage door and did some reconnaissance. It was a variation on the tactics that the Countess herself had used—draw attention with a public display and simultaneously make your true move elsewhere. Irene had no objection to stealing a good strategy, any more than to stealing a good book.

As she navigated through the back streets towards the Grand Guignol's stage door, she considered the theatre's history. Based in a convent school destroyed during the Reign of Terror, the performances took place in the old chapel, under the mocking gaze of the wooden cherubim in the rafters. It came from a tradition of naturalistic theatre, celebrating real human dramas rather than flamboyant escapism. But it also fed the human passion for cathartic spectacle and horrific violence. Short plays alternated through the performance, a mixture of farces and bloody horror. There was supposed to always be a doctor and nurses present, in case anyone in the audience had a heart attack. Irene rather wished she'd been able to attend a performance herself. It sounded more interesting than the scheduled opera this evening. The theatre might be a crowd-pleasing carnival of torture and death, but it was also genuinely experimental. (Though possibly she was being overly even-handed. Most of the audience probably came for the blood.)

Still, on reflection it also seemed the *ideal* place for the Blood Countess to pick as a hideout. A theatre that had mock torture and executions on stage? That had a cauldron of stage blood always on the boil because it used so much of it? Perfect. But was it *too* obvious a choice? Or was it a double bluff?

But one thing was certain: if the Countess was here, and had been for a while, then the whole place should have a higher-than-usual level of chaotic power. Silver should have noticed it, if he'd been checking theatres. Although Silver hadn't been seen since this morning . . .

Irene dragged herself back to focus on the current situation. She was reasonably sure she hadn't been followed from the hotel. Reasonably. It was difficult to be entirely certain, with the streets this crowded. At least she couldn't see any cats lurking in the shadows or on the rooftops.

In spite of everything that was going wrong, and the danger to herself and to the Library, Irene found herself relaxing in the crowd. It was reassuring to be back among normal human beings, in the middle of this upswelling of life and enthusiasm and art, away from the frozen hauteur and the gold-and-ivory décor of the costly hotels. She wasn't *meant* to be a diplomat. She was much happier here in the shadows.

If only there wasn't so much at stake.

She checked her pocket watch inconspicuously—Mu Dan should be round the front right now, attracting attention before retreating—and she loitered towards the Grand Guignol's stage door. There was already a queue outside it, though it would be a while till the interval. Placards in black and white listing the night's performances—THE SYSTEM OF DR. GOUDRON AND PROF. PLUME, MEAT-TICKET, THE CARGO FRAUD, MADEMOISELLE FIFI, A KISS IN THE NIGHT—contrasted with the gaudier pictures beside them. A woman hung impaled on a spike. A white-clad surgeon and nurse leered over the body of a patient strapped to the operating table. Two elderly men in grey suits held a third one down and positioned a scalpel at his eye. The flaring gaslight leached the colours out of the artworks, leaving them in black and white, but the postures and expressions still spoke of drama and horror.

Irene sauntered to the front of the queue, ignoring the mutters from the people she passed, and lowered her voice to speak to the burly stage doorman. **"You perceive that I am a person who has a right to go inside and should not be stopped,"** she murmured.

"Right you are," the man said with a nod, and held the door open for Irene, his cigarette still dangling from the corner of his mouth. She slipped through quickly into the narrow hallway beyond, and the rising tide of complaints was cut off by the door closing behind her.

It took her less than a minute to realize that something was badly wrong. While she was hardly an expert in theatrical backstage corridors, she did know that there shouldn't be so many people in them. It wasn't just the stagehands carrying props through, or the actors and actresses getting into position. It wasn't even the pair of nurses, crisply uniformed, making their way to the front of house. (Apparently that bit of the story was true.) There was a constant flow of men—*all men, not women, interesting*—filtering through the crowded maze of corridors.

And nobody seemed to *notice*. This was abnormal in itself. Actors and stagehands were territorial; Irene had expected to be challenged half a dozen times in the first few minutes, and the words *you perceive that . . .* were on the tip of her tongue. But nobody seemed to notice her, or any of the men drifting through, who were treating the place like some sort of antechamber.

The lights dimmed. The performance was about to start.

Irene couldn't sense any notable level of chaotic power. The place felt much like the rest of Paris, and certainly nothing like the Fae base at the Grand Hôtel du Louvre. But she was sure she was on to something. This might not be the Countess's actual lair, but it could be a gathering point for her servants. She wandered down the current corridor, trying to look as if she knew where she was going, while watching for a possible target to follow.

Then a scream ripped through the air. There was nothing fake about it. The sound was one of genuine pain, genuine insanity, distilled into one single shriek that froze Irene in her tracks. She flinched before she could stop herself.

Two men had just turned the corner—just in from outside, slush still wet on their boots, in the same sort of rough clothing as she was. They both looked at her suspiciously, and Irene realized that she had just identified herself as a total newcomer. A habitué of this place would be blasé about screams from the stage.

She could run. Or she could try to use this to her advantage.

"Do you know where we should go?" she said softly, advancing to meet them. She was grateful that the ongoing play meant they had to keep their voices down. It was easier to fake a man's tones while whispering. "I'm new here."

They exchanged glances—the look of conspirators, rather than stagehands. "Go where, and why?" the larger one demanded.

Time for a gamble. "To see *her*," Irene said, and tried to put hopeless worship into her voice. "You've got to help me. I've got to see her again. I *need* to see her." She reached for the man's sleeve, doing her best to imitate the fervour of addiction, practically snivelling. "Look, I can pay . . ."

He shrugged her off contemptuously, but the suspicion had gone from his eyes. "No need for that, you little rat. Follow us and mind your manners."

"We'd better get on down," the second man said. "Come on, let's get moving."

He led the way, turning off in a new direction. Irene followed, lagging a few steps behind, conscious of just how close her escape had been. She was surprised they hadn't even tried to check her identity; they'd just accepted her as one of them without a moment's hesitation. Did they assume that anyone backstage here was part of the conspiracy? If that was the case, Irene was deep in the middle of a hornets' nest, and it was going to be very difficult to extricate herself.

The first man pushed aside a rack of costumes—bloodstained shirts, strait jackets, uniforms, nuns' habits—to reveal a door in the wall behind it. The door opened silently, without even the smallest creak, but the air that came from behind it smelled of the sewers, and dust, and blood. Both the men breathed it in and smiled.

The stairs behind the door, leading down, were of the same stone as the walls outside and the foundations of this building: the basement must date back to when this place had first been built as a chapel. Oil lanterns lit the way as they made their way downwards, flickering with every draught, filling the corners with jumping shadows. A hushed murmur of voices came from ahead, like celebrants waiting in a church for the service to begin.

At the bottom of the stairs, a small anteroom led into a larger cellar beyond. Grand Guignol posters were slathered across the stone walls; leering faces and dead eyes peered at Irene and her companions as they entered.

And suddenly Irene could taste chaotic power like acid in the air. Her Library brand flared up across her back like poison ivy. She looked around quickly, trying to find a reason for the abrupt change in power level, but nothing jumped out to explain it. Not for the first time, she wished for a convenient Library course in Reasons for Fluctuations in Chaos Level and How Fast to Run Away.

The men in front of her drifted forward as if they were pulled by a magnet. Irene hung back: if something in this anteroom could explain how the Countess was hiding herself, then she needed to know what it was. She ignored the inner voice that pointed out that she just didn't want to go forward into the lair of the Countess. Cowardice and common sense were on the same wavelength here.

But how *was* the Countess suppressing this level of chaos? Horror literature suggested all sorts of unpleasant ideas: a corpse beneath the stones of the floor, dragon blood circulated in some sort of contraption behind the walls . . . all right, perhaps the dragon-blood thing was grossly unlikely, not to mention simply gross, but there weren't any textbooks on what was possible and what wasn't. Especially when Fae were involved.

Irene decided to investigate the most obvious incongruity and examined the posters on the walls. As far as she could tell in the dim light, they were standard Grand Guignol fare, with predatory poses and mouths open in screams or laughter. They didn't have strange runes painted on them, or their ink mixed with blood, or . . .

She thoughtfully ran the tips of her fingers across the biggest of them, criss-crossing it in a regular pattern. Yes, she'd *thought* she'd seen something odd in the shifting lamplight—there was a small rectangular extra thickness at the bottom left corner. Hastily she dug her fingernails under the edge of the poster, peeling it back. It came away easily, the paste crumbling and weakened. There was another piece of paper beneath it. No, parchment. She teased it out, sliding it carefully so as not to tear it, and smoothed the poster back in place; then she looked at what she'd just uncovered.

Irene's breath caught in her throat. It was in the Language. She swallowed and set her back against the wall, trying to calm the sudden panicked hammering of her heart. It was signed ***Alberich.***

The darkness seemed to close in on her. No. *No.* He was dead. She'd seen him die.

The rising noise of voices from the large chamber beyond forced Irene to drag herself away from rising panic and back to reality. She couldn't afford to be caught loitering here; she had to hurry. She made herself read the rest of the script. It contained words in the Language that she didn't know (and wasn't *that* interesting?) but basically seemed to be a ward of some sort, constraining chaos to remain within its boundaries. Interesting; it was referring to itself in the plural. Did that mean that there were several of these, delimiting the area and letting the Countess hide herself within it? That explained a lot.

The parchment was hard and dry under her fingers. It was old, not new. Irene tucked it into her coat pocket, breathing a silent prayer that it was indeed as old as it felt and that the person who'd written it was a thing of the past as well. If *he* was here . . .

It was almost a relief when she made herself walk forward into the inner chamber.

Her first impression was *throne room*, but, incongruously, her second impression was *lion's cage in the zoo*. Men lounged on the plain stone floor as though they were drugged with opium, exchanging slow, rambling sentences or playing endless games of dice or cards. The cats that wandered between them were the only real energy in the room, patterns of moving shadow in the flaring light of the dangling oil lamps. As Irene's eyes adjusted to the dimness, the throne at the far end of the room came into focus, draped with tricolour banners. But empty. For the moment.

The room's dimensions were uncertain. It wasn't just the light. The entire space was liminal, vague around the edges, defined by possibility and horror just as much as by reality. It buzzed against her skin and tasted *wrong* as she breathed it in. She'd been in high-chaos zones before, and they'd all been created and sustained for specific purposes. This one bore the mark of its mistress. It was a place for the Blood Countess to do what she liked best. To do what defined her.

More oddities: iron maidens flanking the throne, their doors shut for the moment but their purpose evident enough. The shadows in the corner, which suggested warped pieces of machinery more appropriate to the theatre above. A table of weapons next to the door, as though inviting visitors to pick one that suited their taste. Flick-knives, brass knuckles, garrottes, and twisted pieces of metal where the only identifiable parts were the blunt end one held. Irene took a small flick-knife, slipping it into a pocket of her coat. She stepped away from the doorway, edging farther into the room.

Then she froze as she saw them, chained in alcoves to the wall behind the throne. Kai, slumped unconscious and dangling from his shackles. Vale, watching the room and with half a dozen cats watching him back. Had he made an attempt to escape already? He'd certainly have lockpicks up his sleeve. His cane was propped near him, just out of reach, as though to taunt him by its presence. Both of them were in the sort of clothing that a working man or a low-grade clerk would have worn, rather than suits—an attempt at disguise? It apparently hadn't worked.

Her gaze followed along the wall. Silver was there too, in chains as well, with the air of a man who was waiting to speak to the management and make a complaint about his accommodation.

At least she knew where all three of them were. Now she just had to work out—somehow—how to get them out of there. Given a roomful of accomplices (and cats), this could be difficult. Perhaps the best course of action would be retreat, followed by a call on Inspector Maillon . . .

Irene rapidly abandoned that plan as she heard noises coming from the stairs behind her. She drifted across to a nearby group of gamblers and folded down to sit next to them. They barely noticed her.

Mu Dan was hustled into the room. She carried herself like an aristocrat heading for the tumbrel, all anger and affronted pride, but her face was pale, even in the dim lamplight. She would be feeling the chaos like a sickness, much worse than Irene's own perceptions of it. A man on either side of her held her arms, while a third was directly behind her: Irene saw the glint of metal in his hand, pressed into her back. Even a dragon would have problems with a close-up bullet while in human form. Or maybe, like Irene herself, she'd intended to play along with capture in order to find out the enemy's plans, and abruptly found herself in far more danger than she'd expected.

So much for reinforcements. So much for fetching help. So much, possibly, for Mu Dan and Irene and all the rest of them.

Mu Dan caught sight of Kai in his chains. "Your Highness!" she called desperately. "Your Highness, wake up—"

Chaotic power washed through the room, and Mu Dan recoiled mid-shout, turning her head as if she had been slapped. And abruptly the throne at the end of the chamber was occupied.

Irene recognized the Countess from their previous meeting, though it would be inaccurate to say she recognized the woman's *face*—it was her *presence* that was familiar, like the taste or smell of blood. She occupied the throne like an invading army. Her hair and dress were the same colour as the dried blood on the base of a guillotine, and she held herself like a naked blade. Men across the room fell or scrambled to their knees, turning towards her, and murmurs of *liberty* and *revolution* filled the air like prayers. Dorotya lurked at the base of the throne, an animate mass of shawls. Cats swarmed from all quarters of the room to stretch and grovel at the feet of their mistress.

Irene cowered like the rest of the englamoured audience, keeping her head down and her face hidden, struggling with panic. She could feel the net of glamour washing across the surface of her mind, seducing with dreams of blood and violence and anarchy—

shouting and killing and revelling in it—but her Library brand and training gave her the will to withstand them.

The Countess extended a lazy hand, and the audience fell silent. "An endless stream of visitors today," she remarked. "Bring the prisoner before me."

Mu Dan looked as if she was considering resistance, but the gun jabbed into her spine again, and she reluctantly marched forward until she stood before the Countess's throne. But not too close—the Countess clearly had more sense than to allow an enraged dragon within arm's length of her. Mu Dan stood there, tolerating the grasp on her arms, her eyes burning with suppressed fury.

"Well?" the Countess asked. "Have you nothing to say?"

"To you? Unlikely."

The Countess smiled. "I understand that you are a judge-investigator, or so my cats tell me. I have some ability in that line myself. I imagine that in a little while you will be very willing to unburden yourself and tell me anything that I might want to know. Of course, by that point I may not be interested in listening."

"Your threats are pointless," Mu Dan answered flatly. "Bring on your tortures. I and my colleagues will laugh them to scorn."

"Excuse *me*," Silver muttered, quite audibly.

"You have been found out," Mu Dan continued, raising her voice to carry over Silver's interruption. "Your lair is discovered. I have allowed myself to be brought down here to negotiate with you. If you surrender and allow your followers to be cleansed, I am empowered to offer terms."

Since it was unfeasible to actually do so, Irene allowed herself to visualise beating her head against the floor. Mu Dan was not a good bluffer. Irene thought that she herself *might* have been able to get away with that, but then she'd had a lot more experience at lying to people . . .

The Countess laughed, and her voice somehow held the echo of trickling blood. "Except there is *nobody* in the streets above who should not be there. The theatre is full of people watching their beloved Guignol plays, celebrating pain and torture and death. You are desperate, little dragon, and it will not save you. Do you have a single reason why I should not kill you here and now, and make better use of your blood than you are doing?"

Irene rose to her feet. "She may not," she said, "but I do."

CHAPTER 23

The Countess was frozen for a moment, the light reflecting on her eyes, and the smell of blood rose till Irene could taste it in her own mouth. Finally she said, "Is there a single reason why I shouldn't tell my followers to seize you and rip you limb from limb?"

"Self-interest," Irene said. She began to pace through the kneeling crowd towards the throne. "You might say that it's my own driving interest as well. Good evening, your ladyship. I trust that you're enjoying Paris."

"I find it suits me very well. Better than it's about to suit you, perhaps."

Irene rated that threat as little more than hot air. The Countess had *not* ordered her minions to rip Irene limb from limb; ergo, she was interested in what Irene had to say—for the moment.

"I apologise for retreating so rapidly earlier," she said. She nodded towards Dorotya, who was still skulking to one side. "The odds weren't in my favour, and I don't like negotiating from a position of weakness."

"Then either your current strength is very well hidden up your sleeve, or this is one of the biggest bluffs I've ever seen," the Countess said, cutting to the root of Irene's position.

Irene removed her cap and bowed. "Would your ladyship say that I was suicidal?"

"Not at first glance," the Countess mused, "but there's a point at which anyone will beg for death."

Irene felt her flesh creep. She made an effort not to show it. "Your ladyship, I am a low-ranking Librarian. My superiors are all old, and are likely to live for decades yet, if not centuries. I fetch and carry at their orders. I run their errands. But, your ladyship . . . I am ambitious."

"Interesting," the Countess said. "Approach."

Irene came to stand a few paces away from Mu Dan—but, unlike the dragon, unrestrained. "Your ladyship wants something. I want something. It seems to me that at least for the moment, we could negotiate."

"I've negotiated with Librarians before," the Countess mused. She leaned forward. "Very well. What are your terms?"

"I would request the lives of your hostages," Irene said. "And safe passage out of here, of course."

"That is quite a large demand." The Countess swept a hand in the direction of the chained prisoners. "A dragon prince. A Fae lordling. A human detective. And the maiden beside you, of course." Her voice lingered over the word *maiden* obsessively. "You ask for a great deal. What do you offer me in return?"

"To clear your name, your ladyship." Irene bowed again. "To shame your detractors by showing their false accusations for the lies they are . . . I'll *ensure* that you aren't blamed for Ren Shun's murder. But it'll be a great deal easier for me to do so with the rest of my team to help me."

"Don't trust her, milady," Dorotya hissed, scuttling forward to snarl in Irene's direction. "She's a tricksy one, she is, sneaky and treacherous. If you want my advice, milady, you'll hang her up by her heels and slit her throat right this minute."

"You always give me good advice, Dorotya," the Countess agreed. "Why should I trust you, Librarian? You've already thwarted me once."

Irene felt the weight of all the eyes on her: Countess, Fae, humans, dragons, cats . . . Her throat was almost too dry to speak. "As I said, madam, I'm ambitious. I'm in a position where powerful people will see what I've managed to achieve. And the world is changing." She gestured at Kai and Silver in their chains. "The Library has to change with it. We're not going to be just book thieves any longer. We'll be deal makers, go-betweens, manipulators." *I must thank Prutkov at some point for giving me such an excellent script,* she thought. "This is my big chance to pull off a coup in front of a dragon king and some very powerful Fae. And if I manage to embarrass my superiors in the process, so much the better."

The Countess was silent, considering. Even the cats were still. Finally she asked, "How would your superiors react, if we made a deal?"

Irene held up two fingers. "Possibility one, they won't know anything about it. My colleagues here will keep their mouths shut. Or else." She smiled, trying to imitate the way the Countess's own lips curved in a red arc. "Possibility two, they find out—but by that point we should have signed our little peace treaty, and they'll have to keep it secret for their own sakes. And that's assuming my superiors will be my superiors for much longer. There could be an accident. Leaving the Library to enter an alternate world is a risky business."

Part of Irene was silently hysterical with disbelief at this performance she was giving. It was almost a complete list of things she'd never do. *What do I suggest for an encore? Seduce Kai and steal a dragon throne? Actually, she might believe that more readily . . .* But the more pragmatic part of her mind was running on controlled panic. The Countess was not going to listen to pleas for mercy or threats. But she *might* temporarily cooperate with someone as self-interested and malicious as she was. As long as it was to the Countess's advantage. And only for that long.

It just had to be long enough for Irene to get everyone out of here alive.

"You remind me of someone I once knew, centuries ago," the Countess murmured. She sounded almost wistful. A cat wound its way up into her lap, and she began to stroke it. "As I said, I've made bargains with a Librarian before."

"Then you know we can be trusted," Irene said hopefully.

"Actually, he double-crossed me and stole from my personal collection. And then I had him chased across the country by my personal guards with whips—with instructions to knout him till there wasn't enough skin on his back to bind a pamphlet, let alone a folio. And when he got away, he set the Inquisition on me. Ah, how I miss him . . ."

Irene could see the blank disbelief on Mu Dan's face. But Irene herself had encountered this sort of behaviour from Fae before. Sometimes they didn't care whether their interaction with other people was positive or negative, as long as it was *intense*. Also, if the Librarian (or ex-Librarian) in question had been Alberich, that explained where the warding scripts had come from—which took a weight off Irene's mind. They *were* really old. One less reason for panic.

"Your ladyship," Irene interjected, "time presses. If I am to clear your name, I need to do it soon. There are far too many people who hunger to blame you and blacken your name."

"So what do you actually require? Besides me letting you and yours go, that is." The Countess paused. "In one piece. With your blood. And your vital organs. And . . . you know, I think you're getting rather the better part of the deal here."

Irene felt the danger level in the room begin to rise again. The Countess might have been impressed by Irene's promises, but it wouldn't last. It was time to go on the attack.

Metaphorically. For the moment.

"What I require, your ladyship, is information," she said briskly. "You've been set up, wrongly branded as the culprit for this terrible crime. But for that to happen, the person responsible must have known you were going to be here to blame. So—why *did* you come here?"

From the darkness of Vale's alcove, she saw the very faint inclination of his head. He'd pieced that together too. She wasn't surprised.

The haze of light around the Countess thickened. She was a mature woman now, with the gleam of forbidden knowledge and secrets in her eyes. "I was told that there would be people here whose blood I could . . . use. It can be difficult to find victims of quality."

That made sense. Powerful Fae liked interacting with each other, repeating and enacting their favourite narrative patterns. But stories that ended up with one participant drained of their blood—and dead—might have significantly fewer volunteers to take part. And the Princess would be the *perfect* victim for the Countess. "But the bomb under the hotel?" Irene asked, confused. "That would have killed everyone."

"Not the *strong* ones," the Countess said, with a bare-shouldered shrug. "The resulting chaos and confusion would have allowed me to take prisoners. Besides, doesn't everyone like blowing up peace conferences?"

Her gaze challenged Irene to contradict her. Potential violence hung in the air. The Countess might want all her audience to kneel and adore her for the moment, but if she changed her mind they'd swarm Irene. And that wasn't even counting the cats.

Irene reminded herself that her job here was to get everyone out alive, and acquire useful evidence, not indulge in sarcasm. "I understand, your ladyship. But you still haven't explained how you found out about these potential victims in the first place." This was the crucial question. "*Who* told you?"

"Oh, I have spies listening out for that sort of thing . . ." the Countess said deliberately. Too deliberately? It felt like a test. Maybe she wouldn't let them go unless Irene could prove she had what it took to find the truth.

Admittedly, Irene hadn't had a great deal of success so far. But information was coming together now.

"You wouldn't risk coming here in person unless you had something *solid* in the way of interest," Irene hazarded. "And you said *I was told* at first, not *my spies discovered*. You *knew* who passed you the information, and whether or not you could trust them—whether or not they knew that you knew."

The Countess considered, then waved a hand at Dorotya. "Fetch the letter, Dorotya. Yes, you're right, Librarian. I traced the information back to the person who leaked it to me. People think of me as a blunt instrument, whom they can employ against their enemies. Yet I am *extremely* sharp. And even the most cunning of my kind can have imprudent agents."

A dizzying flush of success swept through Irene. She felt as if she'd just stepped back from the top of a skyscraper. She stiffened her knees before they could tremble; this was no time to suggest weakness. "I will try to be more prudent myself."

The Countess laughed. "You're here, surrounded by my servants, talking to me, *bargaining* with me, and you call yourself prudent? You're almost entertaining enough to leave alive . . . after this is over, of course."

Her voice was sweet and confiding, demanding respect, somehow bridging the obvious threat in her words and making them sound reasonable. The Library brand on Irene's back flared up in response, and Irene set her teeth, resisting the Countess's will. "Please don't do that, your ladyship," she said. "If I go out of here with your power smeared all over me, someone's going to notice. I have to look impartial, for the moment."

"For the moment," the Countess agreed. "Very well. To business, then. The letter Dorotya holds can be traced to the Cardinal. That's what you suspected, isn't it?"

It was indeed what Irene had guessed. She would have liked to claim that she'd deduced it, but her theory had been based on personalities and possibilities rather than solid proof. "He seemed a more logical candidate than the Princess," she agreed. "And certainly more so than Ao Ji."

The Countess smirked. "Never trust any ruler, Librarian. They're all untrustworthy. I will enjoy seeing what happens next.

The Cardinal shouldn't have tried to endanger me. Dorotya, give her the letter."

Dorotya twitched forward and offered Irene the envelope as if she wished it were drenched in contact poison. Irene took it and tucked it inside her coat. "Thank you, your ladyship."

"But I still think that the bargain's in your favour," the Countess mused. "Yet I can be generous. You may go. And you may take two of your friends with you."

"Two?" Irene said, startled.

"Yes. Two. I think that's a *fair* deal for what you'll do for me. But as I said, I'm generous. I'll let you choose which two you take away with you . . . and which two will remain here with me."

"But they're all valuable to me, your ladyship," Irene argued. Her mind was racing. She could tell the Countess wasn't going to give way on this one. Forcing Irene to make a sadistic choice like this was her ideal entertainment—at least, until one got to the stage involving sharp edges and iron maidens. "I beg you to reconsider—"

"I think not." The Countess rose to her feet, tipping the cat to the floor. She dominated the room. "Pick your favourites. Or leave without any of them and listen to them screaming as you go."

"Leave me," Mu Dan said through gritted teeth. "Take His Highness and the detective. You need them more than you need me."

Irene glanced to Silver. He shrugged. "My little mouse, you will no doubt do precisely as you wish—but your political life will be very difficult if you have to explain my absence."

"You're wasting your time, Lord Silver," Vale commented. "It's quite obvious what choice Winters will make. We will be left to the mercy of this common or garden psychopath."

"Common?" the Countess murmured. A bloody light gleamed in her eyes and was reflected in the pupils of the surrounding felines. "I will be proving otherwise to you very shortly."

Time for the plan of last resort.

"I'd appreciate it if you wait till I've gone," Irene said, doing her best to sound bored. "The sound of screaming does not excite me. As for my choice, I'll take the dragon prince and the other dragon here beside me. I've invested too much . . . time in him, to waste it now."

"Like that, mm?" The Countess smiled. "In that case, I'll tell you a secret." She stepped down, approaching Irene.

Every muscle in Irene's body wanted to flinch away. The buzz of ambient chaos around the Countess made her skin crawl. This was far worse than the Princess; the Princess's aura had at least been relatively benign. But the Countess carried the echo of distant screams with her, the memory of pain, the shadows of torture and despair. If the Princess was a dream, and the Cardinal was a bad dream, then the Countess was a full-fledged screaming nightmare with no hope of waking up. She took a deep breath, tasting the stink of blood and sweat that filled the room, and braced herself.

The Countess stopped barely a foot away from Irene. Her pale flesh was the colour of rotten fungus and pollution, and her dress and hair were the shade of dried blood. The darkness seethed in the corners of the room, ready to rush in and bury Irene forever. Mu Dan had flinched away, hanging in the arms of the men holding her like a victim of radiation sickness.

"Do you want to know a secret?" the Countess breathed.

"Always." The word came out harsh and ragged.

"I had a warning that the princeling and the detective were

coming. A letter." Her hand fluttered to her bodice, in the sort of gesture that Vale would have classified as highly revealing of where she'd hidden it. "You should take better care of your investments, Librarian. They can be taken away from you so very, very easily."

And just like that, Irene's priorities altered. She *needed* that letter. The stakes had risen. And she could tell that the Countess wanted her to ask for it. No doubt there would be a promised favour in return—one that Irene couldn't afford.

The odds were not in her favour. A hugely powerful Fae was within arm's reach of her. The room was full of hostile agents—Dorotya, humans, cats. *Kits, cats, sacks, and wives, how many were there going to St. Ives?* a nursery rhyme echoed at the back of her mind. Her allies were in chains, or incapacitated by the ambient level of chaos, or both. And the whole situation was hidden from the eyes of everyone else in Paris who might have helped her, by the wards that Alberich had created long ago.

Library wards. Written in the Language.

"I appreciate the warning," she said, gathering her will. "And I can only say—" She shifted to the Language. **"Wards of Alberich, force out chaos!"**

It was like being in an aeroplane or an express lift that had dropped thousands of feet in a single second. Even though there was no physical gravity or pressure to the change, it felt as if Irene's ears had popped. She abruptly lacked the strength to stand: her head buzzed with weakness, and she wanted to simply lie down and close her eyes. She'd fallen to her knees, swaying with the effort to even stay upright.

It took her a moment to realize that the reason she was still looking into the Countess's eyes was that the Countess was on her knees as well. Alberich must have done very impressive work with those wards, to be able to inconvenience a Fae of her power. But it wouldn't last: either the wards would revert to their original nature, or they'd burn out, or both.

For the moment everything was still in confusion. Irene fumbled the flick-knife out of her pocket, leaning forward to grab the Countess by the shoulder and press it against her throat. A sharp edge was a sharp edge, and at this precise moment, robbed of her normal power, the Countess would bleed. "Don't move," she ordered. "Don't try anything. Mu Dan!"

There were thuds. "Here," the dragon said. Her skirts brushed against Irene's back. "I'm loose. What next?"

"We kill you!" Dorotya screamed, huddling behind the throne. She wasn't as powerful a Fae as the Countess, so was less affected by the sudden change in the metaphysical atmosphere. "Kill the—"

A gunshot cracked. Dorotya fell silent. Irene couldn't tell if she'd been hit or had simply taken cover. There wasn't time to find out. She pulled herself together, trying to ignore the gaze that the Countess was levelling at her. It promised the sort of death that would last for days or even weeks. Instead she shifted to Chinese to address Mu Dan—the Countess would probably understand it, but Dorotya and the mob might not. "Be ready to use your affinity with the earth to raise the floor towards the ceiling. I'll handle the rest. **Chains, unlock and release the captives!**"

This time the drain of energy wasn't as bad. There was apparently nothing special about the shackles. But a prickle of warning began to tingle in Irene's hand where she held the Countess: the return of the Fae's power, or just Alberich's ward failing? Her time was limited.

"Mu Dan, help me up," she ordered. She felt the dragon's arm round her waist, supporting her till she was upright, and she dragged the Countess up as well, keeping the knife to her throat. "Nobody try anything," she said more loudly, "or the Countess dies."

"You seriously think you can kill me?" the Countess snarled. Her face was like a mask now, white porcelain over something depraved and rotting beneath.

"I can certainly try," Irene retorted. "And I'm sure you know more than I do about what a knife can do to skin. Vale! Silver! Get Kai over here!" She saw Vale and Silver supporting Kai, pushing through the crowd towards them. Nobody was trying to hold them back: her threat to the Countess had cowed the audience for the moment.

Mu Dan released Irene and backed away. "I can't call the earth to help me so close to that creature," she murmured, still in Chinese.

The Countess laughed like fracturing glass. Around them, the men and cats shifted, like a pride of lions moving into position, waiting for the moment to spring. "This is not the sort of story where anyone comes to help you, maiden. This is my story. This is my domain. *You are a victim here!*"

"No," Irene said softly. Her hand ached as if she was trying to hold on to a live power cable, and her Library brand vibrated in her bones. Chaos was strengthening, but she could see a way to use it. The Countess was blinded by her own narrative and hadn't seen Mu Dan as anything other than a maiden and a victim. But that was only half the story. "No, you're wrong, your ladyship, and do you know why? Mu Dan *has* the power here, she has all the power she needs—because this is the part of the story where the law comes to take you down and imprison you, and she's a *judge-investigator*!"

And the floor trembled. It rippled as if Mu Dan was the single still point, with a wave of motion sweeping out through flagstones and earth, swelling and expanding to shudder against the walls. Humans fell to their knees, crying out in shock, their thrall broken fur the moment; cats pressed themselves against the floor, their fur bristling, as if they could somehow make themselves invisible. Dorotya screamed curses, pulling herself away and scrabbling against the wall.

The Countess herself reared back and struck at Irene, claw-like fingers extended to rake at her face. Irene lost her balance and, more important, lost her position; she had to fall back, the knife still clasped in her hand, shifting her balance to stay on her feet.

"Winters!" Vale's voice cut through the noise, and out of the corner of her eye she saw something spinning through the air towards her. She extended her free hand and, by a miracle, caught it—it was Vale's cane.

The aura of chaos in the air was thickening with every breath. "Are you going to try to beat me to death with *that*?" the Countess taunted her.

With her words came the impulse to *do it*; Irene felt the urge to see blood run and hear pleas for mercy. The cane seemed weightless in her hand, and all her hatred for this Fae, for what she *was*, and for what she'd threatened to do to Irene's hands, came together in a blinding flash of purpose. This was what Irene had come here for. To see the Countess dead, to gut her, to hear her screaming . . .

No. No, it wasn't.

Irene dropped the knife, letting it clatter to the floor, and swung the cane towards the Countess's outstretched arm, triggering the switch in the handle that electrified it just as it hit her.

The Countess went down with a shriek. It didn't kill her—it didn't even knock her out, which was a testament to her unnatural nature—but for a moment it inconvenienced her, and that was all Irene needed. She bent down and thrust her hand into the Fae's bodice, forgetting any ideas of decency or proper conduct. Her fingers brushed hard folded paper, and she pulled it out.

She didn't pause to read it. Instead she retreated towards Mu Dan and the others, who had formed a defensive ring. Silver had Mu Dan's pistol now; he shot one man in the head as he attempted to charge.

Vale plucked his cane from Irene's hand as she came within reach, pushing her behind him and next to Mu Dan. "Winters, if you have a way to get us out of here, this would be a good moment."

"Take us up!" Irene gasped to Mu Dan, pointing at the ceiling.

Mu Dan's stern features creased with effort. The ground beneath them rippled again and then *rose* into a small hillock under the influence of her power, climbing farther with every second. A couple of the mob threw themselves at it, trying to get to Irene before she was out of reach, but within a moment the slope of the rising earth was too steep.

Irene looked at the ceiling above. She could only hope she had guessed their location accurately and that they were directly under the stage. She summoned the last of her strength. **"Ceiling of this room, and floor of the theatre above us, part to let us through!"**

The ceiling above their heads split apart in a ripple of layers—rafters, timbers, stones, pipes, cement, and mortar flaking away, earth tumbling down . . .

Light came with it, harshly bright after the dim redness of the Countess's lair. Irene raised her arm to shield her head as the five of them rose through the floor of the theatre and into the room above. It wasn't the stage; it was the theatre's cellars. But there must be a cellar beneath the stage for storage and for sudden exits via trapdoors above. Lines of light showed through the ceiling—the stage floor—marking the outlines of those trapdoors and planking. But Mu Dan's mound of earth wasn't slowing; it was still rising towards the stage floor above, filling the gap that they'd come through in the floor and cutting off the screams and screeching, but still not stopping.

"Stage floor, open for us!" Irene gasped, an instant before they hit it.

The wood peeled back. The stage lights shone down. They emerged into a domestic scene—some sort of family household, probably the setting of one of the social comedy *russe* plays. Except, of course, that the play had not previously involved a group of battered strangers emerging from the bowels of the earth.

Silver stepped forward and bowed to the stunned audience. "Gas leak," he said. "The theatre must be evacuated at once."

They escaped in the screaming and confusion.

CHAPTER 24

The carriage was uncomfortably crowded with five people in it, but nobody had even suggested splitting up to take a second one. Kai had come round from the chloroform he'd been dosed with and now merely had a sick headache. He was complaining about it every couple of minutes. Irene knew from experience that he rarely had any trivial illnesses and was very bad at coping when he did.

She hadn't told him about the note yet. She hadn't told him that he'd been betrayed.

They had all been sharing information. Silver was going over the details of his own capture in heroic detail, but basically it came down to the fact that he'd traced the cake to the theatre, walked in there, and had a gun shoved in his ribs. That had been this morning. "The afternoon was lacking in interest and information," he finished. "Until the detective and the prince showed up."

"Hardly voluntarily," Vale noted. "We were captured in the streets around the theatre while we were investigating."

"I don't understand why you couldn't just make them free you," Mu Dan said. She was somewhere between exhausted and jittering with nerves, making her an awkward coach-seat companion. "You are one of them, after all."

"My talents lie in a different direction," Silver said haughtily. "You may ask Miss Winters for further details. And the Countess already had firm control over everyone she'd allowed down there."

"She was also more powerful than you are," Vale said. He had sunk into a brooding reverie and was staring out of the carriage window. Flakes of snow were beginning to fall, and the night sky was thickly blanketed with cloud.

"She was more powerful than *any* of us," Silver snapped back. "I still don't understand how Miss Winters managed to do whatever it was she did. And why none of us could see her power until we were past her doorstep and into her parlour."

"When I reached the threshold of her hiding-place, I had the chance to examine it," Irene explained. "I found some sort of ward script which had been created by Alberich, probably a long time ago, in order to conceal chaotic power. I took a chance that something which had been created in the Language could be repurposed with the Language." She wondered whether she should mention that she still had the ward in her pocket. Along with the Cardinal's letter to the Countess, and the note betraying Kai . . . she was turning into a walking storehouse of dangerous documents. "It worked. Fortunately. Really, I was quite impressed. Alberich was a master craftsman. I wonder if I could manage anything that powerful . . ."

"What would you have done if it hadn't worked?" Kai asked.

"Kai, that sort of question never helps," Irene said firmly.

In spite of the cold air outside, the five people crammed into it kept the carriage warm. But it wasn't the temperature that made Irene shiver and chafe her hands together. She knew that she had been avoiding this and that she had no time left to do so. "Right. Next item on the agenda. Kai, you were unconscious and you missed this. Someone sent the Countess a message saying that you and Vale were coming. I think that was how she managed to ambush you. I have the note here—at least, I hope I do." She reached into the inner pocket where she'd stashed it. "Unless the Countess is in the habit of hiding multiple billets-doux in her bodice and I grabbed the wrong one."

Kai froze, abruptly more of a statue than a living being. She could feel the tautness of his muscles where he was crammed against her. "Who sent it?"

"Let's have a look." She unfolded the paper, holding it out so everyone could see in the flickering light of passing street lamps.

Vale leaned forward till his nose was practically touching the paper, clearly only just resisting the urge to rip it out of Irene's hands and scrutinise it in more detail. "Good notepaper," he said, "though not watermarked, I think—hold it up a moment, Winters? No, not watermarked, and all three of the hotels have their own watermarked stationery. So we cannot trace it that way. The seal is simply plain wax, with no use of a seal-ring or any other form of identification. The handwriting is formalised and calligraphic, no doubt because the original writer's hand is recognizable. Black ink, no further detail possible at the moment without analysis. The text gives little away. 'The detective and the dragon prince who are investigating the murder are heading to the Grand Guignol to look for culprits there. I hope you will find them entertaining. From one of your kin who wishes you well.' Not signed, of course."

"Would we believe the signature if it was?" Kai's hand closed on Irene's arm. "Irene, what is the *purpose* of this betrayal? Even if we'd vanished at the theatre, someone would have discovered we were going there—Mu Dan, or you, or my uncle. Why didn't whoever it was just tell her to abandon her hide-out and leave? We'd never have found her."

Irene glanced over to Vale and saw that he was frowning, his deep-set eyes in shadow. "You ask some very interesting questions," he said. "We need answers."

But Irene thought she might already know what those answers were. And if she was right . . . then she had good reason to be afraid. A message like this—so detailed, so specific—was intended to get Kai and Vale killed. More murders. "The end result is what we should be looking at," she said.

"Since I am neither a detective nor a judge-investigator—much to my relief—you may need to explain more fully," Silver said.

Mu Dan was nodding. "Irene's right. I realize that you don't want to get involved in the politics of this, Your Highness, but if *you* were killed in the middle of this investigation, and by a Fae, even if the delegation claims not to be involved with her—"

"*Isn't* involved with her," Silver said. "She *was* going to kill me too, in case you didn't notice."

Irene suppressed a sigh. "Mu Dan's just being technical. Just as she was when nobody except me had actually witnessed the Countess last night. Even if you witnessed her bomb."

"I think we can all testify to her presence now," Vale agreed.

Kai looked between them. "You're avoiding the point," he said.

"You don't think she killed Ren Shun, do you, Irene? The person who did it was the same person who betrayed us. They're still trying to disrupt the truce and trigger a war."

Irene wondered how many of the others in the carriage were following the same train of thought she was. Vale, probably. Silver, possibly, but he was the last person who could actually suggest the name that she was thinking. Mu Dan wouldn't cast her suspicions in that direction—even if she was a judge-investigator. And Kai himself . . .

"Kai," she said, "can you tell me how you and Vale came to suspect the Grand Guignol? That's one bit of information I haven't caught up with yet."

Kai went through the details, with Vale confirming them: a disregarded report from Ren Shun, found while going through his papers at Ao Ji's request—and contributory evidence that Vale had discovered. "But you and Mu Dan weren't at Le Meurice when we looked for you, before going out," he finished, a little too self-justifyingly.

Irene felt a twinge of guilt. "I was lured out by Dorotya, a Fae who works for the Countess. She wanted information. And Mu Dan was looking for me. Sorry." She hurried on before Kai could start giving his opinion on her wandering off alone. "But this betrayal does support the theory that the Countess isn't guilty of the murder—whatever else she may have done or be going to do. I hope that the gendarmes can deal with her nest, now that it's been exposed."

They were nearly at Le Meurice now. At least here, together, inside this carriage, they could speak in confidence. Irene had to decide what she was going to say. Her eyes strayed to Kai's taut face again. She'd gotten him into this, and she might be about to hurt him in the worst way possible . . .

But reality slapped her in the face. *The worlds are at risk, this peace treaty's on the brink of failing, my parents may be put to death, and I'm wasting my time worrying about hurting his feelings?*

"I went to the Library," she continued. "Prutkov's unreliable. And our security people are investigating him. But also—and this is *important*—remember the book that was mentioned on the note in Ren Shun's pocket? Herodotus's *Myths*? We've found a copy of it—it was saved from the Richelieu Library, the Enfer section, before the place was bombed. But we *don't* think the edition we've found is from the world referenced in that note—Beta-001. We have that edition in the Library itself—and there's nothing interesting about it at all."

"Your point?" Silver asked, looking perplexed.

"Someone wrote Ren Shun's note and planted it to incriminate the Library. Someone who knew how we classify worlds but didn't know the *right* classification to quote. Which wasn't Beta-001."

"Winters," Vale said sharply, a warning note in his voice. She met his eyes and saw certainty in them. He knew what she was thinking. He'd probably worked it all out already. "Be careful about making accusations without proof. Whether it refers to current affairs—or to the murder of Minister Zhao."

"They're linked?" Kai asked.

"I am certain of it," Vale said. "And while I am not sure who was directly responsible for the minister's poisoning, I believe I know the hand behind them."

"Then we need proof," Irene said. She worked her cold hands together in her lap. "Back at the Library, I told Melusine that if we try to build this peace treaty on a lie, it will eventually fall apart. I haven't changed my mind about that."

The carriage drew up outside Le Meurice, and the driver hammered on the top of the cab. "Here we are, messieurs, mesdames!"

Kai didn't move. "Could the rest of you leave the carriage?" he asked. "I'd like a private word with Irene."

A moment later, the two of them were alone in the carriage, the driver audibly sighing above and the horses stamping their feet in the cold. More snow came twisting down past the windows, and the wind whistled down the broad avenue.

"You've never insulted my intelligence," Kai said abruptly. "If anything, you've expected me to keep up with you and been disappointed when I haven't. Yet tonight you're avoiding my questions. And it's because you think someone in the dragon delegation is responsible."

"It would be pointless to ask which questions, wouldn't it?" Irene replied. "That would just be avoiding them further . . . I'm sorry, Kai." She didn't have to say what for, as she'd never kept secrets from him before. And she was relieved he hadn't followed her chain of logic through to the end—and to *which* dragon was responsible.

"It's clear Vale agrees with you too, about the culprit. But he's letting you handle it. I suppose he doesn't want to deal with the emotional consequences of telling me that I was betrayed by someone I know."

"Kai, *I* don't want to deal with the emotional consequences." She met his eyes. "I don't want consequences, full stop. Give me a way out of this and I'll take it." She found, to her surprise, that she was entirely sincere. If he could think of an answer to the current situation—to naming the potential murderer—then she would be glad to accept it. "I'm not proud."

"The Countess did it," Kai proposed. "We've got all the proof we need that she's here. Somehow she lured Ren Shun out. She suborned some of his spies, perhaps, and that's why they were murdered too . . ."

It was so very tempting. It was the sort of lie that made more sense than the truth. "But if we put that forward as an answer and it's not true, and the treaty gets that much closer to being signed, will there be any more murders? Any more attempts to stop it?"

"You're implying that a dragon's behind it and was trying to frame the Fae. But a motive could just as easily be found for your own people," Kai said, changing tack. "You've admitted Prutkov's unreliable. He told *you* that he was in favour of the treaty, but he could have been lying. The Library could be even *more* of a power broker if we dragons and the Fae remain at war. You say you know he *did* lie to you—but how can you know how much he lied about? Where better to sabotage negotiations than from an apparently neutral position?"

He had put aside his first emotional reaction and was arguing like a courtier, knowing his feelings alone wouldn't be enough to convince her. Irene respected that. She also knew that all the other dragons would agree with him; they wouldn't even consider her new hypothesis plausible. Kai at least was pointing out the possible holes in it. Li Ming or Mei Feng would simply shrug in disdain and have her shown out of the room.

"It seems unrealistic that the one side we aren't considering blaming here is the Fae delegation," she said. "But it's true. The Princess . . . well, I grant you that she's Fae, but she's as trapped in her role as any of them. Treachery isn't in her nature. And I believe the Cardinal would know the possible consequences if you were killed—thinking of your capture by the Countess. He might endanger you, but I can't see him handing you over to *her* . . ."

A sudden realization of just how narrow their escape had been seized Irene by the throat and nearly choked her. She had carefully, very carefully, been avoiding thinking about what might have happened. From the moment she'd entered the Countess's lair and seen Kai and the others in chains, she'd put the brakes on her own imagination so that she could *function*. She hadn't allowed herself to think what might happen if she failed. And now here she was, talking about it so casually, so lightly, as if it was just another clever political move and not the very real possible torture and death of people she cared about.

For a moment it was as if she was back there in the red-lit room, her lungs full of the smell of blood and sweat and malice. She wanted to hold on to Kai, to shield him, to keep him from being endangered like that again. She was the one who'd brought him here, and so far not only had she put him into deadly danger, but she was on the verge of accusing his *uncle* of murder—and trying to ruin the negotiations. *Good job, Irene. Impressive. What do you do for an encore?*

As if from a great distance, she pushed the latent hysteria down and walled it away. "I'm sorry," she said. "Whatever happens, I think this is going to be messy."

"Will you stop apologising!" Kai grabbed her shoulder, dragging her round to face him. "You just saved my *life*. You're wrong about which faction is harbouring the murderer, but that's not something you should be *apologising* for! And you're not the only person responsible for making things right around here . . ."

"I am the person who's had all this dumped in her lap," Irene said through gritted teeth, "and I'm the person whose parents might get *killed* if I get this wrong. Do not lose your temper at me, Kai. I'm not in the mood to be nice. And I'm running out of consideration for your feelings. For *anyone's* feelings. Very soon, I'm going to have to be strategic, rather than kind, and I thought I might at least apologise for that first. But by all means take responsibility for sorting things out as well. I am all in favour of other people being responsible!" She considered the last couple of days wearily. "I'm just not going to count on it."

"No," Kai said bitterly, "you're just going to try to shoulder everything yourself and then take the blame if it all goes wrong."

"That's unfair." Irene was aware that their conversation had veered into the sort of painful emotional argument she'd always detested, but she wasn't sure how to steer it out again. "You have no right to criticise me for doing my job."

"Except that you're not my superior officer in the Library any more," Kai said. "I've left the Library. We're independent now."

"I wasn't talking about our positions in the Library. I meant the *investigation*. And if you ask Vale or Silver, or even Mu Dan, I think they'll all agree that I'm giving the orders there." Honesty compelled her to add, "Until I tell them to do something that they don't want to do, of course."

Kai let go of her shoulder with a sigh. "So where do *we* stand on this?"

Irene could only hope that the answer wasn't going to ultimately be *on opposite sides*. "My position is that I have to find out the truth," she said. "Even if it's Prutkov. And believe me, I will throw him to the wolves if he's responsible. But it would reassure me to know that you were genuinely supporting this attempt to make peace—and not just because you know I want it."

Kai flushed but inclined his head in agreement. "I still detest most of the Fae that I've ever met," he said, "but if they're willing to deal in good faith and try to make peace, then I can do no less."

When it came to motives for building a new future, *retaining the moral high ground* was a bit underwhelming. Still, Irene was prepared to count end results as what mattered in this case. "Thank you," she said. "I needed to hear that."

"I will help." He touched her chin, his fingers warm. "I'll do what I can. But you and Vale need to prove your findings. Li Ming, Mei Feng, my uncle . . . if you accuse anyone in our delegation, and I support you, then they'll say I'm biased. And they'd be right."

"So noted," Irene said. She reached for the door handle. "We'd better get moving. There's no time to lose." She knew that it wasn't settled yet, that the whole question hung between them like an unexploded bomb. But . . . they'd have to deal with that when they came to it.

In the hotel foyer, Irene ignored an argument between Silver and Mu Dan, and a brooding Vale slumped in a chair, and made her way to the desk. "Can you tell me if Monsieur Prutkov is present?" she asked.

The desk clerk was delighted to inform her that yes, Monsieur Prutkov was indeed present and had not gone out, and that they could send a pageboy up to fetch him.

"No, thank you," Irene said. "I'll go up myself."

She was aware that she was attracting glances due to her battered male attire, but fortunately Mu Dan and Silver were with her and well-dressed enough to shield her from challenges. She was also aware that from a self-serving Library point of view, she should question Prutkov in private first. But if he *was* the murderer, then she wanted backup. And if he wasn't, then she needed his help—and having the rest of the group with her might be useful in persuading him to give it.

The few words she managed to exchange with Vale on the way upstairs, out of hearing of the others, confirmed her thoughts. He'd come at it from a different angle, but certain matters had solidified his theory. A discussion with the hotel laundry. A review of the weather patterns on the night of the murder. The post-mortem reports on Ren Shun's agents.

And, of course, the note from Ren Shun's pocket.

What Irene hadn't expected was the man waiting outside Prutkov's room. He was thin—gaunt, even—and in his sixties, with an old scar that ran down the right side of his face. It ran from the top to the bottom of his right eye socket, pale against his dark skin. What remained of his hair was grey and wispy, combed back from his face. His suit was battered, but his cuffs and collar were spotlessly clean and white. He nodded slightly as he caught sight of them. Before Kai could sweep Irene behind him protectively, the man stepped forward. "Irene Winters, I think?" he said.

"Yes," Irene admitted. "But we haven't had the pleasure, so you are . . ."

"Azevedo," he said. "From the Library. I hope the word *Nevksy* means something to you."

Relief filled Irene like oxygen, giving her new energy. "It does. Thank goodness. You've spoken with Prutkov?"

"I have. You were correct." He glanced over the rest of the group. "Normally we'd want to keep certain matters private, but under the circumstances I suppose it would cause more suspicion than it's worth. Please come in."

Prutkov was hunched over in a chair, and he didn't bother to rise as they filed in. His expression was sour to the point of viciousness, and there was a grey undertone to his skin that Irene wasn't sure how to interpret. Shock? She nodded in his direction. "We have some questions to ask," she said.

"You won't be the first person this evening," he said. His gaze moved to Azevedo, who was carefully shutting the door. "Melusine is not going to approve of everyone being present while I'm . . ."

He seemed to be casting around for the right words. "Getting an earful?" Irene suggested helpfully.

"And *you* are proving that you have no discretion."

Irene looked down at him, her suddenly rising anger boiling in her stomach like acid. "You know, under some circumstances I'd be annoyed by that. But given that it's *you* who's accusing *me,* I will only say that you have done a *piss-poor* job of organising an undercover operation." She heard Vale's intake of breath at her vulgarity but ignored it. "You remember the Blood Countess? We've just broken open her lair while we were escaping, because—thanks to *someone* who let them walk into a trap—she was about to kill Kai and Vale here. And Silver too, as a matter of fact. But she wasn't warned that *he* was coming—presumably because he's a Fae. Which leads to a question I need to ask here. Well, one of them."

Prutkov's frown was growing. He picked up a glass of water from the side table by his chair and sipped it. "What questions do you need to ask?"

"First question, and I would like you to answer in the Language." Both Azevedo and Prutkov frowned at that, and Irene knew why. It was impossible for a Librarian to lie in the Language—even though they could, theoretically, make an honest mistake while using it. If Prutkov accepted her demands, then he'd be speaking absolute truth in front of a room full of outsiders. And since they'd all hear the Language as their own native tongue, they'd understand whatever he was saying. But it had to be done. "Did you kill Ren Shun?"

Prutkov's eyes widened. Apparently he hadn't expected *that* question. **"I did not kill Ren Shun,"** he said in the Language, without hesitation.

Kai hissed between his teeth. He knew what that meant. Irene had just knocked the main suspect in his theory out of contention. "Ask him if any of his minions might have done it," he suggested.

Prutkov shot Kai a look of plain dislike. **"I did not give any orders for Ren Shun to be killed, either directly or by implication,"** he said. "You aren't seriously saying that I'm a suspect here?"

"You're unreliable. Given the stakes we're dealing with, I have to be sure." Irene wanted to say more than that—to ask him what the hell he thought he'd been doing, playing with these stakes, with so many lives at risk. But that would have been self-indulgence, when there were more important questions to which she needed answers. "Second question. Did you—or anyone under your orders—send a message to the Blood Countess under the Theatre of the Grand Guignol to let her know that Vale and Kai were coming?"

"She *can't* have been there," Prutkov objected. "We had the place checked for chaos. Twice. It was too obvious!"

"She'd obtained wards from Alberich, in the past, which allowed her to suppress chaos in her local area." Irene pulled the remaining ward-script out of her coat and offered it to Azevedo. His expression darkened further as he looked it over. "That's why none of us could find her there. But trust me, she *was* there, we can all vouch for that. Now please answer my question."

It was strange how her vocabulary and usage defaulted to *please* and *thank you,* Irene reflected grimly, as Prutkov hesitated over his words. *Once it's been ground into you as a child, you can never break free . . .*

"I have never sent any sort of message to the Countess, nor did I order one to be sent." Prutkov took a deep breath. **"And I didn't know where she was based. Nor did I know that the dragon and the detective had gone to the theatre."** He dropped back to English. "Satisfied?"

"I'm surprised you didn't know they'd gone out, or where they'd gone," Mu Dan said. "It seems the sort of thing you would track."

"That may be my fault," Vale put in. "I was already suspicious of Mr. Prutkov here, and I did my best to avoid our coming to his attention."

Irene nodded, her brain whirling as pieces settled into a new configuration. "Kai," she said, "I know that this won't be enough to convince others in the delegations, but will you accept this as evidence for now?"

"Yes. Unwillingly, but yes." There was a glint of dragon-red in Kai's eyes, and he looked as if he would like to be pacing the room. If he had been a cat, he would have been lashing his tail. "My lord uncle will not be happy if he learns one of the Library's own people was manipulating events to his advantage."

"And while it's scarcely necessary to point it out, nor will the Cardinal," Silver remarked.

"These accusations are unjustified," Prutkov said, straightening his shoulders. "I've hardly been 'manipulating events.' I've been defending the Library's interests. Just because one Librarian here dislikes the precise manner in which I've been doing it—"

There was a rapping at the door. Everyone looked at each other. Then Azevedo gestured to Prutkov to answer it.

"Who's there?" Prutkov called.

"Deborah." Irene recognized the voice—she'd been talking to Prutkov while Irene hid behind the curtain with the Princess.

Prutkov sighed. "Come in," he said flatly. Either he'd given up on any further concealment or he realized how suspicious it would look to send her away.

Azevedo opened the door. The woman beyond paused to see a stranger standing there, and her eyes widened further as she saw how full the room was. She hesitated, as if considering bolting, then shrugged and stepped inside. Fresh snow crusted her hat and the shoulders of her coat, and she left a damp trail behind her. "Prutkov, I don't know what's going on, but something's turned bad. Ao Ji's left the opera and he's on his way here now."

"Why?" Prutkov checked his watch. "It'll only just be the interval. It's not even nine o'clock yet."

"I don't know and nor do his people, but something's gone wrong. He's not in a good mood." She brushed snow meaningfully from her coat. "And if the Fae get the idea that something's up and leave the opera too, they'll be coming right here as well. What's going on?"

Time seemed to slow as Irene came to a decision.

"I think I know what to do," she said, "but I'm going to require everyone's cooperation on this one. And that means you too, Prutkov, because you have something I need."

CHAPTER 25

It was yet another hotel room—pale, perfect, expensive, bloodless—and Irene was, once again, the most human and imperfect thing in it. There hadn't been time to change her clothing or even brush her hair. She rose and bowed as Ao Ji entered, and waited for his gesture before she took a seat.

Hsien and his men had swept the room for surveillance devices first, of course. Royalty had its privileges. And its paranoias.

"You have requested a private meeting with me," he said without preamble. "I would know your reasons."

"I thought that Your Majesty might want a report of the evening's events so far, without witnesses," Irene lied blandly. "There have been a number of developments."

His face was impassive. If Kai or Li Ming occasionally looked like a statue carved from marble, then Ao Ji was one carved from ice and snow, in some distant winter where the sun gave light but no warmth. "I felt an upswelling in chaos from across the city. I would not waste time at a theatrical performance while such a threat exists. You were involved?"

"I was, Your Majesty. We discovered the lair of the Fae who was trying to interfere with the peace talks, the Blood Countess."

"Then why are you here and not rooting her out?" Ao Ji demanded. "Why is such a foul creature allowed to continue with her work? The Library promised to protect these negotiations. Or was I mistaken?"

"Your Majesty, forgive me for being imprecise," Irene said quickly. "We located her hiding-place and penetrated it but were forced to retreat due to insufficient strength and numbers. We believe we have hampered her operations and penetrated her disguises—so we can now locate her at our convenience."

Ao Ji's eyes were slivers of ruby as he watched her. "Are you leaving anything out, Librarian?"

Irene had been thinking how to phrase this. "Your nephew's courage is notable, Your Majesty. He was among the first to find where the Countess was based and investigate it."

"Flattering my nephew won't advance your cause in my eyes," Ao Ji said coldly. "Is there some point to this?"

"He was also the one who found a particularly interesting clue, Your Majesty. He said that he found the information while he was going through Lord Ren Shun's papers."

A breath of icy air moved through the room, as though someone had entered silently and brought the outside chill with them. "And?"

"I believe that Lord Ren Shun may have located the Countess himself, Your Majesty. It is logical to draw a connection between this and his subsequent death."

Ao Ji's hand clenched on the arm of his chair, and Irene saw the glitter of claws on his fingertips. "You speak very casually of my liegeman's murder."

"Please forgive me, Your Majesty," Irene said quickly. "Perhaps as a human, I will never fully understand the sort of loyalty which is forged by centuries of service."

Ao Ji paused, tilting his head as though trying to find fault with that statement. "At least you acknowledge it," he finally said ungraciously.

Now it was time to take a risk. "It would be understandable if Your Majesty's loss had prejudiced you against the Fae. But this is a treaty which depends on fair and unbiased dealing from both sides of the table."

"*If* it takes place," Ao Ji said flatly. "So far I have seen nothing but attempts by the Fae to sabotage it and murder those of us who came in good faith. If the Library expects fair dealing from them, then they are deluded. You would do better to spend your time hunting down old books. That is where your talents lie, after all."

"The Library is acting as mediators because we are *human*, Your Majesty," Irene said. Looking at the dragon opposite her—his features perfect and inhuman, his manner as distant as one would expect from a creature near to immortal—she felt her own weakness, her own mortality. But there was nobody else here to make this argument. "We are mortal. And as a human, as a mortal being, I have an interest in general peace and stability. It is vital to me that this treaty takes place. Not just because of my parents, held as hostages to guarantee good behaviour. Not just because of the Library. But because of everyone who may suffer if this falls apart. I've seen what happens when dragons and Fae go to war. Everyone suffers."

"Your attitude is virtuous," Ao Ji acknowledged. "But you are failing to consider the larger picture."

"Would you explain, sire?"

"You said you had entered the lair of the creature who calls herself the Blood Countess. You witnessed her depravity, her sadism. Surely you must realize that by giving half the worlds over to beings like that, you are condemning them to be her victims? You are arguing that both sides are equal, Librarian. Be honest and admit that they are not."

"And you're arguing that one of the worst people from one side is a typical representative of that side, Your Majesty," Irene countered. "After dining in the same room as the Princess, how can you say that she has the same nature as the Countess?"

"She has as much regard for you humans as the Countess does," Ao Ji said dismissively. "Or as little, to be specific. You are merely toys to amuse her."

Irene thought of the time she'd witnessed two dragons fighting in the sky over New York. They hadn't been remotely concerned about the safety or the welfare of the humans beneath them. The city could have been torn apart, and they wouldn't have cared. "And you, Your Majesty? What are humans to you?"

Ao Ji looked at her from a thousand years away. "We would practise good governance," he said, "and you are sorely in need of it. Look at this city, this Paris. How many wars have passed through it in the last hundred years? How many tyrants? The so-called bohemian class live in waste and self-indulgence. The artists waste their time in folly. The poor scratch for a living and celebrate their criminal gangs. The literary classes slip into decadence and spread its philosophies. This is a city where a place like that Theatre of the Grand Guignol can be founded and *admired*."

The theatre's name brought an expression of disgust to his face. "No wonder the Countess found safe haven there; it is an abscess, a mark of everything that is worst about this place. Surely you can see that this is not acceptable. It would be laxness on our part to allow it to continue."

He was speaking to her as if she was a student who needed instruction and he was the teacher whose words were obviously right. He was choosing to spend the time to enlighten her because he considered her worthwhile, and he wanted her to understand. When he paused, he seemed to be expecting agreement as the only possible response.

And he had also confirmed what Irene had suspected. No doubt he could explain how he'd known about the Grand Guignol—but his mention of the theatre had felt somehow *personal*. There had been a direct venom in his voice, a specific and deeply felt abhorrence. He knew about the place. He *must* know about the Countess, even if he'd tried to claim otherwise.

"Your Majesty," she said, "humanity is indeed weak, and we mortals are creatures of the moment. Yet humanity has created works of art, works of literature, philosophical structures, and stories that last. The Fae do not create—they merely imitate. And from what I have seen, the dragons collect what humans have made."

"And you Librarians steal their books," Ao Ji noted. "This is hardly a good argument for either your ethics or your inspiration. Apparently you would give a starving child a storybook—when what she needs is bread and peace. We would enforce that peace."

He hesitated for just a moment on the *we would*: Irene wondered if he'd been about to say *I will*, and make it a declaration of personal intent rather than a vaguer hope for the future. But of course that would be quite inappropriate from someone who was supposed to be prepared to sign a peace treaty. Even if it would be a far more accurate statement of his views.

Irene had to hurry on to the next stage of her plan before Ao Ji grew bored—or decided that she might be a danger to him.

"Returning to current events, sire," she said, "perhaps we shouldn't look so much at what crimes were committed, but what they were meant to achieve."

"Oh?" His expression of curiosity was beyond reproach, but Irene felt the additional coldness in the air. Outside the window, snow reflected a thousand tiny sparkles in the street lights.

Her mouth was dry. She swallowed. "Your Majesty, these crimes were designed to give you reasons to refuse to sign the treaty—or reasons why you shouldn't negotiate at all. It would have been natural for you to walk out, after your trusted servant was murdered. And if your nephew had been killed by one of the Fae currently in Paris, then again you would have had an excellent reason to break off negotiations, and even to declare outright war."

"You think this was done by someone who was trying to manipulate me?" Ao Ji said slowly. "But who would *dare*?"

"There is also the question of the snow," Irene went on. "Ren Shun's body was found in the Salon Pompadour, but he wasn't killed there. He was either brought in through the hotel itself, or through the glass doors leading outside. It wouldn't have been hard to get hold of a key to those doors. The real danger would have been if someone outside noticed. But with all the snow that night, even the usual Paris nightlife was driven off the streets. The murderer had a free hand to work unobserved."

"He took advantage of the weather, then?" Ao Ji asked. "He

waited for a night when the storm would be severe enough to conceal his crime?"

"Along those lines," Irene said. "And he also took care to dispose of Ren Shun's servants, in case they knew too much. Our murderer is very direct, Your Majesty. He sweeps the board clean of evidence."

Ao Ji nodded slowly. "Have you a name for him?"

"I can give one."

Irene's heart was hammering so fast with nerves that she thought her hands should be shaking. But they were steady. She reached into an inner pocket and removed a folded paper. "I retrieved this from the Countess, Your Majesty. It is the letter she received which betrayed your nephew and Vale to her. Of course it is not signed."

Ao Ji's eyes were fixed on it. He was as still as an ice statue, as merciless as a mountain eagle. "That anyone should have dared—*dared*—to threaten my family in that way . . ."

Irene waited to see if he was going to finish the sentence. She didn't want to be struck down for interrupting a dragon king mid-threat. When he fell silent again, she lowered her hand to the table between them, putting the paper there and keeping her fingers on it. "Your Majesty, I said that I could give you the name of the killer."

"And how do you propose to do that, if the note is unsigned?"

"I can use the Language." Irene met his eyes. "I can tell this piece of paper to return to the hand of the one who wrote it. In front of as many witnesses as necessary."

Dead silence filled the room.

And she knew she was right. If he had been innocent and had truly cared for Kai—or for his family blood—as much as he'd suggested, he would have told her to do it. Possibly in private, with only dragons present, but he would have ordered her to identify the guilty party. But this silence? It was an admission of guilt. And he knew that she knew.

Which now brought up the question of her own life expectancy, and whether she would survive to leave this room.

He looked at her. An inhuman anger crawled behind his eyes. "What do you want?" he said.

"Your Majesty," she said. The cold was deeper now, brisk enough to make her hands sting. "These negotiations have been a source of tension for all of us, and you have lost a servant whom you trusted. Might it be a wise choice for one of your brothers to take your place as leader of your delegation? Or one of the queens?"

"I notice you do not speak of justice for those who have died." He didn't move, but Irene had the sense of a great raptor or mountain cat poised to spring at a moment's notice. "Yet my nephew said that you were an idealist . . ."

"I don't believe I could obtain such justice." Irene thought of Ren Shun, of his servants, all cleared away without hesitation—to provide Ao Ji with the motivation he required to break off the peace talks. She wondered if Ao Ji actually felt any regret, or if he had simply decided their sacrifice was . . . necessary. "I'll settle for what I can get. And what I want is that treaty signed and stable."

"Your dedication is worthy of a more noble cause. Any treaty will be temporary. When the eventual war does come, it will end in flames and your Library will fall with it." The sound of future destruction echoed in his voice. "Give me your allegiance now, and you can save yourself. I will take you into my own household—or my nephew's, if you prefer. You will have stability and safety."

"Ren Shun was in your household," Irene countered. She felt a distant anger for the sake of someone who had, by all accounts, been a good man and a faithful servant. "That didn't save him."

"He was a loyal servant who obeyed my will," Ao Ji growled. "He understood the necessity."

"Did he?" Irene wondered aloud. "The knife wound in his back was from *behind*. Your Majesty."

The anger in his face was clear now: snow rasped against the window, a driving river of bitterness that swept down from the heavens to scour the streets. "And what of the evidence against the Library—your own people? What of the words Ren Shun heard, about a book being even more important than the negotiations, and the evidence found on his body?"

Irene folded her free hand in her lap, her fingers numb from the cold. "The paper in Ren Shun's pocket does name a particular book, and gives a Library designation for where it can be found. But the only edition of that book which is of interest doesn't actually come from that world designation. The note was written and placed there by someone who wanted to incriminate the Library, and who knew how we classify worlds, but didn't know which world to name. And as for what Ren Shun heard—that securing a book was more important than the negotiations? Your Majesty, you are the *only* person who has told us about that. *You* wished to incriminate the Library." Ao Ji must have arranged for the *Myths* to be left in the Richelieu Library—ready to be conveniently found as proof. And if Prutkov hadn't removed the book from the Enfer section, the scheme could have succeeded. Irene might almost have been grateful for that, despite Prutkov's lack of ethics—or at least, him not *telling her about it*.

"State your case," Ao Ji said. He held himself like a monarch prepared to give dispassionate judgement, but there was far too much controlled fury in his voice and eyes.

Irene had no time left for fear. The numbing cold lapped round her like winter's deepest heart. "Your Majesty did not wish this treaty to take place. You hoped to find a reason to call it off, but none presented itself. But your fellow monarchs would not accept it, if you simply refused to agree. *You* had already arranged the death of Minister Zhao in another court, but that hadn't stopped it. So you killed Ren Shun, under cover of the blizzard that you yourself called, in order to claim Fae treachery. You either killed his servants or had them killed too, for fear they might know too much. And in case even that didn't give you sufficient leverage, you tried to incriminate the Library too—by suggesting that we were in league with the Fae, or with some other faction, because we wanted a book more than peace. Or we wanted power. Or possibly both. And today, you tried to send your nephew to his death at the hands of a Fae—again, just so you'd have a reason to break off the negotiations.

"You are partial to my nephew," Ao Ji said. "You are moved by sentiment."

Irene lifted her chin and stared him down. "I care about him, yes. I care about a great many people. I care about my parents, who are hostages for the sake of these negotiations. I care about the Library. I care about all Paris outside these walls! Your Majesty, with the utmost respect, I request that someone else take your place. I don't wish to give the Fae unfair advantage by revealing all this—and disgracing you. I don't want to weaken your faction's side. But I *will* have that peace treaty."

Ao Ji rose. Irene tried to stand in turn, but the cold pinned her in her chair; it had come on her inch by inch, and now it held her there, unable to muster the strength or warmth to move. "Enough," he said. He reached into his jacket and removed a flat silver flask. "You know what this is, I think?"

"I would guess that it is a potion which will prevent me from speaking," Irene said. Her voice shook. She'd been forced to drink such a thing once before. It wasn't a pleasant memory.

"Yes. You will be silent when we leave this room. I will say that you insulted me. My account of events will be believed, and I will have my servants take you into our custody. You will be kept safe. I honour your filial respect for your parents: that moves me to spare you." He looked down at her from the distance of a thousand years of coldness. "But there will be no peace. I cannot allow that. And as for the note you think you have . . ."

He reached down and slid it from under her fingers. "That will no longer be an issue."

"Your Majesty," Irene said. "I beg you to change your mind before it is too late."

"It is already too late," Ao Ji said. He unfolded the paper, casually inspecting it.

When he spoke again, there was true anger in his voice. *"What is this?"*

"A blank piece of paper," Irene said. "Hotel stationery all looks very similar, doesn't it?" She tried to work her hands together, to make her fingers move. She couldn't. "But you thought it *was* the note. Which means you knew what it would look like. Your Majesty."

"What game is this?" His voice was not loud, but it made the windowpanes shiver in their sockets.

The door opened. Irene managed to turn her head. Li Ming and Mei Feng were standing there, their faces frozen in simultaneous disapproval and judgement, and other figures waited behind them. She could finally breathe again, move again, her body thrumming with released tension. It had worked.

And all I had to do was destroy Kai's uncle. All I had to do was prove to Kai—someone who thinks family ties are everything, the most important loyalty that could possibly exist—that his uncle tried to kill him.

There is nothing I could say that will ever make him forgive me for this.

"Your Majesty," Li Ming said. "We must speak urgently in private."

"Explain yourself," Ao Ji said, still looking at Irene.

Irene touched the collar of her coat, her fingers numb but functional now. "Your Majesty, I was wearing a wire when I came in here. Everything we said in this room has been heard by these nobles, and by others. It's all very well to say that your account of events will be believed—but they've just heard the truth."

CHAPTER 26

Ao Ji's face was blank, as impassive as a clouded sky: he might have been trying to process what had just happened, or he might simply be choosing not to share his thoughts. He turned away, his shoulders and back stiff and unbending.

Li Ming touched Irene's shoulder, and the cold that had lapped around her faded. "Please leave us, Miss Winters," he said. "There are matters we must discuss in private."

Irene staggered to her feet. She knew that without her present numbness she would be shaking with released tension. But the part of her mind that reckoned political calculus decided Li Ming's *please* was a positive sign. She jerked her head in a nod and began to move towards the door.

Then Ao Ji turned again, raising his hand, and a roaring wave of whiteness swept through the room.

Irene tried to blink. She couldn't open her eyes. She was on the floor. She had fallen, somewhere between that moment of force and the terrible cold, and now. And she couldn't get up. Her brain wasn't processing things properly. It seemed to be stuttering, like a record jolting back over the same few notes again and again. She could hear wind and footsteps, and a distant shouting, but she couldn't make herself focus on it. And she was so numb. Her cheek was pressed against the carpet, but she could barely feel the tickle of the fibres against her skin. There was some sort of weight across her back, a faint warmth against the surrounding cold, but even that was uncertain.

The sound of the wind rose. She forced her eyes open, but for a moment she couldn't interpret what she was seeing. Where there should have been wall and window and paintings, there was now an empty hole, a gap leading out into the open air and whirling snow. Between her and the outside storm was a tall figure wrapped in snow, his back to her, light catching on his hands as though they were sheathed in ice.

He glanced back in Irene's direction. Self-preservation seized her like a vice, and she let her eyes flicker closed, slowing her breathing to the minimum possible. It wasn't hard. It was easy to relax into the cold, to lie there still and unmoving, to barely even think . . .

Light seared her closed eyes. There was a sound like thunder, and then silence again.

The noise of people shoving through the door was almost tame by comparison. There were too many voices. It was difficult to work out who was shouting what. She tried to open her eyes again, but it was harder this time. She was farther away from the room, farther away from everything. She was conscious of hands grabbing her, turning her over, someone's fingers warm against the pulse in her neck, but everything seemed too much trouble for it to be worth waking up. Even the voices were unclear now, running into each other and blending into confusion.

"If you think I'll let you touch her—"

"She's going to die if you don't let me—"

"Strongrock, if he can save her, then we have no choice—"

An arm slid behind her back, pulling her up to a half-seated position, and someone kissed her, lips parting against hers. *How stupid,* she thought distantly, *that only works in fairy tales . . .*

Raw urgent passion and need ran through her body like fire. She jolted in the arms that were holding her, abruptly *feeling* again, and her eyes blinked open to meet Silver's. She was still cold—shivering, terribly cold—but she could think again, and she could move.

"You did it!" That was Kai. He tore Irene out of Silver's arms, dragging her firmly against him. Out of the corner of her eye, Irene saw Silver draw back with a rather satisfied look. Which was more than she felt. Part of her still wanted that kiss. The stupid, physical, brainless part of her. She was aching all over, half-frozen, and her Library brand throbbed with her pulse.

"Well," Silver said smugly. His eyes sparkled, and his whole body seemed to glow with warmth. Irene curled her fingers into fists to stop herself from reaching out to touch him and pull him nearer. "Sometimes the whole *point* of being a libertine is having a kiss which could bring the dead back to life. Or the nearly dead. Speaking of which, my little mouse, you're welcome."

"Thank you." The words came with difficulty. Irene was still too busy cursing her own misjudgement. She'd assumed that Ao Ji would do the sensible, political thing when his guilt was proved—that he'd quietly make some sort of deal behind the scenes, or retire from the negotiations to be replaced by one of his brothers. Li Ming and Mei Feng must have thought the same. And they were now unconscious on the floor, and Ao Ji was at liberty to do heaven knew what . . .

She shivered as she realized that the weight on her body must have been Li Ming. He'd happened to be standing between her and Ao Ji at the moment of the blast. *If he hadn't . . .*

Irene deliberately rejected the thought. If she wasted her time thinking about all the times she'd escaped death, she'd never get anything done. "Situation," she said, shaking her head and making herself focus. "Situation report, Kai. Vale. What's going on?"

Kai turned so that she had a better view of the hole in the wall. To be honest, there wasn't much wall left. The hotel management was not going to be happy. "My lord uncle has left us," he said, his voice clipped and controlled. "Li Ming and Mei Feng are unconscious, and likely to remain that way for hours. Unless Silver can wake them too?"

Silver sighed. "You have no idea how much I'd like to try. But I don't think I could do it. A human or a Librarian, yes, but not a dragon."

"Scratch that idea, then," Irene said. She had a feeling of impending doom that was growing worse by the second. "Where's everyone else? The Fae? The other Librarians?"

Vale went down on one knee next to her, so she didn't have to stare up at him. "Your colleague Azevedo is reasoning with the remaining dragons, assisted by Mu Dan. I gave them the benefit of my own deductions during the pauses in your interview with Ao Ji. I think they are convinced, but I cannot say they are happy. The Fae are presumably still at the opera, or returning to their hotel, as are the other Librarians. And as for Ao Ji . . ." His gaze moved to the snow that was swirling into the room. "Is it my imagination, or is the storm getting worse?"

"It's not your imagination," Kai said.

Irene remembered what Kai had done on one of their missions. "Kai, there was that time with Alberich, when you warded a whole area against chaos. Would your uncle do the same thing? To force the Fae out of this world?"

"He might," Kai admitted, "but in that case I'm surprised he hasn't done it yet."

"Yet?" Vale queried.

Kai shrugged. Irene felt the motion against her body. "He knows where the Fae are. It wouldn't take long . . ."

Irene raised her hand to stop him. A dreadful realization was shaping itself in her mind. She remembered her earlier words to Ao Ji: *Our murderer is very direct, Your Majesty. He sweeps the board clean of evidence.* They seemed to echo in harmony with Kai's comment. *He knows where they are.*

"Kai," she said. Her voice shook. "I apologise for asking you this . . . But if Ao Ji was the only survivor of this peace conference, would his account of events be believed?"

She looked up into Kai's eyes and saw him make the same connections that she had.

He took a deep breath, then carefully released her, rising to his feet. "Irene, you need to get everyone under cover. I'll reason with my uncle—"

"Out of the question," Vale snapped before Irene could get her own disagreement in. "Strongrock, have you forgotten what he's already *done*?"

It was kind of Vale, Irene reflected, to avoid directly saying *have you forgotten he's already tried to kill you*, but it didn't make a great deal of difference. Kai still winced. "I will do this," he said through gritted teeth. "I have a responsibility."

"You'll get *killed*," Irene said flatly, dragging herself to her feet. She swayed, and Kai put a hand out to catch her before she could fall. "Thank you. You'll get killed, and the situation still won't be improved." She saw the desperate resolution in his eyes, the urge to take any sort of action that would let him escape from his current pain and betrayal, and tried to find some words that would get through to him. "Kai, your responsibility is to bring us all out of this alive! *That's* what needs doing here."

"The Librarian is correct." Duan Zheng shouldered his way into the room, with Ao Ji's human servant Hsien a few steps behind him. Hsien looked confused. Duan Zheng looked . . . calm. Past all despair, fixed on his resolution. "Your Highness." He stressed the title. "Your duty is to the negotiations, and to your family's honour. I will try to reason with His Majesty, and buy you what time I can."

Kai hesitated. "As his nephew, I should be the one to try—"

"We've seen how little that means to him." Duan Zheng's curt words held their own shading of pain. *He feels as betrayed as Kai does. Ren Shun would have been his friend too.* "Hsien, you are to obey the prince as you would me, until some other person of superior rank arrives."

He didn't say anything further. He walked through the room, snowflakes whistling round him, till he came to the gap in the wall, and then he stepped out. Light flashed again, and he was gone, a golden dragon rising through the snow until he was lost to view.

"Your Highness," Hsien said, bowing to Kai. "Your orders?"

Kai was still staring out into the storm, and Irene knew, without having to ask, that in a moment he would follow Duan Zheng, whatever the older dragon had said.

Someone had to take command in this mess.

"Kai," she said firmly. "May I make some very urgent suggestions?"

Kai rounded on her. "I'm not under your command any longer," he snapped. "If you think that I'm—ow!"

Irene had slapped him across the face. Hard. His hand caught her wrist, and she felt the bone-crushing strength of his grip. Redness flickered in the depths of his eyes.

"Pull yourself together," she said softly. "Your job is to save your uncle's honour by stopping anyone else being killed during this madness. I know I'm not your superior any longer. But I'm a Librarian, and I'm appealing to *you* as the ranking dragon representative here. And I have a plan."

He slowly unpeeled his fingers from her wrist. "What's the plan?" he asked.

Everyone else—Vale, Silver, Hsien, the people now crowding at the doorway—were looking at her in the same way. Expectant. Hopeful. Waiting for *her* to sort it out. *Can't anyone else have a plan? Why does it have to be my plan? It's not even a very good plan, it's as half-baked and thrown together in an emergency as Ao Ji's own "kill them all and sort it out later" plan . . .*

"His Majesty Ao Ji can't manipulate the weather if the local chaos level is too high," she said. That had, after all, been one of the reasons why a neutral world had been chosen for the conference—so that neither side would be inconvenienced or given too much power at the other's expense. "So we need to find the Fae delegation and work with them to raise the chaos level. Right now. Before Ao Ji finds them first and . . . neutralizes them. And if one of the dragons could make a run for it, to find another dragon royal who could stop Ao Ji, that would be a good idea."

"It wouldn't work," Mu Dan said, poking her head round the door. "If any of us tried to take on proper form and fly, Ao Ji would see us. He dominates the air at the moment."

"Damn. All right. Next step, find the Fae delegation." Irene looked around at everyone who was listening to her. "We all go and we all stick together. We may need everyone for this. And bring Li Ming and Mei Feng. We can't leave them here." *Especially since they're vital witnesses to Ao Ji's guilt, and Ao Ji knows it.* "Move, people, *move,* there's no time to lose!"

In the hustling and running downstairs, she managed to find her way to Vale's side. "Any further suggestions?" she asked quietly.

"No," Vale said. "And I fear they wouldn't listen to me if I did. I am, after all, merely *human.*" Irony laced his words. "At the moment, Winters, I think you may be the only person whom all three sides *will* listen to here."

Irene muttered something under her breath that made Vale raise an eyebrow. "How do you plan to raise the chaos level?" he asked.

"With the Language," Irene said. "And this is one of those experimental things which has never been tried before and I wish I wasn't going to have to try now. So for pity's sake don't ask me if I'm sure about it. First of all we need to *find* the Fae . . ."

But as they stumbled into the hotel atrium, Irene realized that they wouldn't have to go looking. Everyone else was just returning here, Fae and senior Librarians both. They were crowding in from outside, mingling with ordinary hotel guests whose enthusiasm for a night out in Paris had been dimmed by the sudden storm. She saw Coppelia being helped to a chair, stumbling with exhaustion, cold, and rheumatism, and for a moment she had a sudden delusion that she could hand over her responsibilities to the senior Librarians.

Then the whole building shuddered: the noise from above was like some great canvas being ripped apart. Irene's imagination supplied images of a dragon's claws ripping through the sky, even as she frantically tried to find some more plausible explanation. People screamed, fell to their knees, or ran in all directions. The atrium dissolved into a heaving mob. Over in one corner the Princess and Cardinal were surrounded by a solid wall of Fae and human servants, but the Librarians caught in the middle of the crowd were on their own.

"He's hitting the place with lightning!" Vale declared, catching Irene's arm and keeping her upright as someone else staggered against her.

"You can't *get* lightning in a snowstorm," Irene shouted, trying to make herself heard over the crowd.

"You can if you get the weather conditions just right!" Kai answered. "Irene, if we stay here he'll bring the building down round our ears . . ."

There's nowhere to run, no way to defend this place. Why didn't we have this wretched peace conference in a fort? A castle? An underground nuclear shelter? We're damned if we stay here, damned if we go outside—no, wait, that's not true. With the snow as thick as it is out there, Ao Ji can't possibly track every single pedestrian on the streets. But he could probably spot a group of Fae by their aura of chaos. So that won't work. "Mu Dan, get a couple of dragons to help you carry Li Ming and Mei Feng somewhere safe," she ordered. "Prutkov, Azevedo, get the rest of the Librarians, bring them along with me, explain as much as you can. Silver, Kai, Vale, with me, we're going to talk to the Fae."

The prickle of chaos was thick in the air as Vale and Kai forced a path through the crowd for her, as they headed for the Princess and the Cardinal. Sterrington was with them, and Thomson and Thompson, and a dozen others she'd never been introduced to.

It was Erda, the Fae's human head of security, who stepped forward to bar Irene's way. "What's going on?" she demanded.

"His Majesty Ao Ji has run mad," Irene said. She looked over Erda's shoulder to catch the Cardinal's eyes. "I believe the Countess has somehow poisoned him. I have direct evidence of her interference. But if we don't all work together to stop him, then we're all dead."

Should I be concerned about blaming the Countess, given how much she hates false accusations? Irene thought. *Probably. But let's worry about surviving today first.*

The Cardinal might have chosen to look like a normal man for the moment, but he still had the presence of a Fae noble, someone who could twist human souls around his little finger with the greatest of ease. Yet when Irene said *evidence,* his eyes narrowed. "Are you sure?" he called from behind Erda.

"I've got proof," Irene said, struggling with the urge to push past Erda, grab him by the shoulders, and shout it in his face. "And eyewitness testimony from the rest of my team."

The Princess rested a hand on the Cardinal's shoulder and smiled at Irene, her eyes calm and full of gentle patience. "Of course we'll help," she said, and the world was suddenly so much milder, so much more peaceful. It was possible to ignore the rolling thunder above, the sounds of collapsing masonry, the screaming of the hotel being evacuated. Not sensible, but under the spell of her power, so utterly possible. "Just tell us what you want us to do."

"I need you all to focus your natures," Irene said, "and we Librarians will use the Language to boost it. If we can raise the level of chaos in this world, then Ao Ji can't sustain the storm or his dragon form."

A bony finger tapped Irene on the shoulder, and she turned to see Coppelia. "Do you have any idea what you've just suggested?" the old Librarian demanded, as sotto voce as was feasible in the middle of a shouting mob.

"Pull yourself together," Irene muttered. "You're talking like a character from a melodrama."

Coppelia made a sour face. "Blasted Fae and their narrative auras . . . Azevedo explained the basics. You realize that if we help them raise the level of chaos, then we're putting ourselves at risk? It's hardly our natural environment."

"Neither is a blizzard," Irene retorted. "And we can't use the Language on Ao Ji unless he comes somewhere within reach of our voices, which he's not going to do. What do you suggest? Climbing the Eiffel Tower and getting a really big megaphone?"

Then wind struck the side of the hotel like an explosion, bursting the windows and slamming the doors open. Shards of glass sliced through the crowd, but their screams were drowned in the howling of the gale. The lights trembled, flaring and jumping, and the room was a mad confusion of people who didn't know where to go—upstairs, into the falling masonry and thunder, or outside, into the blizzard—but who very definitely wanted to be somewhere else.

"Right," Kostchei growled. He'd come up to stand at Irene's shoulder. The whole mingled group—dragons, Fae, Librarians—were crowding into the corner of the room, as far as possible from windows and doors. "Give us the words to use."

There was a growing sound of crackling from above. Irene was afraid it might be fire—but if it was, at least they'd probably die from the storm or the collapse before they could be burned alive, so all in all, things could be worse. She suppressed inappropriate laughter at the thought, filing it under *stupid attempts to think about anything but imminent death, when in danger of imminent death,* and forced herself back to the present. "I'd suggest 'Chaos, increase,' when I give the signal. Is everyone all right with that?"

There were nods. Not very happy nods, but nods. The Princess and Cardinal were nodding as well, and so were the other Fae around them. It was the sort of agreement that comes a second after you're certain what your superiors want you to say. One of the dragons grabbed Kai's arm. "Your Highness, are you sure this is a good idea—"

"Yes," Kai said with all the firmness of royalty, all the assurance of his uncle. "The Librarians are acting with my permission. My uncle has been poisoned and is acting unwisely. We must stop him before he destroys the alliance."

It would have spoiled the effect if she'd given him a nod or smile of approval, but she caught his eyes for a moment, and the trust in them—after what she'd done, how she'd forced his uncle to admit to murder—it twisted like a knife inside her.

Outside, through the broken windows and swinging doors, the whole sky was a mass of falling snow, so thick that it veiled the clouds beyond. A distant lightning danced through it, like threads of blue and green embroidery in white silk, and thunder rolled barely a second behind. Flakes blew into Irene's eyes, and she forced herself to look away, to return to her duty. But for a moment she thought she could see a great serpentine form moving through the sky, whiter than the snow, colder than the winter, as elegant and perfect as a master calligrapher's writing.

She raised one hand like an orchestral conductor and spoke in unison with all the other Librarians. **"Chaos, increase!"**

CHAPTER 27

The word *chaos* hung in Irene's mouth like the taste of a rotten, overripe pear. The Librarians' words seemed to coalesce, as though some exterior force was blending them into a single voice. It wasn't like orchestral music, with multiple harmonies working together to contribute to the ultimate effect. It was as if they were one person, with one set of words, all and forever in unison.

And chaos answered. It fizzed in the air like the tension climbing before a storm; it was a physical heat against the skin, an aftertaste in the mouth, a heaviness in the lungs, a weight across the shoulders, a sensation that was impossible to describe except that it was *wrong*. Librarians around Irene staggered, going down to their knees. But the Princess and the Cardinal and the other Fae stood there, their faces exultant, *transcendent*. The world was suddenly hospitable to them, where before it had been only neutral—or increasingly unfriendly. Now they were at home, and the universe bent itself around them in an attempt to make their lives more convenient.

Irene had never wasted her time asking local chaos to *decrease* before. She'd been told as a student how stupid and pointless such a thing was. One human being couldn't change the power level of an entire world. One Librarian couldn't alter reality *that* much. And she'd never even considered trying to tell it to *increase*. After all, why would any sane Librarian want to do such a thing? (Besides Alberich, of course, but he wasn't sane. Everyone agreed on that point.)

But sometimes the stupid, pointless, impossible option was the only one available.

The dragons around her were collapsing, curling up on themselves; only a few were still conscious. Kai was on his feet, though only barely. Now he was the one clinging to *her* for support.

The air *pulsed*. An invisible wave of power rippled outwards from the group of Fae, moving through living beings and walls alike, and swelled out into the icy streets with the growing, unstoppable force of a tidal wave, spreading through Paris. It came in an ever-thickening swell, one that lured Irene with a sense of possibility even as it made her tremble and shake with a kind of spiritual sickness.

It was answered by a roar. The sound was even louder than the earlier thunder or the noise of collapsing buildings. And for a moment Kai was able to hold himself up straight again, his legs steady, and the snow blew in like a thousand diamond-edged fragments, driven by a will that desired to scour Fae, Librarians, and dragons alike from the surface of this earth.

The two forces strained against each other . . .

And the snow gave way. The roaring fell silent. Lesser things were audible once again. The snow drifting in through the windows was pretty—romantic, even—a drift of flakes, a charming sign of winter rather than a lethal weather condition. Snow still fell, and the storm still danced through the streets of Paris and along its boulevards, but now the whole perspective seemed to have changed. A little more of this influence, Irene thought sourly, and there would probably be art students out sketching naked women in it. The crowd had quietened to some degree, probably because most of them had evacuated the room for upper floors or cellars, and one could actually hear other people speaking now.

But the immediate danger was gone. Admittedly they *were* still in a collapsing hotel that had been struck by lightning and might be on fire, but things could be worse. She bent down to check Coppelia's pulse, then Kostchei's. Both of them were unconscious but breathing. Azevedo and Prutkov were down too, and Sarashina, and a couple of other Librarians Irene didn't recognize: Bradamant, Medea, and Rongomai were all still upright, though none of them looked happy or healthy. Generally the older Librarians hadn't been able to tolerate the strain, while the younger ones were affected but conscious.

"I feel as if I've gone too deep underwater," Vale commented. "Are you all right, Strongrock?"

"Coping," Kai said through gritted teeth, only barely on his feet. Each breath came with an effort, and he had to lean on her and Vale to hold himself up. Whether it was his royal blood, his strength, his youth, or painful experience in other high-chaos areas, he was still functioning, though the other dragons were out for the count. "Frankly, I'd rather *be* deep underwater. How much longer will we have to abide this abom—" He caught Irene's eye. "Unnatural state," he corrected himself.

"I don't know," Irene had to admit. "But as long as we keep this up, Ao Ji can't use the storm to kill us."

Kai swallowed, looking sick to his stomach, and as if he was strongly considering being killed by the storm as the lesser evil. But he nodded.

"Miss Winters." The Cardinal's voice carried across their murmuring. "Perhaps you could come here and explain precisely what is going on?"

"I'm looking forward to hearing all the details myself," Silver said. He was positively glowing. His mouth was a temptation, his cheekbones were a mortal sin, his hair begged to be stroked, and in every way Irene wanted to throw herself into his arms and let him do as he wished with her body. *Fae attraction,* she reminded herself desperately. *Every single Fae within range has been strengthened, not just the Cardinal and Princess. I have to remember all the many reasons why I don't want to let him take advantage of me, which is difficult when I can't think of them right now . . .*

Something about that thought rankled at the back of her mind, with the nagging ache of an unextracted splinter. She let it marinate for the moment, focusing on what she was going to tell the Fae; she needed a version of the truth that would allow for future negotiations. "Vale, I think I'm going to need your help."

"Of course," Vale said. He paused, tilting his head. "But can you hear something?"

"Hear what?" Irene said, tilting her own head as she tried to listen.

However, Kai had heard something too. He visibly pulled himself together, forcing his sickness down and dragging himself back to focus. *"To arms,"* he shouted at Hsien and his group. "Attackers are approaching!"

A silence seized the room. The few remaining normal Parisians were gripped by it, falling away from the inner entrance to the hotel like grains of sand in a river current, shifting back against the walls. A new flavour touched the chaos of the room. *I need a better word for this,* Irene thought. But she recognized it. It smelled—tasted—of blood, pain, and fear. It was the Countess.

Damn. It didn't cross my mind that when we empowered the other Fae, we'd empower her too. Damn, damn, damn.

Men leaked into the room, cats mingling around their feet, drifting in silently, their eyes—human and feline—avid and hungry. They must have come up from the cellars, and the sewers beyond. None of them spoke. They clustered at the far end, around the inner entrance, like an honour guard.

Irene didn't want to be the first to break the stand-off, especially as she couldn't think of any use of the Language that would neutralize the enemy. Instead she leaned down and grabbed Coppelia's shoulders, pulling her towards the inner ring of Fae, past the mingled line of Erda's guards and Hsien's followers. Out of the immediate line of attack. From the corner of her eye she saw those Librarians who were still mobile doing the same with the others who were unconscious or incapable. She racked her brain for what to do. *If I try to lower the chaos level again, assuming that even works, Ao Ji can raise another storm. But if I don't, the Countess can turn her followers loose on us . . .*

A click. The lights went out.

"This is my Paris now." The Countess's voice came from the darkness, echoing in the room and seeming to rebound from every wall—as though she was surrounding them on every side. The wind was a mere whisper in the background, drowned out by the power of her presence. "And now I settle things once and for all. Little Princess, your time has run out . . ."

Irene found herself shuddering—not from the cold, but from a fear she couldn't shake loose, a horror that was rooting itself in her bones. She couldn't see. She was trapped in the darkness together with that voice, with a woman who was going to take a very long time to make everyone present die, just because she'd enjoy Irene's pain. And all her friends were trapped there with her. They were all going to die, in fear and pain and blood, and Irene's parents and the Library would go down with them, and it had all been for nothing in the first place . . . and Irene knew that all of this was the counsel of despair, that she was the victim of a Fae controlling her emotions and will, and yet she could not, *could* not break free . . .

"I think not!" It was the Princess who spoke. The leash of terror that had held the room in thrall snapped. Moonlight impossibly pierced the clouds and came driving in through the window to halo her in silver, casting long shadows across the floor. She *shone.* Her hair was a torrent of brilliance down her back. Her dress was as white as snowdrops. Her voice was a singing trumpet calling everyone present to arms, inspiring them to courage and honour. "Men of Paris! Defend me against this evil woman!"

And as the Fae on both sides stood back and watched, their human servants threw themselves into battle.

Irene had no room left in her head for some clever use of the Language; she was too busy trying to stop herself from diving into the erupting fight. The room was a morass of moonlight and darkness, full of people struggling in silence, a half-glimpsed nightmare. Cats bit at ankles or sprang at faces. Knives flashed momentarily in the light before disappearing into the shadows again. It wasn't even just devotees on both sides doing the fighting—ordinary Parisians and hotel staff had been pulled into the fray, swayed by either the Countess or the Princess, their faces full of blind faith and passion.

The two Fae were focused on each other, barely conscious of others in the room except as servants or tools. Rongomai was clutching his head and swaying; Bradamant had drawn a pistol and was firing into the press, choosing her shots carefully. Irene's own conscious thoughts were at war with her urge to protect the Princess at any cost. The whole situation seemed somehow formalised and theatrical, a scene being played out by humans in front of the appreciative observing Fae.

Ao Ji's earlier words whispered at the back of Irene's head. *Is this really better than letting the dragons take control? Being toys for the Fae instead?*

She clenched her fist. No. That was the thinking of despair, the easy attraction of false binaries. She wasn't fighting for either side. The Library was fighting for the right of humans to exist in the middle—to make their own mistakes, perhaps, but to have the *choice* to do so.

With returned clarity, she was able to think. This was wrong. The Countess didn't stage frontal assaults. Her modus operandi was to create diversions while her attack came from an unexpected direction . . .

And at the moment, everyone was looking towards the interior of the hotel, and nobody was looking outside.

Supporting Kai and dragging Vale, Irene edged along the wall to the door, grateful for the concealing shadows. They broke out into the snow outside, and Kai turned his face to it, breathing in the bitter air with a sigh of relief.

Vale scanned along the rue de Rivoli, then raised his cane to point. "There—*down,* Winters!"

They hit the snow together as bullets cracked against the wall behind them. From her position on the icy pavement, Irene could see the shadows approaching through the falling snow. There were only half a dozen of them, but they had guns. Dorotya's hunched silhouette was recognizable, her voice a yammer of encouragement and threats as she goaded them on.

An attack from behind with guns could have done serious damage to the defending Fae—and to the Librarians, the dragons, and everyone else. But guns were vulnerable to the Language, and the attackers were now within scope of Irene's voice.

She spat out snow. "Vale, you're not carrying a gun, are you?"

"Absolutely not," Vale answered. "Do your worst, Winters."

It was nice to be appreciated. She rolled to the side as another bullet whistled through the falling snow, and shouted, **"Guns, jam!"**

A high-chaos environment was very sensitive to the Language, even if it was uncomfortable for Librarians. Irene couldn't clearly see what had happened, but she could hear the yells of confusion and fury. Above them, Dorotya's voice carried. "Curse you, Librarian!"

Irene pulled herself up into a crouch, assessing the situation. There were half a dozen men. Possibly lethal with guns. But without them? She and Kai and Vale could take them. "Dorotya," she called, "I'd get out of here while you can. You've lost the advantage of surprise. Save us the trouble of killing you and your men."

"You expect me to leave my mistress in danger?" Dorotya whined. She was a scuttling blotch against the whirling snow, a dark tangle of shawls and skirts. "Tell you what, dearie, why don't *you* run for it and we'll give you a ten-minutes head start?"

"Stop bluffing." Irene was tired and angry, and she'd been on the verge of panic for so long that it had nearly burned her out.

Dorotya won't understand mercy, so perhaps I need another angle . . . She rose to her full height and stepped forward, ignoring Kai's hiss to stay back. "You don't get it. Your mistress is already losing; she's going to have to retreat. I am offering you a chance to escape, and in return you will owe me a favour. Otherwise you can stand there and I'll turn all my allies loose on you. The ball's in your court, madam. But don't waste my time."

The wind hissed down the street, driving the snow with it. Dorotya hesitated, and then, to Irene's immense relief, she nodded. "It's a deal, dearie. I owe you one, you little bitch, but you'd better be damned careful if you try to collect it. Take yourself home, boys—the show's over for tonight."

She faded backwards into a gap between two buildings. The men stumbled after her, leaving the wide street empty. Inspector Maillon would just have to deal with them later. With Dorotya and the Countess gone, the men should go back to their normal patterns of behaviour. And the sound of fighting from inside the hotel was quietening down, which—hopefully—meant that was under control. For a moment, Irene dared to believe it might be over.

Then she turned to Kai and Vale, saw where they were staring, and knew that it wasn't. And she knew why Dorotya had chosen to run.

Ao Ji was in partly human form—his skin was ice-white and scaled, and his eyes pure blood-red, and two horns stood out on his forehead. The light around him owed nothing to the street lights or the fragile moonlight. The shadow that he cast was long and serpentine, very far from being human.

It wasn't enough, the chaos didn't last long enough, ran through Irene's head, in a futile repetition building towards panic. *How can we stop him now?* But chaos and order were still unbalanced; she had more power to change things than usual, until Ao Ji's mere presence forced more order back into the world. Then he'd harness the weather again and they'd all be dead.

Either she despaired and gave up here and now, or she found some words that might yet save them.

Kai straightened and put himself between her and Vale and Ao Ji. There was no convenient water here to aid him—the nearest quantities were in the sewers, locked under stone and pavement. He had nothing except his own strength—and it wouldn't be enough. "Uncle, you cannot do this."

"Nephew," Ao Ji answered, "I regret your sacrifice. But if your father truly understood the danger of the Fae, then he would do no less than I."

He tilted his head in a gesture that was curious rather than immediately lethal. "You have seen how chaos turns on itself," he said, his voice echoing in a way no human voice could. "You have seen the Fae fighting each other and using humans as tools. Do you not see that you are mistaken in opposing me?"

"No," Irene said. "I don't." Her throat was dry with fear. She still had the Language, but what could she say that would stop him? "Human beings need both order and chaos."

"Nephew?" Ao Ji honestly seemed to want some sign of approval—or at least understanding.

"You have ignored my father's wishes," Kai said coldly. "You have chosen to disobey your elder brother's command. You may claim he would approve of your actions, but I disagree."

"And you?" He looked at Vale. A flicker in his crimson eyes suggested that he truly wanted Vale's opinion. That even if he was a dragon monarch, and thus the only one who would ever be qualified to judge, he still sought some kind of approval from the ordinary humans he claimed to protect. "You are the only true human here. You are neither dragon nor Librarian but mortal. What would you choose?"

Vale tapped his cane against the icy paving stones. "As far as I am concerned," he said, his voice as calm and dry as if he had been in his rooms and giving an opinion on a newspaper article, "you and the Countess are both murderers."

Anger flashed across Ao Ji's face at the comparison, clearer than it had ever been before, and Irene knew with a sick chill that though Kai might possibly survive this, and she had gained his mercy before, Vale had just doomed himself. Those words had just tipped the balance. "Insolence and folly!" the dragon said, his attention now fully on them rather than the hotel beyond. "You will be little loss."

Inspiration came. Irene flung herself forward, clasping Kai from behind and pressing herself against him. She saw Ao Ji's lips twist at the emotional, human gesture, and she knew that he wouldn't be able to hear her at this distance as she whispered, "Buy me what time you can," into Kai's ear.

Kai stiffened in her clasp and his head jerked in a nod of understanding. She released him and stepped back.

"Very well," Ao Ji said wearily. He raised his hand to point at them. Snow blossomed out towards them in a pattern as intricate as a mandala or an unfolding camellia, but pitiless and lethal. The petals were edged with ice, lethal claws reaching out to scythe them down. It was slow. It had no need to hurry. There was nowhere for them to run.

Kai crossed his arms in front of him, his feet shifting as he steadied himself with a huge effort. The road beneath them trembled and then split apart, and a gush of filthy water rose before him from the sewers, a fountain climbing towards the rooftops. It was too cold to smell it properly, and in the moonlight and snow it looked almost charming, a moving sculpture of ebony that curved to come down towards Ao Ji.

But the cold wind seized the water and froze it mid-fall; it became ice, crashing down in a thousand shards, splintering across the width of the road and spraying in all directions. The rush of snow and wind beat on through the remnants of the water, laying ice across the hole ripped in the pavement as it rushed towards them. Irene felt the bite of the air like fire against her skin. She flung up an arm to shield her eyes and heard Kai cry out.

But he'd bought her the moments she needed. Four words were enough. She put all her will and power behind them, all her anger, all her fear for her friends, her parents, her Library—everything that she *had*. **"Paris,"** she shouted, her voice carrying over the howl of the wind and the smashing of the ice, **"stop Ao Ji!"**

What were the requirements for using the Language? That the Librarian using it should be able to name and describe what they wanted to happen, and that the Librarian should have the strength to compel reality to change itself. And that the universe could hear her words.

Paris had a name. Paris had been named by human beings, thousands of years ago—not Fae, not dragons, but mortals living and dying there. There was no question that Paris knew what it was. And Paris heard her. In this world, with the powers of chaos and order contending against each other like two opposing tidal waves, she could seize that strength and bridle it for just a moment. She could *use* it.

Buildings shuddered and the street trembled. The huge grinding of stone against stone drowned out the shattering of ice and the shrieks of human beings across Paris who felt their city shaking. Irene fell to her knees, struggling for the energy to *breathe,* as strength drained out of her. She felt heat across her back and smelled burning cloth, and she realized—dimly, on another layer of perception—that her Library brand was scorching through her clothing.

The road rose around Ao Ji, stone taking on life of its own and shouldering aside snow and ice to clench around him like a fist. The frontages of buildings—old, expensive, heavy buildings that had survived Napoléon and the Commune and the Revolution—shook loose their tiles and came cascading down. Ice and snow and wind raved against them, shattering rock to powder and grinding masonry to dust, turning glass to splinters and fragmenting lampposts.

Irene coughed. Blood was in her mouth. She kept coughing, unable to stop herself, spitting out blood onto the ice-crusted pavement in front of her, her body shaking with every breath of bitter air, the cold reaching round her hands and up her arms, pressing against her heart. It was almost gentle against the racking inhalations and coughing that convulsed her; it was an offer to stop, to give up, to let it go. Perhaps this was all just a nightmare—the storm, the earthquake, Kai lying unmoving in front of her, the blood dark against the snow. Perhaps she was still simply lying there in the hotel room, having one last painful hallucination as she slipped towards death. Perhaps none of this was real. She just had to accept that and give in. She was only human. There was only so much she could do. There was no shame in losing.

Her hands clenched. There might be no shame in losing, but there *was* shame in surrendering with so much at stake. She was not going to . . .

More blood. Her throat was raw.

Not . . .

Her eyes had closed. She forced them open. There was nothing to see except whiteness, nothing to hear except the sounds of stone and wind. The only things that defined her were her pain and her will, her choice to hold on, to keep pouring her strength into her words, to throw what was left of herself into the storm.

And then there was silence. Snow kept on falling. It drifted across her blood on the ground, melting as it touched it, letting the dark stain spread. But the wind had hushed; the fury behind it had dissipated. For a moment, quiet lay across Paris like an eiderdown, and nobody dared move or break the stillness.

There was a mound of stone and snow in the street ahead of her. Somewhere under that . . .

"Winters?" That was Vale's voice from behind her. Good. He was alive.

"Check on Kai," she said. Her voice cracked as she spoke—it was a hoarse whisper, barely audible, and dear gods, her throat *hurt*. "Then help me. Please. We need to see what's become of Ao Ji."

Vale lumbered into her line of sight, staggering through the snow with difficulty. Streaks of blood marked his hands and cheeks where they had been scored by the snow or fragments of stone, and his clothing was ripped and torn. He went down on one knee next to Kai, checking his pulse. "Alive but unconscious," he reported, and she could hear the relief in his voice. "But he could do with medical attention."

Irene tried not to laugh. It hurt too much. "So could we all."

"Don't waste your breath on trivialities," Vale advised her. He got an arm round her and helped her to her feet, assisting her along. There was no thought or energy left to claim a strength she didn't have. There was no way she could have walked on her own. She wasn't even sure if she could have crawled.

Ao Ji was sprawled under a pile of masonry. He was unconscious, but a twitch from one outstretched hand suggested that he was still alive. Cuts and scratches marred his white skin. His hair had come undone from its braid and flowed out across the stone like a drift of snow.

"We need to . . ." Irene tried to think what to do next. Her mind was empty. She was exhausted beyond words. "If we . . ."

"You need do no more, Miss Winters," said the Cardinal from behind her. "You have completed your task."

Vale and Irene turned. The Cardinal was there, unmarked, untouched, though the group of human servants and lesser Fae behind him showed the signs of battle, limping, wounded, and bloodied. "Have no fear," he went on. "Your friend the prince is unharmed. He will be taken to safety."

"And what about Ao Ji?" Irene pressed her hand against her throat, trying to control another coughing fit.

"He was found dead," the Cardinal said. The moonlight began filtering through the clouds again, pooling his shadow darkly around his feet. "It is as simple as that."

At first Irene wanted to agree. It would be so simple, so easy: Li Ming and Mei Feng had heard the evidence and could attest to it, and everyone in Paris had witnessed the storm. But then . . . what about Ao Ji's family? His brothers? Whatever he'd done, if he died like this, would they ever accept the peace treaty or forgive the Library for his death? It wasn't just her life that would be at stake for killing him. It would be everyone connected with her. Vale, her *parents*, the Library . . .

"You're mistaken, Your Eminence," she said. Her voice was a thin thread in the cold air. "He was found alive and taken into custody."

The Cardinal shook his head gently. "You are overwrought, Miss Winters. You will be taken back to the hotel where you can rest. Peregrine Vale, assist her."

"We can both testify that Ao Ji was alive and well when we left him," Vale said sharply. "Unless you wish to add us both to the tally of deceased."

"Certainly an option," the Cardinal agreed, "though hardly my preference. Surely you must see that this is the easiest way out? Wouldn't your family and your world agree?"

If Irene had been able—or willing—she could have given the Cardinal some helpful advice. Attempting to blackmail Vale would only set him more firmly on his chosen course. But advice wouldn't save their lives here and now.

Blackmail, she thought, and a card at the back of her mind turned itself over.

"Your Eminence," she croaked, "you aren't in full possession of the facts."

"Oh?" He paused. "Is this where you reveal a note in my handwriting, saying that what you have done was for the good of the state and on my orders?"

"Not exactly." She coughed again and noted the blood that spattered onto her hand. *I hope that's not too serious. Assuming I survive the next couple of minutes.* "Would you—please—have your people step back a moment?"

The Cardinal glanced over his shoulder and nodded. His followers backed away. "You had better have a very good reason to prevent what needs to happen here," he said quietly. "What have you to say that can convince me to change my mind?"

Irene supported herself on Vale. "You deliberately lured the Countess here, to create a mutual enemy against which everyone could unite. And I can prove it—if you insist on this course of action."

"You can?"

"A letter."

Irene saw the cold decision in his eyes. "Then it is a very great pity that neither of you survived this battle."

Irene held up one shaking hand before he could give any orders. "I don't have it."

"Oh?" The Cardinal's voice was calm and unshaken, but there was just a fragment of uncertainty behind it. "Then who does? The prince? Peregrine Vale?"

"Neither of them." Irene bared her teeth in a smile. "I gave it to Silver. And I don't think . . ." She coughed again, her body shaking. "I don't think he likes you very much. I think he'd love the excuse to give that letter to the Princess. And when she finds out that you were prepared to endanger her, at the hands of the Countess? What then?"

Seconds ticked away. Irene watched the snow falling around the Cardinal as he stood there, contemplating, considering, a model for an ecclesiastical statue, weighing her words like playing pieces and judging their worth. Each breath came with more pain and the taste of blood. She was afraid that she was going to start coughing again and that she wouldn't be able to stop.

Finally the Cardinal spoke. "Well played, Milady. I look forward to future games." He raised his voice. "Erda! Have someone fetch one of the dragons from the hotel. His Majesty Ao Ji is alive, and we require witnesses while we take him into custody."

CHAPTER 28

The treaty signing took place in the middle of the Jardin des Tuileries, next to a large pond surrounded by statues. It was past three o'clock in the morning, but the snow was still falling. The group—Fae, dragons, humans—had moved far enough away from the rue de Rivoli to avoid the rescue efforts and repair work that were still going on there. The Cardinal had had a pleasant "little chat" with Inspector Maillon, and Inspector Maillon was now utterly convinced of everyone's innocence in the recent anarchist disruptions. Certainly the crater spanning the street and the shattered surrounding buildings were more reminiscent of bombs than anything else. Such as a dragon attack.

Irene would have felt guiltier about the widespread destruction they'd brought to Paris if she'd had any energy left to do it with. She was running on caffeine and brandy, and even though she'd been wrapped in borrowed coats and had her frostbite bandaged, the cold had settled into her bones. Unfortunately, given the presence of royalty on both sides, only the very elderly or badly injured got to sit down, and she didn't quite rate that level of consideration. The fatigue-stupid part of her brain almost wished that she *had* been injured enough to deserve a chair, but common sense strangled that train of thought. The area buzzed with the same mixture of order and chaos that had filled the dining room last night, but it didn't feel quite as claustrophobic or condensed. Yet it was still a tingle in the air, a frisson on the nerves.

Ao Ji had been removed by a group of dragons, led by his royal brother Ao Guang, who had arrived shortly after all the fighting was over. The official story was that the Countess had poisoned Ao Ji, resulting in temporary insanity. The fact that absolutely nobody believed this didn't stop it from being a good story. The Countess had vanished, but nobody was trying to hunt her down; they were all too busy with immediate emergencies. Irene had reported the full story to Kostchei and Coppelia—as far as she knew it—with Vale's assistance. And it was amazing how smoothly final negotiations had gone, with both sides being culpable of *something* and wanting to smooth it over.

Kai's father Ao Guang was . . . impressive. He had the same colouring as Kai—and Irene suspected that he was blue in his dragon form as well, but she hadn't had a chance to see that. He possessed a bearing and power that came with age and with the knowledge that, if he really wanted to, he could take the world apart. Very much like Ao Ji, in fact. Irene had been doing her best to find other people to stand behind, whenever she was anywhere near him. It probably didn't do much good, but it made her feel slightly better.

Vale was standing near her now. He occasionally offered an elbow when she looked as if she was starting to sway. Irene wasn't too proud to take it. She was counting the seconds till this was done.

And then it was. Ao Guang signed. The Princess signed. Coppelia and Kostchei signed as witnesses. Li Ming brushed snow off the documents—three copies, one for each group—and rolled them up to slide them into scroll tubes, his motions still slow and pained. Irene breathed a sigh of relief: very carefully, through her nose, so as not to hurt her throat any further. She still had difficulty speaking.

There were mutual gestures of courtesy and formal speeches, which Irene mostly tuned out while keeping a vague awareness of the situation. Kai remained at his father's side at all times, and he was far too aware of scrutiny to even glance at Irene, just as she was far too politically sensible to spend her time gazing at him. *Official neutrality. Right.* She had no idea what his father would say to him once they were alone. Determined optimism let her hope that there were *some* prospects for them both, for the future. They were all still alive, after all. That was better than things had looked a few hours ago. She would just have to get on with her job and wait till his father let him go his own way again . . .

And if it's decades? At least we had one night together. At least I'll know he's safe and well.

"And we have one more decision to announce," Coppelia wound up her speech. "Step forward, Irene."

Irene's stomach dropped as everyone's eyes turned to her. Being noticed at events like this was rarely good news. She pasted a polite smile on her face and tried to step forward gracefully but staggered, and Vale had to catch her.

"Kindly forgive Miss Winters," Vale said. "She *was* injured."

"Her service has been noted," Ao Guang said. "What is your decision, Madam Librarian?"

It was too much to hope for a reward, Irene decided. This wasn't the sort of school prize-giving where one was handed a book and an improving homily about hard work. A pity. She'd have liked a book. But she didn't *think* that she'd done anything deserving punishment—or at least, she hadn't been caught doing it officially. She tried to slow her pulse and act as if she knew what was going on.

Coppelia leaned forward in her chair. A thin crust of snow covered her shoulders and dusted the folds of her skirt. The moonlight brought out all the lines of her face. "The Library has decided to create an official embassy. It will be a clearing-house, if you like, for peaceful questions and complaints from all treaty signatories. Naturally this requires a younger Librarian who is capable of living outside the Library and who is on good terms with both Your Majesty's kindred and the Fae."

She paused, possibly to allow objections. Nobody made any.

"We have therefore decided to appoint Irene, also known as Miss Winters, currently Librarian-in-Residence to B-395 by our classification, to this position. Miss Winters will maintain her current job, though of course without infringing on the rights of any treaty signatories. We hope this is acceptable to all parties."

Irene fixed her gaze at a point somewhere over Coppelia's shoulder and struggled to keep her breathing even and not have a coughing fit. Actually, would a coughing fit get her invalided out of this presumptive position? Tempting thought. This job she was being offered—no, assigned—was not *remotely* safe. She was going to be a public target for anyone with a grudge against the Library or the peace treaty.

I'm doomed.

"We entirely approve," Ao Guang said.

They probably all set this up beforehand.

"As do we," the Princess agreed.

Sheer panic took over. *I wonder if my budget will extend to building fortifications and machine-gun emplacements?*

"And you, Irene?" Coppelia queried. "If you honestly feel that you are not suited to this task, then we will assign someone else."

Irene took a deep breath. "I hardly feel competent," she said honestly. "I'm still very young and inexperienced compared to other Librarians." Though, really, was she *that* inexperienced? Choosing to avoid responsibility by labelling herself as unworthy might be the easy choice . . . but was it the right choice?

She met Coppelia's eyes. "But I will do my best to serve the Library in this position," she finished.

"A wise choice," Ao Guang said. He didn't comment on *whose* choice. "And in order to facilitate these lines of communication, I will assign one of my own sons to the same task. Kai, this will be a duty for you. You will share the embassy with Miss Winters here. As will the eventual Fae representative."

Kai went down to one knee in the snow and pressed a fist to his shoulder. "As my lord and father commands," he said. His manner was perfectly appropriate, but Irene knew him well enough to hear the suppressed undertone of eagerness in his voice.

"And of course we will assign some loyal servant of our own for a similar purpose," the Princess said. Her eyes were practically glowing with sweet harmony and love for all living things. Birds would have been singing if it wasn't snowing and the middle of winter. "But for the moment, let us say our farewells. I truly feel that we have achieved something great today."

And when she said it, her words really sounded *true*. Irene could actually believe in . . . happy endings?

We have a peace treaty. The Library's safe. My parents are safe.

I get to be with Kai. He gets to be with me. This can't be coincidence. There has to be some sort of plan behind it.

Or could it really be the closest thing to a reward they can give us? Am I risking my own happiness because I'm too paranoid to accept a gift?

She backed away politely as the royalty on both sides turned its attention away from her. For a moment she caught Kai's eyes, and she saw the same awareness—and the same hope—in his face. Then he stepped back to answer a question from his father, and she looked away before she could be caught staring.

"Well, Winters," Vale said softly. "It sounds as if you will be causing my world some inconvenience for a while yet."

Apparently he'd made the same calculus of potential dangers that she had. "I could request that this theoretical embassy be positioned elsewhere," Irene said reluctantly. "So long as I take the job, that is."

Vale snorted. "Hardly necessary. Simply exercise your customary caution." He glanced at the rue de Rivoli beyond the trees. "And do your best to avoid blowing up London, if at all possible."

Silver slid through the crowd towards them, giving Irene his most affectionate and enticing smile. "I have to admit, my little mouse, that I've seldom been so relieved in my life."

"For which of many possible reasons?" Irene asked.

"Not being given any official appointment regarding our new treaty. It's really not my *style*." He reached inside his coat and slid out an envelope, offering it to Irene. "And speaking of things I'd rather not hold on to—here you are. I'm sure you can find a safe place to keep it."

Irene flipped the envelope open. The contents were reassuringly the same as earlier: the letter the Countess had given her. She hadn't actually read it, and she wasn't sure that she wanted to. She could feel the Cardinal's eyes on her from across the crowd, even if he wasn't currently looking at her. "Somewhere very safe, I think." She slid it into her own coat. "No talk of favours?"

Silver flashed his teeth in a smile. "After some study of your personality, my dear Irene Winters, I'm coming to the conclusion I might prefer to have your goodwill instead. The world is changing. I will watch with interest. Do come by the embassy when we're back in London. I'm sure I can host a party that would . . . entertain you. Bring your pet dragon. And the Princess has told me to make sure you get paid, detective, so I'll see to that."

He tipped his hat and wandered away.

"Do you believe his affirmations of goodwill?" Vale asked, austere and suspicious.

"I think the strength of his intentions may depend on the seriousness of the situation," Irene answered quietly. "But he has come out ahead for the moment, so let's not rock the boat. Could you help me across to Coppelia, please?"

A gap formed around Coppelia as Irene and Vale approached, with surrounding Librarians and bystanders melting away.

Coppelia looked up and her face creased in a smile. "You know, for a moment I honestly thought you'd refuse."

"You're my teacher," Irene responded. She knew that people around her were listening to the conversation, even if they were tactfully pretending not to. "Of all the people here, you should know which way I'd jump."

"You might have claimed that you weren't up to it. You've done it before. I'm glad that you didn't do it this time. After a certain point, it becomes a habit." Coppelia offered her hand to Vale. "And thank *you* very much for your help. I hope that we can call on you again if necessary. I believe your fees are on a fixed scale, except when you remit them entirely?"

Vale gave her a small bow. "You are correct, madam, though I would expect nothing less from you. I am glad I could be of assistance."

"Excellent. My agent will be calling on you later."

Irene passed Coppelia the letter. "This needs to go somewhere very safe indeed."

"Ah yes," Coppelia said, tucking it under the blanket that covered her skirts. "Another document for the files . . . You can call on me in your own time, you know, Irene." Her voice softened. "There's no need to be a stranger."

Irene thought about all the people in her future. "I promise that I won't," she said quietly. "Some things may change, but others will stay the same."

She felt the brush of orderly power behind her and turned to see Ao Guang, with Kai behind him. Automatically she dipped in a bow, and Vale perforce did the same.

Ao Guang nodded to them both. "There is no need to detain you further," he said, in a tone of voice that Irene decided to class as friendly. "I can see that you are both injured, and the night is cold. I will be glad to escort Madam Coppelia and her friends to the Bibliothèque nationale, to exit this world."

And the Cardinal's letter. Right. "Thank you, Your Majesty," Irene said. She tried to meet his eyes without having any thoughts about

Kai whatever. Or about Ao Ji. Or about anything to which Ao Guang could take exception.

"Your fee will be dispatched to you," Ao Guang informed Vale. "Kai, see to it. I will not require you for the rest of the night."

"Yes, my lord father," Kai said, with another bow.

Ao Guang turned from them to Coppelia with the calm assurance of a man who knew they'd vanish into social invisibility the moment he looked away. Kai took Irene's other arm, and the three of them retreated to the shelter of one of the statues.

"I can get all three of us home," Kai said quietly. "Irene's obviously not up to much travel—"

"Excuse *me,*" Irene muttered, and coughed.

"Ignore Winters," Vale advised Kai. "After being ordered around just now, she feels the need to assert her independence."

Irene glared at him but didn't trust her throat enough to speak.

"Or we could find another hotel for the next few hours," Kai suggested. "Enough to catch some sleep. My father has given me leave."

"Yes, we heard," Vale said. "Tell me, Strongrock, what do *you* make of this embassy business?"

"Experimental," Kai said thoughtfully. "But it's worth a try, I think. And it keeps me out of court for the moment. The matter of my uncle . . ."

"I'm sorry about that," Irene said hoarsely.

Kai looked at her, choosing his words carefully. "Irene, I would be lying if I said I was at all comfortable with what has happened. But my father came to help. He has publicly acknowledged me and given me a worthy task. Things are never going to be the same—

but I know that he feels I acted properly. And his opinion is the most important thing to me."

More important than me? The words rose in Irene's throat, but before they could pass her lips she saw just how stupid they were. There were different *sorts* of importance. Kai would never ask her to compare her affection for him to her loyalty to the Library. Mortal beings could have more than one thing that they cared about. Immortal ones, like dragon kings, might be carried away by their ruling passions and be prepared to sacrifice everything else—all other loves, all loyalties, all honour—to that consuming flame.

But she was mortal.

She nodded.

In the distance, down along the Seine and on one of the further bridges, far-away noises drifted through the snow. The grinding of cartwheels, the noise of horses' hooves, and above it, singing and shouts of enthusiasm.

"What's going on?" Kai asked.

"The early-morning market vendors," Vale answered. "They're bringing their vegetables and other food to the markets at Les Halles. They usually go along the boulevard Saint-Michel—but perhaps the snow has closed it. And I'm told the more bohemian students often accompany them." The disapproving lines of his face suggested that he'd never done any such thing himself when he'd been studying.

Irene, however, had. "Life goes on," she said philosophically, giving up on resting her voice, "and Paris will be here long after we've left it. I think a hotel might be the best idea. We can get back to London tomorrow."

"Probably wise," Vale agreed. He looked at the group of people in front of them. Fae, dragons, Librarians—and all of them interacting with each other. If not warmly, then at least politely. "I dare-say nobody will notice that we have gone."

Irene nodded. She smiled at both of them, more genuinely than she'd managed yet this evening. It was difficult to let fear go. Yet she was willing to try. "Tomorrow's going to be a busy day. But . . . I think I'm looking forward to it."

ABOUT THE AUTHOR

Genevieve Cogman is a freelance author who has written for several role-playing game companies. She currently works for the National Health Service in England as a clinical classifications specialist. She is the author of *The Invisible Library, The Masked City, The Burning Page, The Lost Plot,* and *The Mortal Word.*